FRESHMEN HONEYS

BY: MAHOGANY WOODLAND

Manufactured in the United States of America

Please visit my website at: www.mahoganywoodland.com

Facebook: Mahogany Woodland

Library of Congress Control Number: 2009940149

ISBN Number: 9780983431800

Book Cover Design by Lonnie Woods

Edited by Asha Taylor and Jacquia Frink

Layout and Design by Delaney-Designs

Website Design by Davo Productions

DEDICATION

I dedicate this book to three fallen soldiers who I will dearly miss. My two cousins: Marcus and Edward Woodland and my best friend of 8 years, Kofi Brown. Marcus and Edward, we might not have been that close as we got older, but if I needed anything, ya'll were there, and I will miss you both dearly.

Kofi you were always there for me whenever I needed you and were a big support of all my endeavors, this book included. I know you're in heaven smiling down on me. I love you and you will always have a place in my heart.

ACKNOWLEDGEMENTS

First and foremost I would like to give thanks to my Lord and Savior Jesus Christ for placing this vision into my life and making it a reality. If it was not for Him, there would be no book to be writing acknowledgements for. Therefore, I am so grateful for everything you have done in my life, and will continue to try my best to live my life in a way that honors you, God.

Next, I have to thank my mother, Thelma Woodland, for always believing in me and standing by me no matter what choices I made in my life. I love you forever and I am so grateful to have you as a mother. I want to thank my friends and family for always believing in me. I have to give a special shout out to Jacquia Frink, Olivia Crosby, and Monique Young. You may not even remember this but you three were some of the first people to read the beginning phases of the book and your excitement and encouragement inspired me to finish the book.

Next, I have to give a big thanks to Asha Taylor for editing the first versions of my book and to Jacquia again for editing the last version of the book for me. I truly appreciate all your help and the time you put in to help me out. Also, thank you to Mrs. Thelma Johnson for proofreading my book for me. I truly appreciate your generosity.

I definitely have to give a huge shout out to my girls, Olivia, Octavia, Tiffani, Jacquia, and Sharelle for being models on the cover of my book. Thank you for taking time out of your busy lives to help make my dream come true. Another big shout out to Mahadeo Lanz for doing all the hair and make-up for the cover shoot and also for introducing me to Stef Williams who put me into contact with Toya Evans; which got this whole process rolling. Thank you so much Lonnie Woods for designing the book cover. It was a long and tedious process and I thank you for all your help.

I would also like to thank my Zion Church family, especially the Remnant ☺, for your support, love and prayers. Thank you for always being there for me if I needed anything and believing in me.

Lastly, I would like to thank Toya Evans, my publisher, for helping to make this dream come true.

To those whose names might not have been included in the above list, please do not think that you are not important to me. There are just so many of you, that I could not possibly name you all. Please know that you all have had a major impact on my life giving me encouraging words along the way and supporting me in my various endeavors. To each of you, I say I love and appreciate you. I am grateful for each and every one of you in my life.

INTRODUCTION

*I've never had any female friends, and until now, never really
cared for any. When you're raised in the suburbs of Maryland,
you learn early on not to trust chicks because they mostly hate. I
was born in the used-to-be murder capital of the U.S., but unlike
most Prince Georges County natives, I don't claim D.C.; since my
mother and I moved out of the city when I was five. My father hasn't
been in the picture, but that's cool since you can't miss what you've
never had. It's all good. My mother handles everything. Not only is
she a beautiful, strong, intelligent, and ambitious black woman, but
if it had not been for her waking me up every morning for school,
and motivating me to do my work, I would not have a full academic
scholarship to XU now. I owe everything to my mother and tell
her that almost daily. And when I say everything, I mean EVERY-
THING; thank God I inherited her intelligence and her looks—at
least that's what everybody says who's ever seen my mother and
me. Just being real, I KNOW I got it! Who can deny a five-foot,
eight-inch, honey with flawless caramel skin, engaging hazel eyes,
and long, healthy brown hair with honey blonde highlights. Oh,
and don't sleep! The curves are in all the right places. Yeah, I
got it from my mama. A lot of people call me conceited, well most
of my graduating class; but I like to refer to it as being very ...
"confident." So that's how I got used to not trusting females, and
it also explains why my best friend is a guy, Mike Wood; who will*

also be joining me at XU on a full basketball scholarship. But back to my "confidence"; I sometimes wonder if my confidence intimidates a lot of the females around me and if that's the reason they don't like me, but regardless of the reason, I've gotten more than used to having only male friends or being by myself. It wasn't until my first week here at XU that I met a group of girls that made my males-only policy—and life—begin to change.

It was the first day of school for freshmen at XU, and what started off as a fun and exciting day took a turn for the worst. Me and six other girls, as different as night and day and who probably wouldn't have spoken to each other under normal circumstances, soon found ourselves in a predicament that forced us to bond. The university had screwed up, already, and misplaced our housing assignments, which led to us being temporarily placed in a small, two-bedroom, on-campus apartment until our housing predicament was solved. I was suddenly faced with having to learn not just a few, but SIX new personalities: Kelly, Ashley, Ebony, Melissa, Angel, and Dana. Over the next couple of days, I came to know who each girl was and what she was about. Kelly Brown was born in Newark, but moved to the suburbs of South Jersey when she was a little girl—too young for her to remember. She is the youngest of two, and her older brother also attends XU, which is one of the main reasons she chose to come here. Kelly, like me, is a beautiful girl. When I first met her, I had to give it to her; she was fly. Her 5'7" dancer physique went perfectly with her shoulder-length hair, which was nicely styled. She is what we refer to as "light-skinned." She had a lot of people fooled with her innocent, brown eyes and deep dimples, but I knew that Kelly was definitely somebody to look out for. Angel Perez is a sexy and *feisty Puerto Rican "mami" who carries herself with a toughness that is so characteristic of those who grow up in the Bronx; but once you got to know her, she is a softy at heart. Angel is mixed: her father is Puerto Rican and her mother is black, so she has that sexy, "exotic" look that music video directors love to exploit. With her long wavy hair, tall model physique, and tiny waist, Angel acts as if she's never seen her own reflection. I guess that's the thing that draws most people to her: her humility. Angel is undoubtedly a beautiful girl, but it hasn't gone to her head. Then there are the ATL cousins: Ashley and Ebony Johnson. They are as different as night and day, but thick as thieves. Ashley is loud, rambunctious, and always ready for a good time, while Ebony is quiet, soft-spoken and would rather stay home reading her Bible than hit up a good party. Like ying and yang, you rarely saw one without the other (unless Ashley was going to a party, and then she would be with the rest of the girls). Dana Lewis is a bold and aggressive female who has no problem going after what she wants, even if what she wants happens to belong to somebody else. I guess she had to be that way growing up on the rough streets of Newark, New Jersey. I could tell we were going to have to watch her since she was known for her loud mouth, and has a problem with saying the first thing that comes to her mind. Trust, if there is anything that she doesn't like about something or somebody, she will tell you. Although she's really pretty, her attitude sometimes takes away from that. Dana keeps her hair styled in beautiful Senegalese twists highlighted with red tips. She has a beautiful smile accentuated by her high cheekbones, and a curvaceous body that was doubly emphasized by her lack of height. She's only about 5'4" and is one of the thicker girls of the crew; unfortunately, she* uses that thickness to attract every sexy brother who walks by her—even if he has a girlfriend. Lastly, there is Melissa Wood, a seemingly quiet yet confident female, or at least that's what she portrays herself to be. She could be aloof and secretive at times, but I'm sure that's related to something deeper from her home life, which she rarely discussed. Melissa was from the rough part of East Orange, New Jersey, but she never let that hold her back and would never use that as an excuse for anything. In my opinion, she wasn't as attractive as the other girls, but she was far from ugly. It's hard to describe because I'm not a guy, but she had a sexiness about her that drove all the guys on campus wild. It was in the way that she carried herself, as if nothing fazed her.

With all of the different personalities, you would think that it would have been automatic chaos in that matchbox they called an apartment, but instead the exact opposite happened. For the next week, the length of time that it took the housing department to find housing assignments for all of us, we formed an unbreakable bond and vowed not to let anything get between our friendships. Or so we thought...

FIRST SEMESTER

SEPTEMBER
CHAPTER ONE

"How does this look?" Keisha asked Kelly as she admired her reflection in the mirror. She had on a black halter top that showed a little bit of cleavage, just enough to keep them guessing, and some Seven stretch jeans that accentuated her waist. A couple of weeks had passed since the girls arrived at XU, and Keisha and Kelly were now roommates. When the housing director found rooms for the girls, they all had the option of either rooming together or being placed in a room with a girl that they didn't know. When Keisha was made aware of the housing gossip, she jumped at the chance to have Kelly as her roommate because Kelly was the one who she built the strongest bond with. Of course the ATL cousins, Ebony and Ashley, became roommates; whereas the other girls opted not to room together. After living together for that week, the other girls knew that if they wanted to remain friends they were better off avoiding the conflict of becoming roommates. In the end, everything worked out for the best: Keisha, Kelly, Ashley, and Ebony all lived on the same floor in Tower A. Angel also lived in Tower A. Dana and Melissa lived in Tower C, which was walking distance from Tower A.

"That is cute, girl!" Kelly responded excitedly, giving Keisha her stamp of approval. It was a Friday night, and the girls' first official week of classes was now over. Keisha and Kelly were now getting ready to go to their first "official" college party. There had been a couple of social gatherings thrown by the Department of Housing during freshmen week—the week when all the freshmen arrive, but no classes are held—but no real parties had been thrown until tonight. This party was supposed to be one of the best parties this semester, and everybody was talking about it—even people at nearby colleges knew about it! Two of the most popular black fraternities on campus were sponsoring the party, so you had to come dressed to impress. Kelly matched Keisha's sex appeal with a pink see-through shirt with a matching tube top under it, dark blue skinny jeans, and pink BCBG pumps to top it off.

"What time are the other girls supposed to get here?" Kelly asked Keisha as she applied the finishing touches of her flawless make-up. Everybody had agreed to meet in Keisha and Kelly's room before heading over to the party at the student center.

"Umm…it's nine o'clock now….so probably around…now," Keisha answered nonchalantly while glancing over at the clock. Keisha still couldn't believe that she had gained so many close female friends. There used to be a time when her only close friend was her best friend Mike, but that had all changed now. It felt like she knew the girls forever, but it was only two weeks ago that her mother was driving her up to Jersey from Maryland. As if on cue, somebody knocked at their dorm room door.

"Come in," the girls shouted in unison excited for the night to begin. The party started at nine o'clock. The girls knew they wouldn't be on time however. College parties didn't usually start jumping until at least an hour after they got started; especially black parties.

"Hey ya'll!" Ashley and Dana greeted the girls as they walked in the room with Melissa trailing behind them.

"You're not ready yet?" Dana playfully asked Keisha shaking her head with a smirk. In just two weeks, Keisha had become infamous for being the last one ready when it came time to go somewhere, and Dana was always the one to point it out.

"Whatever! I'm almost ready. All I have left to do is put on my shoes. Plus, what's the rush? It's only nine o'clock and the party starts at nine, so you know it's not gon' be jumping til' like ten or so," Keisha playfully snapped.

"I don't know about that Keisha, this party isn't like the other ones we went to. I heard that you better get there early because this party is sure to sell out, and without a wrist band you will not get in." Ashley had done her research and was hoping her subtle comment would speed up the process.

"Ight, chill out. I'm almost done; plus Angel and Ebony aren't even here yet," Keisha replied starting to get irritated; she hated being rushed.

"Uh, hey ya'll," Angel greeted them apprehensively. They had been so engrossed in their conversation that they didn't even realize that she had slipped into the room.

"Oh that reminds me, Ebony's not coming," Ashley told them, after everybody greeted Angel. She had just remembered that Ebony changed her mind at the last minute about going out with them tonight.

"What! Why not?" Kelly asked disappointed that Ebony wouldn't be joining them.

"Girl you know Ebony ain't going out to no party." Ashley said matter-of-factly. "She's in the room reading her bible or something." Ever since Ebony's boyfriend of two years broke up with her this summer, Ebony had found herself back into the church and was working on developing a closer relationship with God. Although Ashley didn't agree with Ebony's decision to avoid going out because she was into church, she thoroughly respected her cousin's choice.

"Oh boy, we really need to get her out one night," Dana replied condescendingly. It wasn't that the girls didn't believe in God or anything, they even made it a point to go to church with Ebony on some Sundays. They felt like Ebony should continue to come and hang out with the girls on the weekends.

"Yeah, I know." Ashley agreed. Every time the girls went out, Ebony refused to come.

"No offense to God, but this is college -- a time when you don't have to worry about any major responsibilities. College is probably the only time in your life when you can let go of all of your inhibitions; plus we're young and we have plenty of time for that! Right now it's our time to just be young, dumb, and have some fun" Dana stated bluntly. Dana believed in God, but she wasn't trying to hear all of that right now. Angel quickly came to Ebony's defense.

"Girl, leave Ebony alone. I think what she's doing is admirable."

"Really? Then why don't you stay in tonight *with* Ebony?" Dana asked with a smirk.

"Hey, I said it was admirable. I didn't say that I was ready to take that step too," Angel replied with a sly grin that made the girls laugh because they were all thinking the same thing.

By that time, Keisha had finally finished primping in the mirror. With one final look at her stunning reflection, she turned around on her toes and dramatically snatched her purse off the bed and headed towards the door.

"Ight! Are ya'll ready to go or what?" Keisha asked in a manner that was nothing short of the diva that she was. Dana rolled her eyes at Keisha's dramatic ways. While the other girls snatched up their purses and followed suit.

~~~~~

"Daaaaaaggg! You wasn't lying, girl. This line is long as cra-a-a-p-p," Keisha emphasized to the girls. She was in disbelief when they reached the Student Center and saw the ridiculously long line for tonight's party.

"Mmm hmm," Ashley said rolling her eyes. She was pissed at the thought of having to wait in that long line. "I tried to tell you."

"Hey ya'll, don't even worry about that line. I just called my brother and he said we can skip the line and walk right up to the front," Kelly told them with a mischievous grin. She had known all along that her brother could get them in for free, but she didn't want to say anything too soon just in case he couldn't get them all in. Kelly's brother, TJ, was a junior at XU and a member of one of the hottest frats on campus, who also happened to be one of the frats hosting the party, so it was no problem for him to get them in. Plus, since their clique was the flyest group of freshmen females on campus, his frat brothers had no complaints. The upperclassmen guys on campus had started calling them the "freshmen honeys" since they were all some of the sexiest freshmen at XU. It had been determined that every single one of them had it going on;

they were smart, ambitious, fine, and could dress their butts off.

"Thanks TJ," Keisha purred flirtatiously into TJ's ear as she walked by him and into the party. Keisha had a humongous crush on TJ ever since the first time Kelly had introduced him to her. However, with his six-foot frame, smooth light-brown complexion, dimples, and taut athletic build, she was hardly the only one who had an eye on him. Matter fact, just about every female on campus had a little crush on him, including Dana. Which explained why, Dana made sure to strut her healthy hips and wink at TJ when she walked by, completely disregarding the fact that her girl, Keisha, had a crush on him. The way she looked at it, any guy was free game until one of them was actually talking to him. In this short amount of time, Dana noticed that this wasn't the first time her and Keisha had eyes for the same guy, and she doubted it would be the last. The party was jumping when they walked into the multi-purpose room. All the students were partying to "Make It Rain" – a hot new joint by Fat Joe.

Wow! The party is jumping already, and it's only ten o'clock. Ashley wasn't lying, Keisha thought to herself as she looked around seeing who was there. In the back of the party, there were football players for days just standing around ogling over the various female physiques grooving to the latest sounds around them. While Keisha was scanning the room in amusement, she spotted Mike on the opposite side of the room with some of his teammates. The tall basketball players were doing their thing on the wall, while different Greek fraternities and sororities competed for attention in the middle of the dance floor, doing their party strolls through any open spaces they could find. It was kind of funny observing all of the different male groups on the dance floor. Surrounding each one was a pack of groupies hovering by, dancing around them and vying for their attention. Keisha just shook her head and laughed. As far as she was concerned, everybody was equal in God's eyes, so why put anyone on a pedestal? She could never allow herself to stoop so low as to be a groupie, and neither could the rest of her girls. That was one of the main reasons why they were regarded so highly on campus; not one of the "honeys" had accepted any of the many offers from the desire and lust-filled males on campus—even upperclassmen. But some of the girls had plans to change that tonight.

"What ya'll wanna do first? Walk around the room and see whose here or start partyin'?" Kelly asked the girls while fighting the urge to let her hips wind to the reggae rhythms reverberating through the room.

The girls agreed to see who was there, and laughed at the fact that a couple of them had said the same thing at the same time. That seemed to be happening a lot lately. It was a ritual they had started when they arrived at any party. First, they would walk around the premises to see who was there, or more importantly, to scope out the cute guys that were in attendance. The next move was to begin dancing around the section that had the most cuties. Thirty seconds into their walk through, Dana and Melissa made a detour claiming that they were going to say 'hi' to some girls they knew, but everybody knew the real deal; they were on their way over to see Ray and P—a couple of sexy football players that they always flirted with whenever they had a chance.

"I don't know why they like those dudes so much," Keisha whispered to Kelly, who nonchalantly shrugged her shoulders while moving through the crowd. It wasn't that Keisha didn't like Ray and P, but she didn't like the fact that they were football players. Everybody knew football players were the worst guys to talk to at XU because the majority of them were "hoes" -- plain and simple! But honestly why wouldn't they be? They had the most groupies of any male clique in the entire school, and they were young so they took advantage of it. Keisha knew that all the football players weren't "hoes," and that there were some good ones out there. However, they were few and far in between so Keisha opted to stay away from them just in case. Mike, Keisha's best-friend, was on the basketball team and had to arrive at XU early in the summer. He ended up having the opportunity to chill with a lot of the football players, considering they were the only other males on campus besides his teammates. From that, Mike got to hear about how a lot of those guys viewed females, and see how they acted when females came around. He made it a point to inform Keisha when she arrived at XU on how those dudes got down, and warned her to stay away from them. Thinking of Mike and him looking out for her, Keisha made her way over to see him and his sexy teammates. It felt like forever since Keisha had chilled with Mike. She was always with her new girls hanging out now, and didn't find much time to spend with him anymore.

"Hey, what's up?" Keisha greeted Mike with outstretched arms.

"What's up, girl? I thought you were going to call me when you were on your way over here," he said giving her a mean mug and acting as if he wasn't going to hug her.

"I was…but then, all the girls came in the room and distracted me, so I figured I would just see you up in here," she said giving him the puppy dog face that he could never stay mad at.

"You are so stupid," he said referring to her look. "You're lucky that I came over here with my boys; otherwise, I would have

still been sitting in my room waiting for you to call." He tried
to fake a serious tone. She just gave him the *boy, you know you
lying*-look, and they both started laughing.

"Whatever, you know I still love you. We'll get up after the
party. I promise!" Keisha told Mike while making the scouts honor
sign with her fingers.

"Ight, that's a bet. And make sure you bring your sexy new
friends with you too." He shook his head in admiration of Kelly,
Angel and Ashley's beauty as they passed by. Before Keisha could
comment, she was distracted by Juvenile's gritty grunt signaling
the beginning of his hit "Slow Motion."

This song will definitely get the crowd hype, Keisha thought;
the crowded room erupted in shouts of excitement confirming her
prediction. For the first few moments, all that could be seen were
females and males alike scurrying to find a dance partner to "slow-
motion" grind with. Keisha didn't have much time to look because
Jaden, one of Mike's teammates, swiftly made a place behind
Keisha's ample behind and started grinding on her backside.
Keisha had no problem with that though considering that Jaden
was six-four, with a sexy, muscular physique, and some of the
biggest and cutest puppy-dog eyes she had ever seen. She noticed
him around campus, but never spoke to him before. Guys like
him, you had to let make the first move, especially since he was on
the basketball team, and had plenty of females approaching him
on a daily basis, trying to get with him in some form or another.
Keisha didn't want to be seen as one of the many, so she kept her
distance from him and figured that if he wanted to holler at her
then he would approach her, and if he didn't…oh well! There were
too many dudes out here to be tripping off one!

"Hey, beautiful," Jaden whispered into Keisha's ear before slowly turning her around to face him so that he could gaze deeply into her hazel eyes.

"Hey, cutie," she whispered back. As if on cue, Usher's voice serenaded the room with a tease *"Can you handle it, if I go there baby with you-u-u-u-u?"* Jaden began to hold her tighter as he slow danced with her personalizing the message of the song with his body.

"I've noticed you around campus," Jaden whispered into her ear and then paused. "And I like how you carry yourself."

"Really? Why's that?" Keisha seductively whispered back, turning Jaden on to the point that he had to step back a little bit unbeknownst to Keisha.

"Because, you're not like these other girls out here…flaunting themselves at any attractive and available guy on campus. You carry yourself with class, and I like that in a potential wifey."

Keisha knew he was just gaming her up, but it still sounded good. Good enough that she accepted an invitation for the crew to hang out with him, Mike, and the rest of their teammates at T.G.I. Friday's after the party ended. Keisha soon found out, Dana and Melissa had other plans though.

CHAPTER TWO

Ray is so sexy. I have to make him mine tonight, Dana thought to herself as she and Melissa made their way to Ray and P's apartment. Both girls had already decided earlier that night that they were going to leave the party early to hang out with the guys. They didn't tell the other girls about it until they were actually leaving out in order to avoid listening to their reasons on why they shouldn't go. Dana and Melissa both had already made up their minds, so it would have been nothing they could've said to convince them otherwise. Ray and P stayed in a three-bedroom, on-campus apartment that was only about a two-minute walk from the Student Center. Their other roommate, Ace, was at the party, so it would just be the four of them in the apartment chilling.

"So ya'll want to watch a movie while we chill?" Ray asked the other three, with special interest in Dana's reply.

"I don't care," Dana replied smoothly trying to conceal her excitement. She had had a crush on Ray since the first day she met him. She and Keisha were on their way back to the dorm from the Dining Hall one evening, when Ray approached them. At the time, it seemed like he was more interested in Keisha than Dana; but the second Ray mentioned he was on the football team; Keisha lost complete interest in him. She discretely passed him over to Dana by excusing herself from the conversation, claiming she had to make a phone call. Dana had no problem with that because ever since that day, whenever she and Ray would see each other, they would flirt incessantly.

"Hey Dana, come in here and help me pick out a movie," Ray yelled to her from his room.

As she sauntered towards the room his voice had come from, she noticed Melissa and P walking towards P's room. Melissa gave her a little wink, as she closed the door. *Uh-oh let me find out Melissa gets down like that,* Dana thought with a smirk. She thought she was a little goodie-good, but she guessed it was true what they say; it's always the quiet ones! But then again, Melissa *was* pretty secretive; so Dana wouldn't put it past her if she were a closet freak. The thought put a big grin on her face.

"What you grinnin' 'bout?" Ray asked Dana as she walked into his room in his deep gritty southern accent.

"Oh, nothing," Dana responded breathily.

The sexual tension was thick between the two of them. She noticed that he couldn't make eye contact for staring at her lips, but she had her eyes elsewhere too. Ray had taken his shirt off while she was out in the living room, giving her a clear view of his six-pack abs. *Hmm, just looking at him is making me hot,* she thought to herself while trying to keep her hormones under control.

"So, what movie you wanna watch?" he repeated. This time, he sounded even sexier with his country drawl. Ray and P were both from Miami. The football scholarships are what landed them at XU.

"Let me look," Dana responded while purposely bending over

in front of him, so that he could get a good look at her supple
booty. She had been told by many sources that she had an onion;
in other words, just looking at her booty would make a grown man
cry. Turning around suddenly and catching Ray off guard, Dana
could see that her tactic had worked. "How 'bout we just put a CD
in and talk…since you *did* say you were trying to get to know me
better?"

"Ight, that's wassup," Ray replied as he slipped in R. Kelly's
"TP2" album. Ray always put that CD on when he had a female
over; it always seemed to put them in a sensual mood. It had never
failed him in the past, and he was hoping it wouldn't fail him
tonight. He walked around Dana and sat on the edge of his bed.

"Come here," he said as he patted his knee for her to sit on.

"Dana, you have some of the most supple lips I have ever
seen," he barely whispered while gazing into her eyes and glancing
at her lips hungrily.

"Really…" she started speaking, but was cut off by his
lips as he gave her one of the most sensual kisses she had ever
experienced. *Hmmph, his lips feel so good*, Dana thought to
herself as a light moan escaped her lips.

"Oh, Ray, that feels so good," Dana moaned as Ray started
kissing her on her neck and working his way down while laying her
flat on the bed. She wondered how far down he was going to go, but
before she had any more time to wonder, he unbuttoned her pants.

"You want me to stop?" Ray knew the answer before it came
out of her mouth.

"Nooo," she moaned despite her intuition telling her to leave.

Deep within her heart, Dana knew it was way too soon for
her to be doing this with him. So much was running through her

mind. Even though she knew she shouldn't be doing this so soon with a random dude she just met, it just *felt* so right. Her mind was saying "Stop," while her body was saying, "Go!" It looked like her body was going to win this one. *Plus, it's not like I'm a virgin or anything,* Dana thought as she tried to rationalize her impulsive behavior to herself; but this was the first time that she had ever been in a situation like this—intimate with somebody she barely knew. It was too late for Dana to change her mind now though. Ray had just put a condom on and proceeded to finish the "deal." Ray made it a habit to never run up in a chick raw. A couple of his boys back home made that mistake; and now had little ones running around from chicks they cared nothing about. *Dat sho' nuff ain't about to be me*, Ray thought snidely with a triumphant smirk.

~~~~

"Where Dana and Melissa at?" Ashley whispered to Keisha so that nobody else would hear their conversation. Keisha, Ashley, Angel, and Kelly were just getting out of the party and walking with Mike, Jaden, and the rest of the basketball team as they all walked to get something to eat. Ashley was just noticing that Dana and Melissa weren't with them. She was busy dancing when Dana and Melissa told the rest of the girls that they were leaving early to chill with Ray and P.

"They left early to go chill with Ray and P," Keisha whispered back nonchalantly.

"Hmmm, I don't even know what to think about that. But I do know that they are missing out tonight," Ashley said referring to them hanging out with some of the most attractive guys on campus. Keisha didn't respond. The way she saw it was who Dana and Melissa chilled with was their business. She just told them to be careful, have fun, and hit her up when they left so she would know that they were all right. Although she didn't trust Ray and P, they were big girls and she trusted they could fend for themselves. She left it at that.

"What ya'll over here whispering about?" Jaden asked Keisha out of nowhere. Being quick on her toes Keisha swiftly responded, "I was just telling Ashley how sexy you are."

"Ah-h, let me find out you got a lil' game," Jaden laughed impressed by her quick wit. T.G.I. Friday's was in walking distance to campus, so they got there in no time. When they were finally seated, it ended up being like twenty people: the majority of the basketball team—which was like twelve guys—five of the guys' female friends, and the four of them. All the girls were cool, except for this stuck up and bougie one, Nadine. She had a complaint about everything the waiter did or didn't do. Keisha wanted to tell her to chill out and just enjoy herself, but it was too late to be making a scene. Plus, Nadine was the girlfriend of one of the senior basketball players, Chris, so she definitely had more clout than Keisha had with the other guys. Chris was one of the stars on the team and was supposed to be good enough to go to the league, which is why Nadine was like a pit-bull when it came to her man. Anybody who got too close to him would feel her wrath.

I'm sure hell hath no fury like a Nadine scorned, Keisha thought to herself with a laugh. Another NBA prospect on the team is RaShawn. RaShawn wasn't that cute, but his personality made up for that. For him to have so many people sweating him, and still be so laid back and chill was impressive. Those two were the only two seniors on the team; the rest of the team was made up of four juniors, a couple sophomores, and four freshmen.

The girls ended up being spread out at the table, but Keisha got to sit next to Jaden. Keisha never could have fathomed that she and Jaden had so much in common until that night. They ended up talking about everything. She told him that she planned on majoring in sports management, and then going to law school to become a sports and entertainment lawyer. He told her how he was majoring in business because he was going to need something to do with all the money he would be making from the NBA. It seemed like everybody on this team had hoop dreams, and thought that he was going to make it to the NBA. Keisha entertained the possibility. She had to give it to them; they did make it to the final four of the NCAA tournament last year, and were undoubtedly expected to do the same this year. Keisha was really surprised that Jaden hadn't said anything to tick her off yet, especially since she usually avoided talking to athletes. Having one for a best friend, she knew all about how they liked to get down. Mike used to have girls throwing the *booty* at him, and that was only high school. She could only imagine what college was like. It was funny because Jaden swore up and down that he was not like one of those guys, and while Keisha was skeptical to the truth in that, she was seriously thinking about making an exception for him. The way she looked at it, this was her freshmen year! She wasn't looking to get wifed up, she just wanted to have some fun.

~~~~

"Wow! That was, by far, the best sex I have ever had."
Ray lay impressed by the beauty lying beside him.
"Ray?"
"Wassup, sexy?"
"I just wanted to tell you that I don't normally do that with

people I barely know."

"Don't worry about it. I'm not going to think any differently of you," Ray easily lied. On the real, he just lost a lot of the respect he had for the girl. She should have at least tried to hold off for a couple of weeks, made him work for it. Still, he couldn't deny the sex was off the hook and the head was crazy. *Umph! I might have to keep her around a lil' longer just off the strength of her skills!*

"What you smiling about?" Dana asked snuggling closer to him.

"I'm just sitting here thinking about how much I'm feeling you," Ray quickly gamed her up, telling her exactly what she wanted to hear even though it was furthest from the truth; while kissing on her neck gearing her up for round two.

I love freshmen girls! They are so easy, he thought to himself as he dove for more.

~~~~

"Wake up! Wake up!" Ray whispered in Dana's ear trying to wake her up from her nap. *What can I say? I wore that lil' young joint out. I had her screaming my name all night, while I gave it to her in every position,* he thought with pride. "Get up girl. It's time for you to go home."

"Whyyy?" Dana whined.

"I got practice in the morning," he told her. That, plus the fact that it was against house rules to let chicken heads stay overnight. That privilege was saved for wifey's only.

"Can't I just sleep here till you get back?" Ray shook his head wondering if it was boldness or just plain stupidity that had prompted her to ask such a ridiculous question. Usually he would have just let a chick know that all she was to him was some booty. It was some good booty, but still booty nonetheless—and just because they had sex did not mean that she was his girl. A lot of girls had it mixed up thinking that dudes were like them. *They* got their emotions all entangled after they got some, thinking the dude would feel the same. The way Ray saw it was if a girl gave him some this fast, what would make him think that every other dude couldn't get it that fast? That's what girls failed to realize! A "wifey" is a female that respects herself enough to wait until she gets to know a guy before she gives him some. This isn't saying she has to wait until they're in a relationship to give it up, but a wifey knows better than giving it up on the first night, especially when a real conversation hasn't even occurred. Dana was young; she'd learn the rules of the game sooner or later. Since this *was* her first time in a situation like this, Ray decided to be nice and not kick her out like he did some of those groupie broads. There was a difference between a chicken head and a groupie. A groupie was somebody who would do anything it took (meaning having sex or even pleasuring your boys just to be in your presence) because you're on the football team, basketball team, or if you basically have some type of higher status than the average guy. A chicken head, on the other hand, was just a young and dumb chick that gave it up too fast, thinking that it was going to make the two of you closer. A chicken head was just naïve, and for that reason Ray just gave her a BS excuse, instead of hurting her feelings like he would usually do.

"I'm sorry, but coach doesn't allow us to have girls stay overnight and he sends someone to check each room at three o'clock every night to make sure that everybody is in the bed sleep with no company. It's two forty-five now, so you gotta hurry," he easily lied to her. *If she believes this then she really is dumb.*

Why the heck would a coach wake his players up at 3 am just to see whether there are girls in their rooms? Ray thought to himself with a smirk. The only time they had curfew and a checker was the night before a game, and most of the time the coaches had them put up in a hotel the night before a game.

"Oh okay," Dana conceded as she got up reluctantly and started dressing. Ray had to admit, lil' mama had a banging body with a fatty to boot. He was definitely going to have to keep her around for a little while longer. If she was lucky, he just might school her to the game. *But for now its time to send these chicks on the walk of shame*, Ray thought as he and P kicked Dana and Melissa out. For those who didn't know, the walk of shame was when a female realized that she had sex with somebody that didn't care about her, and so instead of being cuddled up in bed next to him, she was walking back to her room all by herself with her pride gone and ego bruised.

Sorry to say, I have sent a lot of girls on that walk, Ray thought with a smirk. It takes two to tango though!

~~~~

What a night, what a night, Melissa thought to herself as she and Dana walked back to the dorms. Melissa knew when she and Dana were going over to P and Ray's apartment that P wanted to do more than just "talk." But it was cool with her since P was sexy as crap with his long, honey-tipped dreads, and tall, lean physique. She wanted him the second she saw him at the party. A lot of people saw Melissa as the quiet, cute girl so her actions surprised P tonight. As soon as Melissa and P got into his room, she began a little strip tease for him.

"I know why you brought me here," she had told him. So after she had stripped to her Vicky bra and panties she closed the door and took care of her business. Unlike some other girls, Melissa was not afraid to get hers. She was like a dude when it came to sex; if she saw something she wanted, then she was going to go after it— even if it was taken. She didn't care. Melissa had a lot of people fooled with her shy, insecure act. If her girls really knew the real her, she's not sure if they would still want to be as close with her. For that reason, she planned on keeping that side of her on the low for a while. She chuckled thinking about how she had him knocked out by one thirty.

He is definitely going to be sweating me for some later. Too bad I don't usually go back after I have sex with a guy on the first night, Melissa thought to herself with a smirk. *That's when they think they got you.* So, what she did was flip the script on them. Her policy was to not call them, and when she saw them she'd just give a head nod to say what's up and kept it moving. She treated them like she didn't even know them, which was the same way dudes be treating females. *That mess be pissing them off!* Like tonight, while P was sleep, she just went out to their living room, watched TV, and waited for Dana to come out. When P finally woke up and realized that Melissa wasn't there lying next to him it confused the mess out of him, but he couldn't even say anything because Dana and Ray came out at the same time he did. Melissa just said, "bye" and rolled out leaving P standing there baffled about what just happened. *I think he was expecting a kiss goodbye or at least a hug or something,* Melissa laughed as she thought about the night's events.

"So, what did you and P do?" Dana asked Melissa nosily while making that trek back to their dorm. Dana was quickly becoming one of Melissa's closest friends out of the crew.

"Well, before I tell you… you have to promise me you won't tell anybody else and you have to tell me what you and Ray did. Agreed?" Melissa asked her.

"Okay," Dana agreed. "Now get to the juicy stuff." Melissa then proceeded to tell Dana the whole story of what went down, blow for blow.

"For real, girl? Was it good?" Dana asked laughing.

"Girl, was it! So what did you and Ray do?"

Dana then proceeded to tell Melissa all the details of how her and Ray ended up doing it. *Wow, who would have thought that me and Dana would have ended up bonding at the end of the night over having sex with Ray and P?* Melissa thought.

"So what happens now?" Dana asked hesitantly, like she didn't want to know the real answer to that question.

"Well, if you're smart you won't trip off of em'. Just chalk it up to a in-the-heat-of-the-moment thing because you need to remember although he made you feel special tonight, it's about twenty other girls on this campus thinking that they're just as special to him," Melissa told Dana, giving it to her straight. "And that's real!"

"Daggit, I usually don't let myself slip up like that. I at least play with a guy's mind first before doing anything with him. That way I at least have em' on me and doing whatever for me to get with me; and then, and ONLY then, do I usually give it up." Dana told Melissa exasperated. Melissa scoffed at Dana's frantic reaction, but a previously nonexistent thought came to both of their minds; there might be unwanted consequences later on down the road because of what they did tonight.

CHAPTER THREE

Although the Greek party tonight was supposed to be one of the best parties of the semester, Ebony was glad that she didn't go. She had just finished reading the book of James in her Bible, and James 1:12 promised, *"The lord blesses those who patiently endure testing...."* Closing the Holy Book, she reclined against her pillow knowing that this was exactly what she was going through right now: a test. Her girls just couldn't seem to understand that in order to be a *true* follower of Christ, you had to make sacrifices. Although she did miss going out to parties and grooving, the desire to be dancing and grinding all up on some random guy (or guys) was no longer there. It just wasn't something that she thought she should be doing.

I just wish my girls *could understand and respect that, instead of always trying to pressure me into going out with them every weekend.* What a lot of them didn't know was *why* their pressure was a test to Ebony. A bittersweet smile crept on her face as she glanced across the room at nothing in particular, reminiscing on the days when she didn't live her life so innocent. The smile was one of happiness from recognizing her growth, but sadness from how that growth was obtained. It wasn't until her boyfriend of two years broke up with her over the summer that she threw herself back into the church and her religion. What was ironic was that her ex-boyfriend, Darren, was actually the reason that she had grown apart from the church in the first place. When Darren first entered her life, she had just made a vow to remain a virgin until marriage and was diligently pursuing a close relationship with God. That lasted about a month, until she broke that vow and began having sex with Darren on a regular basis. At first she felt guilty about what she had done, and would cry herself to sleep at night, but the more time she spent with him, and the more they had sex, the less guilty she began to feel, and eventually ended up pulling herself away from the church altogether. And honestly, if Darren hadn't had broken up with her claiming that a long distance relationship would mess up their "intellectual and social growth" in college, she would still be living that life.

Initially, his reason for breaking up with her had pissed her off; like the Toni Braxton song, she wished he'd just be a man about it. She had wanted the truth; and the truth was that he would be attending Clark University in Atlanta, with seventy percent of the student body being females. That meant for every ten people at Clark, seven of them were females—and at least five had to be homegrown, southern girls who were known for being stacked like grown women at the age of like fifteen. It took a while for the anger to subside, and when it did, she saw the reality of how hurt she really was because this was the guy who she had given her virginity to, and he was supposed to be there with her for the long haul. It wasn't until she forced herself to get back into the Word and into the church that she realized that everything—including the break-up—happens for a reason. She was now learning that

God is a jealous God, and He wants to be first in your life. If you are investing more time into something else that does not honor Him, He will take it away from you; but God is also a loving and forgiving God that blesses those who put Him first. She could feel His grace and mercy on her life, even in the most difficult times.

Knock-Knock! The sound startled Ebony from her thoughts. Not waiting for Ebony to open the door, Ashley, Keisha, Kelly, and Angel barged into the room all talking at the same time announcing that they were having a sleepover in her room. Ebony's mood welcomed the chattering girls; she had to admit, it *was* kind of lonely being in the room by herself all night. She did miss her girls.

"So, how was the party?" Ebony asked the girls. The girls erupted into their different versions of the party simultaneously. "Please! One at a time," Ebony said laughing at how excited each of the girls were. Ashley skipped all of the details of the party, and went right into their evening with the basketball team at Fridays and how much fun they had there.

"What's wrong Ebony?" Angel asked Ebony concerned, after noticing a distraught expression on her face.

"Nothing," Ebony replied plastering a phony smile on her face to conceal her true thoughts. Truthfully, she was a little upset that her friends left her out when they went to Friday's. Just because she didn't want to party didn't mean that she wanted to be alienated from all the social events—she would've gone to the restaurant had she known. In addition to that, she thought that Ashley would know that, since they *were* cousins and so close.

"Come on Eb, I know you, what's wrong?" Ashley scooted closer to make eye contact with Ebony. She hadn't fallen for the quick-smile trick.

"I just wish you guys would have invited me to Friday's at least. I mean, I'm not allergic to social gatherings."

"Aww, girl I'm sorry. We just figured that since you didn't go to the party you wouldn't have wanted to go to Friday's." Ashley and the girls didn't mean to leave her out; they just got caught up in all the excitement, and didn't even think to ask if Ebony would want to go.

"Yeah, we're sorry girl. Next time we'll make sure to call you after a party to see if you want to come," Keisha promised Ebony, while all of the other girls nodded their heads in agreement.

"It's cool ya'll." Ebony felt better now that she had been open enough to tell them the deal; she had always had problems with that—especially if she thought it would cause conflict. "By the way, where are Dana and Melissa?" Ebony asked the group, just noticing that they still hadn't came into the room yet.

"They decided to chill with Ray and P after the party," Keisha replied nonchalantly.

"I just talked to them, and they're on their way over here," Ashley said as she hung up the phone with them. She had just called to make sure that they were okay.

"Hmm, I wonder from where?" Angel said sarcastically. Keisha and Kelly giggled at the comment, while Ashley scolded them; Ebony was just plain ole' confused.

"What's that supposed to mean?" Ebony asked them, still not understanding the joke.

"Nothing, Angel is just trying to be funny," Ashley responded to Ebony chiding the other three girls. Before anybody could say anything else, Dana and Melissa walked into the room.

"Speaking of the devils," Keisha said playfully. "So how was *ya'll* night?"

"It was cool," Dana answered vaguely, glancing surreptitiously at Melissa. They already suspected that the girls would want to know blow for blow what happened, but Melissa was preoccupied with her suspicion of what the girls had said about them.

"What were ya'll saying about us?"

"Nothing. We were just telling Ebony where ya'll went," Kelly answered honestly.

"Oh." Melissa conceded, but she didn't really believe Kelly.

"So, what did ya'll end up getting into?" Keisha asked curiously with a mischievous smile. Although all the other girls wanted to know the same thing, Keisha was the only one that was bold enough to ask them. Melissa and Dana shared secret smiles with each other before Dana answered, "We chilled at their apartment and watched some movies." Melissa and Dana were going to tell them the truth about what happened tonight, but after they walked in on the other girls talking about them, they weren't too sure if they could trust them completely. So before any of the girls could ask them any more questions, Dana changed the focus.

"What did ya'll do after the party?"

Ashley excitedly began to tell them all of the details of the night, and the other girls, with the exception of Keisha, soon forgot about the questions they had for Dana and Melissa. Keisha wasn't fooled; she just decided to let it rest for now. *Everything done in the dark eventually comes to light,* she thought to herself with a knowing smirk.

"Do ya'll know how many girls who would have loved to have been in our place tonight?" Ashley randomly asked the group.

"I know I do! Plenty of them groupie chicks would have done

anything to be where we were tonight and probably have. I'm telling ya'll, these groupie chicks out here are funny." Keisha told the girls, as she felt a slight disgust creep up in her throat as she recalled a story that Mike had told her about when he first got up at XU.

"Mike told me the first week he was up here these groupie chicks came to each of the freshmen basketball players dorm room and knocked on their doors wearing nothing but trench coats. He was like the chick that came to his door didn't even say hi or nothing. She just dropped the trench coat and went straight to his room, with no words said."

"Whatever girl, you lying," Kelly exclaimed with disbelief, but humored by Keisha's seriousness. There was an outburst of mixed responses, but Keisha knew her best friend, and he was NOT a liar.

"Whatever! I don't believe that. Mike had to have exaggerated that story. Come on let's be real now, who does that?" Ashley adamantly stated while shaking her head in disbelief.

"That's just trifling," Ebony commented while scrunching up her face in disgust.

"Believe what you want, but my boy ain't no liar. And that's how they be getting down out here," Keisha confirmed. "And I heard the football players are the worst ones." The girls were oblivious to Dana and Melissa's waning involvement in the conversation after Keisha made her comment. They couldn't forget what had gone down earlier that night and where they had just came from. Even though Melissa was up on her game, she, with Dana, silently hoped that what they did wouldn't come back to haunt them.

After that died down, Kelly began giggling out of nowhere.

"What is so funny?" Keisha asked curiously as she looked

at Kelly like she was crazy.

"Oh, my bad, I was just thinking about how confused ya'll looked when they started playing some New Jersey club music," Kelly responded pointing at Keisha and Ashley. Angel, Dana, and Melissa began cracking up laughing too, while Keisha and Ashley rolled their eyes. New Jersey club music belonged to the genre of house and dance music, only with a hip-hop twist. But if you were not from the tri-state area, it was something that you had to get accustomed to; Keisha and Ashley found out the hard way. Angel, Melissa, Dana, and Kelly being from around the area had no problem getting into the groove when the club music came on at the party. Angel was especially amused.

"Ya'll looked like ya'll had just entered a foreign country or something and everybody was talking a language that ya'll didn't know."

"That's how it felt," Ashley responded laughing. "When everybody started dancing to that trash I was like, what the heck are they playing?"

"I feel you girl. We definitely don't listen to that back in Maryland where I'm from, although club music *did* originate in Baltimore; but the P.G./DC area, where I'm from, crank that Go-Go."

"You mean like stripper music?" Ebony asked confused. The girls fell out laughing, while Ashley pretended to be a stripper and danced around an imaginary pole. Still laughing, Keisha clarified what she meant by "Go-Go."

"No, it's like a live band playing their own version of popular songs that are out. Like, it's a Go-Go version of Fat Joe's 'Lean Back'. You got to hear it to understand."

"Trust me; you guys do not want to hear it." Kelly said twisting up her face. Kelly, being Keisha's roommate, was forced to listen to Go-Go and could not stand it. It sounded like a bunch of people banging on pots and pans to her. The next thing Kelly knew a pillow hit her in the face.

"Stop hatin'!" Keisha screamed while laughing, and trying to duck the pillow Kelly threw back at her. What started as Kelly and Keisha throwing the pillow back and forth became a full-blown pillow fight with everybody. *I guess you can't have a sleep-over without a pillow fight*, Keisha thought to herself amused and observing the love going around the room; *I hope it's always like this.*

CHAPTER FOUR

"You guys want to play a game?" Ashley asked after everybody had settled down from the pillow fight. The girls had decided that since nobody was ready to go to sleep, they might as well have an "official" sleepover.

"What type of game?" Keisha asked her. Ashley gave a devious smile and looked over at Ebony before replying, "A game called Twenty Questions."

"I don't think they're ready for that," Ebony said returning the same devious smile.

"Ya'll *must* not know! I was born ready," Keisha bragged. "So what are the rules of this little game?"

"Okay, here are the rules; each of us writes down five questions on a piece of paper that we want everybody in this room to answer. It can be any type of question you want to ask. The juicier the better! Then, after everybody finishes writing their question, we put them in a bowl and one person picks a question out of the bowl and reads it out loud to everybody. Everybody then has a choice. They can either answer the question or pass. The only thing, though, is that if you pass, you have to reach into another bowl which has a whole bunch of crazy dares on pieces of paper. You cannot back down from whatever you pick! The game is only fun when everybody agrees to follow all the rules. So do ya'll want to play?" All of the girls agreed, although some looked apprehensive. "Before we start though, everybody has to agree that what is said in this room stays in this room. Cool?" Once again everybody agreed, and Ashley began the game.

"Ight. Everybody write out 5 juicy questions, and 5 crazy and wild dares that you would never want to do yourself."

Hmm, what questions do I want to ask? This is kind of hard, Kelly thought while she spotted each of her friends busy scribbling things down. She had never been too good at daring—something she learned in high school playing Truth or Dare. *Ooh!* She frantically wrote down under dare: Go downstairs to the vending machine and get some snacks, wearing nothing but a towel and flip flops. *This is going to be fun,* Kelly thought with butterflies in her stomach as she turned in the rest of her dares and questions. Sitting on the other side of the room, Keisha was just as puzzled as she thought about some of the dares she put into the basket. One of them was: run around this floor in nothing but a bra and some panties screaming, "I'm a pretty princess!" *I plan on answering all of the questions because if their dares are as crazy as mine, then I know that I'm not trying to do a dare. Plus, I ain't got no cut cards, so you can ask me anything and I have no problem telling you the answer,* Keisha thought to herself self-righteously.

"Okay is everybody ready?" Ashley asked the girls, assuming the role as moderator. After she was satisfied with their response, Ashley started the game by pulling out the first question. "Alright, the first question is an easy one. What do you aspire to be?" The girls laughed heartily at the safety level of the question, which actually made it cheesy in this context; but the rules required them to answer it. Ashley answered first, stating that she wanted to be a forensic detective and be like the people on CSI. Kelly, as expected, wanted to become a renowned dancer and choreographer with her very own studio. Keisha wanted to "get paid off the people who make the most money" or in other words, be a sports and entertainment lawyer. Dana was also planning to go into law. Ebony wanted to be a doctor and Melissa couldn't decide between a doctor or a psychologist. Angel wanted to be a model, but would settle for journalism if that didn't work out.

"How hot would that be?!" Angel went on excitedly about the idea of winning on Tyra Banks' *America's Next Top Model.* The girls talked over each other about the idea of their home girl being the next Eva Pigford. No one could deny that she definitely possessed the beauty, height, and attitude for the profession. The next couple of questions were pretty easy to answer, and everybody answered 'no' to questions like: have you ever had a STD? And are you in a relationship? It was starting to get kind of boring. Keisha was the first one to speak up.

"Ey' ya'll, I'm sorry but this is starting to get just a *little* boring for me, so how about we switch the rules up some?" Dana started talking before Keisha could even finish.

"I agree! I thought this game was supposed to be 'juicy'," Dana glanced at Ashley in a semi-mocking way.

"What you thinking?" Ashley asked Keisha, ignoring Dana altogether.

"Okay, instead of waiting for somebody to take a pass on a dare, how about we combine both the question bowl and the dare bowl. That'll make the game a lot more exciting," Keisha suggested. Judging by everybody's facial expression, it appeared as if they liked the idea. "So, we'll keep the question part the same, but if somebody pick's a dare instead of a question then they have to do the dare," Keisha finished up.

"Ight, that sounds good," Ashley said agreeing with the new twist on the game. All the girls nodded their heads in agreement. So, Keisha stuck her hand into the dare-mixed-with-questions bowl, and mixed all of the pieces up really well with her hand.

"Since, I suggested the new twist on the game, I'll go next." Keisha said as she picked the next piece of paper out of the bowl. *Dag! I hope I get a question because I am definitely not in the mood to be running around campus acting a fool,* Keisha thought to herself. "Yes!" Keisha slightly whispered to herself happily as she saw that she picked a question. *Hmm, this question is definitely juicier than the last ones;* Keisha thought as she read the question to herself first, then read it aloud to the rest of the girls.

"Alright, the question is 'Where, when and with who did you lose your virginity to?'" Since Keisha picked the question, she had to answer first. "The first time I had sex was when I was sixteen, with Mike…" Keisha started.

"Mike your best friend?" Kelly asked interrupting Keisha.

"Yes, my best friend. Anyway, we were chilling at my house one day after school while my mother was at work. We were both virgins and kind of curious about what it would feel like. So, we started messing around, and one thing led to another and then it happened," Keisha finished with a smile.

"Wow, so what happened between you and Mike?" A curious Kelly asked, while everybody else looked at Keisha with eager eyes.

"Well, we went together for awhile, but the chemistry just wasn't there. We both decided that we were just better off as friends. Now, who's next?" Keisha hurriedly asked with a devious grin, ready to hear everybody else's stories. Angel raised her hand, signaling that she wanted to go next.

"Sorry guys, I don't have a story for ya'll because I'm a virgin," She answered with a sheepish grin. Everybody's mouths dropped in astonishment. No one would have guessed that any of them hadn't done 'the do' yet.

"Yup," Angel reiterated as if someone had asked her a question.

"Are you waiting until you get married?" Dana asked.

"Nah, it's nothing like that. I just haven't found the right person. Ya feel me?" Even though the rest of the girls couldn't relate through experience, they understood the logic behind Angel's pure state.

"Well trust me, you should definitely wait until you get married," Ebony told Angel in a voice tinged with regret, as she went into the story of her first time.

"Well, me and Darren met the beginning of our junior year in high school. He was in one of my classes. Everyday for a couple of weeks he would ask me if he could take me out, and I would tell him no, since I was really into my Christian walk at that time. But by the third week, I couldn't resist those pretty brown eyes and handsome features. About a month later, we were chilling at his house and it just happened," Ebony concluded with a nostalgic look on her face. She didn't want to go to into too much detail for the fear that it would have taken her back to a time in her life that she vowed to leave in the past.

"Well, I guess I'm next," Dana declared to the group to break the uncomfortable silence. "Let me think, my first time was with sexy Joe Brown," Dana started her story with a look in her eye like she was back in that night. "It happened on the night of my junior prom, which was a magical night in itself. Prom was held at this nice hotel near Newark Airport, and we decided to get a room there afterwards. And, let's just say we ended a magical night with a magical experience." Dana said with a wink.

"Awwww," everybody wooed over Dana's storybook experience with 'Sexy Joe Brown.'

"Well, my experience is definitely not as sweet and romantic as that one," Kelly said after everybody quieted down. "It was my sophomore year in high school and I had this huge crush on this senior named Dj. Dj was *super* fine. He was one of them guys that all the girls wanted and would do anything to get. Dj was also one of my brother's closest friends, so he would always be at the house, but I was always too scared to say anything to him. But, even if I wasn't scared, my brother would have kicked my butt for talking to him—for good reason, I found out later on. So one day, my brother had a big get-together at the house, and I finally got up enough courage to strike up a conversation with him. My brother didn't notice because he was too busy gamin' up some chick. We had a nice long conversation and after that, he started calling me. Of course I thought I was in love, so a couple weeks into us talking he got me to skip school with him and we went to his house. Let's just say one thing led to another and I said goodbye to my virginity." After a few minutes of silence, the other girls finally realized that she was finished with the story.

"Man, you can't leave us hanging like that. What happened between you and Dj?" Keisha asked her. *Damn, she got me sitting*

on the edge of my seat wondering what happened with them,
Keisha thought to herself as she looked around the room. She
could see that everybody else was just as curious as her—if not,
more so—to know what happened after it all went down.

"Ya'll don't really want to hear the rest," Kelly said while
sucking her teeth and looking around the room with a devilish grin.
The room bubbled over with pleas from the girls: "Come on!"
"Tell us!" and then they all started in with "Pleeeeeeeeeeeeeeease!"

"Alright, alright, since ya'll are begging me," Kelly said
with a satisfied laugh. "Well, basically after that day, me and Dj
continued talking and having sex for the next couple of months
whenever he wanted it. I soon found out that Dj had three other
girls that he was having sex with. I know this sounds stupid, but
at that time I didn't care, because Dj's game was so tight that
he could make you feel so special when he was with you, that
you didn't even mind sharing him. Plus Dj only messed with the
tightest, prettiest, and sexiest girls; if you were one of his girls it
instantly boosted your popularity. I had so many chicks coming
up to me like you are so lucky."

"Wow! Dj must've been the ish' then," Dana said interrupting
her. "This negro must have looked better than Boris Kodjoe,
Usher, and Morris Chestnut combined the way she describing it."
The girls looked at each other and then fell out laughing at Dana's
candid opinion.

"Trust me he was. I'll show ya'll a picture later. But anyway,
just being considered one of Dj's girls was a privilege. But that
feeling was short-lived because my brother soon found out and
straight up blacked on me."

"Hol' up, hol' up! He did *what* on you?" Keisha interrupted her with a hand in the air. She was still just getting used to this Jersey slang. She never thought each state would have a different slang vocabulary until she got up there. Just the other day when she told Kelly she was "lunchin" Kelly looked at her like she was stupid. "Lunchin" back in Maryland meant that someone was tripping, but up in Jersey it literally meant going to lunch.

"Oh, I forgot I gotta translate for ya'll. It means he screamed on me."

"Oh ok. My bad, you can finish your story now. I promise I won't interrupt again." Laughing, Kelly continued, "Ight, so basically to make a long story short, my brother put some sense into my head. He told me that I was better than that, and it was no reason why I should be proud of sharing a man and allowing him to have control of my body whenever he wanted it. My brother then schooled me to the game, and taught me the difference between being a wifey and a chick on the side. After that little talk, I definitely decided that I was a 'wifey' and deserved to be treated like one. I told Dj that, and after he laughed in my face I stopped messing with him and vowed to never let another Negro have control over my body the way Dj did."

"Dag, that story was on point." Ashley said. "Right on!" She threw up her right fist, giving the infamous 'Black Power' sign. Everyone laughed and chimed in throwing their pseudo-feminist fists in the air, mocking Kelly's firm resolve.

"I'm curious, what's the difference between a 'wifey' and a 'chick on the side?'" Melissa asked.

"Well 'wifey' is a girl that gets treated with respect, gets taken out, and basically is a girl that all the guys want to have. In order to be wifey material, though, you have to treat yourself with respect by not letting anybody else disrespect you. You gotta be something like untouchable. Meaning, a lot of guys may come at you, but only a chosen few actually get you. On the other hand, a 'chick on the side' is basically what it sounds like. It's a girl that a guy just has around to smash. He doesn't take her out, introduce her to his boys, and the only time he spends time with her is so he can smash. That's what I was, and I'm not going back to it."

"I know that's right," Keisha said in agreement. "That is definitely the way to go!"

"I guess I'll go next!" Melissa exclaimed grudgingly. She had already decided to herself that she wasn't going to tell the girls the real story of how she lost her virginity. How her first real boyfriend in high school had forced her to have sex with him in his car one night, after a date when she was fifteen. Nah, she had already decided she didn't want their sympathy or for them to look at her any differently. She had had enough of that with her friends back home. Plus, they were having such a fun time; she didn't want to put a downer on the night by telling her story. So she told them a BS story about how after school one day, she and her first real boyfriend had had sex and that was that.

"Ight, Ashley it's your turn. You're the last one up." Angel said, after Melissa told her story.

"Well, my story is definitely not as romantic as Dana's or as entertaining as Kelly's." Ashley started off.

"Hmph!" Ebony huffed as she rolled her eyes and tried to keep herself from laughing.

"Anyway!" Ashley said while rolling her eyes at her cousin, and ignoring her giggles. "My first was a guy named Ron Oakley. Ron was my first real boyfriend. We were together from my sophomore year in high school to the beginning of my senior year. In the middle of junior year, Ron's parents were supposed to be going away for the weekend, so I lied to my parents and said I was staying at a friend's house, but instead I stayed over there. I thought my first time was going to be this magical experience, but instead it was the worst experience ever. First, Ron had trouble getting the condom on. I had to help him, which threw the mood off a little bit. Then he couldn't find the right hole to put it in. And just when it seemed like things couldn't get any worst, his parents walked in mid stroke." That had to have been one of the funniest stories of the night. The laughter began at the condom part, and by the end of the story the girls were rolling around the floor, kicking their legs and crying from laughing so hard.

"That may not have been the most romantic or entertaining story, but it was definitely the funniest," Keisha said laughing.

"I agree," Dana said while wiping the tears from her eyes from laughing so hard.

"Oh my gosh! So what happened after that?" Kelly asked her.

"His parents looked at us, walked right back out, and then came back in and started screaming for us to get dressed. They then called my parents and we had to sit through a long lecture on why sex before marriage was wrong." She answered stone-faced, which started a whole new bout of laughter. "It's not funny. That experience traumatized us so bad, that we didn't attempt to have sex ever again." Although she tried to keep a serious face, she couldn't help but to eventually join the girls and start laughing.

"So why did ya'll break up?" Angel asked.

"Oh, we just got tired of each other."

"Ight, who's next to pick?" Keisha was focused on getting

them back on track.

"I'll go." Angel said. "No dare, no dare, no dare," she repeated as she stuck her hand in the bowl.

"Daggit, it's a dare. It says: I dare you to open up the window and yell, "Look at me" while flashing your boobies to the people outside.""

You would have thought since it was two-something in the morning that there would be nobody outside, but this is college, and people were out and about until like four in the morning or later some nights. The worst thing about it was that Ebony and Ashley's room faced the front of the building where everybody sat and smoked their cigarettes, since Tower A was a smoke-free resident hall. The girls soon began clapping and cheering Angel on, as she slowly walked over to the window and began inching up her shirt. She just looked back at them with the I'ma-get-each-and-every-one-of-you-chicks- back-while-you're-sleep look.

"Hold up, let me get my video camera," Ashley said laughing.

"You better not put my boobies on camera," Angel screamed. All the girls cracked up. *Man, I haven't laughed this hard in a long time*, Keisha thought to herself with a smile, happy to have this group of women as friends in her life.

"Don't worry I'm not going to put your 'boobies' on camera. I'm just going to tape us laughing at you," Ashley responded sincerely with a smile.

"Thanks! Like that's not as bad," Angel replied to Ashley sarcastically. Angel then opened the window and screamed "Hey, look at me." It had to have been like twenty, drunken guys out there because all the girls could hear was all kinds of cat calls and whistles from outside. The girls all applauded Angel for not backing out.

"Kelly it's your go," Keisha said continuing the clockwise rotation that they had started going in. Everybody started clapping and whooping in anticipation of what she might pick. After Angel's dare, everybody was hoping that she would get a dare too. They were not disappointed.

"Oh boyyy! I got a dare… My dare says: I have to knock on Aaron's door down the hall and ask if I can borrow his soap," Kelly said looking real distraught.

"Boooo, what kind of dare is that?" Keisha asked disappointed.

"I'm not done yet," she said pouting. "I have to do this wearing nothing, but a bath towel and a shower cap," Kelly finished with an exasperated look on her face. The girls squealed with delight and amusement.

"Oh no! Isn't Aaron that cute guy down the hall?" Angel gushed.

"Hold up, I definitely gotta get the video camera ready for this," Ashley said laughing while Kelly went into the bathroom that they shared to change into the towel; but left her undergarments on. There was no way she was walking down the hall with a towel on and nothing under it. Ashley had just turned the video camera off, but quickly got it ready to record Kelly. "This is going to be classic. Something that we'll always remember, even when we're all old and grey," Ashley gushed.

"You can be so corny at times," Dana told Ashley laughing.

I guess the saying just might be true: the friends you meet in college are the friends you will have for a lifetime, Keisha thought to herself as she watched Ashley chase Dana around with a pillow and anxiously waited for Kelly to walk down the hall.

CHAPTER FIVE

I can't believe I'm doing this, Kelly thought to herself as she walked down the hall to Aaron's room with nothing on but a towel and a shower cap. *Keisha would be the one to suggest switching the rules of the game. She better not fall asleep before me,* Kelly thought with a laugh. *She is going to wake up with all types of toothpaste, shaving cream and whatever else I can think of on her.*

"It's almost three o'clock in the morning. What if he's asleep?" Kelly hissed back down the hall to where they were standing laughing at her.

"Don't worry he's always up late," Keisha promised her.

"How you know?" Angel asked Keisha with a smirk, insinuating that Keisha liked Aaron.

"Shut up, you know that's just my peoples," Keisha replied, while rolling her eyes at Angel. Keisha and Ashley hung out with Aaron all the time, so they knew he stayed up late.

"Even worse, what if he has a girl in there?" Kelly paused to hiss back at them before she made her way down the hallway. She was starting to rethink what she was about to do. Aaron had his own room by default, since his roommate decided not to attend

XU anymore at the last minute. Because of that, you could usually catch a female sneaking out of there on the late night.

"That's why I said he's not sleep," Keisha responded laughing. *Oh boy! Am I really about to do this?* Kelly asked herself in disbelief as she began knocking on his door. There were some shuffling sounds coming from inside the room before Aaron came to the door with an amused look on his face, as he looked Kelly up and down admiring her slim physique in the towel. *Thank God, nobody else was in his room. This was embarrassing enough with just him seeing me like this,* was all Kelly could think, almost forgetting what she came down there to do.

"Um, how can I help you?" he asked with a smirk.

"Uh, I ran out of soap, and I was wondering if I could borrow yours?" Kelly asked sheepishly.

"Are you serious?" He replied laughing. Then he looked down the hall and saw the rest of the girls rolling around the floor, dying from laughter.

"Oh, I get it. Ya'll must be playing truth or dare or something," he said while shaking his head thoroughly amused.

"Yeah, something like that," Kelly replied barely audible and utterly embarrassed. "Well, thanks, I guess, I'll see you later," Kelly stuttered and then quickly ran back to the room before she could make even more of a fool out of herself.

"Hey Aaron," Dana greeted Aaron, with a wave, while still on the floor laughing.

"Ya'll are crazy," Aaron said laughing and then shut his door.

"I CANNOT BELIEVE YOU ACTUALLY DID THAT," Ashley screamed while tears streamed down her face from laughing so hard. By that point, Ashley had put the camcorder down, too busy laughing to tape anything else.

"Um, 'scuse me, but can you guys keep it down? It is damn near three o'clock in the morning. Some of us are trying to sleep!" The obnoxious, nasal voice came from an angry neighbor who was clearly trying to get some sleep next door. They all got quiet for a moment and then roared with laughter even louder.

"That's it! I'm calling the R.A.," the obnoxious voice declared before slamming the door.

"*That's it, I'm calling the R.A.*," Dana mocked the girl in the same nasal voice, which caused the group to fall out and laugh even harder.

"Come on you guys, get in the room before you get us written up," Kelly said and then went into the bathroom to put her nightclothes back on. After Kelly got out of the bathroom, there was a loud knock on the door—more like a bang. Everybody in the room got dead silent, while Ashley walked over and opened the door.

"Oh no, it's the R.A.," Ebony whispered. They couldn't hear what she was saying, but it didn't look good.

"Sorry guys, but your little 'sleepover' is over. I have gotten too many complaints and I'm dead tired right now. So, I am not a happy camper, but I'm going to be nice tonight since it's still just the first month. So instead of writing you guys up, I'm just going to need for everybody who doesn't live in here to go back to their room right now. Okay?" She was obviously pissed off about being woken up from her sleep this late. They were all having so much fun, that they were sad it had to end like this. Then the R.A. went and stood at the door while she waited for Keisha, Kelly, Dana, Melissa and Angel to gather their stuff up and go back to their own rooms.

"We'll finish our game later," Ashley told them

"Man, this sucks. Just when it was starting to get good," Keisha mumbled under her breath as she walked out.

"Hey, Kelly why don't you go see if Aaron will let you sleepover in his room," Dana said being funny. Kelly didn't even respond, she just rolled her eyes at Dana and made her way to her room, while the other girls laughed.

"Bye guys," Angel said while shaking her head at the exchange between Dana and Kelly.

~~~~

"Man, I'm mad," Kelly told Keisha. They were in their room and were each lying in their beds.

"I know me too. The sleepover was just starting to get fun and that little witch next door had to call the RA."

"No, I'm mad because I was the only person who ended up doing a dare that truly embarrassed me," Kelly said pouting.

"Hmm…mmm," Keisha sputtered as she unsuccessfully attempted to hold in her laugh, which caused them both to burst into fits of laughter.

CHAPTER SIX

Wow! This class has a lot of people in it, Kelly thought as she
walked in to her Calculus 101 class. This happened to be her first
time in this particular class because the professor had a death in
the family and canceled the class for the first week. Kelly knew
college courses had a lot of people, but it had to be close to a
couple hundred people in there. She was used to classes within
her dance major, which only had about twenty or so people in
them. That was because the dance school was very competitive,
and only accepted 250 freshmen out of 10,000 applicants a year.
Kelly quickly found a seat in the fifth row close to the aisle. As she
sat down, she glanced around the classroom to see if there were
any familiar faces, but she didn't see any. Class began. Kelly
felt as if she had been dropped into the Twilight Zone because she
couldn't understand a word the professor was saying. She looked
around to see if she was alone in her struggle, but everyone else
was either pretending or really good at deciphering some form of
Hindi dialect. Her difficulty wasn't because the class was hard
or anything; Kelly was really strong in math, and even took AP
Calculus in high school. It was because the professor just didn't

speak English clearly. He was this short, Indian guy with a thick accent. Just as she was about to ask the person on the right side of her if they understood anything the teacher was saying, Kelly felt somebody sit down in the seat on her left side.

"Hey!" Aaron whispered. Shocked, Kelly whispered back, "I didn't know you had this class."

"Yeah. Is it me, or do you not understand anything this guy is saying?"

"That's funny. I was just sitting here thinking that very same thing," Kelly replied.

"Shhhh," an aggravated student trying to listen to the lecture, hissed at them.

"Come on let's get out of here. We can't understand him anyway, and I'm sure we can find something better to do with our time," Aaron whispered to Kelly with a smirk, trying to hold in his laughter so not to aggravate the student even more. He didn't have to ask her twice; Kelly wrote down the homework assignment that was due for the next class, and led the way to the nearest exit. Kelly wasn't really tripping off missing the class because she learned from her brother that you don't need to *go* to class to get an 'A.'

"So, what do you want to do? It better be good since you got me skipping class," Kelly said teasingly to Aaron.

"Well we could go back to my room and —" Kelly quickly gave him the, "I-know-you- didn't-just-come-at-me-like-that" look. "Sike naw, I'm just playing girl. You ain't have to look at me like you was going to kill me or something. Damn! But nah, I got my car on campus, so how about I take you to the movies?" Aaron asked.

"Yeah, that sounds cool," Kelly was more than willing to break the monotony of the school day.

~~~~

"So, you're telling me that ya'll skipped class and went to the movies?" Keisha asked Kelly amused. The girls—except Dana and Melissa—were on their way to the Glen Dining Hall to get something to eat, while listening to Kelly tell a story about skipping class and going to the movies with Aaron. Dana and Melissa had class, and were going to meet up with them later. After the night of the sleepover, Aaron started stopping by Keisha and Kelly's room to chill with Kelly, and earlier today he finally asked her out; now the girls were teasing her about it.

"Yup," she said with a dreamy glimmer in her eye.

"I don't believe you," Ashley squealed, "Well how was it? And don't leave anything out."

"*Well,* there's nothing to tell. It was a regular date." Kelly replied.

"Aww boooo," Keisha yelled. "You are so boring. Ya'll didn't kiss or anything." Laughing and with a sly wink Kelly replied, "I don't kiss and tell."

They walked into the Glen causing a ruckus with their boisterous laughter. Keisha knew everybody was looking at them like something was wrong with them, but she could care less what they thought. *Shoot, we ain't got half the problems some of these fools lookin' at us got!*

~~~~

"Man, I can't stand when girls walk in a room acting all loud and ghetto," TJ, Kelly's brother, told his best friend, David, as these loud girls walked in. He swore it was the same thing every year. These young, freshmen chicks come in thinking they're cute and that they can automatically run things up here. They were definitely in for a rude awakening.

"I know man," David responded. "Hey! Ain't that your sister over thurr?" David still couldn't shake his Midwest accent. David was from St. Louis and was at XU on a basketball scholarship. TJ and David were roommates their freshmen year, and had instantly clicked. Now, even in their junior year, they still hung tight.

"Where? OH NO! What is she doing?" TJ was completely disgusted that his sister was among the group of rowdy, chickenhead-acting females that had completely made a fool of themselves with their uncouth behavior. TJ had specifically told Kelly on her first day not to be one of those loud, obnoxious freshmen girls. Apparently she didn't listen very well, and they were going to have to have another talk. It might seem like he was being too uptight and hard on her, but it was for a good reason. He knew the game: the upperclassmen guys use the first couple months of the semester to observe and prey on the incoming freshmen girls. They then point out the ones that seem to be the most immature, curious, naïve, and overly excited. Those are the easiest to turn out and have on their dicks. TJ knew this for a fact because that's what him and his boys did last year, but that was a completely different story.

"Damn, your sister got some sexy ass friends," David commented with a gleam in his eye like he was already thinking up a plan about how to get one of them. TJ didn't say anything. He just looked over to where they were standing. *Damn, David ain't lying. I mean her crew was some straight dimes*, TJ thought to himself. They had all the brothas' attention up in that joint. He was just going to have to make sure that they didn't let those upperclassmen take advantage of em'. Kelly's roommate had to be the sexiest one to him, though. With her beautiful hazel eyes, long silky hair, and banging body. *Shorty has it going on. She is without a doubt wifey material,* TJ thought to himself while biting his lip. He might have to bend his don't-mess-with- any-of-his-little-sister's-friends rule this one time. TJ had noticed Keisha at the party over the weekend, but never got a chance to talk to her that night. He didn't plan to let that happen today, though.

"Hey TJ," Kelly greeted him as she sat down at the table with her friends. "You already met Keisha," who just so happened to sit down right next to him "and this is Ebony," she continued while pointing to a *real* cute but quiet looking chick. "And this is Ashley," she then pointed to another very attractive female that looked a lot more outgoing. "Lastly this is Angel."

"Hey ya'll. This is my best friend David," TJ said so everybody would be familiar with one another. He noticed David staring at Ebony, which was funny because she was definitely not his type. That was not to say that she was unattractive or anything. It's just that David usually went for the aggressive-type girls who took chances and had sex appeal oozing off of them. That reminded TJ that he needed to check them on walking up in the dining hall all loud.

"Hey D, you think I should school 'em?" TJ asked David warming up his speech he was about to give them.

"Yeah, I think they cool enough," David replied with a smirk, playing along.

"School us on what?" Keisha asked, giving TJ the eye.

"Ight, I'ma let ya'll know how things go down up here at XU. Ya'll can't walk in a building or a room laughing and talking all loud. It brings too much negative attention to your-selves."

"What's wrong with laughing with friends? If other people

don't like how loud we are, then that's on them. Na'mean?" Keisha stated plainly.

"I feel ya, but hear me out. I'm not finished." His eyes begged for Keisha's permission, and with a nod, she granted it. "The upperclassmen prey on beautiful freshmen girls like your-selves, and they especially take advantage of the ones who are really loud and draw attention to themselves. And trust me; you do not want to be one of those chicks who get picked out in the beginning." The girls still didn't seem to get a clear understanding about why they had to be so careful; TJ and David just looked at each other and shook their heads. All the girls needed to do was heed the advice given, they didn't need to know anything more than that. Telling them all of that would be breaking the rules in the player handbook.

"Ya'll don't need to know all of the 'whys' 'hows' and all that, just know that ya'll are a beautiful group of young ladies and a lot of guys are going to be trying to get at you. Just make sure that you don't holla at all of em' and be careful of who you talk to, because a lot of these dudes up here are grimy."

"Whatchu mean by that?" Kelly asked. She most definitely wasn't trying to get caught up by some trifling, lying no-good Negros in school. That was the last thing she needed after what she had been through with her first boyfriend.

"That means that they will game you up until they hit it, and then go at your roommate right in front of you like you don't exist."

"Damn, it's like that!" Ashley exclaimed.

"Yeah some dudes up here really be goin' like that."

"Are ya'll like that?" Keisha asked looking directly at TJ.

"Who? Us!?!?! Oh, nahhh, me and my mans not grimy like that," TJ replied in mock shock, giving the appearance that he was surprised that she would even suggest such a thing.

"Hmm mmm." It was clear that Keisha wasn't buying his act, but she was still flirting: a green light.

"What you don't believe me?" TJ and Keisha were now conversing with each other in privacy because the rest of the group had broken into different conversations.

"So you're telling me that you have never taken advantage of one of the 'young and dumb' freshmen chicks that came in last year and hit it and quit it?" Keisha asked TJ flirtatiously. TJ could tell by the way she was flirting with him that regardless of the answer he was going to get her number anyway; so he decided to just evade the question and get at the real reason she was asking him the question.

"Why are you so concerned with who I'm hittin' and quittin'?" Keisha knew that TJ wasn't ready to handle her. *This dude think he 'got' me*, she thought haughtily. Rather than fighting the truth, Keisha told TJ exactly what he wanted to hear.

She leaned over and whispered, "Well, I need to know what type of person my future boyfriend is." *Damn, she got me aroused like I don't know what,* TJ thought to himself. Usually a warning sign went off in TJ's head when any chick mentioned the "b word," but when Keisha said it, he could envision it. He had to give it to her: she had game. Just that moment, David kicked TJ under the table interrupting TJ from his thoughts, and gave him the man *you better holla at that* look. TJ laughed to himself that his man would think he'd let an opportunity like Keisha pass him by. What David didn't know was that TJ was already a step ahead of him as he discretely slid Keisha his cell phone under the table to put her number in.

~~~~

"Yeah, I saw you over there, son," David said to TJ while dapping him up as they gathered their things to leave. Laughing TJ replied, "Yeah, Miss Keisha definitely has it going on, but what's up with Ebony? I saw you peeping her out, while she was sitting at the table." It took a nudge to get the response out of David. "Ey, man! Wake up! I said what's up with Miss Ebony?"

"I don't know, son." The crazy thing was that David really didn't know what to say or how to describe it. He didn't understand it himself; he sure didn't know how to explain it to his boy. "She's one of those church girls, and I usually try to stay clear of that kind, but it's something about her that just pulls me to her. Son, I know that sounds crazy, but that's real." David let his voice drift off as he digested everything he just said.

"What!? Let me find out the pimp himself, is catching feelings for a chick—a freshman, church girl, at that!" TJ teasingly chided David. Ever since TJ had known David, David had never had a girlfriend or even expressed interest in being in a relationship. He never spoke against being in one, but his actions spoke for him. He changed girls like he changed his drawers, which was one of the many benefits of being a starting basketball player. So, it surprised TJ, to see his boy this into a chick that he wasn't even talking to yet.

"Nah, man, it ain't even like that. I just think shorty is cute and would like to see what she's about," David knew he wasn't believable, but he tried to play it off before TJ had a chance to respond. "Man come on, let's roll." With that, David got up from the table with his tray and headed out the cafeteria.

~~~~

"Ebony what's up with you and David," Ashley teased Ebony as the girls walked into the dorm and made their way upstairs to Ashley and Ebony's room, which had become the unspoken hang out spot for the girls.

"Yeah, I saw ya'll over there flirting," Kelly co-signed with a silly grin.

"What are ya'll talking about?" Ebony asked Ashley in genuine confusion. "Why would something 'be up' with me and David?"

"Come on, Eb, don't tell me you didn't see the way David was all up in your face asking you questions? I started to ask him if he wanted to change seats with me," Angel huffed playfully. She had been sitting in between David and Ebony while they were at the Glen earlier.

"Well, I'm not interested in him if he is interested in me," Ebony stated plainly.

"Why not? David is beyond fine. You better snatch that up girl!" Kelly exclaimed, while Keisha high-fived her in agreement.

"I'm not interested in talking to any guys right now. I'm just trying to stay focused on God," Ebony replied starting to become frustrated.

"Damn girl, I knew you were into church, but I didn't think you were becoming a nun," Keisha joked. The rest of the girls started laughing so hard, that Ebony eventually did too.

"Whatever! I see ya'll got jokes, but it's cool though…And that reminds me I didn't appreciate that comment ya'll made when David had asked me why I didn't go to the party." Ebony said semi-serious.

"What comment?" Keisha asked. She had been so involved in her intimate conversation with TJ that she missed everything the others were discussing.

"Ashley was like 'Ebony would rather sit in her room and read the Bible than party'," Ebony reiterated not amused. Ebony didn't expect the girls to up and change and start living their life for God like she was, but she did expect them to respect her lifestyle.

"Dag, Ashley why was you hating like that?" Keisha asked Ashley jokingly.

"Nah, I was just playing," Ashley apologized and walked over to hug her cousin. She hadn't meant to be disrespectful. "For real, I was playing. Eb, girl you know I didn't mean it in a spiteful way. I'm sorry if that offended you." Ebony just nodded her head, to signify that she accepted the apology.

"I just got one question, if you're not interested in talking to him, then why did you give him your number?" Angel asked Ebony mischievously with a grin.

"What? I said I'm not interested in talking to any guys. I didn't say I wasn't interested in having any friends. Besides, he asked if he could go to church with us this Sunday, so I gave him my number and told him to give me a call."

"Mmm hmm, well you better watch out for that girl. A guy will act as if he's into God and church one second, and the next he'll be trying to get you into the bed," Keisha stated seriously.

"You ain't never lied," Kelly shouted in agreement.

"What ya'll in here shouting about?" Dana asked amused, as she walked through the open dorm room door and into the room with Melissa in tow. Angel then proceeded to update Dana and Melissa about what went on in the Glen earlier.

"So, you're talking to TJ now?" Dana asked Keisha, trying to conceal her jealousy. Dana couldn't understand why all the guys she liked always seemed to like Keisha instead.

"Yeah girl," Keisha responded ecstatically. "Oh yeah that reminds me, is it okay with you Kelly that I'm talking to your brother."

"Yeah girl, you know I don't care. I rather see you talking to him than any of these trifling heifers on campus," Kelly replied sincerely. All the while, Dana sat seething to herself disgusted at the interaction between Keisha and Kelly, burning with envy and jealousy.

OCTOBER

CHAPTER SEVEN

It was the middle of October, and Keisha was finally starting to get used to the whole college thing. The being on her own and responsible for every little thing from waking herself up in the morning to making sure she turned in the right assignments on time, which was a tough feat at times, especially since some of the professors could care less if students attended class or not. They got paid regardless of the numbers in attendance. Keisha did have to admit that having great friends like Kelly, Ashley, Ebony, Melissa, Dana and Angel helped her immensely in making the transition from high school to college. After the weekend of the sleepover, the girls had been pretty much inseparable. Two other people that Keisha had also been getting closer to were Jaden and TJ. They were the only guys that Keisha 'messed with' at the moment. Keisha was talking to this Puerto Rican 'papi' as well, but he started sweating her just a little bit too much, so she decided to cut him off. At first, Keisha was approaching her situation with a carefree mindset. After all, this was her first year in college, so she just wanted to chill, have fun, and do the little pimp thing; not worry about the guys. But now Keisha was starting to change her mind because she found herself beginning to fall for both TJ and Jaden, which was crazy to her. She would have never thought that she would be falling for both of these dudes this soon. A week ago, she knew for sure she was about to be caught up because she didn't realize that David, TJ's best friend, was on the basketball team with Jaden; since he wasn't at the Friday's that night. After she panicked and called Mike for some advice, he told her that she had nothing to worry about because TJ and Jaden didn't really chill like that with each other. It had something to do with some undisclosed issue that happened their sophomore year. Whatever it was, it kept the two guys from knowing about each other, or maybe they knew about each other and just didn't care since neither one had said anything to her about it. The more she thought about it, the more Keisha concluded that she didn't have to tell one that she talked to the other because it wasn't like they told her the other girls that they talked to. Keisha knew they had some other girls they messed with even though Jaden tried to make it seem as if it was all about her. TJ on the other hand acknowledged that there were other girls that he talked to, but he liked to make it seem as if they didn't compare to her. Plus, with TJ being in a popular frat and Jaden being on the basketball team, she could trust that they both had girls coming at them everyday, sweating them, and some willing to do whatever for them. Keisha was pretty sure that they were doing their thing when they weren't with her, and, honestly, she didn't have a problem with that considering that she wasn't either one of their girlfriends and she hadn't had sex with either one of them. As far as she was concerned, they could do whatever they wanted. *Speak of the devil,* Keisha thought to herself as TJ knocked on their open dorm room door.

"What's up?" TJ said walking into the room.

"Hey," Keisha, Kelly and Ashley replied in unison. Kelly was over at her desk typing up a paper, while Keisha was lying on her bed talking to Ashley, who was sitting at Keisha's desk playing on the Internet. TJ gave Kelly a hug first, and then came and sat down on Keisha's bed next to her. Keisha always felt awkward about being affectionate with TJ in front of Kelly, even though Kelly was cool with them talking.

"You ready?" TJ asked Keisha playfully tapping her thigh. They were supposed to be going to the movies tonight to see this new scary movie. It was a Saturday night, so they had to get there early because it was sure to be sold out.

"Yeah, I'm ready. I just gotta put my shoes on," Keisha answered while sitting up and reaching down to put on her black, Nine West boots. She was already dressed in some dark blue, Express jeans and a tight-fitting, low-cut black top. The boots just topped the outfit off.

"You look nice," TJ complimented her, while admiring her body at the same time.

"Thanks."

"Oh yeah, before we go, I need to ask ya'll something," TJ announced looking at Keisha and Ashley, and then at Kelly.

"What's up?" Kelly asked him while turning her back to her computer and facing him.

"Are ya'll real tight with those girls Dana and Melissa?" Kelly noticed that look; TJ meant business.

"Yeah, those are my girls. Why?" Kelly asked him hesitantly.

"Well, I heard some stories about them, and from what I've heard, I don't think it's in your best interest to be associated with them," TJ stated bluntly.

"What kind of stories?" Kelly asked. She had started playing with her hair, which indicated the beginning of irritation. She was irked that the first semester hadn't even passed before somebody had started spreading rumors about their girls that were serious enough for her brother to suggest that they stop hanging with them. TJ first looked at Keisha, and then looked back at Kelly, like he didn't want to tell them.

After Kelly gave him a look that said, "Look, I ain't got all day," he replied.

"Ya'll didn't hear this from me, but I heard that the night of my frat party a month ago, they gave it up easily to a couple of football players I know, and whenever the guys want some easy pussy, they were like they can just call them up. Then the following weekend Melissa got with one of my line brothers. The funny thing about it is that he wasn't even going at her like that, but after he walked Melissa to her room she came at him trying to smash."

"What! Are you serious?" Ashley asked with disbelief. It wasn't a secret to her that the girls had had sex with them; she was more shocked at the way Ray and P tried to play them. Just the other day, they saw Ray and he was claiming how Dana was his "boo" and how much he cared about her. Melissa on the other hand never even talked to P again after that night, so it was no reason for him to make it seem like she was at his beck and call. Plus the other girls already knew Melissa liked sex, and that was how she got down.

"Dead serious," TJ replied solemnly.

"Wow," was all Kelly could muster. Keisha on the other hand was not surprised. She had tried to warn Dana from the get-go that it was something wrong with those dudes.

"The worst part is that a lot of the upperclassmen on campus are referring to them as J.O.'s, which stands for jump-off, and a girl that is classified as a J.O. is a girl that Niggas just hit up when they trynna smash. They don't get taken out, and they most definitely don't get wifed up. And, sorry to say it but if you're seen chilling with a J.O., then sometimes you will be guilty by association. That's why I would rather ya'll not be associated with them chicks, for real." TJ really hoped that they listened to him because he didn't need his baby sister or a girl he was interested in being labeled as a J.O. That would not be a good look for him.

"Hmm, well J.O. or not those are my girls and I'm not gonna diss them because some dude started a rumor after he got his feelings hurt," Keisha stated irately, referring to P.

"Yeah, TJ, I'm sorry but I can't just disown my friends because a couple of guys on campus might look at me different. And if they don't want to talk to me because I'm associated with Dana and Melissa, then they weren't worth talking to in the first place." Kelly exclaimed with her neck rolling to emphasize what she was saying.

"Ight, that's cool. I respect that lil' sis, I was just letting ya'll know what's up. You are all big girls and grown enough to make your own decisions. Just don't say I didn't tell you so." He wasn't going to push the issue. After all, there was only so much he could say.

"Well, what I don't understand is why it's okay for a dude to sex as many girls as he wants, but when a girl does it, she's all of a sudden a slut?" Kelly asked getting upset. Ashley nodded her head in agreement.

"Well, dudes are called man whores, but it doesn't have the

same impact. I know, it's a double standard, and it'll probably be a double standard for a long time," TJ just decided to stop after his feeble and futile attempt to defend the male gender. No man ever won this debate, especially in a three-to-one match. He didn't want to change the mood before he and Keisha went out. He had seen many women assume another woman's emotions and then bring that attitude back to the man they were with. That always confused him.

"Hmm, see that's what I'm talking about and it's not fair," Kelly exclaimed while shaking her head.

"I know girl it's not," Ashley co-signed.

"Not saying that that's something I want to do though," Kelly quickly replied with a smile after she thought about what she had just said. The girls laughed, and TJ was thankful for the decrease in the tension level.

"Well, which one of ya'll want to tell Dana and Melissa about this?" Keisha asked the other girls, as she put her jacket on.

"Why can't you do it?" Kelly playfully retorted back to Keisha, not missing that Keisha purposely left herself out of it.

"I'm bout to go out," Keisha replied with a sly smile and laughed.

"Well, I'm writing a paper," Kelly playfully snapped back.

"Well, how about we all do it together tomorrow 'cause I think Dana went home this weekend, and Melissa went with her. And I think it would be better doing it face to face," Ashley suggested, ending their back-and-forth comments.

"That works for me," Kelly chirped.

"Me too," Keisha stated, and then left out with TJ.

~~~~

That movie was so scary, Keisha thought to herself as she rode with TJ to his place. They had just come from seeing *Saw III*, and were now about to chill at TJ's place. Since the movie theater was only five minutes from school, before Keisha knew it she was following TJ up the steps to his two-bedroom, on-campus apartment, which he shared with David. She hoped David wasn't there so that they could have some privacy, but decided not to think about it too much.

"Can I ask you something?" TJ asked Keisha after they had gotten settled in on his couch, and saw that they did have the place to themselves.

"What's up?" Keisha asked him, feeling nervous.

"Is it true, that you mess with Jaden, the one on the basketball team?" He sounded so emotionless asking such a serious question. *Damn, I knew that this would come up sooner or later,* Keisha thought to herself as she stared at his expressionless face. She wasn't sure how she should answer his question, but quickly decided to just be honest with him.

"Yeah," Keisha barely whispered.

"Oh," was all TJ stated.

"Why?" Keisha finally asked him just to break the silence. Ignoring Keisha's question, TJ asked her, "So when were you going to tell me?"

"I didn't know I had to tell you. You don't tell me who you be talking to or going out with," she replied slightly annoyed.

"But you know me and him are cool." *What! I'm going to kill Mike. He told me that they were beefing and that they probably wouldn't even care,* Keisha thought to herself angrily.

"I didn't know ya'll were cool. If that were the case, I wouldn't have continued talking to both of ya'll. I don't even roll like that. I heard ya'll weren't friends because ya'll were beefing or something," Keisha told TJ straight up.

"Nah, we *were* beefing, but now we're cool. That's how I found out that you mess with him too. I was telling him that I was going out with a girl named Keisha tonight and he started telling me about this girl he was feeling, also named Keisha. Then we put two and two together." *Hmm, that explains why Jaden called me earlier tonight and was all up in my business about what I was doing tonight,* Keisha thought, putting it all together. Things were now starting to make sense to her. Luckily she didn't lie to Jaden; she just told him she was going to the movies with one of her friends. When Jaden asked her who she was going with, Keisha just told him that it wasn't any of his business just like it wasn't any of her business who he took out when he wasn't with her. She was so relieved that she didn't lie to him because she would have been so caught up right now. Honesty really was the best policy. 'A true pimp doesn't have to lie,' is what Mike always told Keisha, and she planned to stick to that advice now. *Hold up, rewind, did he just say that Jaden was 'feeling' me,* Keisha thought with a smile, knowing that she shouldn't be thinking about Jaden while she was with TJ.

Still, something inside of her fluttered around at the thought that Jaden was digging her enough to speak about it with one of his boys.

"So, where do we go from here?" she asked TJ while snuggling up to him.

"I mean, me and Jaden were upset at first, but we talked about it and for right now we don't have a problem with it," TJ responded smiling while placing his arm around her. "I just wanted to test you and see if you were going to try and lie about it." *It's a good thing that I didn't*, Keisha thought smiling back. *Wait! Why don't they have a problem with it?*

"Why don't ya'll have a problem with it?" Keisha asked hesitantly, pulling back from his embrace.

"Oh, because neither one of us wanted to stop talking to you, so we just decided to let things flow," he answered all too easily. Keisha didn't really know how she felt about the vibe she was getting from TJ. It was almost as if she were some type of non-entity to be conquered. She pictured them standing around her like a car at a dealership, bidding on her. Keisha wasn't feeling that too much, and it was beginning to put a damper on the mood for her.

"Really?" Keisha wasn't sure if she trusted his answer. For all she knew they both could just be gaming her up and trying to play her like she was a dumb, naïve freshman. Keisha might be young and a freshman, but she was far from dumb.

"I know you probably think we're trying to game you up and then hit it and quit it," TJ responded, as if he could read her mind. "I can't speak for Jaden, but trust me it's not like that with me. If that was the case I would have been made some moves on you and tried to hit."

"Mmm hmm really, is that so?" Keisha replied flirtatiously, as she became at ease again.

"Yeah." At this point, he was staring deeply into her eyes, testing her will power.

"Let me ask you something," Keisha asked him in a sultry voice, while backing away from him so that she could look into his eyes.

"What's that?"

"What do you want from me?"

"Huh?" TJ choked out, and inched back a little bit. Keisha had caught him off guard; he wasn't ready to answer that question yet.

"You said that you're not trynna game me up, hit it and quit it. So my question is what *do* you want from me? What am I to you?" Keisha persisted.

"Look, shorty…I like you a lot and all, so I can see you as a potential girlfriend down the road. But…I'm going to be real with you; I'm not going to want a girlfriend for a *long* time." Keisha took that to basically mean: 'I like and respect you. If we have sex, I'll still be here; but don't expect for me to be your boyfriend after it goes down.' She had been there and done that before, and that was a sure fire way to get your feelings hurt because as soon as you catch feelings for the dude and tell him that you're trying to be with him, that's when he pulls out the 'I told you I wasn't ready for a relationship' card and you end up sitting there looking stupid. That also meant that Keisha was going to make sure that TJ didn't get any from her until that *long* time occurred.

"That's cool," Keisha said in a disinterested tone. "Well, I'm getting kind of tired. Can you walk me back to my dorm now?"

"Why don't you sleep over instead?" TJ asked her while giving her the puppy dog eyes, oblivious to her obvious change in mood. *Aww, he is so cute. I would but as sexy as he is, I don't know if I have that much self-control to stop me from doing something that I may regret in the morning*, Keisha thought as she fiddled with the idea of spending the night.

"Maybe next time," she said winking at him and making her way to the door.

"Ight, that's cool. I'ma hold you to it," TJ said seductively while following her to the door. *Yeah, whateva Negro. I'ma hold you 'to it.'* The thought made Keisha giggle out loud; TJ thought it was in response to what he had said, but he was so mistaken.

CHAPTER EIGHT

"Yes! I'm finally finished writing this stupid paper," Kelly said aloud to herself as she glanced at the clock to see what time it was. *Damn, it's eleven o'clock already.* That meant Kelly had been sitting there writing her paper for damn near four hours. She started around seven, and then took a short break when her brother came thru to take Keisha out. After that, she talked to Ashley for a little bit about the best way to approach Dana and Melissa regarding what TJ had told them. After Ashley left and went back to her room down the hall, she had gotten serious about finishing her paper. *My brother and Keisha look so cute together*, Kelly thought to herself as she saved her paper to a disk. Kelly just hoped that he didn't break Keisha's heart like he did to so many other girls he messed with, but she doubted that because from what she had seen, Keisha was pretty smart. *She may be a well-needed challenge for him.*

"Okay, all I have left to do now is print the paper out," Kelly said out loud to herself as she put her shoes on. She had run out of paper for her printer, so she had to walk to the 24-hour computer lab that was in the Student Center to print her paper out. *'You must*

not know bout me, you must not know bout me. Cause I can have
another you in a minute, matter fact he'll be here in a minute...'
Kelly's cell phone began to ring with her Beyonce ring tone. As
Kelly walked over to get her phone off her bed, she wondered who
was calling her. Keisha and her brother were at the movies, Aaron
went home for the weekend, and she had told her girls that she
would call them when she finished the paper. Kelly looked at the
screen, but didn't recognize the number.

"Hello?"

"Hey, can I speak to Kelly?" A smooth masculine voice replied.

"Yeah, who's this?" Kelly asked trying to distinguish who the
voice belonged to. It sounded familiar, but she couldn't quite make
it out.

"It's your future boyfriend," the masculine voice replied. *Oh*
boy somebody's playing on my phone. I really am not in the mood
for this BS, Kelly fumed silently.

"Look I'm not in the mood to be playing games. I just spent four
hours writing a paper, so..." Kelly responded about to get indignant.

"My bad girl, calm down. It's Mike," he said with a soft laugh.
Just hearing his name put Kelly in a better mood. She didn't know
why, but it was just something magnetic about Mike, even though
she knew he wasn't her type. Mike was too showy for her; she
liked the more low key and laid-back type guys.

"How did you get my number?" Kelly asked. She was hoping
he couldn't tell she was excited that he was on the other line.

"I got my sources," he replied with a chuckle. "So what are you
doing, Miss Kelly?"

"I'm about to walk to the computer lab and print this paper
out," she told him.

"What are you doing after that?"

"Nothing."

"Well, how about I walk you to the computer lab, so that you don't have to walk all-l-l the way over there by yourself, and after that you chill with me for awhile."

"Hmm, let me think about that...Well I don't want to make that *lo-ong* thirty-second walk all by myself, so I guess you can walk with me," Kelly said sarcastically. They both began laughing because the computer lab was literally a hop, skip, and a jump away, but he made it seem like it was thirty minutes away.

"Ight, I'll be there in five minutes. See you soon," Mike responded and then hung up before Kelly had a chance to change her mind. Just then it occurred to Kelly that she had on her scarf, some old tattered sweatpants, and her Class of 2006 t-shirt. She only left out the room once today, and that was to go eat brunch earlier that day, around one. When Kelly got back from brunch, she took a shower and put on some comfy clothes because she knew she was going to be working on this paper all day long. Since it was due on Monday morning and she had other work to do tomorrow, she figured she might as well get suited up. *Damnit, he's going to be here in less than five minutes, and I look a hot mess*, Kelly thought as she stared at her reflection in the mirror. *Well, it's time to change that quick, fast and in a hurry.* In less than five minutes, Kelly combed her dubey-wrap out and put on a white, tank top with a cute pink and gray Rocawear sweat suit. It was still pretty nice outside, so Kelly just slid on some pink, Old Navy flip-flops to match the pink in the sweat suit. Just as Kelly finished beautifying herself, she heard him knocking at the door.

"Hey!" Kelly greeted Mike cheerfully, but awkwardly.

"Hey beautiful," he said smiling down at her. Mike had such a pretty smile; Kelly swore it was infectious because she couldn't stop smiling at him. They were both just standing there staring at each other for a while, until Kelly finally broke the trance and went to get her disk out of the computer.

"You ready?" she asked him nervously. This was the first time that the two of them had hung out alone, without Keisha present.

"Yeah let's go."

~~~~~

After Kelly and Mike left the computer lab, they ended up walking around campus for a while, just talking and getting to know each other. *It feels like I've known him forever, but I can't allow myself to fall for him,* Kelly thought to herself. *At least not yet.* Plus, judging by the things that Kelly had heard about Mike from Keisha, she couldn't even take him seriously, which was one of the main reasons why Kelly didn't understand why she was out there with him right now. *Plus, I'm really feeling Aaron, and I don't want to mess things up with him for a fleeting feeling of companionship,* Kelly thought. She was completely aware of her inner struggle over liking Mike, when she felt his hand slip into hers. His touch startled her from her thoughts. She looked up at him and smiled; he just stared intently like he was thinking something that he wasn't ready to say. They were walking back to her dorm room blanketed with a comfortable silence when Mike abruptly stopped walking, yanking Kelly's arm in the process.

"Kelly, I feel so comfortable around you. I feel like I can open up and tell you anything. I never felt like that with anybody," Mike said calmly as he gazed into her eyes. Shocked, Kelly just stood there and stared at him to see if he was serious or just trying to run game on her. What Kelly didn't know was that Mike was just as surprised by his confession as she was. He never opened up to a female like this, especially on his first night really chilling with her. *But, it's just something about her,* Mike thought to himself. *Maybe it was her sweetness, or her innocence, or the fact that she has been one of the only girls up here, other than Keisha, that I've had a real conversation with that didn't involve basketball.* Mike didn't know what it was. All he knew was that he had to have Kelly for himself. *Man this girl got me already and I haven't even kissed her yet,* Mike thought to himself with a smirk while shaking his head.

"What are you smiling about?" Kelly asked Mike, confused. Mike contemplated whether or not he should tell her what he was really thinking or just keep that to himself for awhile. He knew how some girls got when they thought that they had you all early in the game, but for some reason Mike didn't think that Kelly was like that.

"I was just thinking about what it would be like if you were my girl," Mike told Kelly truthfully, while holding his breath the whole time he waited for her reply.

"Whatever, you're probably just running game. You *are* a basketball player, and you could have as many females as you want so why should I believe that you want to settle down with me?" Kelly responded matter-of-factly.

"I'ma keep it real with you, ma, and you can take it how you wanna take it. When I look at you I see something different from when I look at all the rest of these youngins up here. It's like you see me for me and like me for me. I know I just met you, but I just get this strong vibe from you and I don't want to lose that. I'm not asking you to be my girl right now because I know we just met and I don't want to rush things, but I would like you to consider me as being your boyfriend in the future." *What the hell? I can't believe I just said all that,* Mike thought as he realized that he meant every word of it. Mike couldn't believe that Kelly had him this open, but he had to admit he was on her ever since the first time he chilled with her and Keisha in their room the first couple of weeks of school. Although he wasn't the mushy, soft type, there was something about the way she just, *was* that made him not act like himself. When he looked at Kelly though, the last thing on his mind was running game and moving onto the next girl.

It's just something about her though that got me wanting to change my ways, Mike thought, still in disbelief. He pictured how Keisha was going to go crazy when Mike told her about his feeling for Kelly; since Mike had told her when they first got up there that he didn't plan on settling down with anybody until maybe his senior year. At that time, his rationale was that it was just too many females for him to 'get at' to be worried about being in a relationship with any one of them. Now Mike realized that majority of the females who came at him lacked substance. They only liked him because he was on the basketball team, and that's all they cared about.

"It's like I want to believe you, but…" Kelly started saying, but before she could finish Mike softly caressed her face with his hand and leaned in for a kiss. As Mike parted her lips with his tongue, he experienced one of the sweetest and sensual kisses ever. Kelly couldn't believe he had just kissed her, but she wasn't complaining. She felt like she was dreaming. When they finally pulled away from each other, Mike could see in Kelly's eyes that she felt the same way for him as he felt for her.

"Wooo-ooooo!" Obviously, some drunken guys passing by had witnessed the action and started screaming at them and whistling. That's when they both realized that it was about twenty people outside of the Towers watching them kiss. They were both so caught up in the moment that they hadn't even noticed them.

"Can we go upstairs and finish this… uhh…conversation, in a more private setting?" Mike asked Kelly while eyeing all the people surrounding them. As they rode the elevator up to her dorm room, Mike couldn't help but pull her into his arms for another kiss.

This feels so right, Kelly thought to herself as she lay on her bed kissing Mike. Kelly still wasn't sure if she totally trusted what Mike was saying, but what she did know was that kissing him felt too good to stop. As Mike's hands sensually massaged Kelly's body and his lips softly kissed her neck, Kelly couldn't help but to let out a soft moan. Kelly wanted him so badly, but she couldn't give in too soon. It was like her mind was in a battle with her body. At that moment, her body was winning though, especially since he was sliding her tank top up and kissing on her navel.

"I want you so bad," Mike whispered into Kelly's ear and then started gliding her sweatpants down. Mike didn't want this to happen so soon, especially since he knew she thought that that was all he was trying to do in the first place, but he couldn't control himself; he wanted her so badly. Kelly's brain was shouting, 'NO! It's too soon' but her body was exclaiming just the opposite, so she did nothing to stop him. Just as they both began to really get into it, the door flew open.

"Man, what the hell?! Kelly what are you doing?" TJ started yelling, while Keisha just stood at the door with an amused grin on her face.

"Wow!" was all Keisha could muster. Mike quickly removed his hands from her body and sat up straight. *Oh my gosh, this is so humiliating,* Kelly thought as she quickly put her tank top on and pulled her pants up and hid her face behind her hands in utter embarrassment. Still, in the back of her mind she was thankful that they didn't barge in five minutes from now because who knows what they might have saw. *I guess it's true what they say, 'Everything happens for a reason.' This might have been the only way I wouldn't have had sex with Mike.* Kelly's thoughts were interrupted by TJ's huffing and puffing. All of a sudden TJ started yelling at Kelly and talking about how "dudes" like Mike didn't want anything but sex and how he taught Kelly better than that. Kelly just ignored TJ because his whole argument was hypocritical considering that he was one of those "dudes" he was yelling about right now. He was always telling her to avoid "this dude" and "that dude" because they're only trying to hit it and quit it. *He got some nerve sittin' up here, preachin' to me about not having sex with somebody I barely know, when he does it all the time*, Kelly mumbled to herself.

"How you going to sit up here and tell me how I'm going to treat your sister?" Mike yelled back at TJ, beginning to get defensive.

"Yo, Son! I'm not talking to you. I'm talking to my little sister. But, since you want to go there…let's go back to last night! Why don't you tell my little sister what you *were* doing then?" TJ was getting louder, his anger evident in his eyes. Instead of yelling back, Mike got really quiet, which raised Kelly's suspicion.

"Yeah, that's what I thought," TJ sneered at him. Keisha, realizing how upset TJ really was, tried to drag him out in the hallway to try and calm him down.

"Kelly, I'm going to go for a short walk with Keisha to calm down. When I get back, that Nigga better be gone," TJ hissed at Kelly, and then left with Keisha as he slammed the door behind them. Mike just sat on the bed glaring at the empty doorway with anger in his eyes.

"What the hell is my brother talking about? What were you doing last night?" Kelly asked Mike slowly, not wanting to jump to conclusions. Mike had hoped that Kelly didn't hear or had forgotten that tidbit of info that her brother threw at him.

"Don't worry about that. It was before I realized my feelings for you," Mike replied still glaring at the door. TJ had really gotten to him; he couldn't stand when dudes started hatin' and assuming things.

"Nah, I'm not trying to hear that. If you want to be with me, then you need to be completely honest with me," Kelly retorted back.

"Or what?" Mike replied playfully trying to take some of the seriousness away from the situation.

"Or you can step," Kelly said getting up and pointing towards the door, not realizing that Mike was playing. *I know he is not going to sit up in here and play me like that, especially after I almost gave it up to him,* Kelly seethed to herself.

"Calm down, calm down. You are so cute when you're mad," Mike said sitting Kelly down on his laps. "Look if I tell you what happened last night, you have to promise me that you won't fault me for it because I promise you starting today I am only about you."

"Okay," Kelly told him not really believing the whole 'I am only about you' line that he was spitting.

"Last night, I was chilling with some of the guys on the team at David's crib."—*Oh, now I see how my brother knows so much,* Kelly thought as he told his story—"And some girls came over. It was this really pretty chick that was clocking me, so I went over to her and spit my regular game. I later found out that she was your brother's ex, Tiffany. So, me and her left the get-together and went back to her room to get to know each other, uh, better. But, I went over there with one thing in mind. She seemed to have the same thing on her mind, as well, because one thing led to another and me and her ended up having sex. But she means nothing to me, I swear." *Damn, he had sex with Tiffany. Man, Tiffany is like the big sister I never had,* Kelly thought sadly. Even though Tiffany and TJ broke up a year ago, they had remained friends so Tiffany was over Kelly's house all the time. *Damn, how can I mess with him after he got with one of my friends? I can't get with a dude that my play sister got with,* Kelly thought to herself, as she shook her head despondently.

"I can't believe you had sex with Tiffany," Kelly mumbled barely audible.

"You know her?"

"Yeah I know her! She's practically like family," Kelly responded irately. "So, let me ask you something? When you came over here to 'chill' with me, did you just have one thing on your mind then, too?"

"Na-a-ahh," Mike stammered out of nervousness, but Kelly took it to mean that he had been lying the whole time.

"Get out," Kelly stated calmly as she clenched her teeth to prevent her from screaming, and pointed her finger towards the door.

"It's not even like that with you, I swear," Mike pleaded as he searched her eyes for a hint of compassion. "Get the eff out of my room now, before I call security to escort you out," Kelly screamed, losing her composure.

She didn't want to hear any of his explanations. She should have listened to her first instincts about Mike and not have let him come over in the first place. As Mike walked over to the door slowly, Kelly felt something rise up inside of her: a wall. *If I don't take care of me, no one will,* she thought. *From now on I am going to follow my mind and not my body.*

~~~~

I love college, Dana thought to herself while leaving another great party. Dana and Melissa had decided to come back to campus earlier that night, so they could go to this party. They had been at Dana's house in Newark since Thursday since they didn't have any Friday classes. But there was only so much that they could do at home, so they made a last-minute decision to come back to campus tonight for the party. Luckily, Dana only lived about thirty minutes away, which allowed them ample time to get to campus and get ready for it. It was around three o'clock in the morning and the party was still jumping, but they were ready to leave. Because it was an off-campus party, it would just go on until everybody left or until the police came to shut it down—which might be soon since the police were always shutting down the black parties. Another black fraternity threw tonight's party, at one of the frat houses. Although it wasn't an "official" frat house, it was an off-campus house that about four fraternity guys lived in, so everybody just called it that frat's house. They even had a DJ. After Dana missed a great majority of the first party messing around with Ray, she made it a point to be at all the rest of the parties since then. It had been a party every weekend since then. Dana and Melissa had made an appearance at each and every one of them, even when the other girls didn't feel like going—like tonight.

Since school had started, Dana and Melissa had become tighter than ever. Melissa was by far Dana's closest friend out of the group of girls. As time went on, the girls began to separate into little cliques of their own. They were all still tight, but some just had more in common than others. Dana and Melissa had become a clique; while Keisha, Kelly and Ashley had become one; Angel and Ebony usually just stayed to themselves if they weren't hanging out with the rest of the girls.

"What you 'bout to do?" Dana asked Melissa when they got into Melissa's car. "Or should I ask *who*?" Dana added laughing. Melissa always ended up creeping with one of her 'boys' after a party. First, there was P, who Melissa had cut off after that first night like she said she would, but he kept begging for another chance. Finally she relented and started talking to him again, but didn't have sex with him anymore. Then there was Malcolm, one of TJ's frat brothers, whom she met at this gathering the girls went to a while ago. She let him stick around for a couple of weeks before she got bored. Finally, there was Jay whom she met last weekend at a Student Center party. The funny thing was when Melissa cut each one of them off, she didn't call or even speak to them when she saw them on campus. That was her M.O. -- she treated guys the same way they treated girls as if she flipped the script on them. What was even funnier to Dana was that after she did cut them off, they would be straight sweating her—calling her all the time and even showing up at her room from time to time. A lot of people judged Melissa and misunderstood her behavior as being "loose," but Dana called her a revolutionary because she was courageous enough to go against the grain and do her, without caring about others' opinions.

"Ha-ha-ha, that was cute," Melissa said sticking her tongue out at Dana. "I'll probably get up with Jay tonight. What about you?"

"I'll probably hang out with Ray," Dana responded. Melissa gave Dana a disapproving look, but didn't say anything. They had been through it before. After that night at the party, Dana had tried to take Melissa's advice and chalk it up to a heat-of-the-moment thing and not call him. She was doing well with not calling until she saw Ray one day in the dining hall looking all good in his XU football sweats. He came over to her that day flirting and talking about, "You can't call nobody?" Dana had held it down telling him that if he really wanted to hear from her, he would have called her. All Ray did was step back, laugh and reply, "True," and then walked away. After that, Dana couldn't get Ray off of her mind, even though he basically played her on the sly. Dana eventually ended up calling Ray the next night, and it was evident that he knew she would because when she called he said, "It's about time you called." One part of Dana was mad that she fell into Ray's plan, and that he assumed he had her pegged as one of those "young and dumb chicks." The other side of her was secretly turned on by it. Dana ended up going over to his apartment that same night, and the rest was history. They started having sex just about every other day since then. Unlike Melissa, Dana didn't like sleeping around, so Ray was the only guy that she dealt with. Melissa didn't like the fact that Dana gave into Ray, and she definitely wasn't feeling the idea of Ray using her. Dana saw things differently. She was getting just as much out of it as

Ray so she figured why not just live in the moment and enjoy it. Eventually, Dana figured that she would stop messing with Ray and get with somebody who took her seriously. Right now she was just having fun. That was good enough for her.

CHAPTER NINE

Last night was a long night for Keisha. It took her over a half hour to calm TJ down and convince him to let Kelly make her own mistakes. Kelly was a grown woman, and it was time for TJ to stop looking at her like she was still a little girl that needed his protection. By the time Keisha and TJ had returned to the room, TJ had agreed to apologize. However, Mike was gone and Kelly was knocked out. Keisha wasn't expecting that. She was half expecting them to walk in on the same scene as before, with Kelly and Mike on the verge of having sex. Keisha couldn't help but to laugh out loud just thinking about the expressions that Kelly and Mike had on their faces when they got caught. At first Keisha was mad at Mike for trying to get with her friend because she figured Mike was just going to do Kelly like he did all of his girls. But when she called Mike last night, after TJ had left, he assured her that Kelly was different. Mike explained to Keisha how no girl had ever made him feel this way before, and how he even revealed his feelings to Kelly. That was something that Mike never did unless he *really* liked a girl. Keisha was happy for Mike until he told her how he would never get to be with Kelly because of what he did the night before. Mike's past was finally catching up to him. Keisha had warned him that he couldn't keep dogging these girls out and expect for nothing to happen to him in return. She felt bad because the only thing that she could do for Mike was promise him that she would talk to Kelly for him. Honestly, Keisha didn't blame Kelly for not wanting to deal with Mike. From what Mike told her, Tiffany was like a sister to Kelly. That made Keisha pretty sure that Kelly wasn't going to mess with Mike, regardless of how she might feel. Kelly was pretty loyal to her friends. After they finished their conversation about Kelly, Keisha told Mike about the whole Jaden and TJ situation. Mike told her that the two of them becoming friends again must have just happened because he didn't even notice it, and that he would keep his ears open for anything sounding like they might be trying to play her.

"What are you doing up so early?" Kelly asked Keisha as she started waking up, interrupting Keisha from her thoughts. It wasn't really that early, it was only ten o'clock in the morning, but in college time it might as well have been six.

"I didn't feel like lying down any longer, so I got up and started doing some homework," Keisha responded, although she was dazing off more than she was doing homework. "You alright?" Kelly knew she was referring to the previous night.

"I don't feel like talking about it right now," Kelly replied dejectedly.

"True. Well you want to go to brunch after I finish?" Keisha asked her, respecting her space.

"Ight, give me another hour."

"Ight," Keisha responded, and then called Angel, Ashley, and Ebony to see if they wanted to meet them for brunch. Keisha wanted to wait until after they ate to tell Dana and Melissa about the rumors, which is why she didn't call them for brunch. Besides they always slept in late on Sundays, so they wouldn't think anything of it.

~~~~~

"Are you serious? Your brother walked in on ya'll," Ashley exclaimed, while listening to Kelly tell her story about what happened last night. During brunch, the girls had decided that it would be better to tell Dana and Melissa about the rumors in a familiar spot, so they were now sitting in Ebony's and Ashley's room, listening to Kelly tell her story while they waited for Dana and Melissa to arrive. Keisha wanted to laugh at that part of Kelly's story because it was so funny to her, but she knew Kelly was really upset over what happened, so she just held it in. Earlier that afternoon, Keisha had tried to convince Kelly that Mike was really feeling her, and that he had changed his player ways, but Kelly wasn't trying to hear that. Kelly didn't doubt that Mike felt the way Keisha said he did, but she couldn't get with him—at least not so soon after he got with her play sister, Tiffany. *Well, I tried,* Keisha thought, *but Mike should have just kept that thing in his pants.* After everybody finished sympathizing with Kelly, Keisha brought up the dilemma at hand and went over exactly how they planned to tell Dana and Melissa about the rumors.

"I still can't believe Ray and P would try and play Dana and Mel like that," Ashley said in disbelief while shaking her head.

"I can," Keisha stated matter-of-factly.

"Oh boy, here we go again," Kelly said playfully while rolling her eyes. Keisha had been told the girls that it was something not right about Ray and P, but they didn't want to listen to her, so ever since TJ had told them about the rumor she had been using every chance she had to say, "I told you so."

"What? I'm just saying! Did I not say there was something shady about them dudes?"

"What dudes?" Melissa asked as she walked in through the cracked door and into the room with Dana right behind her. *We really need to stop leaving the door open when we're in here talking*, Keisha thought to herself, glad she didn't say anything incriminating. Dana and Melissa's presence startled the rest of the girls. They were expecting Dana and Melissa to call when they got outside of the dorm; not walk right in. Since they lived in a different dorm than the rest of the girls, they didn't have a card to swipe to get into it. The room became dead silent for about two minutes while the girls exchanged nervous glances with each other; nobody wanted to be the one to bring it up and possibly bring pain to their friends. Dana, growing tired of the silence, finally spoke up and asked the rest of the girls what was wrong as she and Melissa took a seat on the fluffy rug in the middle of the floor facing the other girls.

"Well it's something we need to tell ya'll," Keisha said hesitantly, as she urged Ashley with her eyes to speak up, and not make her be the one that had to tell them.

"What's up?" Melissa asked tentatively, not sure what they had to do with the shady dudes that they were discussing before she walked in.

"Go ahead, Ashley, you tell them," Keisha said passing it over to Ashley after Ashley didn't take her hints. Keisha felt that it would be better coming from Ashley than her. Ashley was more sympathetic and soft-spoken than she was, and Keisha didn't want to come off cocky in any way for telling them that she knew something like this was going to happen all along.

"Um...well...Kelly, why don't you tell them since it came from your brother," Ashley stumbled out, not wanting to carry the burden either.

"Will somebody tell us?" Dana screamed, becoming more annoyed by the second with all of their secrecy. She couldn't understand why they were acting as if they were in elementary school. Anything that they had to tell them, she figured that she and Melissa could handle. They were all grown.

"Fine, I'll tell ya'll," Kelly finally replied annoyed with Keisha and Ashley for acting like little immature girls. "Last night, when my brother came to pick Keisha up for their date, he told us some rumors about ya'll that have been going around campus," Kelly then sat silent for awhile, not really wanting to tell them that most of the guys on campus saw them as jump-offs.

"Well, what are the rumors?" Melissa sneered with exasperation.

"He told us what went down with Ray and P that night of the big frat party, and that Ray and P told a bunch of guys on campus about it. Also, about what went down with you and his frat brother Malcolm,"-- She directed that comment to Melissa-- "And that Ray and P have been going around campus telling the upper classmen guys that ya'll are J.O's, and that we shouldn't associate ourselves with ya'll because then we will be guilty by association," Kelly finished quickly, while avoiding eye contact with Dana and Melissa.

"What's a 'J.O'" Dana's face had confusion written all over it.

"It stands for Jump-off," Kelly whispered. Both Dana and Melissa knew what a jump-off was, but they had never heard it abbreviated like that. Both the girls sat silent for a while, just taking in what Kelly had just told them. Dana looked hurt by it; and Melissa did too, surprisingly. Melissa had always carried herself with such a mental toughness that they didn't think anything could affect her, especially a rumor. They soon found out that it was Dana being hurt that made her feel that way.

"Are you serious? I can't believe Ray would play me like that!" Dana screamed angrily.

The rest of the girls just nodded their heads looking back and forth at each other, not knowing what else they could say to make her feel better.

"Man forget those punks! I told ya'll not to trust them anyway. They're just like all the rest of these football Niggas out here," Keisha told them, while standing up outraged. She then started pacing back and forth like she was thinking about something.

"What I don't understand is how P can go around calling me a 'jump-off' when I haven't even had sex with him since that night. Especially when this Negro is leaving messages on my cell phone talking about he misses me and he wants to see me again," Melissa stated perturbed. Her anger had already begun to fizzle to mere agitation; she wasn't tripping off these lying Negroes. She was more upset for Dana because she knew Dana really liked Ray.

"Man, that dudes just salty," Angel stated plainly. "He's mad cause you sexed him and played him like he was the female." Angel's statement brought a much needed laugh and eased a lot of the tension in the room.

"I don't understand why Ray is trying to make it seem like Dana's a hoe, when he's the only one she's messing with up here," Keisha said, still pacing.

"Can you stop that?" Ashley asked Keisha, referring to her pacing. "It's starting to irk me." Ashley was sitting on a throw pillow on the floor right next to where Keisha kept pacing.

"Oh, my bad," Keisha told Ashley, stopping abruptly and taking a seat on the desk that was right next to her.

"I know my sentiments exactly! Dana, you do know you're going to have to leave Ray alone now, right?" Melissa told Dana soothingly, ignoring the interaction that just took place between Keisha and Ashley.

"I know! But, it's not that easy," Dana replied softly, beginning to cry.

"What do you mean it's not that easy?" Keisha almost screamed, not understanding what the problem was, and why Dana didn't want to leave Ray alone. She figured Ray was somebody that Dana was just having fun and passing the time with. That meant he should've been disposable.

"I really like him," Dana whispered, barely audible.

"Oh…" was all Keisha could muster. Keisha really thought that Dana was stronger than that, but she guessed she was wrong. She didn't say it out loud, but it really bothered her that Dana would allow somebody like Ray to get to her like that.

"Wow! I'm sorry girl. We didn't realize that it was that deep with him," Ashley told Dana sympathetically and then scooted over to her to give her a hug. The rest of the girls followed her lead, even Keisha.

"So what now? Are ya'll going to stop hanging around us?" Dana asked the group insecurely through her tears. She knew the detriments that being called a J.O could have on a female's reputation. Dana actually used to be one of those people that wouldn't associate with any girls that were classified as J.Os when she was in high school, so as Dana waited to hear their response, she figured it was all coming back on her now. After a suspenseful pause and the other girls exchanging surreptitious glances with one another, they broke out into a chorus of remarks that made it more than clear that they had her back. Each girl took time to tell Dana and Melissa how nothing could ever break up their friendship, especially not a stupid rumor. Dana felt so blessed to have such a wonderful group of friends that she couldn't help but to have a big smile on her face, as she wiped away the remainder of her tears.

"Now we just have to think of a way to get them back," Keisha replied devilishly. *After all, isn't this what college is about,* Keisha thought laughing to herself.

~~~~

As Dana and Melissa walked back to their dorm that night, they still couldn't believe that Ray and P would do them like that. Melissa hadn't taken it as bad as Dana because she was used to little boys acting and reacting to things the way little boys do. *They get some and run and tell all of their friends about it; same stuff, different day,* Melissa thought to herself when she first heard the news. It was clear that Dana wasn't prepared for that though. The messed up thing to Melissa was that Ray knew that Dana wasn't a hoe. He was the only person at XU that Dana had sex with or had even talked to for that matter. Plus, Dana really liked Ray for a reason unknown to Melissa, so to know that Ray would see Dana as a "jump-off" hurt Dana to the core. That was the only reason Melissa was really mad; she didn't like seeing any of her friends hurt, especially Dana. Melissa on the other hand was nowhere near hurt, and could care less what P or any of his friends thought about her, especially since P had been sweating her ever since that night -- calling her twenty-four seven and trying to take her out. She bet he didn't tell his boys that. Now everything was cool with Melissa because after the girls initiated their plan to get them back, Ray and P would think twice about spreading rumors about them. After everybody had settled down from the all the emotional interactions, the girls came up with an elaborate plan to get Ray and P back for spreading those rumors. The upcoming weekend was homecoming and would be the optimal time to put their plan into action. The homecoming festivities began on Thursday night with a step show with all of the black frats and sororities. Friday night's festivities would include Midnight Madness, which was basically something that was celebrated in every college/university across the nation that had a basketball team and was apart of the NCAA. On that day at midnight was when all teams were allowed to start practicing, marking the start of the basketball season. Students gather in the gym and watch the basketball team's first practice of the season, along with other festivities to get the student body involved. There would also be parties galore on Friday. Saturday would be homecoming, so everybody would go to the football game and then to the homecoming parties. Since, Ray and P played on the football team, Saturday was going to be a big day for them. *It was also going to be the day that they realized that they picked the wrong chicks to screw over,* Melissa thought to herself spitefully.

CHAPTER TEN

"Dag, ya'll have got to be the slowest people ever when it comes to getting ready to go out," Angel exclaimed as she walked in to Keisha and Kelly's room, and saw that they weren't ready to go yet. Keisha, Kelly, and Angel were headed to the step show. They were supposed to be meeting Dana, Melissa and Ashley outside the gym, where the event was being held, but they were running late.

"Calm down, I'm almost ready. I just have to put my shoes on," Kelly told Angel playfully. It was obviously an exaggeration. Kelly still had her scarf on, which meant that after she put her shoes on she was going to have to do her hair. That task in itself was going to take her an extra ten minutes.

"Just call Ashley and tell them to go on in without us, and to save us some seats," Keisha told Angel, while rolling her eyes at Kelly. She knew that messing with Kelly, they probably wouldn't be leaving their dorm room for another ten minutes, let alone getting to the step show any time soon. Angel quickly agreed with Keisha and called the girls.

"They said okay," Angel reported as she sat down on Keisha's bed and watched her across the room applying the finishing touches to her make up. "But ya'll still need to hurry up." Angel was really excited about the step show and just wanted to get there. It was supposed to be one of the premier events for homecoming weekend, not to mention it was expected to be off the chain. Greeks from other schools were participating in it, which meant the girls would get to see some new faces. Although when Angel thought about it, she still hadn't seen all the faces at XU yet. Since XU was such a big school, she saw somebody new everyday.

"Why are you in such a rush tonight anyway? You knew they would most likely end up holding our seats for us," Keisha asked Angel curiously; knowing that it had to be some other motive behind Angel rushing them

"She wants to see her boo-oooo," Kelly responded teasing Angel and then started singing the Usher and Alicia Keys song "My Boo". Angel had just started talking to this sexy dude named Shawn, who also happened to be performing in the step show tonight. Now Keisha understood why Angel was rushing; usually, Angel wasn't in a rush to go anywhere.

"Aww, so how are things going with that?" Keisha asked Angel referring to her new boo.

"Ya'll be blowing things out of proportion. You know Shawn and me just started talking. And he is far from being 'my boo'," Angel replied while rolling her eyes at them.

"Maybe not right now, but you want him to be," Keisha said teasingly, while laughing. Angel just sucked her teeth and ignored her comment.

"Since you all up in my business, who's gonna be your date at the end of the night, TJ or Jaden?" Angel asked Keisha playfully with a sly grin.

"Oh you went there with it?" Keisha responded laughing. Kelly just laughed and shook her head at them, not caring that it was her brother that they were discussing.

"Yeah, so what's up with you and the sexy two?" Angel wasn't giving up without an answer.

"Well, if you must know," Keisha paused for effect, "I'm going to be chilling with TJ tonight and Jaden tomorrow after Midnight Madness."

"Wow! Miss P-I-M-P over here," Angel declared while laughing.

"I try, I try," Keisha responded jokingly. "But nah, for real I like them both a whole lot, and its starting to really take a toll on me."

"Well what do you want right now? Because I thought you said you didn't want a boyfriend, and you were too cute to be tied down," Kelly asked Keisha, while mocking her. Kelly then stopped doing her hair and gave Keisha her full attention while she waited for Keisha to answer her question. *See, that's Keisha's problem,* Kelly thought. *She doesn't know the answer her damn self.* Keisha came into this school year with just chilling and having fun on her mind. Next thing she knew, she met these two sexy, intelligent, and just all-around cool guys, and they threw her whole mind frame out of sync.

"Well, I don't know. It's like I don't want a boyfriend, but then I wouldn't mind if TJ or Jaden was my boyfriend. I don't know, man. I am so confused right now."

"Okay, since you don't know what you want, what do they want?" Angel asked gently.

"Well, TJ doesn't want anything serious right now. I haven't gotten a chance to talk to Jaden about it yet. I'm going to talk to him tomorrow after Midnight Madness when we chill," Keisha replied. She hadn't seen Jaden since Monday. She had been so busy with school and he'd been busy with school and basketball. Keisha didn't even know if he was coming out tonight.

"I'ma be real with you girl, Jaden is probably your best bet. TJ isn't going to be ready for a relationship for awhile," Kelly commented bluntly.

"Why you say that?" Keisha asked her, feeling some type of way from that comment.

"After he and Tiffany broke up last year, he's basically just been playing the field," Kelly answered truthfully, but it seemed like she was holding something back.

"I know it's more to the story, I can tell by how you keep looking down," Keisha persisted. Kelly was a really bad liar, and Keisha could always tell when it was something else to a story with her.

"Ight, if I tell you this, you have to promise you won't bring this up to my brother. And I'm only telling you this because I don't want to see you get hurt."

"Okay, what is it?" Keisha asked, starting to get upset. Keisha really liked TJ and although she was talking to somebody else, she still didn't like to hear about him liking somebody else more than her.

"I think, and this is only my opinion, that TJ is not over Tiffany yet and that's why ever since they broke up he hasn't gotten into any new relationships."

"The Tiffany that Mike just smashed?" Keisha asked astounded. Cringing, Kelly nodded her head 'yes.' *Dag, I forgot that she's really feeling Mike and that whole situation hits a nerve every time I bring it up,* Keisha thought as she realized how inconsiderate her last comment was to Kelly.

"Sorry," Keisha whispered meekly. Keisha couldn't believe that TJ still had feelings for that girl Tiffany after all these years. It would explain why TJ reacted so outrageously with the whole Mike and Kelly thing, though. *He was probably madder at the fact that Mike had just hit his ex-girl than he was about Mike and Kelly getting together,* Keisha fumed. This gave Keisha a whole new outlook on her situation concerning TJ and Jaden.

"I'm ready," Kelly said, finally.

"About time!" Angel said playfully.

"Where's Ebony? I thought she was walking over with us?" Angel asked them.

"She was, but she said that she'll meet us there," Keisha answered.

"Why? What is she doing?" Kelly asked nosily.

"I don't know. But, I do know that I'm ready to go. So, let's make some moves," Keisha replied, and they made their way to the step show.

~~~~~

Ring-ring, Ring-ring. Ebony's room telephone rang.

"You going to answer that?" David asked Ebony as he glanced at the ringing phone. Ebony just shook hear head 'no' and continued to ignore the ringing phone. She would've gotten up and answered the phone, but she already knew who was calling her, and she was comfortable where she was. It was more than likely just Ashley calling to see if Ebony had left the room yet to come to the step show. Ebony would call her back later. Right now she was enjoying the conversation that she was having with David, and she didn't want to mess that up. Ever since that night in the Glen when David had gotten Ebony's number, they had become really good friends. David admired the fact that Ebony was really into her religion and went to church every Sunday. He even became a regular attendee at her church. David was even starting to fall for Ebony, but Ebony had told him off the break that she didn't want anything or anybody to come between her relationship with God; if something seemed like it was then she was going to have to cut it off. So, David kept his feelings to himself and just continued to enjoy their friendship. Although Ebony didn't like David in that way, she kept their time spent with each other to herself, but her girls had their suspicions—especially Keisha, since she always thought she knew everything anyway. It wasn't like Ebony was trying to keep it a secret or anything. She just didn't want them to blow it out of proportion, as they tended to do with everything.

"Do you still want to go to the step show tonight?" David asked Ebony in his cute St. Louis accent. They were supposed to be on their way to the step show right now, but Ebony didn't really feel like going anymore.

"Wouldn't you rather stay in here tonight and watch a movie?" Ebony asked David innocently. Ebony really wasn't in the mood to be out and about, especially at a rowdy step show. The way she saw it was if you've seen one, you've seen them all. Ebony had been to a ton of step shows down in Atlanta, at Clark, Spellman, and Morehouse Colleges.

"Yeah…but I did want to see my boy step," David said, referring to TJ who was stepping in the show.

"Well, I wouldn't want to hold you back from seeing that,"

Ebony said slightly sad, but she didn't understand why.

"Um…nah, it's cool. I'll chill with you, I don't really feel like being around a bunch of people either," David said, adding a little white lie. The truth was he just loved spending time with Ebony, and he could care less what they decided to do.

~~~~

Tonight had to be one of my worst nights, ever! Keisha thought as the girls walked back to the dorms. Keisha was still trying to figure out how she went from having a great time at the step show to being kicked out of the step show. When they arrived at the gym, where the step show was being held, there was a long line to get in. Thanks to Angel's 'new boo' Shawn, the girls received the VIP treatment and didn't have to wait in the line at all since his frat was one of the co-sponsors for the event. When the girls walked into the gym, the DJ had the place jumping, and it seemed like all the frats and sororities were doing their party strolls around the gym as they waited for the step show to begin. Some students were even dancing in the bleachers. Keisha wasn't sure if she had just walked into a step show or a party, but whatever it was she knew she was going to have a good time. It took them awhile to find Ashley, Dana, and Melissa because it was just so much going on and it seemed like every five seconds, one of the girls would run into somebody that they knew to stop and chat with. About thirty minutes later, Keisha, Kelly and Angel eventually found the rest of the girls sitting in the front row of the bleachers that were closest to the stage, which was located at the opposite end of the gym.

"What took ya'll so long?" Dana asked the girls, slightly irritated. While the other girls had been taking their good ole time, Dana, Melissa, and Ashley had to fend off the masses for the seats that they were holding for them. Black people could get real ignorant when it came to having good seats at an event. That alone had brought Dana's mood down a little bit, even though she was trying not to let their tardiness ruin her night.

"Our fault, we've been here for about thirty minutes or so, we just kept running into people as we tried to find ya'll. But thank you sweetie," Keisha told her as she, Angel, and Kelly took their seats right behind the other girls.

"Unh huh," Dana mumbled, a little upset by their inconsiderateness. Keisha and the other girls just ignored Dana. They were used to her attitudes by now. Plus the deejay had just announced that the step show was about to begin and for everybody to take their seats. The step show started. The Sigma's and Delta's killed it; they shut it down. Keisha wished she could have seen how well the other fraternities and sororities did, but that was all she got to see. After the Delta's went off, Ray came over and sat down on the steps next to her, since she was sitting right next to the aisle. He started talking normally, just asking her how she had been and seeing what was going on with her, like he always did when he saw her around campus. Keisha was wondering why he was talking to her, and not talking to Dana who was sitting a couple seats over in the row in front of Keisha. She stopped stressing and figured that he must not have seen her. Keisha started to go off on him for spreading the rumors about her girls, but the girls had collectively decided that they would act as if they knew nothing about the rumors and act normal towards Ray and P, which was the only reason that Keisha even continued to have the cordial conversation with him. Meanwhile, Dana was sitting in her seat fuming. Dana couldn't hear everything that

Keisha and Ray were saying to each other, but from where she was sitting, it looked as if Keisha was flirting with him. The rest of the girls braced themselves, knowing that some drama was about to pop off, from the heated expression that was now on Dana's face.

"You know Dana is sitting right there, right?" Keisha asked Ray, hoping that he would get the hint, and leave her alone.

"I know, but I came over here to talk to you. So when are you going to stop playing games, and let me take you out?" Ray boldly asked Keisha, who was now dumbstruck and in disbelief that he would just ask her that with Dana sitting right in front of them. She wasn't the only one: Kelly (who was sitting right next to her) and Ashley (who was right in front of her) turned their heads around and gave Ray the 'are you serious' facial expression. That's when all hell broke loose. Keisha was hoping that it was too loud for Dana to hear what Ray had just said, and she tried to play it off, at first, by laughing and acting as if Ray were just playing. She really didn't want any drama that night or to bring any unnecessary attention to herself. Then Ray started telling Keisha how he wished he would have hollered at her that day that he had met her and Dana, and that Dana was just some smut he got with because he was bored. All Keisha could do was sit there in shock for a second; she really couldn't believe this Negro had the audacity to come at her like that right in front of her girl. What made it worse was that by that time Dana was standing directly in front of them and had heard everything that he had just said. Dana told Ashley and Melissa that she wasn't fazed by Ray, and that she was going to the concession stand so that they would let her through. At first they weren't going to let her through to the aisle at all because, like Keisha, they didn't want any drama that night. Dana was so persistent that they let her through, but they soon regretted it. Just when Keisha was about to tell Ray's ass off for disrespecting Dana and having the audacity to come and holler at one of Dana's friends in front of her, Dana jumped into their conversation. Keisha thought that Dana was about to go off on Ray right along with her. But Dana surprised Keisha and Ray by jumping down Keisha's throat, calling Keisha fake, saying that Keisha was a hater, and asking how Keisha was going to sit up there and holler at her man. It took everything in Keisha not to knock Dana out right then and there, but Kelly was beside her telling her to calm down and not do anything, while Ashley began trying to hold Dana back. *Dana needs a serious reality check because this dude doesn't even claim her,* Keisha thought to herself heatedly, while contemplating knocking the hell out of Dana.

"Dana, are you seriously that hung up over this trifling Nigga that you're going to jump down my throat for *him* trying to get at *me* and not the other way around?" Keisha asked Dana as she squinted her face in utter disgust.

"Whatever Keisha, don't try and sit up here like you weren't entertaining it. You are such a fake bitch," Dana spat the piercing words at Keisha. She was so emotional that she wasn't trying to hear anything that Keisha was saying. Before Keisha even knew what she was doing, her instinct kicked in and she slapped the mess out of Dana in front of everybody. By that point, the students in their section were paying more attention to them than to step show. They had even started adding their own insight about the situation, instigating the issue and fanning the fire. One girl shouted for Dana not to believe Keisha; that she saw it with her own eyes, and that Keisha was flirting with the dude. Another girl called Dana a "stupid freshman" and that everybody knew that Ray was a hoe. All the while, Ray stood back and enjoyed the fireworks until security finally came over and picked both Keisha and Dana up and carried them out of the gym.

Keisha had never been so embarrassed in her life! Her phone was ringing off the hook now from people calling to see if that was really her and Dana who had been carried out of the gymnasium for fighting. By that point, she just decided to turn her phone off.

"I can't believe that bitch hit me," Keisha heard Dana yell behind her. Keisha started to turn around and hit her again, but Kelly and Angel were on both sides of her pulling her back to the dorms. The rest of the girls had followed quickly behind them as the security carried them out, with their heads held down from embarrassment. They knew that somebody was going to have to keep the two separated as they made the ten-minute walk back to the dorms. Keisha had never been in a fight before, and wouldn't have thought her first one would be with somebody that she called a friend. Keisha wasn't even sure if she could call Dana a friend anymore.

"You had it coming to you," Melissa responded to Dana truthfully. Melissa knew that that wasn't what Dana wanted to hear, especially coming from her of all people. But at the same time, Dana was wrong. Melissa had been sitting right next to them and she had heard everything Ray said.

"WHAT?! ARE YOU CRAZY…?" Dana screamed. *Wow, she is really tripping; I have never seen her like this,* Melissa thought, not liking this side of Dana. Nobody did, and that was obvious from the looks of disgust that all the girls had on their faces as they looked over at Dana, while walking back to the dorm.

"Look Dana, I'm your girl, so I'm gonna keep it real with you. *You* were out of line, plain and simple!" Melissa exclaimed trying to remain calm, before being interrupted by Dana.

"I can't believe you're taking her side," Dana cried, snatching her arm away angrily from Melissa's grasp.

"It's not about sides. Ray tried to talk to her and not the other way around, and you know that. But instead of getting mad at him, you jumped all up in Keisha face. That's not cool, man," Melissa told Dana straight up, shaking her head with contempt.

"Whatever…" Dana was not trying to hear what Melissa was saying.

"Melissa's right, Dana! I mean look how Ray acted after you jumped up in Keisha's face. He just sat there and laughed all amused and ish, dapping up his boys. He doesn't care about you, because if he did he wouldn't have disrespected you like that," Ashley turned and yelled at Dana, losing her patience.

"Look! I don't understand you Dana." Keisha had gotten fed up with listening to Dana act as if she had done something wrong. "I thought we were friends. How are you going to come at me like that tonight, even after I defended you to TJ, and stuck by your side after we found out about the J.O. rumors? I did nothing wrong!" Keisha screamed, walking closer to Dana, waiting for an answer. "Answer me!" After Dana didn't say anything for a while, Keisha screamed in utter frustration and threw her hands up in the air, as to say I'm done with this. At that moment, it finally hit Dana that she was acting out of her jealousy towards Keisha. Keisha really didn't do anything wrong. It wasn't until Dana saw the pain and frustration in Keisha's eyes that she realized she had jumped to conclusions, acted out of jealousy, and possibly ruined a good friendship in the process. Dana couldn't even look Keisha in the eye anymore, so she just dropped her head in utter disappointment with herself.

"I know, I know, you did nothing wrong. I don't know what came over me, but I was wrong. And I am so sorry girl," Dana whimpered as she covered her face with her hands to hide the tears that were now streaming down her face. "Its just that I like him so much, and when I saw him talking to you and trying to holler at you, I lost all train of thought. My first instinct was just to yell at you because I was angry and jealous of you, Keisha, for him liking you. I know it sounds stupid but…I guess my jealousy and insecurities took control over me….and I am just so-o sorry," Dana broke down even more, and fell down to her knees with loud sobs. The rest of the girls didn't know what to say or do at that point. It appeared that Dana was really in love with this dude, but the other girls couldn't understand why. Ray hadn't done anything for her at all. All the two of them did was chill in the dorm and have sex. But they also knew that love makes you do crazy things. Love would have the most sound, intelligent female out hiding behind bushes spying on some man. So, the girls could relate to what she was going through.

There had been times in all of their lives when they did something stupid and embarrassing in the name of love. So all of the rest of the girls could forgive Dana for her actions; the only question was, could Keisha? Keisha wasn't the type to be easily moved by tears, so Dana's crying didn't really faze her too much. She just had one thing that she needed to let Dana know.

"Look girl, I'm going to keep it real with you right now. Prior to tonight, I viewed you as a strong, intelligent, and beautiful black woman. Now I'm trying to figure out if you're just a little girl disguised as a woman. You see because a real *WOMAN* does not allow a trifling Negro like Ray to come between her and her friends. A real *WOMAN* is not for all the drama, and doesn't make a scene like that in front of everybody and their mother. And a real *WOMAN* doesn't allow little boys to treat her with disrespect because real *WOMEN* don't deal with little boys. The way you acted tonight was like a little girl. Because we all have our little girl moments, I forgive you, because just now by admitting that you were wrong, you proved yourself to be a woman and not the latter." Keisha saying that she forgave Dana, prompted Dana to lift her tear-drenched face out her hands and to look up at Keisha with hope that they could put this whole night behind them. As Dana opened her mouth to comment, Keisha abruptly cut her off. "Hold up, I'm not done," Keisha said while looking directly into Dana's eyes. "Yeah, I do forgive you for tonight and I do want to remain friends...but if you *ever* disrespect me and come at me like that again, us being friends is not an option." With that, Keisha turned on her heels and made her way back to the dorm by herself, leaving a sobbing Dana on the ground and the rest of the girls dumbfounded, not knowing whether they should comfort Dana or chase Keisha down.

CHAPTER ELEVEN

"Whoa, this is crazy," Mike said to nobody in particular as he watched the crowd screaming from the locker room entrance. Tonight was Midnight Madness: the night when practice started for all NCAA basketball teams across the nation. This was Mike's first Midnight Madness, so he wasn't sure what to expect, but so far it felt great.

"This is only for a practice. Imagine how it's going to be at our first game," Charlie, one of the other freshman players, said next to Mike. Mike just smiled and nodded his head in agreement.

"Forget Midnight Madness, I can't wait till the after parties," Mike's teammate Bryan said to him. Bryan was a junior, so he was used to the hoopla already.

"Why? What's so good about the after parties?" Mike asked him baffled by why Bryan would be more excited about an after party than their first practice of the season in front of thousands of fans.

"Let me school you young boys real quick. You see all of these females out there screaming right?" Bryan put his arm around Mike's shoulder and pointed out towards the crowd. Mike and the other freshmen players all nodded their heads to signify that they saw them. "Well, *all* of them will be at the after parties. And after we go out there and perform tonight, all we'll have to do is step in the building and majority of them will be standing in line and begging for us to hit that." Mike just laughed while Charlie dapped Bryan up getting hyped up about all the girls he was about to get. *That Nigga Bryan is such a hoe; all he thinks about is getting some,* Mike thought to himself with a smile and shook his head.

"Man, I don't even know why you so hyped you know this Nigga exaggerating," Mike told Charlie.

"Ight, you ain't got to believe me, son. You'll see for yourself at the party tonight," Bryan retorted with a knowing smirk and walked back into the locker room where the rest of the team was. Mike just shook his head at him. On some realness, Mike could care less if Bryan was telling the truth or not. After the whole Kelly blow up, Mike had just been chilling by himself for awhile. Out there being a hoe is what messed up things with him and Kelly in the first place. Thinking back to that night with Kelly's "play" sister, it was Bryan who encouraged Mike to get with Tiffany in the first place. Mike was chilling that night, but Bryan was like *"Go ahead son, you can use my room if you need to. Look she is on you. Don't punk out on that one."* *Ugh, it just blows me every time I think about that night*, Mike thought to himself sadly. But Mike was tired of thinking about that; now it was time for him to focus on what he came to XU for: basketball.

"Come on," Mike said to Charlie as he saw his other teammates lining up to go out.

It's game time!

~~~~~

"Wow, these Niggas weren't lying," Mike said to Keisha as they walked into another after party. They had been to two parties already, and at both parties girls were throwing themselves at Mike and the other guys on the team; it was crazy! The way these girls were coming at them, you would think that they were in the NBA. Mike had run into Keisha and Angel at the first party, and they had been partying and chilling ever since. Keisha needed a good party after what happened last night between her and Dana. Mike still couldn't believe Dana had jumped out there with Keisha like that, especially in front of all of those people. A lot of the guys on campus were talking about how dumb Dana looked last night for trying to fight Keisha when it was so obvious that Ray was trying to holler at her, and not the other way around. What was even more surprising to Mike was that Keisha was still friends with the girl. Back in the day, she would have cut the chick off with no questions about it, but Mike guessed Keisha really had formed a bond with all of the girls, including Dana. Thinking about Keisha's friends made Mike think about Kelly. He was still disappointed that Kelly wasn't with Keisha and Angel tonight. Keisha told Mike that Kelly was out with some dude. Mike couldn't even front, that mess made him sad as hell to hear that she was out with another dude instead of with him. Still, Mike had no one to blame but himself. *I can't believe I'm sitting here thinking about this girl when it's all these beautiful girls in here smiling at me and making sexual advances towards me. Damn, I got it bad*, Mike thought to himself sadly as he turned down yet another chick.

"I know! This is crazy. It must be ten girls to every dude in here," Keisha exclaimed to Mike, regarding Mike's earlier comment. Mike just smirked as he looked around the party, realizing what she had said was true. By this point, it was just Mike and Keisha left as they walked into a third party. Angel had left with some frat boy at the second party, claiming that she was tired. Judging by the look on dudes face though, she wasn't going to be getting much sleep. The only reason Keisha was still hanging out was because she was meeting Jaden at this third party.

"Where Jaden at?" Mike asked Keisha, since he didn't see him in there.

"He said he was on his way over now," Keisha answered him. Keisha really didn't feel like being out at a party anymore, she just wanted to go back to Jaden's apartment and chill.

"You need to tell that dude to hurry up," Mike told her, impatiently. He only came to this third after party because she was trying to get up with Jaden, and he wasn't going to leave her by herself.

"There he goes right there," Keisha snapped while rolling her eyes at Mike, a little irked by his impatience.

"Ight, well I'm bout to go then," Mike told her, and then gave her a hug goodbye.

"Hey, get your hands off my girl," Jaden yelled playfully as he walked over to them and playfully pushed Mike off of Keisha. After Jaden dapped Mike up, he then pulled Keisha in for a hug while giving her a passionate kiss on the lips, and then put his arm around her protectively when he was done. *Wow, this dude is really feeling her. That move that he just made just proved that to me,* Mike thought with a smile. Mike believed that you could tell a lot about how a guy felt about a girl just by how he greeted her. And by Jaden giving Keisha a passionate kiss in front of all these other girls in the party, showed Mike that Jaden had no concern for those other chicks at all and that Keisha was the main female that he was dealing with. Jaden putting his arm around Keisha protectively was a sign to all of the other guys in the room that that was his girl and nobody better try and come at her. Now, on the other hand, if Jaden would have just came over there and gave Keisha a friendly hug and kept a friendly distance, then it would have meant that Jaden had another girl in the room or one that he was trying to kick it to later, and that Keisha was free game to any of the guys in there. Judging by Keisha's puzzled facial expression to his kiss; she was just as surprised by his move. Mike schooled Keisha a long time ago on to what guy's different gestures meant, which probably explained the smug smirk that she was wearing on her face as she snuggled in closer to Jaden.

"Ight, I'll see ya'll later," Mike told them as he left the party.

~~~~

Tonight was definitely an improvement from last night's escapade, Keisha thought happily to herself as she rode back to Jaden's apartment with him. Keisha had had so much fun tonight at Midnight Madness and at the after parties she went to. She was so proud of her boy, Mike, tonight out there doing his thing. Mike had come a long way from that little boy that she used to know, out there shooting hoops in the driveway. After they left the athletic center, where Midnight Madness was held, Keisha, Kelly and Angel went to one of the after parties. The first party was okay, but it was way too many girls in there. Jaden had warned her it was going to be like that when she talked to him earlier, saying, "It's like all of the basketball groupies come out of hibernation when the season starts." Keisha had just laughed at his remark, thinking he was exaggerating, but she soon found out that Jaden was downplaying it; the way them girls were pushing and shoving just to get a glimpse of one of the players, you would have thought

Kobe was in the place or something. Keisha and the girls were ready to go after the first thirty minutes of the party. That's when Kelly rolled and met up with Aaron. Keisha was getting ready to do the same thing, but she and Angel ran into Mike by the door and he had told them about a second party. That party was much better than the first one. That was probably because it was more exclusive than the other one, and had all of the top players on campus including the athletes, Greeks, and pretty boys. You had to be specially invited or friends of the team to even get into the second party. The only downfall of the party was how the girls were giving Keisha and Angel mean mugs all night just because they were cool with some of the players, and the guys weren't paying them any mind. Keisha was about to ask them if they had a problem, but she quickly remembered what happened the night prior and promptly decided against that notion. She had had enough drama last night to last her a year; there was no need to start any more. So, Keisha just ignored them chicks and started talking to TJ, who was in attendance. Mike was teasing her all night calling her a pimp because Keisha was at the second party bunned up with TJ, knowing all the while that she was going to meet up with Jaden later on. Mike even had her paranoid most of the night too, by acting like Jaden had just walked in the room while she was with TJ. After an hour of watching her back, Keisha told TJ that she had to go. Not wanting to get caught up. Keisha was surprised Jaden didn't show up at that party; half of the team was there. She was going to have to ask him about that when they got to his place. Jaden had told her earlier that night when she talked to him that he had to talk to her about something, which is why they were on their way to his place at the moment. His apartment was more private than her dorm room. Keisha wondered what it could possibly be that Jaden wanted to talk about, since they had already talked about the whole TJ thing, and he was cool with that—or so she thought.

~~~~

"You can open your eyes now," Jaden whispered in Keisha's ear as he removed his hands from in front of her eyes. They had just gotten into his apartment and before they walked into Jaden's room, Jaden made Keisha promise to keep her eyes closed until he told her to open them.

"Oh my gosh!" Keisha gushed as she saw roses, candles, and balloons everywhere. Jaden had placed a mixture of white, pink, and red roses in vases and placed them along his dressers and he had even scattered rose petals on his bed. He even had rose petals on his bedroom floor leading a path from the doorway to the bed. He had two bouquets of "I love you" balloons strategically placed on both sides of his bed. Before she could say anything, Jaden went in and lit the candles that were on his dresser, and almost immediately, Keisha was comforted by the nostalgic scent of cherries. Keisha was in pure heaven, and could not believe that he did all of this for her.

"When did you possibly have time to do all of this? Or better yet, what's this for?" Keisha asked him excitedly as she took another look around the room and noticed a small wrapped gift on the bed.

Looking deep into Keisha eyes and taking her hand into his hands, Jaden responded, "I just wanted to show you how special you are to me. I know we've only been talking for a month and a half now, but the thought of you with somebody else is unbearable. I want you all to myself, Keisha. So, what I'm trying to say is…will you be my girl?" *Whoa!* Keisha wasn't expecting that to come out of Jaden's mouth. Keisha had never had a guy go out of his way like this, just to ask her be his girl. Now, she saw what he was doing instead of attending the after parties tonight. This had to have been the sweetest thing anybody had ever done for Keisha. So, with no hesitation Keisha happily responded, "Yes, I'll be your girl," and gave him a sensual hug and tantalizing kiss. Smiling, Jaden pointed to the gift on the bed and said, "Open it. It's for you." Excited, Keisha quickly opened the box and what she found in it was amazing; it was a diamond encrusted heart pendant.

"Wo-o-w! I can't possibly accept this gift, Jaden. It's way too expensive," Keisha whispered in awe.

"Don't worry about that, I can afford it. This pendant represents my heart, so don't look at it as me giving you an expensive gift, look at it as me entrusting you with my heart." Before Keisha could protest anymore, Jaden gently pulled her in for one of the most alluring and passionate kisses Keisha had ever experienced. *Hmm, I want him so bad*, Keisha thought as he started undressing her.

"You are so beautiful," Jaden told her, while gently caressing her face, staring into her hazel eyes.

"You don't know how long, I've wanted to do this, sweetheart," Jaden whispered as he proceeded to end the romantic night off right. *Man, he doesn't even know how long I've wanted to do this,* Keisha thought, her body and mind filled with lust. Jaden was so sexy to Keisha, and his six-pack abs had not gone unnoticed. Lucky for Keisha she possessed such 'self-control', which is why it had taken him until now to get some. *And it was definitely worth the wait,* Keisha thought to herself after they had finished making passionate love. It was just one thing left on Keisha's mind: when and how was she going to break the news to TJ.

CHAPTER TWELVE

"Wake up, sleepyhead," Kelly yelled to Keisha as she walked into their room, this morning. It was six o'clock and extremely early for the both of them, but they had promised the other girls that they would meet them outside the dorm at six-fifty to initiate their plan. Kelly had ended up falling asleep in Aaron's room last night watching movies, after they had gotten in from a wonderful evening together. She had randomly run into Aaron last night at the first after party she went to with Keisha and Angel. After about ten minutes of talking inside of the party, Aaron asked Kelly if she wanted to leave and take a walk around the campus since it was such a nice night outside, and the party was so loud. Kelly immediately jumped at that opportunity because she really wasn't feeling the party and she didn't want to chance running into Mike. After the night that Mike had told Kelly that he had slept with Tiffany, Kelly had been avoiding Mike's phone calls and ignoring him whenever she saw him. It took a lot of energy to avoid somebody, and last night, Kelly wasn't up to exerting that much energy. After Kelly and Aaron left the party, they walked around campus for hours laughing and joking with each other and just enjoying each other's company. It was amazing to Kelly how much they had in common. Now that Kelly thought about it, she was glad that Mike had turned out to be a jerk because she almost cut Aaron off for him, and she would have missed out on a great guy.

"I am awake," Keisha whined groggily. "Where have you been?" Keisha had made it a point to come back to her room last night from Jaden's since she knew she had to meet the girls early in the morning, and she didn't want to oversleep messing around with Jaden.

"I should be asking you the same thing, missy. I called the room last night when I got in and you didn't pick up," Kelly replied playfully.

"Well, me and Jaden made it official last night," Keisha told Kelly in a dream like trance, as she remembered how special last night was. Keisha went on telling Kelly about how romantic Jaden had made last night for her, and how they had made passionate love all night.

"Aww, that is so sweet, Keisha," Kelly gushed.

"And the sex was so good; it brought tears to my eyes," Keisha added for good measure.

"Dag, it was *that* good. But wait, what are you going to do about TJ?" Kelly asked Keisha, concerned about her brother's feelings.

"I called him later that night, while Jaden was sleep, and I told him everything. He was upset at first, but he knew he wasn't ready to make that commitment to me so he settled for just being friends," Keisha responded solemnly. Calling TJ to break the news had to be one of the hardest things Keisha had to do. Especially since Keisha really did care about TJ, but Jaden came with an offer that she couldn't refuse.

"Wow, so it's really official?" Kelly asked Keisha, still a little surprised that the pimp of the group was the first to settle down.

"Yeah…and don't think I forgot my question. Where were you at last night, missy?" Keisha asked Kelly as she finally got out of the bed and threw on some sweat pants.

"I fell asleep at Aaron's, *mom*," Kelly replied teasingly, as she changed into a black sweat suit as well.

"Hmm mm, so what's up with that?" Keisha was anticipating some juicy news.

"We made it official," Kelly answered smiling at Keisha. Although, it didn't happen as extravagantly as it did for Keisha and Jaden, it was just as meaningful.

"So, how was it?" Keisha pried, knowing there was more to the story.

"How was what?" Kelly asked her confused.

"The sex!" Keisha exclaimed, "I know ya'll did the *nasty* to make it official." Laughing Kelly replied "Actually we didn't. We didn't want to rush things."

"Oh," Keisha simply stated with a thoughtful expression. "What?"

"Do you ever wonder what it would be like if you were still a virgin?" Keisha asked Kelly out of the blue. After shaking her head 'no,' Kelly let Keisha continue. "I mean, things were just so much simpler then, you know? You didn't have to worry about the pressures of wanting to have sex. You could just chill with a guy and know nothing was going to happen. You know what I mean?" Keisha asked as she put her shoes on.

"I guess I never thought about it," Kelly answered her reflectively. "But now that I think about it, you're right. Because now when I chill with any guy that I'm attracted to I have to control myself around them and it wasn't like that before I started having sex."

"Yeah, I know. It was like after I started having sex, my body started feigning for it," Keisha responded.

"True."

"I guess that's why God wanted us to wait until we got married to have sex because he knew how powerful it would be. When you're sharing it with the person that you're going to spend the rest of your life with, you don't have to worry about all of the stresses it brings along with it," Keisha said.

Wisdom was one of the traits that Kelly admired in Keisha. She always had the tendency to switch it up and get real deep like that. Keisha would have a person thinking about things that probably wouldn't cross someone's mind on a regular basis. "Well, it's just something to think about," Keisha said as they made their way out of their dorm room. "Now, let's go initiate this 'plan' of ours."

~~~

Today was the big day! Melissa thought with a sinister grin. When Melissa said that to other XU students, they thought it was because today was homecoming, but for Melissa today was the day when Ray and P would realize they screwed over the wrong chicks.

"Ya'll ready?" Melissa asked Dana, Kelly, Angel, Ashley and Keisha as she glanced both ways to make sure nobody could see them. Even though, it wasn't many people out on campus at seven o'clock in the morning on a Saturday, they had to be cautious. The girls whispered and nodded, acknowledging that it was time to do what they set out to do. They were on their way to sneak into the football locker room, clad in matching black hoodies to cover their

faces. Ray and P had made the mistake of taking Dana and Melissa
to the locker room one night when they were still messing around.
Melissa was bored one night, so she decided to give P another
chance. The boys had thought it would be fun to lounge around
the locker room, which really meant they thought it would be fun
to have sex in the locker room. They ended up doing both, but that
was before the guys started trying to play Melissa and Dana out.
When they had all been in the locker room that time, unbeknownst
to the guys, Melissa watched as they put the pass code in on
the door handle. The locker room was designed as a part of a
larger football facility, so there was a front entrance that any and
everybody could walk through, and get to it by taking the elevator.
Then there was a side entrance that you needed the pass code to get
into it. Mostly players used it because they were allowed access to
the locker room twenty-four hours a day. So, the plan was to have
one girl stand outside the main entrance of the building on look-
out, two girls by the side entrance on look-out, one on the inside by
the other locker room entrance, and Dana and Melissa were going
to sneak into the actual locker room to initiate the plan. When
the girls told Ebony what they were up to, she wanted no parts of
it. Ebony had warned the group that they would reap what they
sowed, and instead of getting revenge on the guys they should just
forgive them and let it go. The other girls weren't trying to hear
that, so here they were taking matters into their own hands.

"Ight, the coast is clear," Melissa whispered to Dana as she
looked around the locker room to make sure nobody was in there.
The locker room was set up with one section for the players'
entertainment, which consisted of a plasma twenty-seven-inch TV,
with leather couches circling it, as well as a pool table and some

other amenities. The other section of the locker room was where the players' actual lockers with uniforms and game equipment were located. Each football player had his own locker with his name on it and, inside was their uniforms and some personal belongings; which was going to make their job a lot easier.

"Are you sure we won't get caught?" Dana asked Melissa getting apprehensive as they walked towards the locker section of the locker room.

"YES I'M SURE! Their game tonight is a late game, and right now all of the team and the coaches are having breakfast, and aren't supposed to show up here until ten, at the earliest," Melissa hissed as they walked into the locker room looking for Ray and P's locker. She had talked to P earlier that week about what his schedule would be for today, just to double check.

"How do you know all of that?" Dana was hesitant to continue, yet perplexed at Melissa's extensive knowledge of the team's schedule.

"Don't worry about all that, just know that we won't get caught, and we'll be out of here in five minutes tops. Give me the itching powder," Melissa told Dana as they finally found Ray and P's locker. Dana pulled out a bottle of itching powder from the pocket of her hoody, and handed the bottle to Melissa. Melissa protected herself with latex gloves that were hanging out the pocket of her sweat pants, and began to pour some of the itching powder into their jock traps, shoulder pads, pants, and everything else that she could get her hands on. She rubbed it in really well, so that the powder was invisible. *Click-clack. Click-clack.*

"Shh, you hear that?" Dana shushed Melissa. Melissa didn't hear anything so she continued doing what she was doing. *Click-clack. Click-clack.* The sound got louder, and then Keisha barged in from her post, and screeched, "Ashley just said that some people just pulled into the parking lot. It's time to go!" With that news, all the girls started running out of the side door and making a break for it. Ashley, Angel and Kelly—who were on lookout outside— had been got up out of there, and were now waiting for the rest of the girls at the agreed meeting spot. Nervous laughter escaped them all when they finally reached safe ground, where the other girls were waiting for them.

"Oh my gosh! I can't believe we just did that," Dana laughed and tried to catch her breath at the same time.

"I know," Keisha replied smiling at Dana, trying to catch her breath also. You would have never known that Keisha and Dana had just gotten into a fight a couple of nights ago. Apparently, all was forgiven between the two, as the girls' escapade seemed to have bonded them. The girls met up outside of the library, which was a good five-minute walk away from the locker room, and they had run the entire way. You would have thought Melissa, Keisha and Dana were Olympic athletes as fast as they got out of the locker room and made it to the library. The girls didn't want to take any chances with somebody seeing them, so the library was a good spot to meet on homecoming Saturday because nobody was there.

"Do you think the itching powder is going to work?" Kelly asked the group as they walked back to their dorms.

"I hope so. I guess we'll find out at the parade," Melissa answered with the corners of her mouth upturned in a satisfied grin. Before every football game, the football team along with the cheerleaders, dance team and marching band walked from the campus circle to the football stadium, while everybody stood on the side and cheered them on. All of the girls usually didn't go to the parade, but today they planned on having front row seats.

"Ight, everybody get changed, and let's meet back here at two."

~~~~~

"Here they come, here they come," Dana screamed excitedly. The girls were now at the parade, with front row seats right by the football stadium. All of the girls were out there, including Ebony. Although Ebony didn't condone what they were doing, she had to admit she was curious to see if the plan was actually going to work.

"Why are you so excited to see them?" Aaron asked Dana questionably. Aaron had come out to the parade with Kelly, and knew nothing about the girls' plan. The girls had promised to take that secret to their grave.

"Aww, we're just excited because it's our first college homecoming game," Dana easily lied to Aaron. The other girls smiled at how smoothly she responded.

"Oh," Aaron replied, not thinking anything of it. "Why are those two Niggas scratching themselves like that?" Aaron asked out loud, squinting his face in disgust as he pointed to two football players walking towards them. The girls looked over to where he was pointing, and saw that the two football players were Ray and P. The girls continued to watch with mischievous grins on their faces, as the two players squirmed uncontrollably and unsuccessfully tried to scratch their leg and groin areas discreetly so nobody could see. The only thing was everybody could see their poor attempts at trying to hide their scratching and started to turn all of their attention towards them. Delighted at that, the girls saw that the first part of their plan was now working; now, it was time to execute the rest.

"Well, it is a rumor going around," Melissa started off, loud enough for the group of black girls standing next to them to hear, "that Ray and P have Chlamydia."

"How'd you hear that?" Ashley asked her, matching her volume. They now had everybody's attention, including another group of girls beside them.

"Well, ya'll can't say anything, but one of my girls works in the health center and she gets to see everybody's file that comes in. She happened to be there one day this week when Ray and P had come in," Melissa told them trying not to laugh, as the group of girls believed her outrageous story.

"Word! I wonder how they both got it." A nosey girl in the group behind them was asking questions. This was perfect.

"They must have run a train on some girl without wrapping it up and both got it," another girl replied with certainty.

"Well, not exactly," Melissa said mysteriously. Her dramatization made it difficult for the rest of the crew to keep a straight face and not laugh because they knew what she was about to say.

"What? How'd they both get it then?"

"I *heard*", Melissa said talking with extra emphasis, "that they gave it to each other."

"WHAT!!" everybody gasped. *Now our plan is complete,* Melissa thought satisfied with their deceit. It was only a matter of time before the whole, black community on campus would know of this little bit of information. Gossip and rumors traveled fast at XU, especially when it was as juicy as this one. And most of the time, the final rumor would end up ten times worst than when it started. Melissa felt like she was back in high school, the way everybody talked about each other, but in this circumstance that was a good thing.

"So you're saying they're GAY???" Aaron asked Melissa incredulously, finding it hard to believe. "But I thought you guys used to mess with them? And in that case how are they gay?" Kelly frowned, and gave Melissa an apologetic look for bringing Aaron, since he was asking too many questions. Unbeknownst to Kelly, Aaron was adding fuel to the fire and helping Melissa out.

"Haven't ya'll heard of 'down low' brothers?" Melissa asked Aaron, and the girls behind them, secretly thanking Aaron for his question that allowed her transition into the last part of the lie. A book on brothers on the down low (DL) was out by J.L. King, and it really opened Melissa's eyes. She would have never thought that so many straight guys were engaging in homosexual sex. That's what gave her the idea to say that Ray and P were on the down low and gave each other the STD. If she had said that they had it, people would have eventually looked at her and Dana like they had it as well, but this way it took them out of the limelight.

"Yeah girl!" Keisha said hyping it up. "It was a lot of brothers in that book who presented themselves as heterosexual men with girlfriends and wives, but were sleeping with their best male friend." The group of girls ate Keisha's line up.

Then, nodding her head one girl added, "Well, now stuff makes sense! Like why they're always together and are always so close up on each other." Those girls behind them were definitely making their job a lot easier with their presumptions. *Ahh, revenge is so sweet!* Melissa smirked to herself.

CHAPTER THIRTEEN

"Hey girls, guess what?" Angel asked Keisha and Kelly, animatedly as she barged into their room.

"Um, did you forget to knock? We could have been getting dressed or something," Keisha said in a mock, serious tone still lying in her bed. After the parade, Keisha made a beeline to her room and hopped in the bed. The rest of the girls had gone to the football game after the parade, but she had only gotten a couple of hours of sleep the night prior, and after they had got back to the dorms this morning, Keisha and Kelly had decided to get something to eat. By the time they had finished talking and got back to their room, it was time to get ready for the parade.

"Oh girl, shut up. It's just me, and if you didn't want people barging into your room you would keep your door locked," Angel snapped back playfully.

"What happened?" Kelly asked Angel after laughing at her and Keisha's interaction. Kelly had gone to the first half of the game with Aaron, but was too tired to sit through the rest of the game and was now lying in her bed as well.

"Well, the word on the street is," Angel started, and then

paused to add suspense, "is that Ray and P gave each other a STD and are on the down low."

"What?" Keisha gasped, playing along with Angel and acting as if she knew nothing about it. Laughter overcame the girls.

"And get this, Brittany from down the hall told me, and said she saw it first hand," Angel told them barely able to get the words out from laughing so hard. The girls' plan was working better than expected, if Brittany had found out. She had one of the biggest mouths on campus, so if she knew and actually believed it, then everybody would know by the end of the day.

"So, Angel what did you and Shawn end up getting into last night?" Keisha asked Angel changing the subject, after their laughter had finally died down.

"Well, we just chilled after we left the party," Angel responded, downplaying her night.

"Boooo, I want to hear details! I know ya'll did more than just 'chill'," Keisha exclaimed, challenging her. Keisha had wanted to ask Angel about her night earlier today, but there was too much stuff going on.

Grinning Angel replied, "We went back to my room and watched a movie. We didn't get to see much of the movie, though, because we were too busy kissing. Before things could go too far, I told him that I was a virgin and that I wasn't ready for that yet."

"What did he say?" Kelly asked her curiously, thinking about the conversation that she and Keisha had earlier that day. They both knew that a guy's reaction to hearing that could range from praising God and being patient to being pressed and pushy.

"He was real cool and understanding about it. I really appreciated that because most guys either get scared off by the fact that I'm a virgin, or they try to sweet talk me into being with them so that they can be 'the first.' He ended up spending the night, was the perfect gentleman and didn't try to pressure me at all. He just told me that he really liked me and that he had no problem waiting until I'm ready."

"That's what's up! He sounds like he's a keeper," Keisha stated, as Kelly nodded her head in agreement.

"Yeah, he definitely is," Angel said wistfully. Changing the subject she asked "Are ya'll going to the homecoming party tonight?"

"Probably not, I'm going out to eat with Jaden tonight," Keisha answered.

"Yeah, I doubt I'll go either. I'll probably just end up hanging out with Aaron. I'm not really in the partying mood," Kelly told Angel.

"Aww, you guys suck." Angel whined and poked out her lips. "You go and get boyfriends, and then forget about your girls."

"Sorry," Kelly said smiling at her little tantrum.

"Well, I'm about to get up with Dana and Melissa, you know they're always down for a party," Angel stated and began making her way to the door.

"Tis' true, tis' true," Kelly nodded her head in agreement.

"Ight girl, let us know how it was," Keisha told Angel as she left.

~~~~~

Our rumor is spreading even faster than I expected, Melissa thought to herself as she heard a group of seniors in line in front of them, talking about Ray and P being on the DL. Ashley, Dana, Angel, and Melissa were all standing in line at the Student Center for the official homecoming party that the BSU (Black Student

Union) was giving.

"Do you guys think they're really on the DL?" Melissa heard one of the girls ask her friend, and watched the friend nod 'yes' in response.

"Oh my gosh, there they go!" some girl behind them exclaimed. Turning around to see what they were talking about, Melissa saw Ray, P, and a few other football players walking over to the line. Ray and P probably thought that everybody was staring at them because they just won the homecoming game. *This should be real interesting*, Melissa thought as she glanced at her girls and they shared a smile.

"What's up?" Melissa overheard Ray greeting this girl and attempting to give her a hug.

"Um, please don't touch me," the girls said disgustedly as she walked away from him.

"What the F is that chick's problem?" Ray asked out loud to nobody in particular.

"Yo son! You not gon' believe what I just heard," one of Ray and P's boys ran over to Ray and told him, after he got a chance to catch his breath.

"What?"

"Somebody started a rumor saying that ya'll two Niggas are gay and gave each other a STD," Ray's boy answered while scrunching his face up in disbelief.

"WHAT THE HELL ARE YOU TALKING ABOUT??" Ray screamed. His outlandish reaction not only made the scene more entertaining, but also made him seem guilty of the deed.

"What happened?" P asked him, not hearing what the boy had just said. The boy repeated it to him and received the same reaction.

"LOOK, THAT 'ISH DOESN'T EVEN *SOUND* BELIEVABLE," Ray yelled outraged before he realized that everybody was staring at him. Then, he started trying to calm himself down.

"So, is it true?" The boy had been standing there the whole time with a skeptical, yet amused look on his face.

"Hell nah, that 'ish ain't true. Nigga, I can't even believe you have the nerve to ask me that," Ray replied. At this point, he was beyond heated. *Our plan worked even better than I thought it was going to, and I have front row seats to see it all fan out,* Melissa thought excitedly with a cynical grin. She was in heaven; she loved to see a man sweat, in more ways than one. "WHAT THE HELL ARE YA'LL STARING AT??" Ray started screaming at the people in line, including them. Everybody was just standing there staring at them in disbelief and shock at the scene that they were now making.

"Don't be mad at us 'cause you burning. You need to be mad at your boy P for that," a random girl in the crowd yelled back at him. Everybody started laughing. The drama was so unreal, like watching a reality series.

"YO, I DON'T KNOW WHO THE HELL YA'LL HEARD THAT CRAP FROM, BUT I AM FAR FROM GAY AND I DEFINITELY DON'T HAVE AN STD. SO FOR ALL OF YA'LL WHO WANT TO BELIEVE THAT BS, I HAVE ONE QUESTION TO ASK YA'LL." Ray said yelling at the stop of his lungs so that everybody outside could hear him.

"If I'm so called "burning", why don't you, you, you, you, and you have this same 'STD' because I smashed all of ya'll hoes this week," Ray said more calmly and pointed out like five girls, who shamefully put their heads down. "The only reason me and this Nigga was itching was because somehow our uniforms got itching powder on it," he paused for a second, nodding his head in satisfaction. "And we have proof of that. So ya'll Niggas think about that. And when I find out who started this BS rumor, they are going to have all hell to pay," Ray threatened as he began to walk away, apparently not in the party mood anymore. *Aww, and he had such a good game. Ha-Ha!* Melissa inwardly laughed to herself. Idle threats in the heat of the moment were nothing to her.

"Yeah right! If that's the case, why the hell were ya'll the only two Niggas scratching?" an attractive guy in a NY fitted shouted out. P started to argue with the dude, but it appeared he decided against it because he just walked away in the same direction as Ray.

"Yeah, go comfort your boyfriend," another guy yelled out to him, which caused a whole new batch of laughter. Dana had a worried expression on her face. Melissa guessed it was because of Ray's threat. Ray and P were from the South, and the down South boys were known to be crazy. Dana knew first hand, that if Ray said that he was going to do something, he definitely did it; but then again, the girls didn't have anything to worry about. They had hoods over their heads and made it a point to keep their heads down the whole time they were in the locker room. Besides Ray and P had told them before that there were no security cameras in that part of the locker room, when they were worried about their sexcapades being caught on tape. So, there was no way Ray and P would find out that it was them. Worst case scenario, the team might conduct a little investigation. Since they had the code, it would look like an inside job. Needless to say, Melissa wasn't worried.

NOVEMBER/DECEMBER

CHAPTER FOURTEEN

I'm so lonely! It's the end of November, and I still haven't met a good guy yet, Ashley thought to herself despondently. Ashley had just gotten back from Thanksgiving break, and was sitting in her room bored while Ebony was out with David. Ashley felt like everybody was 'wifed up' or at least had somebody, but her. Ashley swore it was something wrong with these New Jersey Niggas. She didn't even like to call her black men "Niggas," but she swore the guys up there were just that: Niggas. They were so trifling and most of all, on some BS. Ashley knew they were in college, and times were hard, but couldn't a guy at least come up with a creative way to take her out, even if funds were low. *Damn! Like, ask me to go see one of the movies that the student union shows for free every Friday,* Ashley huffed to herself. But noooo, all the guys up there that she came across, just wanted to chill in the room and try to smash. At first, Ashley didn't mind the sex part because she enjoyed having sex and she was on it the same way they were. That was until Ashley caught feelings for this guy, Siyan, a football player she met at the BSU party. He had everything that Ashley always looked for in a man; and trust he was all man, with his 6'3" muscular frame, and handsome face. He was smart, came from a good family background, a junior, had a prominent future, and most importantly, the sex was crazy. *The things that he did with his tongue...hmm girl,* Ashley smirked as her thoughts went back to those nights with him. Now that Ashley thought back to it, she messed things up with him in the beginning when she told him that she was just chilling right now, enjoying her freshmen year and that she wasn't looking for anything serious. Siyan had said the same, and that was the beginning of Ashley's demise. Ashley didn't know why she thought she wouldn't catch feelings for this guy, especially when the sex was outstanding. It was funny to Ashley now because she'd seen it happen before. A girl would say, "Oh we're just having sex, I don't like him like that," and then, the next week, be all upset when she realized that she really was feeling him and he didn't feel the same way about her. Ashley was starting to realize that females just couldn't continuously have sex with a guy—well, a *good* guy—and not expect to fall for him. It was just inevitable. For some reason, it didn't happen to guys. *Well at least not the ones that matter,* Ashley thought. Guys can sex a girl as many times as they want, and not feel anything towards her. Ashley, on the other hand, ended up getting it bad for this guy; she really fell for him. When Ashley finally told him how she felt, he reminded her that they both had agreed that they didn't want anything serious. Ashley figured that since she was feeling him a lot, he had to be feeling the same way about her. Plus, it wasn't like they were just having sex; they were going out, spending a lot of time together, and talking on the phone a lot. Long story short, Siyan basically said that he liked Ashley, but he didn't want anything serious at that time. Ashley couldn't even be mad at him because her dumbass had told him in the beginning that she didn't want anything serious. The only person she could be mad at was herself. That wasn't the worst part, though. After he told Ashley that he didn't want anything serious, a couple weeks later he ended up getting back together with his ex-girlfriend. Basically he just didn't want anything serious with Ashley. That had to have been one of the worst feelings Ashley had ever experienced: to have somebody tell you that they really like you and if it were a different time you would be the perfect wifey for them. Then have that person turn around and wife somebody else. Ashley was heated. After Siyan played her, Ashley changed her whole mindset. Now, she told guys up front that if they wanted to start talking, then she was going to want something serious eventually, and Ashley had even sworn off sex for a while. She didn't want to have sex with a guy unless she saw something promising.

"I had fun too. I'll see you later," Ashley heard Ebony say to somebody, waking her up from her nap. Ashley must have been tired because she didn't even remember falling asleep. Turning over, Ashley saw Ebony smiling.

"Where are you coming from?" Ashley asked her.

"I just got back from hanging out with David," she answered cheerfully.

"Oh really," Ashley said winking at her. Ashley didn't know why Ebony was trying to act like she didn't have feelings for David. Everybody could see that she did.

"Shut up. How many times do I have to tell ya'll? ME AND DAVID ARE JUST FRIENDS," Ebony said getting loud. Ashley just nodded her head, not believing her.

"Well, if you don't want him, I'll take him. He's probably one of the only good brothers left on campus that's not taken," Ashley told her disappointedly. David was a very good-looking brother, and if Ashley didn't think that he was so into her cousin, she probably would have tried to talk to him herself.

"If you want, I'll hook you up with him," Ebony said with a sneaky grin as she reached for her phone.

"Shut up. You and I both know that boy has it bad for you," Ashley responded not even wanting to entertain that notion.

"How many times do I have to tell you, David and I are just friends?" Ebony said extra slow as if Ashley was mentally challenged.

"Ok, hook it up then," Ashley said calling Ebony's bluff, not thinking that Ebony would seriously call David and tell him that.

"Ok, I'm 'bout to call him now," Ebony said taking out her cell phone. *Wow! She's really serious,* Ashley thought to herself as Ebony called David. Just as Ashley started to tell Ebony never mind and that she was playing, Ebony told David that Ashley was interested in him, and asked him if he would like to go out with Ashley sometime. *Oh boy, what have I gotten myself into,* Ashley thought to herself and shook her head in disbelief. One minute she was just chilling in her room drowning in self-pity and the next minute Ebony was trying to hook her up with David.

"So, what he say?" Ashley asked Ebony wearily, when she got off the phone. Now that Ebony had put it out there to David that she was interested in him, there was no turning back for Ashley. *Ugh! He must have said he doesn't like me like that, judging by the weary expression on her face and the way she keeps looking down,* Ashley thought despondently and laid back down. All Ashley could think about was how she was going to have to duck David every time she saw him for now on, just from sheer embarrassment. She was so deep in her thoughts that she didn't even hear Ebony say that David said that it was cool and that they could go out sometime.

"Hello, Ashley, did you hear what I said?" Ebony asked Ashley while waving her hands back and forth in front of Ashley's face to get her attention.

"Huh? What did you say?"

"I *said* that David said it's cool, and to give him a call later on tonight," Ebony answered breaking a big smile.

"Are you serious?" Ashley asked her finding herself getting a little excited about a possible date.

"Yeah, here's his number," Ebony said, reciting David's number from her cell phone for Ashley. *Well, I'll call him tonight and see what happens*, Ashley thought, hopefully.

~~~~

"Man, I don't believe that ish'," David heard TJ saying to somebody on the phone as he walked into their apartment. He had just gotten back from dropping Ebony off at her dorm.

"What are you in here yelling about?" David asked TJ when he finally got off the phone.

"I was telling this girl how I truly doubt that those Niggas, Ray and P, are gay."

"Oh yeah, I heard about that. I don't know, them Niggas do be acting a little funny," David said jokingly with a chuckle.

"Shut up, man. Ray's my people, and I know he ain't playing for the other team," TJ replied, dead serious.

"Yeah, ight," David responded doubtfully as he heard his cell phone begin to ring.

"Hello," David answered, and smiled just hearing Ebony's rich voice. "Hmm mm, well just tell her to call me tonight." David got off the phone and shook his head slowly. "I can't believe this chick just called me up and tried to hook me up with her cousin," David said to TJ exasperated. David couldn't believe Ebony didn't see how much he was feeling her. It wasn't just on a physical level either; it was deeper than that. Ebony had showed him things that no girl ever had, and she even helped him to get back on the path to grow spiritually. He didn't understand why Ebony couldn't see that they would be perfect together. David was even willing to wait on having sex until marriage, and that was something that he would have never done in his past.

"Who?" TJ asked David amused.

"Ebony, man!"

"Oh! So, what you going to do?" TJ asked David concerned

"I give up on Ebony, son. I'm just going to go ahead and talk to Ashley," David said defeated. He couldn't continue to put his heart on the line just for it to get trampled by Ebony.

"In all seriousness, I would have gone at Ashley first. I'm surprised you even wanted to talk to Ebony. Not that she's ugly or anything, but she's...she's just not your type," TJ said trying to console David.

"I know, but Ebony's different from the other girls out here. She has her convictions and she sticks to them, and I respect her for that. Like, that's what really drew me to her, but I guess she doesn't feel the same way," David replied somberly.

"So now are you going to drop this church boy routine?" TJ joked with David, not believing that David was really into church. All the years TJ had known David, not once had David acted spiritual in anyway or expressed a desire to go to church.

"What routine?" David asked confused.

"The one you been putting on for the past couple of months to get Ebony to like you," David replied seriously.

"Son, this isn't a routine. I truly do love going to church, and I'm going to continue going. That's one good thing that did come out of me spending so much time with Ebony," David told TJ sincerely. "And, you should come with us one Sunday."

"Ight," TJ responded, as he did every time David asked him to go to church, although they both knew he wasn't going to go. That never stopped David from asking. His goal was to get TJ to church at least one Sunday.

To change the subject before David started giving him reasons why he needed to go to church, TJ quickly asked, "Hey son, how are you going to talk to Ashley if you are damn near in love with her cousin? Don't use Ashley to get back at Ebony for not feeling you," TJ was hoping that David wasn't planning on using Ashley to make Ebony jealous. TJ had started to see Ashley and the rest of Kelly's crew as little sisters, and didn't want to see them get hurt. Well, everybody except Dana and Melissa. He still saw them as J.O.'s and only spoke to them when he had to.

"Nah, it's not going to be nothing like that. For a while now I've been checking Ashley out whenever I was over there. I just didn't act on my attraction because I figured I might have something with her cousin in the future, but now that Ebony just slammed that door in my face, I'm going to take advantage of the one that she opened for me."

"Well, you let me know how that goes." TJ said laughing and shaking his head.

"Where are you going?" David asked TJ as he got up and put his coat on.

"I'm bout to go chill with my little sis for awhile. I haven't hung out with her since that Mike incident. Plus she wants me to meet her new little boyfriend."

"Oh word. Baby Kelly is all grown up. Who's her boyfriend?" David asked TJ curiously.

"Some lil' freshman dude, named Aaron," TJ answered shrugging his shoulders.

"Oh. So is *Keisha* going to be there?" David asked teasingly with a smirk.

"Shut up, son. You know that's Jaden's girl now," TJ said playfully trying to conceal his sadness.

"What? I just asked a simple question," David said fawning innocence. TJ just gave him an evil stare in response.

"Seriously though, I really thought that was going to be wifey for you," David told TJ sincerely. The way TJ used to come home talking about Keisha, David just knew TJ was going to wife her up, quick -- especially when TJ found out that Jaden was talking to her too.

"I should have. In retrospect, I see it was my fault. I told her that I wasn't going to be ready for a relationship for a while when in all actuality, I was. Girls, don't want to hear that though because during that 'while' they don't know what's going to happen. You could eventually end up being with her or you might decide over that 'while' that she's not the one for you and pick somebody else. Nobody wants to risk their feelings like that, so when Jaden came to her and said that he wanted to be with her, she had to take that offer. Otherwise, she would have had a fifty-fifty chance with me."

"How do you know she would have picked you over Jaden?" David asked, cutting TJ off.

"I had asked her once, if she had to choose between the two of us, which one would it be? And she said me, with no hesitation. That's why I know, I messed that one up. When I look back on it, though, I realize that I was just scared of making that commitment especially after what happened with Tiffany," TJ stated dejectedly. "When it came down to it, Jaden wasn't scared and he was ready, so in the end he got the girl." David didn't realize that the situation was hurting his boy like this. David had known that TJ was mad that Jaden and Keisha were together, but he didn't know that it was hitting him this hard. The way TJ pranced around the apartment with a different girl every week, David would have never thought that Keisha had affected him that much. Since TJ was leaving, David figured he might as well give Ashley a call and see what she was getting into tonight. Since David didn't have Ashley's cell phone number, he called her dorm room phone hoping that she was in.

"Hello," David heard a charming southern voice answer.

"Can I speak to Ashley?" David asked hesitantly. He was a little nervous about asking Ashley out.

"This is her. Who's this?"

"It's David."

"Oh! What's going on?"

"Nothing much, I was just wondering if you wanted to go out with me tonight?" David asked Ashley, sounding more confident then earlier.

"That's cool, what time were you trying to go out?"

"Is eight cool?"

"Yeah."

"Ight, I'll pick you up at eight," David told her.

"Ight, I'll see you then," she replied, and then hung up.

~~~~

"I thought you said if you weren't playing ball you could be a professional bowler?" Ashley teased David as he bowled another gutter ball. David turned around and gave her the evil eye, making Ashley laugh even harder than she was already. Ashley was beating David by twenty points, and this was the last frame. It was no way that he was going to catch up and win. David walked back over to Ashley smiling sheepishly after he only hit two pins in his second turn.

"Ight, you got it," David said sitting down next to Ashley and holding his hands up in defeat.

"I guess we're going to Friday's then, since I won the bet," Ashley replied flirtatiously. They had a bet that the winner would have to treat the loser to dessert at Friday's. Friday's had this delicious vanilla bean cheesecake that Ashley had been craving for the past week.

"I don't know. I think you hustled me. I thought this was your first time bowling," David said skeptically.

"No, I said that this was my first time bowling in *New Jersey*," Ashley said while flashing him an innocent smile, which evoked laughter from both of them.

"Let me find out, Ashley, hustled me," David said smiling down on her and shaking his head. *Damn, he is so fine. I can't believe Ebony passed this up*, Ashley thought as she admired his handsome features. Ashley knew that Ebony was probably scared that if she let her guard down with David, then the same thing that happened between her and her ex, Darren, was going to happen with David. Ashley could tell that David was different though. It was just too bad that Ebony couldn't.

"You're lucky I like you," David said in a mock threatening tone.

"Or what?" Ashley asked him getting into his face playfully.

"Or this," David replied and began tickling Ashley incessantly.

"Stop," Ashley squealed not able to control her laughter. David finally stopped when the people next to them started staring at them with disapproval.

"You're lucky, there are witnesses," David whispered and stopped tickling her, but didn't let her go.

"I'm glad you called me and asked me out," Ashley whispered to David, while still in his embrace. She was sitting close enough to him to smell his minty breath and his Curve cologne, which was awakening all six of her senses.

"I am too," David whispered into Ashley's ear before pulling her in for a kiss. As David softly pulled away from the embrace, Ashley couldn't move. His passionate kiss had put her in a daze that she never wanted to leave. It almost made her forget that he was into Ebony before he asked her out. Almost!

"Are you ready for dessert?" David asked Ashley, bringing her out of her dreamlike trance. Ashley wasn't sure if he was talking about Friday's or himself.

"Yes," Ashley answered wanting both.

"Ight, let's get your cheesecake," David said leading the way out of the bowling alley.

"Can I ask you a serious question?" Ashley asked David as they sat at the Friday's eating their cheesecake.

"What's up?" David replied with his usual laid back facial

expression, becoming serious.

"Do you have feelings for my cousin?" Ashley quietly asked him the question that had been in the back of her mind all night. Ashley didn't want to bring it up earlier because they had been laughing, joking, and having such a good time that she didn't want to ruin the night, but now the night was coming to an end; it was now or never.

"Yeah, I was feeling your cousin," David replied nonchalantly while staring off at the tables in front of them.

"Oh!" Ashley said dejectedly. She knew this was too good to be true. Ashley didn't even know why she kidded herself into thinking that David wasn't feeling Ebony, although she knew deep down inside that he was.

"So, I guess you just went out with me because Ebony doesn't feel the same way," Ashley said lowering her head feeling like a complete fool and kicking herself for allowing her feelings to get caught up so soon. Lifting Ashley's chin up with his finger and looking into her eyes, David shook his head 'no' in response to Ashley's question.

"I'm going to keep it real with you because I don't like starting anything serious based on lies. I was -- keyword *was*, feeling your cousin. That was until I realized she didn't feel the same way about me."

"So, since you couldn't have my cousin, you wanted the next best thing?" Ashley asked David bitterly while cutting him off.

"I've always had a strong attraction to you, but I never acted on it because of your cousin. So when she called me today and said that you were feeling me, I jumped at that opportunity," David told Ashley genuinely. "I understand if you're skeptical of my feelings for you, but I promise you they're real, and if you give me a chance, you will eventually see that."

"I don't know," Ashley said, confused and skeptical. She really liked him and wanted to believe him, but Ashley didn't want to get her feelings hurt.

"So, what happens in case Ebony changes her mind later? Are you still going to want to talk to me?" Ashley asked David expressing what was on her heart.

"Honestly, sweetheart, I don't like to think about 'what if' questions because for all you know, I might be gone tomorrow. But, what I do know is, right now, I'm with *you* and I'm feeling *you*. That's all there is to it. So what you need to ask yourself is whether you can push that other stuff to the side and still talk to me?" David said flipping everything back onto Ashley. "If not, let me know."

"True. Well, you have to give me some time to think about that," Ashley told David, knowing she was going to have a lot to think about when she got back to her room tonight.

"Ight, I respect that," David told Ashley and then got up. After that conversation, the mood diminished a little, just like Ashley had expected it to. And with that, David took her back to her dorm, and they called it a night!

CHAPTER FIFTEEN

"Are you sure you don't like him?" Ashley asked Ebony one more time, as they waited for Keisha and Kelly to finish getting dressed, which was something that the girls had now become accustomed to. Apparently, Ashley was still concerned about that David had feelings for Ebony, which Keisha already knew that he did. Keisha didn't understand why Ashley would even go out with David in the first place, knowing that Ebony would probably eventually come around and give David a chance. In Keisha's opinion, Ashley must have really been lonely to make that move.

"I'm positive, Ashley. I have no feelings for David," Ebony said convincingly. Although, Ebony might have convinced Ashley that she didn't have feelings for him, she didn't convince Keisha or the other girls, of that fact. Keisha figured that Ebony was just fighting her feelings for David because she was scared to fall for another guy after Darren, which was why she was pushing David onto Ashley. Keisha knew that if Ashley went through with talking to David, nothing but disaster could come from it.

"Okay, because I'm going to tell David tonight that it's cool that me and him talk," Ashley told Ebony wearily. Keisha wanted to express her thoughts, but she learned a while ago, not to intervene in family matters.

"Okay. I don't know why it took you this long," Ebony replied flippantly, rolling her eyes at Ashley. Ashley gave her the eye and was about to say something when Kelly stepped in.

"Alright, ya'll ready to go," Kelly asked. Diffusing what seemed to be a heated argument in the making, judging from the expression on Ashley's face. Keisha, Kelly, Ashley, and Ebony were about to go to a female/male showcase, hosted by BSU. A showcase was when an audience bids on a male/female that comes out on stage, while a host reads their biographies. Sometimes the participants would even do a talent. Angel and Melissa were already at the showcase waiting on them, while Dana had decided to stay in her room and study tonight. Ever since the incident between her, Keisha and Ray, Dana had been keeping her distance and not really going out as much with the rest of the girls. The other girls figured it was because she needed some time to get over Ray, so they didn't really bug her about it. The host of the showcase was supposed to be RaShawn, from the basketball team, which meant that the girls were going to have to get there early, so that they could get a good seat because the groupies would, without a doubt, be out in full force tonight. Angel was also a participant in the showcase, which is why she was there early and Melissa just went with her because she abhorred waiting on Keisha and Kelly.

"Aren't ya'll boyfriends in the showcase tonight?" Ashley asked Keisha and Kelly with a huge grin.

"Yeah," they both said in unison.

"What if somebody bids on them?" Ebony asked with a

nervous laugh. Kelly just shrugged while Keisha answered, "I don't care; I know who he's coming home to. But just in case, he did give me enough money so that I should definitely win." This brought laughter to the group as they made their way out.

"Wow! It's packed in here," Keisha stated as she looked around the auditorium where the showcase was being held, and searched for some empty seats but saw nothing in sight. Keisha's assumption about the groupies being out in full force tonight was correct, and because of that it was also a lot of guys out, since they probably knew a lot of females would be in attendance.

"There's David and Melissa. I told them to hold us some seats," Ashley said, and started walking towards them. As Keisha walked down the aisle to their seats, she bopped along with the pounding music; the deejay was playing some of the hottest songs of the year. One thing Keisha realized about college was that every event was like a party.

"Welcome everyone to the 2006 BSU showcase. I am your host RaShawn, and we will be starting in five minutes so please find a seat," RaShawn announced to the audience. RaShawn was a good choice for host. He had a smooth, baritone voice and gregarious personality. Since RaShawn was hosting, half of the basketball team was in the showcase, which is the only reason Jaden was doing it. Just that instant, Kelly nudged Keisha and darted her eyes towards Ebony, taking Keisha away from her thoughts. At first Keisha was a little bit confused as to why Kelly was doing that because it didn't look like Ebony was doing anything except staring at something. *What is she staring at, especially with that sad expression on her face?* Keisha pondered to herself as she followed Ebony's eye gaze. Keisha finally located Ebony staring at Ashley and David cuddling and sneaking kisses. What she saw made it all clear to her. Although, Ashley and David had only just gone out a week ago, the way they were cuddled up, you would have thought that they had been together for months now. As Keisha examined Ebony's face even further, she saw that it wasn't sadness on Ebony's face, but what appeared to be a twinge of jealousy. *That's what she gets!* Keisha thought to herself as she shook her head knowingly. Keisha and Kelly had tried to tell Ebony once before that she made a big mistake hooking Ashley up with David, but Ebony insisted on lying to herself (because they knew better). They warned her that if she hooked David up with Ashley, when she finally accepted her feelings for him, it would be too late. Although Ebony persistently reassured them that she absolutely had no feelings for David, her eyes betrayed her. Whenever David's name was mentioned around Ebony, she would get a twinkle in her eyes that showed her true feelings for him, whether she wanted to admit them or not. Ebony was in love with David. It just took seeing him with somebody else for her to realize that. It was too late now, in Keisha's eyes, because judging by the way David was giving Ashley all of his attention and only glanced over at Ebony once to say 'hi', he was definitely over her.

"We tried to warn her," Keisha whispered to Kelly. Kelly just nodded her head in agreement.

"Welcome everybody to the BSU male/female showcase. Before we get started, there are some ground rules and guidelines for tonight's event. First, we are all grown and mature adults up in here, so there should be no reason why you cannot place your bid in an orderly fashion. All bids tonight will start at five dollars. After that we will go until we get to the highest bid and no one bids anymore. All winners will get passes to a movie tomorrow night with the male or female that they bid on. All proceeds will benefit the Hurricane Katrina Relief fund so don't be cheap. Alright, is everybody ready?" RaShawn asked as he finished going over all of the rules and guidelines.

"Yeah!" The auditorium roared with excited, Black college students.

"Ight, let's get this show moving. Our first participant tonight is Miss Angel. Angel is a freshman and…." RaShawn said introducing Angel and getting the show started.

"WORK IT GIRL!" Keisha screamed as Angel walked down their little stage looking just as beautiful as ever, in a simple, black, knee-length dress and stiletto heels.

"I'll start the bidding at five dollars," RaShawn announced.

"Five dollars, right here my man," a short unattractive guy yelled from the front row.

"Ten dollars!" Angel's boo Shawn yelled from the back. His frat brothers started shouting their fraternity calls in support for their boy.

"Fifteen dollars!" another guy, who was more attractive than the first, yelled. He was also sitting in the back. The bidding went on like that for a couple more minutes until Shawn raised the stakes to fifty dollars and all the rest of the guys in the crowd sat down.

"Shawn is so silly," Keisha said to Kelly while laughing, as Shawn did a pimp walk to the front of the stage while waving bills in his hand. Kelly just nodded her head in agreement and joined in on the laughter. After Angel walked off the stage to Shawn, RaShawn introduced the next participant.

"Next, for you single ladies out there, I have a treat for you.

He stands tall at 6'5" and is one of the rookies on the squad. We call him 'pretty boy', but all the girls call him, Sexy Mike. Come on out, son!" RaShawn announced, hyping Mike up. When Mike stepped out from behind the curtains wearing a black wife beater that showed off all of his taut muscles, and some True Religion jeans, all of the girls went wild in that place. The way girls were screaming, you would have thought it was a B2K concert. Keisha had to admit though; Mike was looking pretty damn good. She was ready to bid on him herself. Mike even had his cornrows done in a new design that made his face look even more striking.

"Ok, I'll start the bidding at five dollars," RaShawn said with a smirk, knowing that his boy was definitely going to go for way more than that.

"Ugh! Next participant please," Kelly mumbled under her breath, so that only Keisha could hear it. Keisha just laughed her off. She didn't even know why Kelly was faking the funk. She could tell by the way she was over there drooling that she still wanted Mike, but if Kelly wanted to act like she didn't to everybody else, then far be it for Keisha to challenge her.

"Twenty!" a petite girl in the front row yelled trying to end it all early.

"Twenty-five!" a cute Latina chick in the back yelled, walking up the isle. She just knew she was going to win.

"Forty!" Keisha heard a familiar voice in front of her to the left say, but she was too busy text-messaging Jaden to look up and see who it was.

"Forty, going once; forty going twice; and sold. Come get your prize, ma" RaShawn announced to the highest bidder.

"I don't believe this crap," Kelly muttered angrily. *What is she talking about…Oh!* Keisha thought as she saw Melissa go up to stage and meet Mike. Ebony and Ashley, who were also sitting in the row in front of Kelly and Keisha, turned to look at Kelly to see her reaction. However, Kelly had quickly wiped the angry expression off her face, and was now smiling like she wasn't fazed. Keisha didn't know what to think about the situation because Kelly couldn't really be mad, if Melissa started talking to Mike since she *claimed* that she had absolutely no interest in him; plus Kelly was with Aaron now so Mike was fair game.

"Are you okay?" Keisha whispered into her ear, so nobody else could hear.

"Yeah, I'm cool. I told you I have no interest in Mike, so if Melissa wants to talk to him, then that's on her," Kelly replied nonchalantly. While they were talking, a girl that Keisha didn't know came out and was sold for a mere ten dollars. Keisha's baby was called out next.

"Ight, we'll start the bidding at five dollars for my man, Jaden," RaShawn said while dapping Jaden up.

"Fifty dollars," a big butt girl yelled from a couple of rows in front of Keisha. *I know she didn't just bid fifty dollars on my man standing right in front of me. These girls are real thirsty tonight, coming out of their pockets that much,* Keisha thought astonished. All Keisha had was seventy-five dollars that Jaden had given her; which she hoped was enough. Just before Keisha was about to bid seventy-five, a voice in the back of the crowd screamed, "One hundred dollars." Keisha couldn't believe that some chick just bid a hundred dollars on her man. She began to look around the auditorium furiously to see what the chick looked like that bid on him. She then looked back up at the stage at Jaden, who signaled for Keisha to bid something. Keisha held up her hands to him, as if to say I don't have that much money. Jaden then tapped his pocket as to say 'I got you', but by that time it was too late.

"One hundred going once, one hundred going twice and sold, to the young lady in the uh-uh…I didn't see who said it, so just come on up and claim your prize," RaShawn said a little bewildered. Keisha could have died when she finally saw who the girl was that won Jaden as her prize for the night. This girl had to be one of the most unattractive females Keisha had ever seen and that was an understatement. The girl was fat and black as all hell, with these hideous bumps on her face. Her hair was snap short and she had on a skintight dress with rolls hanging out. The look on Jaden's face when the girl walked down the isle was priceless. Keisha wished she had a camera.

"Oh my gosh!" Kelly said while covering her mouth with her hand and trying not to laugh.

"That's what he gets," Keisha said matter-of-factly and burst out laughing. The whole auditorium was laughing, especially Jaden's boys in the crowd. Keisha had told him not to do the auction, but he claimed he couldn't let his boy down. She bet he would think twice again before signing up for one of these things.

"Next up is a freshman from "the bricks", and for you non-New Jerseyians, that's Newark. Please welcome, Aaron."

"Uh-oh look at your boo up there," Ashley turned around and nudged Kelly.

"Again, we will start the bidding at five dollars."

"Twenty dollars!" a cute petite girl in the front bid.

"Twenty-five dollars," Kelly screamed.

"Forty!" A girl on the other side of the auditorium yelled.

"Forty going once…"

"Well that was the highest I planned on bidding," Kelly said to Keisha with a smirk, not caring that another girl was probably about to win. Kelly knew that this event was for a good cause, which is why she didn't mind Aaron doing it. Plus, like Keisha, she knew who he was coming home to.

"Forty going twice, and sold, to pretty in pink on the right. Come on up and claim your prize."

"I can't believe Melissa bid on Mike," Kelly thought out loud later on that night, still in disbelief that her girl would bid on somebody that she used to talk to. Kelly was in Aaron's room chilling with him, and watching a movie. Although Kelly should be focused on enjoying her time with Aaron, she couldn't seem to get Melissa bidding on Mike out of her mind.

"Why are you tripping off of that? I thought you were over Mike," Aaron said beginning to get irritated and slightly jealous. He sat up and faced Kelly, so that he could look at her directly in her eyes, to make sure she answered truthfully. Kelly didn't realize that she had just said that out loud, but she cleaned it up by replying, "Baby, it's not the fact that Mike is going out with Melissa that bothers me. It's the fact that Melissa bid on Mike after she knew me and him used to kind of talk."

Kelly was only partially lying because it did bother her a little bit that Mike was going out with Melissa, but she would never let anybody else know that.

"Oh," Aaron replied, not sure if he believed her or not.

"Baby, you know I don't want anybody else but you. Especially not Mike, so you have nothing to worry about," Kelly told Aaron sincerely as she pulled him closer to her for a kiss. Kelly really didn't want to be with Mike, she just didn't want to see him with somebody that she was close to; at least that's what she liked to tell herself.

"It was just the principle of the matter, baby. I don't know if I can trust her completely now."

"Well, just talk to her about it tomorrow after you cool down," Aaron told Kelly, completely believing her. He began to kiss her on her neck and Kelly was surprised by his show of affection; usually she was the one all up on him. Aaron would always say how they should wait and how he didn't want to rush into things.

"What's gotten into you tonight?" Kelly asked Aaron curiously, enjoying the extra attention, and completely forgetting about Mike.

"Nothing, it's just that Christmas break is quickly approaching and I'm going to miss you," Aaron replied as he started to slowly undress her.

"We still got a week or so," Kelly moaned lightly as Aaron pinned her down on the bed and began to kiss on her neck.

"Yeah, but finals start next week so we'll be focused on studying, so I'm trying to get my time in now," Aaron said and then started kissing lower.

"But…" Kelly started, but was soon cut off by Aaron as he placed his index finger on her lip, signaling for her to be quiet.

"Shh, enough talking," Aaron whispered into her ear, and reached in his dresser next to him for a condom.

"You are so beautiful," Aaron said genuinely to Kelly after they had finished making love. *So that is what it feels like to make love to somebody,* Kelly thought as she lay next to Aaron. At this point, all Kelly could think about was the love she had for this man. She just hoped he felt the same.

"I love you baby," Kelly said, barely audible as she lay in Aaron's arms. For a while, Kelly didn't think that Aaron had heard her because he was so silent. Then Kelly felt a single tear trickle down onto her cheek. When Kelly looked up into Aaron's eyes, she saw something that she had never seen before. Kelly saw so much emotion in his eyes at that moment that she already knew how he felt about her before he said anything.

"I love you too, sweetheart," Aaron replied, kissing her forehead.

"Promise me something?" Kelly asked Aaron feeling protective of her heart at that moment.

"Anything for you. What's up?"

"Promise me that if I give you my heart tonight, that you'll cherish it forever and never break it."

"I promise, as long as you promise the same," Aaron replied lovingly and then pulled her closer as she nodded her head in agreement.

CHAPTER SIXTEEN

"How does this look?" Melissa asked Dana and Ashley, after she tried on yet another outfit. They were in Melissa's dorm room helping her get ready for her movie date with Mike tonight. The BSU was sending all of the participants from the showcase and their dates to see *Freedom Writers*, a new movie featuring Hillary Swank and Mario—the hot R&B singer.

"It's fine, and so were the last two outfits you had on," Dana mumbled, somewhat annoyed. This was the third outfit Melissa had tried on. Melissa knew she was being indecisive, but what she wore tonight was very important. It had to be something that was sexy enough to make Mike forget all about Kelly, and take Melissa home with him tonight after the movie.

"Why are you so picky tonight anyway? It's just Mike," Ashley asked Melissa confused.

"What? I can't want to look nice for my movie date?" Melissa asked her fawning innocence. Ashley just stared at Melissa, not knowing what to say. Ashley still wasn't sure if Melissa really liked Mike or if she just wanted to hit him and quit him like she did her other guys. Dana on the other hand knew the real deal, and just rolled her eyes at Melissa when she said that. Melissa had once confided in Dana that she found Mike incredibly sexy, and just wanted one night with him alone. The only thing was that soon after Melissa had told Dana that, Mike and Kelly had had their little fling, and after that Mike was so hung up on Kelly that he never even looked at Melissa like that, for fear of messing something up with Kelly. But now that Kelly was with Aaron, Melissa just had to jump on that opportunity when it was presented to her at the showcase. Plus, Kelly claimed that she had absolutely no interest in Mike, so that was a green light as far as Melissa was concerned. *Knock-knock,* the sound of Mike knocking on Melissa's dorm room door reverberated throughout the room.

"Well, he's here. I guess this will have to do," Melissa mumbled to herself as Dana went to answer the door and Melissa applied the finishing touches of her makeup.

"Hey Mike," Melissa greeted Mike seductively as he walked into the room.

"What's up?" he replied nonchalantly.

"Bye, ya'll have a fun time, but not too much fun," Ashley said playfully as she left out. Laughing at Ashley, Dana just waved goodbye and left out the room with her.

"So, are you ready?" Mike asked Melissa avoiding eye contact and looking like he just wanted to get this date over with. Mike found Melissa extremely attractive, and had it had been under other circumstances he would have been happy to be going out with her tonight; however, because Melissa was friends with Kelly, he didn't need anything else to make Kelly upset with him. Melissa knew he would probably act apprehensively in the beginning; but that was okay. She was just going to have to loosen him up as the night went on.

When Melissa and Mike arrived at the movie theater, they were greeted by all of the showcase participants and their dates. Melissa quickly went over to Angel and Shawn and greeted them, while Mike went to dap up some of his teammates. When it was time to go inside the theater, it wasn't the romantic scenery that Melissa pictured it being. Melissa had figured that she and Mike would be in a nice dark theater together, in a private, secluded area, where she could convince him that he should want to come home with her tonight. Instead, when they walked into the theater it was packed with not only the BSU winners and their dates, but also plenty of other people from school. On top of all that, of all the contestants in the showcase for Melissa and Mike to sit next to, they ended up sitting next to Aaron, Kelly's boyfriend, and his flirtatious date. It wouldn't have been a problem for Melissa if the chick was flirting with Aaron, but instead she was all up in Mike's face and kept reaching over Melissa to talk to Mike, who happened to be on the other side of Melissa. The girl even had the nerve to move to the empty seat on the other side of Mike, while the previews were still playing. Since Aaron had told the chick when they first got there that he had a girlfriend and wasn't interested in her, the girl had set her eyes on Mike. Melissa was fuming mad, especially since Mike was entertaining the chick and paid no attention to her.

"You okay?" Melissa heard Aaron whisper next to her as he moved into the empty seat beside her.

"Yeah," Melissa whispered back with a smile, trying to console the fact that her night was now ruined. The only upside to Melissa's night was that the movie had been excellent and very inspiring. *Too bad I can't say the same about my night,* Melissa thought as she waited for Mike to finish flirting with Aaron's date, so that he could take her home. All thoughts of Melissa hooking up with Mike tonight flew out the window, as she thought about how he just completely disrespected her earlier. Although Melissa had an agreement with Mike that it would just be two friends going to the movies, he could have at least paid attention to her. She didn't pay forty dollars, to sit and watch him flirt with another female in front of her.

"Hey Melissa, you don't mind riding home with Aaron do you? Kiki and I are going to, uh, hang out some more; Ight? I'll get at you later," Mike told Melissa, not stopping to see if she would have a problem with the change in plans. He made his way out of the movie theater with 'Kiki' and Melissa was beyond heated.

"I *know* this Negro did not just leave me here, so that he could roll out with that hoe," Melissa fumed out loud to herself.

"Um, yeah... I think he did," Aaron responded to Melissa's rant with an amused look on his face. Melissa then turned her anger onto Aaron, giving him an evil look as she stared him down. She did not like Aaron getting amusement out of her misfortune.

"You don't have to worry about taking me home, I'll just get Angel to drop me off," Melissa told Aaron snidely as she looked around the theater in an attempt to locate Angel.

"I guess that would work, if Angel and Shawn hadn't left like ten minutes ago," Aaron replied in a sarcastic tone, trying to hold his laughter in. Aaron didn't mean to get so much enjoyment out of Melissa's unfortunate circumstance, but it was just too funny not to.

"Of course she did," Melissa replied sarcastically, while looking up at the ceiling. *Could my night get any worse?*, Melissa thought.

"You think this is really funny don't you?" Melissa accused

Aaron. It had just become evident to her that he was struggling to keep from laughing.

"No," Aaron replied, but then couldn't hold his laughter in any longer, and let out a loud boisterous laugh. Melissa tried to remain angry, but she couldn't help but to laugh too because the situation was just too messed up not to be funny. After they received a couple of disapproving stares, and got all of their laughter out, Aaron walked Melissa out of the theater and dropped her off at her dorm.

CHAPTER SEVENTEEN

"I can't believe we're done with our first semester in college," Keisha told the girls reminiscently.

"I know," Kelly replied with a faraway stare. The whole crew was lounging in Keisha and Kelly's room, spending their last night at XU before the winter break together. They all wanted to spend some time together, since majority of them wouldn't be seeing each other until they got back up there next semester.

"It seems like just yesterday they got our housing assignments mixed up, and we were all living in that cramped two bedroom apartment," Ashley said with a goofy smile remembering that fateful day. A comfortable silence fell over the room as the girls thought back to that day with half-smiles on their faces. That day had meant a new beginning for each one of them.

"Yeah, I remember that day. I remember I thought Keisha and Kelly were going to be real stuck up, but I soon found out ya'll were the exact opposite," Angel said smiling and waiting to see what the two would say to her comment.

Laughing, Keisha replied "Yeah, and I remember thinking it was no way that I was going to get along with any of ya'll chicks.

But, look at us now." Keisha then looked around the room and smiled at her girls. Although the girls appeared to be real chummy, there was still a lot of tension in the room that they were all trying to ignore. Melissa and Kelly still hadn't talked about the whole Mike situation, and Kelly was still kind of upset with Melissa over that. Then Dana and Keisha still hadn't talked on a one-on-one tip since that night of the fight. Nobody wanted to bring the issues up in fear of starting another fight between them.

"Ha! Remember when we got Kelly to go down to Aaron's room in a towel," Dana squealed. They all broke out into laughter, including Kelly.

"At first I was so embarrassed about that night, but if I hadn't had gone down there in that towel, I might not have met the love of my life," Kelly said with a cheesy grin.

"Aww," Ebony and Angel gushed, while Ashley stuck her finger down her throat, as if she was about to throw up.

"Hey ya'll," Keisha said in a serious tone that got everybody's attention, "I just want to say that I...I have never had close, female friends in my life that weren't family, and I'm glad that I was blessed enough to have ya'll cross my path. I love ya'll," She finished genuinely.

"Aww! You're getting me all teary-eyed over here. I love you too, girl," Kelly told Keisha as she walked over to Keisha's bed where Keisha was sitting at and gave her a hug. One by one, each girl walked over to show her love for the bonds that had been established. For that split second, all the girls forgot any differences or problems that they might have had with each other. It just wasn't important for the night.

"I want us to make a pact, ya'll. That from now until forever we will always be friends and never let anything come between us," Ashley said to the group and extended her right hand into the middle of them as a signal for them to do the same so that they could solidify the pact.

"Deal!" Kelly said and put her hand on top of Ashley's. Angel, Ebony, Dana, Melissa, and Keisha agreed one after another, and put their hands on top. Keisha was definitely going to miss these girls when she left to go home over the break.

"I'm sorry I have to break up our little Hallmark moment, but I promised David that I would spend my last night up here with him," Ashley told the group, regretfully. Ebony instinctively flinched at the mention of David's name, but no one noticed.

"Mmm," Kelly moaned like someone's aunty. "Ya'll seem to have gotten close over these past few weeks."

"Yeah, he is so sweet. He bought me flowers and a Mahogany card telling me how much he was going to miss me while I was gone," Ashley replied dreamily. That reminded Keisha that she was supposed to be getting ready to go over to Jaden's room, so that she could spend her last night with him as well. Jaden was still going to be up there over most of the break since he had basketball practice and games. Keisha would probably come up and visit him over the break and go to some of his games, though.

"I'm happy for you," Keisha told Ashley. Just as Keisha said that, she noticed that Ebony wasn't smiling anymore; and she started to ask her what was wrong, but Keisha already knew the answer. *Ebony is just going to have to get over David and deal with the mistake she made because it didn't seem like Ashley and David were going to stop talking anytime soon,* Keisha thought while shaking her head to herself.

"Well, its okay that you have to leave because I told Aaron that I would spend tonight with him," Kelly said getting excited.

"Forget ya'll," Melissa said playfully. "For those of us who don't have men, we will be chilling in my room watching Black-love movies for the rest of the night."

The single crew consisted of Melissa, Dana and Ebony, because Angel planned on spending the night with Shawn, who was now her boyfriend. Angel was still a virgin though, and he was being real patient with her about it.

"Yeah," Dana said with a playful pout as she got up to get ready to leave.

"Ight, ya'll I guess... I'll see ya'll later," Ashley said sadly as she gathered her things.

"Yeah, I guess I'll see ya'll next semester," Keisha told the girls, with tears trickling down her cheeks. It just hit her that she wouldn't be able to talk to Kelly in the middle of the night, or be able to just walk down the hall when she wanted to see Ebony and Ashley once she got home for the break. The girls gave each other one last group hug, and went their separate ways, to their separate destinations, with their separate thoughts.

SECOND SEMESTER

JANUARY

CHAPTER EIGHTEEN

Keisha loved being back in Maryland, but she had to admit after the first week of being there she was ready to go back to XU. She missed her friends, Jaden, and most of all, the college lifestyle. When you're in school, you set your own rules. You don't have to worry about a curfew or having somebody to answer to. You can stay up and talk on the phone as late as you want to, and best of all, you don't have to do any chores. Keisha swore her mother was irking her by the time the second week rolled around of her being home for break. She always had a demand; and after being away at school she was not used to being on somebody else's time. Constantly she was saying, "Clean up this," "Wash these," "Why are you on the phone so late?" "I don't care what you do at college. You are at home now…" *Yada, yada, yada! Ugh! I had to get out of there, especially since I didn't have a job over winter break, which meant no money to get out of the house,* Keisha thought as she finished unpacking her suitcase. She was happy to be back in her dorm room at XU. Keisha's mother chilled out some when her grades came in though; Keisha got a 3.50 for the semester. Keisha's mother was so proud of her grades that everything else

Keisha did didn't even matter. Keisha wasn't the only one out of
the crew who did well. Kelly got a 3.82, mostly because half of her
classes were related to her dance major, so she excelled in each of
them. The rest of the girls did well, getting 3.0's and up; and of
course Mike did well, since he was on the basketball team. They
wouldn't dare allow him to get lower than a 2.5 especially since
he was starting now, and averaging fourteen points a game. Mike's
game was so good that he had taken one of the junior's starting
spots. Jaden had told Keisha how some of the people on the team
were hating on Mike at first because he came right in and started.
After they saw what he could do on the court, they instantly gave
him the respect that he was due.

Keisha reflected on her winter break; she had had fun seeing
some of her old friends from high school and going to the clubs
in D.C., but it wasn't the same with Mike not being there with
her. She never realized how much stuff she and Mike would get
into when she was at home, until he wasn't there anymore. Keisha
had to admit she really missed her best friend. Mike had to stay
at school for basketball practice and games, so he was only home
for a week out of their month-long break. Keisha had thought she
was going to be able to visit school a lot, but she only made it up
to New Jersey once over the break. She stayed for about a week
at Jaden's apartment. While she was up there she got to see Angel,
Melissa, Kelly, and—of course—Mike. Keisha and Dana weren't
really talking like that, so she didn't bother to call her while in
New Jersey. Jaden was another reason why Keisha couldn't wait
to come back to school. After Keisha had come home from that
week's visit at XU, she had missed Jaden so much, even though
she practically talked to him for hours each night. Jaden was one

of the first people Keisha planned on hanging out with later on that night; but at the moment Keisha was sprawled out on her bed, watching Kelly unpack the last bit of her belongings.

"I'm hungry. You want to get something to eat," Keisha asked Kelly breaking the silence that had occupied the room. For the past thirty minutes, both of the girls had been in their own little worlds as they unpacked their luggage from winter break. Now that Keisha's unpacking was finished, she was growing tired of sitting in the room. She was ready to see everybody, and the best place to do that was in the dining hall.

"Yeah, that's cool. Call the girls and tell them to meet us there," Kelly responded.

"Cool!"

~~~~~

"Ya'll are so silly," Angel said while rolling her eyes at a joke Keisha told. "But, anyway like I was saying, it's so funny how a month away can change so much." The whole crew was sitting at their usual table in the dining hall, catching up with each other, since they hadn't been together as a complete group since the last day of the first semester.

"What do you mean?" Ebony asked Angel baffled.

"For example, have you guys heard anybody mention Ray and P?" Angel asked with a knowing look. *Dag, now that I think about it, nobody has said anything about Ray and P*, Keisha thought as they all shook their heads 'no' in reply to her question. *Shoot, Keisha had forgotten about them to and the rumor they started,* now that she had time to think about it.

"Damn, you're right. Before we left, that's all anybody could talk about," Keisha replied.

"It's probably because the football team won their bowl game over the break. That's all anybody can talk about, now," Kelly said with a thoughtful expression.

"Speak of the devils," Ashley whispered while nodding her head towards the dining hall entrance where Ray and P were walking in with some other players on the football team. They all turned around to get their own glances of the new "superstars." You would have never thought that a month ago there was a rumor about Ray and P being on the DL with each other, by the way girls were running over to them and smiling all up in their faces.

"Another thing that died down is the rumor about you guys," Angel told Dana and Melissa, with a smile. "I heard this cute upperclassmen guy say that if he had the chance to, he would wife Dana up in a heartbeat."

"*Word*! Where is he?" Dana responded while playfully getting up like she was searching the dining hall for him.

"Girl, you are silly," Ashley told her as they all finished laughing at Dana's goofiness.

"Honestly, the rumor had to die down 'cause Dana stopped messing with Ray, and after that she didn't hook up with anybody else," Melissa told the group. "Me, on the other hand…I don't know." That comment brought on a whole new bout of laughter. Keisha missed being around her girls; she had almost forgotten how much fun they had together.

"Anyway, how was ya'll winter break?" Kelly asked everybody, changing the subject after all of the laughter died down.

"You act like you didn't talk to us all at least once a week," Angel stated rolling her eyes. Kelly was about to say she didn't, but decided to keep it cordial at the table, referring to Melissa.

"Fine. How was the last week before we moved back in?" Kelly said with mock annoyance, while playfully sticking her tongue out at Angel. Kelly had talked to everybody, except Melissa, over the break. Since Melissa still hadn't come to Kelly to discuss the "bidding on Mike" situation, the tension between them was thick enough to cut with a knife. When they did speak, it was only to say 'hi', and that was it.

Oblivious to the tension at the table, Ashley replied, "It was great. I came back early and stayed with David. We made our relationship official last night." Ashley was just beaming with happiness. Whenever Ashley mentioned David, Keisha always found herself glancing in Ebony's direction to see her initial facial expression. It always revealed how Ebony was really feeling about something before she had a chance to hide it with a fake smile. This time, Ebony's facial expression read more sadness than jealousy. *Damn, I thought she would have been over this by now,* Keisha thought as she noticed how Ebony had been unusually silent the whole time they were there. *If she can't get over it, she better learn how to hide her feelings before Ashley catches on,* Keisha thought as she kicked Kelly under the table and clandestinely nodded her head toward Ebony. Keisha and Kelly were definitely going to have to have another talk with Ebony. Over the break, Ebony finally admitted to Keisha and Kelly on three-way that she did have feelings for David, and that she didn't know what to do. They advised her to keep her feelings to herself because Ashley and David were happy and all her feelings would do is complicate things and possibly cause a rift between all three of them.

"That's great! I'm so happy for you. Just a couple months ago you were sitting in your room sulking, and now you're all bunned up," Keisha told Ashley teasingly.

"What's bunned up mean?" Melissa asked Keisha confused. Ashley looked at her with the same confused expression that Melissa had.

"My bad, I keep forgetting we all have different slang. Being home for a month made me get used to my DC/PG slang again, but anyway it means, wifed up."

"Oh! Well, yeah. Who would have thought it?" Ashley said in a dreamlike stance, probably thinking back to that night when Ebony hooked her up with David.

"So, did ya'll make it *official, official*, or just *official?*" Kelly asked Ashley with a mischievous wink. Kelly was trying to see if they had had sex, or if they were just boyfriend and girlfriend.

Laughing at Kelly's nosiness, Ashley responded, "No, we didn't have sex, Kelly. David said that he wants to abstain from sex until he gets married."

"Whoa, that's major. Let me find out his church routine isn't a façade," Dana commented, surprised. She wasn't the only one who was surprised.

"So, what about you? What happens when you want some?" Melissa asked Ashley quizzically, knowing that if it was her, she didn't think she could be with a guy who wasn't having sex. Melissa loved sex way too much for that abstinence mess.

"I honestly think it's a good idea, and he's even motivated me to start going to church more and living right," Ashley said thoughtfully. For some reason, hearing that David wanted to wait until marriage really bothered Ebony because it really hit her that David probably wouldn't have gotten in the way with her relationship with God, as she had once thought. Contrarily, he might have even strengthened it. This fact just made Ebony even more miserable than before.

"So Dana, how was your break?" Ebony asked Dana quickly taking advantage of the pause in the conversation. Ebony was tired of hearing about Ashley gush about David. That's all Ashley had talked about over the winter break while they were in Atlanta.

"It was really good. I even met this guy, who happens to go here, and I have a date with him tonight," Dana said with a wistful smile, oblivious to the real reason that Ebony had asked her that question.

"With who?" Melissa asked Dana. This was the first Melissa was hearing about this, and she talked to Dana almost everyday over the break.

"A guy named Jason. He's a junior, and one of Shawn's frat brothers," Dana said beaming while nodding at Angel. "I met him at this party back home a few weeks ago, and it just so happened that we both go to XU. We've been kicking it ever since."

"Hold up! Why are you just telling us about him, if you met him a few weeks ago?" Melissa asked her getting a little indignant.

"Oh, because I didn't want to jinx things. We had just started talking, and I wanted to keep it to myself until I knew if it was going to be serious or not. And before ya'll ask, 'no' I haven't had sex with him yet. I've definitely learned my lesson from messing with Ray," Dana replied humbly, not wanting to go that route again.

"So, how was your break Ebony?" Dana asked Ebony.

"It was cool. I didn't really do much," Ebony answered wearily, still thinking about what Ashley had just said about her and David.

"What! You didn't attend any church revivals?" Dana innocently joked with Ebony. Only Ebony didn't laugh. It wasn't that Ebony was offended by the joke, she was used to them joking like that, but she just wasn't in a joking mood. Keisha and Kelly were the only ones who knew about her feelings for David, so they knew why she was acting so reserved and sullen. However, the other girls did not, so they weren't used to seeing Ebony in a funk like this. Ebony was usually very upbeat, at peace, and happy.

"Are you okay?" Ashley asked Ebony concerned.

"Yeah, I'm fine," Ebony answered Ashley while avoiding eye contact.

"Are you sure? You've been acting different ever since we got back to school," Ashley kept probing Ebony.

"I said I'm alright, dag," Ebony snapped. "Man, I have to go do something. I'm going to see ya'll later." She then walked away from the table leaving the rest of the girls sitting there speechless.

"Was it my joke that got her upset? Because I was just playing," Dana asked the group worriedly.

"Nah, she just has a lot on her mind," Keisha replied and left it at that, even though Ashley looked at her with a questionable look on her face.

～～～～

Ebony felt so bad about walking out on her girls in the dining hall. She couldn't sit there and listen to Ashley talk about David anymore or how happy she was with him, especially when Ebony knew that it could have—and should have—been her. When Ebony went home for the break, she had done some soul searching and realized what Keisha had said was true. Ebony was scared of falling for David because she didn't want him to get into the middle of her relationship with God, as Darren had. However, after Ebony prayed on the situation, she realized that David was nothing like Darren. Darren had persisted and persisted until Ebony had finally given into having sex with him. David, on the other hand, was willing to wait until marriage for her, and for God, as she just found out. Where Darren never wanted to attend church with Ebony, David attended church every Sunday and even continued to go after he knew he didn't have a chance with Ebony. After Ebony had come to that conclusion, she realized that she had made a big mistake hooking Ashley and David up with one another. Ebony knew if she had been honest with herself and had been honest with David, then she wouldn't be in this predicament she was in now.

For the last hour or so Ebony had been walking around campus aimlessly, praying for clarity and trying to figure out what to do about her feelings. She just felt so guilty for being jealous of her own cousin rather than being happy for her. Ebony was even getting to the point where she didn't even like being around Ashley anymore. It was to the point where she was even starting to look for excuses to leave the dorm room when Ashley was in there. She resented her so much for living the dream she wanted. The worst part was that she only had herself to blame. After walking around for an undetermined amount of time, Ebony finally reached a destination and a decision. She wasn't sure if this is what God had in mind, but Ebony knew she had to be true to herself and be honest. *I hope he's here*, Ebony thought as she knocked on his apartment door.

CHAPTER NINETEEN

"Hey D! You got company," David heard TJ yell from the living room. David wondered who it could be, since he had just talked to Ashley and she said that she was going to be chilling with her girls for a little while longer before she came over there.

"Ight, I'm coming." David was walking from his bedroom to the front of the apartment when he stopped mid-stride.

"Ebony!" David said astonished, not believing his eyes. That was the last person David was expecting to see. Although David and Ebony had a pretty close friendship before, it had dwindled after she hooked him up with Ashley. It wasn't on purpose, but once David got a girl, he kind of lost a lot of the free time that he once had and wasn't able to spend as much time with Ebony or call as much. It was that, and out of respect for Ashley that he just kept his distance from her.

"Hi," Ebony replied meekly. Ebony still wasn't exactly sure what she was doing there, but she knew she had to follow her heart.

"What are you doing here?" David asked perplexed; swinging his arms nervously as he awaited her reply.

"Uh…over the break I was able to do a lot of thinking," Ebony started saying and then paused.

"Okay-y," David replied not knowing what Ebony was getting at, and motioned with his right hand for her to continue, for the suspense was killing him.

"And...never mind...I don't even know what I'm doing here," Ebony mumbled out, and turned to leave, but before she could reach the door, David reached out and grabbed her arm, pulling her back to him, and huskily asked her to say what she had come over there to say. He wasn't going to let her off the hook that easily.

"Basically, I came over to tell you that...that I love you. And I'm sorry I didn't tell you that when it really mattered," Ebony confessed, starting off at a normal volume and ending in a whisper. David hadn't realized how close Ebony and him were standing to each other, until he noticed that her face was only inches from his. David couldn't help but to lean in close and plant a soft kiss on her trembling lips. It just felt so natural, he didn't even think about the consequences that would eventually come from that little kiss. All David could think about at that moment was that this was what he had dreamed of happening ever since that first day he had laid eyes on her in the Glen and now it was finally happening. Then, reality set in. *Hold up! What am I doing? I'm with Ashley now, and I love Ashley, not Ebony. Well, at least I think I love Ashley. Ugh, either way I can't be doing this,* David thought as he quickly pulled away from Ebony, now utterly confused about his own feelings.

"Oh my God, what did we just do?" Ebony whispered bewildered, talking to herself more so, than David. "I should have never come over here. I have to go," Ebony whispered, still shook by what had just happened, but made no effort to leave.

"Why are you just telling me how you feel now?" David asked

her incredulously, shaking his head with disbelief.

"Because," Ebony said earnestly, "I was fighting my feelings for you in the beginning because I was scared. That's why I hooked you up with Ashley. I guess I was subconsciously trying to push you away from me."

"Well you succeeded. I'm with Ashley now, and we're happy," David told Ebony spitefully, now becoming upset. The whole time David had wanted to be with Ebony, she had expressed no interest in him what so ever. Now that David was with Ashley, Ebony comes and tells him that she loves him. He couldn't believe her.

"Well, I guess that's that then," Ebony responded sadly. "I just had to be honest with you and let you know how I felt." With that, Ebony turned around and left out of the apartment, before David could say anything.

"I can't believe this ish'," David screamed out loud.

"What happened, son?" TJ asked David as he walked over to the foyer where David was standing, to check and see if everything was okay; obviously eavesdropping the whole time.

"Son, how is she goin' come over herre' and express to me that she loves me, like it's nothing?!" David asked TJ bewildered with his St. Louis accent coming out. David couldn't believe the situation that he was now in. He thought stuff like this only happened in the movies.

"Do you still love her?" TJ asked him blatantly.

"Yes," David answered TJ with no hesitation. David had known he loved Ebony even when he started going with Ashley, but he figured that since Ebony wasn't into him, that those feelings would eventually go away so he just ignored them.

"Do you love Ashley?"

"I really care about …" David started, but then TJ cut him off and asked David the question again.

"Do you *love* Ashley?"

"No," David said somberly as he dropped his head. David had to be honest with himself. Although he cared a lot about Ashley, he knew he would never love her the same way he did Ebony.

"What do I do?" David asked TJ as he went and slouched down onto a nearby couch in the living room and placed his face into his hands.

"I don't know man, that's a tough situation; especially since they *are* cousins *and* roommates at that, son. Meaning that if you do play Ashley for Ebony you're going to have to see Ashley every time you go over there to visit Ebony. Not only that, but Ashley is always going to be in Ebony's life."

"Hold up! Who said anything about me picking Ebony over Ashley?" David said while snapping his head up.

"Son, you said you love Ebony and that you don't love Ashley. It's a no-brainer," TJ responded adamantly while scrunching his face, clearly not understanding why David wouldn't want to be with Ebony.

"Yeah ight. I may still got love for Ebony, but she can't just come back into my life and think that I'm going to drop everything for her," David stated arrogantly, and then stormed out of the living room and back to his bedroom, ending the conversation with that. David had a lot of thinking to do by himself before he could discuss the situation anymore with anybody else.

~~~~~

Why am I so nervous? Dana asked herself as she rode next to Jason in his 96' pearl Lexus sedan. It wasn't like Dana and Jason hadn't gone out before. Dana guessed it was because it was the first time the two of them had gone out while they were at XU, and Dana still felt insecure about what happened between her and Ray. She just didn't want Jason to play her the same way that Ray had. The whole 'hit it' and then make it seem like she was some type of hoe scenario was a nightmare to even think about. That was the main reason why Dana hadn't had sex with Jason yet, although she wanted to really badly. Jason was beyond fine with his six-foot, one inch frame and lean, muscular physique. Dana was getting turned on just imagining his arms around her. She was beginning to feel a lot more secure about the situation though, since the JO rumors about her had died down.

"You okay over there?" Jason asked Dana sweetly while reaching over for her hand. "You've been quieter than usual." *Aww, he's so observant. I like it when a man can read my moods and know when something is wrong with me,* Dana thought as she grabbed his hand and replied, "I'm okay baby, I'm just a little tired."

"Well if you want after we eat, we can just go back to my place and watch a movie," Jason replied thoughtfully. Dana would, but Jason was just too tempting for her to put herself in that predicament. She didn't trust herself with him, and she was trying to turn over a new leaf in life. Dana had promised herself that she wouldn't have sex with anybody unless she was in a relationship with him.

"I would, but I have an early class tomorrow. After we eat, you can just drop me off at my dorm," Dana responded with an innocent smile, hoping that Jason wouldn't be mad at her for saying 'no.' Jason wasn't mad though, he was actually the opposite. He was testing her to see if the rumors his boys had told him were true, and he was glad to see that Dana had passed the test by carrying herself with respect and not allowing him to smash early in the game.

"Oh okay, that's cool. So, where do you want to eat?" Jason asked Dana as they approached a shopping center with three restaurants in it.

"Let's go to Red Lobster. I've been dying for some of their cheese biscuits for a minute," Dana told Jason, as she felt her stomach growl in agreement.

"That was fun. I really enjoyed talking to you tonight; our conversations always flow so easy," Jason told Dana as he pulled in front of her dorm. "I don't run into many girls that I can really sit and just talk with. It's almost always just a physical thing, and I like that we haven't even took it there, yet." *Wow! I guess it's a good thing that I've been holding out on him*, Dana thought as she smiled at him.

"Uh, thanks. I had a good time too," Dana replied nervously, not really knowing how to respond to that.

"Dana, I'm really feeling you," Jason said and then pulled her face gently to his with his forefinger and his thumb and softly placed his lips on top of hers. "I hope you know that?" Jason said after they finished kissing. Dana just nodded hear head 'yes' in acknowledgement to his question, unable to speak after that kiss.

"Ight, I'll see you tomorrow," Jason said smiling and giving her a goodbye kiss on the cheek.

"Bye, Jason," Dana said dreamily and waved goodbye as she walked towards her dorm. *What a beautiful night. I can't wait to call Melissa and tell her all about it*, Dana thought as she rushed upstairs to her room.

CHAPTER TWENTY

It feels so weird to be back in classes, after having that month break, Melissa thought as she sat in class. Melissa had to admit, though, she definitely missed being at school. Melissa hated going home; it was like a jail. After Melissa's high school boyfriend raped her, her mother had become very protective of her and her little sister, and barely let them leave her sight. That's why when Melissa went home with Dana last month she had made it a point not to let her mother know that she was in town. By the end of the first week of break, Melissa couldn't wait to get out of that place. She must have had her bags packed at least two weeks in advance. It was really that serious! Melissa had done pretty well last semester, grade-wise. She had surprisingly got a 3.0, which is really good for somebody who barely goes to class. Dana really surprised her though, because she got a 3.7, and she was right with Melissa when she wasn't in class. Dana's explanation was that majority of the classes she took she didn't need to sit through the class to do well. She just had to study the book when it came to the exams. Plus, towards the end of the semester, that was all Dana did when she stopped hanging out as much with the girls. But this semester was going to be a different story for Melissa. While she did well last semester, she could have done better. Melissa had decided that she wanted to get into medical school after she graduated, so she had to be on point this semester.

"Alright, I'll see ya'll next class," Melissa's Black Experience professor abruptly dismissed the class. *Finally!* Melissa mumbled to herself. The professor had been rambling about his trip to Africa over winter break for the past half hour. If it wasn't going to be on the exam, then Melissa really could care less about it. Melissa knew she had just said that she was going to be more focused this semester, but that excluded non-class topics.

"Hey Melissa, I didn't know you were taking this class," Aaron greeted Melissa with a smile as he approached her seat.

"Hey Aaron. I didn't know you were taking this class either," Melissa replied surprised to see him. Ever since that night at the movies, Aaron and Melissa had become pretty good friends, and every time they saw each other around, they would chill and talk for a while.

"Oh, I'm surprised Kelly didn't tell you, when you told her what classes you were taking," Aaron told Melissa assuming that she and Kelly had discussed their class load like most friends did.

"Yeah, me too," Melissa muttered, while looking downwards. Melissa and Kelly hadn't said more than two words to each other since they got back from break, let alone went over the classes that they were taking this semester.

"So, what are you about to get into?" Aaron asked Melissa as they started walking towards the door together.

"Probably about to get something to eat. You're welcome to join me if you like," Melissa replied smiling.

"Okay, that sounds cool. Hold up let me call Kelly and we can all eat together," Aaron told Melissa as he took out his cell phone to call Kelly. For some reason, Aaron calling Kelly really bothered Melissa, and she didn't know why because Kelly *was* his girlfriend and he had a right to call her and invite her out to eat.

"I'm sorry Melissa. I would join you for something to eat, but Kelly wants to take me out to Olive Garden for a romantic dinner, and then we're going to go to the movies. I guess, I'll see you on Thursday when we have our next class," Aaron told Melissa sympathetically, and then began walking in the opposite direction of her. Melissa knew that the only reason Kelly was taking Aaron to Olive Garden was because she didn't want to be around her. She sighed and tried to ignore the fact that her friendship with Kelly was deteriorating right before her eyes, with no solution to fix it in sight.

~~~~~

Ugh! I missed being at school, but I sure as hell didn't miss going to class, Keisha thought as she sat in her boring accounting class. It was one of those required classes for her major. Actually, accounting itself was pretty interesting to Keisha; it was just the professor who was boring.

"Psst," Keisha heard somebody whisper. It was a large lecture hall style classroom, so Keisha ignored it and continued to listen to the boring lecture not thinking that it was directed towards her.

"Psst," Keisha heard the sound again, but this time she decided to turn around to see who was making that obnoxious sound. *Damn! He's sexy as hell,* was Keisha's first thought when she turned around and saw the cutie who was making the 'psst' sound. Surprisingly, he got up and moved to the empty seat next to her.

Keisha was sitting in the back of the large classroom, so nobody paid him any mind when he moved. Plus, it was only about fifty out of the two hundred students enrolled in the class in attendance that day. Keisha guessed everybody else felt the same way about the class as she did; she was just the only dumb one who decided to subject herself to the torture of sitting through the whole class.

"Is it me, or is this dude one of the most boring professors on earth?" The cute guy asked Keisha.

Laughing quietly, Keisha responded, "I think he might have that title."

"What's your name?"

"Keisha," she replied flirtatiously. Keisha knew she might be wrong, but a little harmless flirting never hurt anybody and she planned on making sure by the end of the conversation that he knew she had a man.

"Oh okay, well Miss Keisha, I'm Jay." By this time, he was flirting back. Keisha knew she had heard that name before or knew him from somewhere, but she just couldn't remember from where.

"Have we met before?" Keisha asked Jay quizzically, while studying his face to see if it would come to her.

"Nah, I don't think so. I never forget a beautiful face," Jay said eyeing Keisha intensely. Keisha loved when a guy made direct and unwavering eye contact. The confidence it indicated turned her on.

"So where are you from?" Keisha asked Jay, still trying to figure out where she recognized him from.

"I'm from North Jersey. I know *you* not from up here, though. I can tell by your accent," he told Keisha teasingly.

"One, I don't have an accent, and yeah I'm definitely not from up here," Keisha replied while scrunching up her nose. By that point

Keisha just gave up on trying to figure out why he was so familiar.

"Aww, you tryna' go on Jersey? Where you from?" Jay asked while laughing quietly.

"I'm from Maryland," Keisha responded, but pronounced Maryland as *mur-len*, and not Mary-land. Keisha never realized she did it until she got to Jersey and everybody kept making it a point to correct her.

"You mean Mary-land," Jay said attempting to correct Keisha.

"No, I said it right the first time. We pronounce it like that back home."

"Huh hunh. You really are country," Jay joked.

"Whateva."

"But anyway, I've been down there a few times. A lot of my fam stays down there," Jay said while nodding his head, like he was giving Keisha his stamp of approval.

"So Miss Keisha, do you have a boyfriend?" Jay asked Keisha while flashing a beautiful smile, even though he already knew the answer to that question.

"Yes, I do," Keisha answered, innocently, knowing that her flirting earlier could have suggested otherwise.

"Damn, I figured you would. Does he go here?" Jay asked Keisha, knowing full well that he did.

"Yeah, he goes here. And before you ask me, his name is Jaden," Keisha told him, assuming what his next question was going to be.

"Jaden on the basketball team?" Jay asked. Keisha then nodded 'yes' in reply.

"Oh, that's cool. That's my man," Jay said smiling, and moving away from her a little bit. *I guess when he figured out whose girl*

I was he didn't want to be seen too close to me, Keisha thought to herself, proud of the clout that her boyfriend had on campus. That wasn't the real reason Jay moved over; it was all a part of his game plan. Jay knew that Keisha was Jaden's girl from the jump. He had seen them on campus multiple times to know that she was Jaden's girl. But the way Jay saw things was that knowing Jaden, he was going to mess things up with Keisha soon anyway. Jaden always did when he found a good girl. So Jay figured he would just play the "friend" role for now so that when Jaden did finally mess up, he would be right there to pick up the pieces.

"Well, we can still be friends," Keisha told Jay as he predicted she would. To Keisha, Jay was cool, and he kept her entertained throughout this boring class, which was now ending. So Keisha didn't want Jay to think that just because Jaden was her boyfriend that Jay couldn't talk to her anymore.

"Ight, friends. I think I can handle that," Jay told Keisha playfully, while standing up and stretching. Jay didn't usually sneak around his friends back, and get at their girls on the sly, but Keisha was different. Keisha just had this unbelievable attractiveness to her, and all of it didn't even have to do with her looks: it was her whole persona that Jay found attractive. Jay had talked to a lot of attractive females—he was even talking to one now—but none of them had had this type of effect on him. And *all* they were doing was talking; Jay couldn't imagine how he would feel if they were in an intimate relationship. Even before Jaden had wifed her, Jay had noticed Keisha around campus last semester; but it was never the right time for him to approach her. That's why when Jay saw her in class, he knew he had to say something to her.

"Well, 'friend' would you like to get something to eat with

me?" Jay asked Keisha, while giving her a puppy dog look.

"Yeah, I was about to head over to the dining hall now anyway," Keisha said while laughing at his silly facial expression.

"Well, lead the way *friend*," Jay said emphasizing friend and extending his arm for Keisha to go first.

"Boy you are crazy," Keisha laughed and led the way to the dining hall.

CHAPTER TWENTY-ONE

I can't believe I allowed things to get like this, Ebony thought as she reflected on a picture that she and David had taken last semester. The picture was taken in front of the dorms, and they both had big silly grins on their faces. Ebony had known then that it was something special about David, but at the time she had fought her feelings for him. It was now a couple of weeks since that spontaneous night that Ebony had barged into David's apartment pronouncing her love for him. David had been avoiding her like the plague, barely speaking two words to her when he did come in contact with her. Ashley was too in love to notice the rift that was vastly growing between Ebony and David. It was starting to get to the point that Ebony couldn't even look Ashley in the eye anymore. Every time Ashley would ask her what was wrong, she would feel worse about hiding the truth from her cousin, whom she loved like a sister. It was a wonder to Ebony that Ashley hadn't put two and two together yet, the way Ebony would automatically shut down from guilt whenever Ashley brought up David, which, recently, was all the time.

Ebony was starting to grow stronger though, and although it

hurt to hear Ashley talk about how in love she was with David, knowing that that could have been her; she was finally starting to come to grips with the situation. As time went on, and as Ebony continued to grow her relationship with God, she finally came to see that the real reason that she pushed David away was because she was trying so hard to be perfect, and not slip up again like she had with her ex. That, in turn, caused her to ignore any feelings that she had for David, and when she started feeling like she couldn't ignore them anymore, she pushed him onto Ashley, figuring that it was no way that she would ever care about him if he was with her cousin. Much to her dismay, she now knew that logic was flawed. Ebony was now lying in her bed with the lights in her room off, meditating on this morning's sermon from church and how it applied so perfectly to her life right now. She could still hear the pastor preaching:

Nobody is perfect, and nobody will EVER be perfect. It is time for us as God's people to stop trying to live our lives as if we're perfect because that's where frustration and backsliding comes into play. The problem is that people think that once they become Christians, that all the sinful thoughts and desires that they used to have are going to just up and disappear. But what they have to realize is that the world is not void of sin, and neither will we live void of sin in our lives. The problem is that once some people realize that some of the "secular" things that they used to do aren't just going to up and go away because they want it to, they give up and stop trying to live their lives right for God. They figure that if they can't stop themselves from having lustful thoughts or listening to secular music, then they're going to hell, and since they're going to hell anyway, they might as well go back to living a life of sin. But that's not the case, at all. Whenever you start feeling like that, you have to step back and realize that Jesus died for that very reason. God knows that we live in a world of sin. Let's not forget that Jesus walked this earth as a man and was tempted by the very things that tempt us. Oh! He understands. The bible says in John 3:16, "for God so loved the world that he sent his one and only begotten son, that whosoever believes in him shall not perish but have eternal life." What that means is that Jesus died for our sins so that we wouldn't have to be bound by them. It is okay not to be perfect, and to fall from time to time. The key is to get back up again, and continue to put God first in your life. God knows your struggles; there is nothing hidden from His eyes. If you never sinned, you wouldn't need Jesus. The Bible says that His strength is made perfect in our weakness. It's okay that we're weak sometimes, as long as we know who the source of our strength is. God is faithful and merciful to forgive AND FORGET, unlike humans. Trust in Him and let Him be God.

Today's sermon had really spoken to Ebony. She was finally able to see that her fight and struggle to be perfect was a losing battle because nobody is perfect, except for Jesus Christ. Ebony realized that she was close to becoming that person her pastor was talking about in his sermon. As the days had passed, she was starting to feel more and more like the harder she tried to live right, the more everything she did seemed wrong. Before today's sermon, she was even considering just saying forget it and enjoying the so called "college lifestyle" like her friends were, who seemed to be pretty happy and had no worries. Thankfully, God kept her through to hear this message. Ebony now knew that it was okay for her to fall from time to time; she just had to make sure that she continued to get up after each time. She also realized that it was okay for her to have feelings for somebody; she just couldn't allow those feelings to come in between her and her relationship with God. Now Ebony was just wishing she had figured that out before she forced David onto Ashley. As Ebony continued to reflect on the revelations she was receiving from God, she heard a soft knock at her door.

I wonder who that could be, Ebony thought to herself as her brow furrowed. She knew that all of the girls were busy doing something tonight, so it couldn't have been any of them. Ebony slowly lifted herself out of bed, and walked cautiously over to the dorm room door. As she opened the door, and saw the figure on the other side of the door she couldn't believe her eyes.

"David," Ebony gasped, "What are you doing here?"

Ebony clearly remembered Ashley telling David on the phone earlier that she was going to be over at the library working on a group project until later on tonight, which left Ebony to ponder, why he was standing in front of her right now? David was wondering the same thing, as they both stared at each other, speechless.

~~~~~

"Baby-y-y, do you have to leave right now," Kelly whined, while attempting to give Aaron the puppy dog look. "Why don't you study later?"

"You are so cute when you whine," Aaron cooed as he gave Kelly a kiss on the cheek, and then continued to prepare his book bag to leave.

"But you know I have a exam Wednesday that I *have* to study for, and this was the only time that she was available," Aaron told Kelly after he finished gathering all of his stuff together.

They were in Aaron's room, and had been lying around in bed, watching movies for most of the day. Aaron wished he didn't have to leave, especially while Kelly was lying in his bed with a revealing camisole and boy shorts set on. He was tempted to cancel his study session and jump back in the in the bed with her, but he had an exam on Wednesday that he hadn't even started studying for yet. That meant he only had three days to study since today was Sunday. If his Black Experience exam wasn't worth forty-five percent of his grade, he would have strongly considered it, but if he failed that then he might as well have failed the class. And after his performance last semester, being put on academic probation with a GPA of 1.9, he couldn't afford to get less than a B in any class, let alone fail one. Aaron's parents had told him that if he didn't drastically improve his GPA from the last semester, they wouldn't be paying for him to come to XU next year. So, it wasn't a game anymore for Aaron. Kelly didn't know that Aaron was on academic probation; he had decided against telling her after he found out how high her GPA was. When she told him that she had gotten a 3.8, he felt so embarrassed and inferior that he had received a meager 1.9 that he lied to her and told her he got a 3.5. Kelly was surprised that he did so well, since Aaron barely studied last semester and went out almost every weekend. She then figured he was one of those people who could just go to class and do well without having to study as much, so she was surprised tonight when he said he had a study session.

"I know, I know. It couldn't hurt to ask," Kelly told Aaron playfully and made her way out of the bed over to his desk where he was standing to give him a hug.

"Ight babe, I gotta go," Aaron moaned and gently pushed her

away, as Kelly attempted to playfully nibble on his neck, knowing that was his spot.

"Okay, okay. I can't help it though. You're just so irresistible," Kelly said with a smile as she retreated back over to the bed. "By the way, who are you studying with tonight?"

"Melissa," Aaron replied nonchalantly, not thinking anything of it.

"What? You didn't tell me you were studying with her tonight!" Kelly exclaimed with a slight swivel of her neck and a hint of jealousy in her tone. By this point, Kelly and Melissa were still cordial with one another when they were with the crew, but the tension between them had escalated to the point that Kelly no longer considered Melissa a close friend anymore. She was more of an associate and Melissa basically felt the same way about Kelly. Kelly just didn't trust her, and she definitely didn't want her boyfriend alone with a female that she didn't trust.

"Yeah, I didn't think it would be a problem. Why are you so upset anyway? I thought Melissa was like one of your best friends?" Aaron responded uncertain to why Kelly was reacting that way.

"Come on Aaron, you know me and her don't even chill like that no more," Kelly said slightly irritated that he was acting so naïve.

"I thought you guys were cool again. Whenever I see ya'll in the group, ya'll are all buddy-buddy, so who am I to assume that ya'll aren't. And please don't tell me that you're still tripping off that whole Mike situation," Aaron told her beginning to get upset. He had told Kelly how Mike acted like a jerk, and basically left Melissa stranded that night of the BSU movie-date, if he wouldn't have taken her home. To Aaron's surprise that night, Kelly seemed more relieved about the situation then bothered.

"Oh boy! HOW MANY TIMES DO I HAVE TO TELL YOU....I'M NOT TRIPPING OFF OF MIKE," Kelly began to shout at Aaron.

"Whatever, I don't have time for this," Aaron mumbled as he grabbed his book bag and made a beeline out of the room, slamming the door behind him; leaving a fuming Kelly alone with her thoughts.

~~~~~

"What's wrong with you?" Melissa asked Aaron after she realized that he had been staring at the same page for about twenty minutes. They were both in the library sitting side by side at one of the back tables studying for their Black Experience Exam. Aaron didn't have one of the books needed for the class, so Melissa was letting him read hers while she went through her study guide. The only thing was Aaron didn't seem to be studying.

"Nothing. Why you ask that?" Aaron looked up from the book and asked Melissa, finally coming out of his dazed state.

"Well, you've been staring at the same page for about twenty minutes. So I was just making sure you were okay," Melissa chuckled at Aaron who just realized that he hadn't been reading. Laughing Aaron responded, "I guess you're right. Me and Kelly just had our first real blow-out, and I guess I'm finding it hard to concentrate," Aaron confided in Melissa. *Wow, I would never think the golden couple would have any problems*, Melissa thought to herself not really knowing what to say.

"Do you want to talk about it?" Melissa asked Aaron hesitantly; wanting to be there for him but not sure if that was such a good idea, giving the current circumstances of her friendship with Kelly.

"It's okay, we don't have to," Aaron replied, trying to hide the fact that the argument was really getting to him. Seeing right through him, Melissa closed up her notebook and pushed her study guide to the side to give him all her attention. She decided to just be there for him, and deal with the consequences later.

"I said we don't have to," Aaron said with a sideways smile, appreciating her efforts.

"Now you and I both know that if you don't get this off your chest now, you're not going to get any studying done. And then I'm not going to get any studying done because I'm going to be worried about you. So go ahead and talk, boy," Melissa insisted, not taking no for an answer.

"Okay, okay. If you insist," Aaron said jokingly, but really grateful that Melissa was loaning her ear to him. Aaron had friends on campus, but none of which he could talk to about stuff like this. His boys would either laugh at him for being too soft for letting the situation get to him, or just advise him to cut Kelly off and avoid the drama. They were all single and couldn't possibly understand why Aaron would choose to be in a serious-committed relationship in his freshmen year of college. Whenever he came to them for relationship advice, they would always tell him, 'leave her alone, there's too many attractive females on campus to be tripping off of one.' Aaron was glad that he finally had somebody to talk to about his relationship problems that would actually give him some real advice. Aaron told Melissa, how the argument started, and how Kelly was mad that he was coming to study with her. Aaron then told her how he thought that it was deeper than that. He felt Kelly was mad at Melissa for going out with Mike, and he felt as if Kelly still had feelings for Mike.

"Honestly, Aaron, in that situation Kelly has a right to be upset with me and not to trust me because I went out with somebody who she used to mess with, without checking to see if it was okay with her," Melissa told Aaron somberly. She realized that she probably lost a friend over her selfishness. At first she was mad that Kelly had gotten so upset over her bidding on Mike, especially when Kelly had a boyfriend anyway. However, after talking the situation over with Keisha, she learned that Kelly had a lot more feelings for Mike than she let on, and if Mike hadn't have slept with Kelly's play sister then they would probably be together right now. Plus, as Keisha so blatantly put it, out of all the sexy guys on campus that were after Melissa, why did she need to go after one that her friend used to mess with. After meditating on that for a while, Melissa realized that she was being selfish, and she was wrong in the situation.

"My thing is why do you even need to check with her about it? The way she explained her situation with Mike to me was that it was just a short-lived fling. They were about to talk, but then she found out that he had got with her play sister, so she stopped messing with him. And Kelly told me that she didn't even have feelings for him like that. Explain to me why would you need to ask for permission to bid on him?" Aaron asked Melissa as he tried to keep his voice to a library whisper, but struggled because he was so frustrated with the entire situation. Melissa didn't know what to tell him, because it was obvious that Kelly had lied to him about her feelings for Mike. However, Melissa didn't feel that it was her place to tell him. If she did that, she would be breaking the girl code and her friendship with Kelly would really be over. However, Melissa just hated to see him so sad and frustrated especially when she knew that although Kelly cared a lot about Aaron, she was in love with Mike. Kelly needed to admit that to herself before she ended up hurting Aaron. As Melissa stared at Aaron, not knowing what to say, it became very apparent to the both of them that their faces were mere inches away from each other; yet neither one made an attempt to move. In the heat of the moment, Aaron had inched closer to her to tell her everything he had to say, so that he wouldn't be talking too loud in the library.

"Melissa," they heard somebody call out, which startled them out of their intense stare. Aaron quickly scooted his chair back away from her, and hurriedly prepared his book bag to leave. "Melissa!" This time they could see Dana sashaying her way over to their table, ignoring the shushes and annoyed stares that she was receiving from other students for being so loud.

"Hey girl, what ya'll over here doing?" Dana asked them, oblivious to the intense moment that the two just shared.

"N-n-nothing," Aaron and Melissa stammered off at the same time. Dana was too busy sitting down at the table and taking her books out to notice the uncomfortable exchange between the two.

"Well, I'm bout to head back to my room. You don't mind if I borrow your book do you?" Aaron asked Melissa, as he quickly stood up to leave and headed off before she could give him an answer.

"Okay," Melissa mumbled to Aaron's retreating back. Melissa wasn't sure what just happened between them, but she was sure of one thing: she had to get Mike and Kelly together, AND SOON.

CHAPTER TWENTY-TWO

"So, what now?" Ebony asked David nervously. The two of them had just finished a deep, much-needed conversation to clear up the tension that had recently grown between them. After Ebony had gotten over the shock of seeing David at the door earlier tonight, she invited him into the room, and after a long uncomfortable silence, they were finally able to discuss all that had occurred between them. They talked about everything from the kiss at David's apartment to what Ebony had realized from today's sermon. David had been at church today too, but he had been so focused on what he should do about the Ebony and Ashley situation that he wasn't able to pay attention to the message. He spent the majority of the sermon praying for God to give him some clarity regarding what he should do about the circumstance that he now found himself in. The clarity finally came to David during the conversation that he and Ebony had just had. That was when David finally admitted to himself and to Ebony that he was in love with her and couldn't be with Ashley anymore. Now the two sat staring at each other contemplating what their next move should be. As Ebony sat on her bed and looked over to the desk in front of her where David was sitting, she knew without a doubt that she wanted a relationship with David and was in love with him as well. The only thing was that David was still with Ebony's cousin and when it came down to it, there was no way that she could ever be with David without hurting Ashley in the process, and Ebony just couldn't do that to Ashley.

David shrugged his shoulders, in response to Ebony's question because he just didn't know. David knew he wanted to be with Ebony, but he also knew that it would be real dirty on his part to break up with Ashley and then turn around and be wifed up with Ebony.

"Well, as far as me and Ashley are concerned, I know that I can't be with her anymore. I would be living a lie if I stayed with her, and that would hurt her more in the end," David confessed to Ebony after he had thought about it for a little while.

"And regarding us," Ebony asked him shyly, curious to know what he was going to say, although she already knew that nothing could happen between the two of them.

"Honestly…Ebony I love you, but I think we both know that it would be wrong for us to act on our feelings right now and start messing with each other because in the end, it's going to lead to a lot of hurt and ruined friendships all across the board. Plus, I have faith that if it is God's will for us to be together, then He will lead us back to one another. Until then, I think it's safe to say that we should just be friends," David answered Ebony speaking with a wisdom and maturity that only comes from spiritual growth. Impressed by his response, Ebony smiled and nodded her head in agreement.

"My thoughts exactly," Ebony replied, and beamed from admiration.

"So, what are you going to tell Ashley?" Ebony asked David after they both had dazed off for some minutes, lost in their thoughts.

"I'm going to tell her the truth. That's all I can tell her, and hopefully I won't hurt her feelings too much," David responded remorsefully as he dropped his head and stared at the floor. David really wished he didn't have to tell Ashley that he couldn't be with her anymore because he was in love with her cousin, and not her. He knew he could take the easy way out, and just tell her that basketball was starting to pick up, and he wasn't going to have time for a girlfriend or some other BS excuse. That would be the cowardly route, and David was far from that, so he was going to tough it out and face the consequences like a man.

"Well, I guess you should probably start heading out then, before she gets back," Ebony told David, as she turned away from him, breaking an intense stare that the two had been sharing. Ebony didn't want Ashley to come back from her study group to find David lovingly gazing at her. At least not before David told her that he didn't want to be with her anymore because he was in love with Ebony.

"Actually I would rather stay, so that I can tell her in person," David responded, as he got up from his seat and paced to Ashley's side of the dorm room and glanced at a picture of himself that Ashley had sitting on a nightstand next to her bed. "I just think that, the mature thing to do is to tell her to her face. So, if you wouldn't mind leaving the room for a few, I would really appreciate it."

"That's cool," Ebony replied as she looked over at him and admired the maturity that David was showing. David had grown a lot since that first day she met him in the Glen. While David had his back turned to her, Ebony couldn't help but to take one last glance at him, as admiration and love filled her heart. "I'll just go down to Keisha and Kelly's room and talk to them for awhile." With that, she got up, put some slippers on, and began to make her way towards the door to go down the hall. Before she could make it all the way out, David pulled her into his arms for an embrace, and whispered in her ear how much he loved her and although he knew that only time would tell if they were ultimately going to be together, he would always have love for her in his heart, and that if she needed anything he would be there for her. With this said, a single tear trickled down Ebony's face as she whispered back 'I love you too.' David affectionately wiped the tear from Ebony's cheek, as he stepped back from their embrace and let her go. Time must have been on their side, because as Ebony made her way out of the dorm room, Ashley was standing outside the door reaching for the door knob to make her way in.

"Where are you going?" a chipper Ashley asked a startled Ebony as she balanced her books in one arm and a poster board and her purse in the other. That's what was taking her so long to open the door.

"Down to Keisha and Kelly's," Ebony responded, quickly concealing her distraught expression, with a plastered on smile. Ashley was too distracted with balancing all of her belongings, to notice.

"By the way David's in the room waiting on you," Ebony told Ashley, avoiding eye contact.

"Oh he is, he knew I had a group project I was doing in the library," Ashley replied with a big grin as she stepped into the room and left Ebony to go down the hall. "Hey sweetie. You missed me so much you had to come over and wait for me to get back from the library?" Ashley greeted David flirtatiously as she finally was able to put all her things down onto her desk. "I *so* hate group projects. I promise you, it took us forever to finally agree on what we wanted to do, and who was going to do what. That's why I'm just finally getting in," Ashley chattered as she stood by her closet and took off her coat and shoes. Ashley was so caught up in her own world that she didn't even notice that David hadn't responded to anything she had said since she got into the room. "Babe, you're kind of quiet over there. What's wrong?" Ashley asked concerned as she made her way back across the room where David was sitting on her bed, finally noticing the solemn expression on his face.

"We need to talk," David whispered somberly.

~~~~~

"Hey," Kelly greeted Keisha glumly as she walked into their dorm room. Kelly was still upset over her argument with Aaron, and was still trying to come to grips with what just happened.

"What's wrong with you?" Keisha asked Kelly as she sat up in her bed to give Kelly her full attention. Keisha had been lying down in her bed, listening to the smooth, rich serenades of Sade, enjoying her solitude. Times like this were few and far between when you had a roommate.

"Nothing, I don't feel like talking about it right now. Where have you been? I haven't seen you in awhile?" Kelly responded. Kelly learned a while ago that if you have an argument or a fight with your boyfriend that it was best to just discuss it with him and not to bring your friends into it. Usually all your friends ended up doing was taking your side and making you more upset about the situation than you were before. Once you get over the situation and forgive your boyfriend, your friends will still be holding a grudge against him and just waiting for him to slip up again to tell you they told you so.

"I've been over at Jaden's spot," Keisha answered nonchalantly. Keisha had been M.I.A. for the past couple of days, not really taking any phone calls from anybody unless it was her mother; she just didn't feel like being bothered. Keisha loved Kelly to death and all, but she just needed her personal space; which seemed few and far between these days. She was truly enjoying the rare moment of solitude in her own dorm room, before Kelly barged in. Being an only child, Keisha was used to having her own personal space and needed that for her sanity. The less alone time she had to herself, the more irritable she noticed herself becoming. To get some space, she had decided to camp out at Jaden's spot for a few days since he was traveling with the team for games.

"So, you couldn't tell anybody or answer your phone?" Kelly asked condescendingly, not letting it go. That's what Keisha was talking about. She shouldn't have to check in with anybody. Kelly wasn't her mother.

"Where else would I be?" Keisha asked sarcastically while scrunching up her face, beginning to get annoyed. She really wasn't in the mood for this right now.

"I don't know. You could have been lying in a ditch somewhere, or worse. Ight, forget it! I don't even know why I bother. You don't have to worry about me caring about your selfish behind, anymore," Kelly yelled with her neck swaying in attitude. Kelly knew she was probably taking out some of her frustration with Aaron out on Keisha; and she knew she was wrong for that but she just needed a release. Kelly wasn't really that upset with Keisha, and was mad at herself now, for letting it get this far. She did know that Keisha was over at Jaden's. That's where Keisha always was when she wasn't in the dorm, just like Kelly was always in Aaron's room. Before Kelly could apologize for her rudeness, somebody knocked at their door.

"Who is it?" Keisha screamed still glaring at Kelly not understanding why Kelly was coming at her like that.

"It's Ebony," Ebony answered as she hesitantly walked into the room. Ebony wasn't sure she still wanted to come in anymore from the way Keisha just screamed 'who is it'. "What's going on in here?" Ebony asked them perplexed. She noticed that Keisha's face was scrunched up with annoyance and she looked like she was going to go off any second.

"I was just about to apologize to Keisha for coming at her wrong," Kelly told Ebony, and then looked over at Keisha and apologized. Keisha quickly calmed downed and accepted the apology after she saw the sincerity in Kelly's eyes. They both realized that it was just a frustrating time for the both of them, which had them on edge.

"So, what brings you here, Ms. Ebony?" Kelly asked as she got comfortable on her bed. Ebony hadn't been down to their room to chat in awhile. It seemed like she was always in her room brooding or too busy to chill with the group anymore.

As Ebony sat down on the bed next to Keisha she responded, "David and Ashley are in my room having a serious talk, so I came down here." Ebony felt bad about concealing the truth, but she wanted to talk to Ashley first before she told the other girls what happened between her and David.

"Oh so you're using us to pass up the time," Kelly retorted playfully.

"Yeah, the only time I seem to see you anymore is when I stop by your room. What you been up to since you don't have time for your girls no more?" Keisha chimed in with her lips pursed. "Well, I've just been doing a lot of soul searching and praying lately. I realized today that I've been trying to live this perfect life and there's no way that I will ever be perfect. But I know now that God understands that," Ebony stated wistfully.

"Hmm, I could have told you that girl. Ain't nobody in this whole world perfect. So does this mean, you goin' to start coming out to parties with us and stuff, instead of being held up in your room all night?" Keisha asked Ebony hopeful that she was about to start living the college lifestyle with the rest of the girls.

Ebony laughed and replied, "No Keisha. Just because God doesn't expect us to be perfect doesn't mean He wants us to give up trying to live our lives right. He still wants us to live our lives in a way that honors Him, but He knows that we're going to mess up sometimes. It's just instead of getting defeated like I used to when I messed up, I know that God still loves me and He forgives me for it. Instead of giving up, I can get back up and try again,"

"So you're saying going out to parties and having fun is dishonoring God," Keisha asked confused, not sure what Ebony meant by that statement. "Nah, I'm not saying that. I honestly don't think it's anything wrong with going out to a party, if you're just dancing by yourself or in your group of girls. But it's just not for me anymore," Ebony stated plainly.

"Whatchu mean?" Kelly asked Ebony curiously.

"Ight, well, before I started living my life for God, I used to party all of the time. I mean I was *partying*; freak dancing with every dude at the club and just plain ole' so called 'having fun.' After I would leave the party, I would always call up my ex, or we would already be together, and we would go and have sex somewhere. I mean for me, I already know that after going to a party and listening to songs like David Banner's 'let me make your p----y wet' or Shawnna's 'I was getting some head', I'ma be ready to get some for real, you know? So, for me it's just best that I avoid going to the parties all together. You feel me?"

"Wow. Yeah, I never thought about it like that. But, yeah I do want to call Jaden or go back to his place whenever I leave a party," Keisha commented with a smirk.

"Yeah, that is true," Kelly cosigned.

"I mean that's why I don't even listen to the radio like that. That's why in church they tell you to be careful of what music and images you take in because it'll stimulate your flesh and have you doing some things that you weren't even thinking about a second before," Ebony added seriously. Ebony didn't like to get too spiritual with her girls because she didn't want it to seem like she was judging them in anyway. She usually only talked about her spirituality when they brought it up, but tonight was different.

"Yeah that is true, 'cause I know if I put my R. Kelly CD in, then I'ma be ready for Jaden to be on his way over here ASAP," Keisha added with a devilish grin.

"Girl, you are a mess," Kelly told Keisha, while rolling her eyes at her as they all laughed. Although Keisha was laughing and making jokes, she knew what Ebony was saying was true. Keisha wanted to start living her life right for God, but it was just so hard for her to give up sex. Keisha used to tell herself that she would start living her life right after she got married, that way at least she didn't have to worry about not having sex anymore, but she knew that she couldn't put God on the backburner for that long. For now she was just going to start making it a point to go to church with Ebony every Sunday. She would just have to handle the sex thing later. *And like Ebony said, God knows that I'm not perfect, so eventually I'll be able to take care of that*, Keisha thought to herself. Before Keisha or Kelly could ask Ebony any more questions, Ashley calmly walked through their open doorway and walked right over to Ebony.

"You knew the whole time what he was going to say? Didn't you?" Ashley yelled at Ebony as she placed her finger in Ebony's face.

"What's going on Ashley?" Kelly asked as she stood up, not knowing if she was going to have to pull Ashley off Ebony in a few seconds. Ashley ignored her and kept talking, not giving Ebony a chance to respond. "The whole time we were in the hallway talking, you knew David was sitting in the room waiting to break up with me. Didn't you?"

"Whoa," Keisha gasped and looked over to Kelly uncomfortably, not knowing what they should do. *Why does drama always seem to happen when I'm around*, Keisha thought to herself as she shook her head really not knowing what she or Kelly should do.

"I *thought* we were family, you could have at least warned me. But why would you when the reason he was breaking up with me is because he's in love with you," Ashley spat out as she finally allowed the tears to trickle down her face. She hadn't wanted to give David the satisfaction of seeing her cry, so she held the tears in, until now.

"Are you serious?" Kelly whispered loudly to herself. She was shocked and unable to hold her tongue on that one. She didn't want to get in the middle of their argument, but she couldn't believe that David broke up with her because he still had feelings for Ebony -- especially, after he had reassured Ashley, plenty of times that he was over her.

"Ashley let me explain," Ebony begged, but was quickly shut down.

"Shut up! So tell me, how long did you know? Huh, Ebony? How long did you know that he was in love with you and not me?" Ashley yelled at Ebony who sat silently, staring at the ground and unable to make eye contact with Ashley.

"Ashley, come on, we all know that David has been in love with Ebony since he first met her. Even when you started to go out with him, he was in love with her," Keisha told Ashley blatantly. She was unable to hold her tongue any longer as she stood up for Ebony. Keisha knew that Ashley was hurting, but she had warned Ashley that this was going to happen if she ended up going with David. Ashley was so desperate for a man that she didn't pay attention to the signs. "Keisha not now," Kelly hissed at Keisha for her inconsideration. Ashley ignored Keisha and Kelly's remarks, and continued on her rambling rampage.

"I can't believe he just broke up with me, a couple weeks before Valentines Day at that; And for what? Because he's in love with you? You don't even want him!" Ashley cried out as she broke down into sobs in front of Ebony. Ashley still didn't know that Ebony had feelings for David, which is why she didn't understand why David would break up with her. Keisha was right. Ashley had known all along that David was in love with Ebony, but she figured that as long as Ebony didn't feel the same way for him, then the feelings would eventually fade away. Ashley guessed wrong.

"So what happened, sweetie? Was that the only reason he had for breaking up with you?" Kelly asked Ashley soothingly as she walked a calmer Ashley over to her bed to sit down.

"He said that although he cares about me a lot, he's in love with Ebony and knows that it would be unfair to me if he stayed with me. But what I don't understand is where all this is coming from? Before we started going together he had said that he didn't have feelings for Ebony, which as Keisha stated, I knew was a lie. I guess I figured that as long as Ebony didn't express feelings back to him then they would eventually fade. I guess I was wrong," Ashley whimpered as she continued to cry on Kelly's shoulder. Ebony buried her head down into her hands, unable to even look at her cousin anymore. As Ashley continued to cry, Kelly looked over at Ebony and threatened her with her eyes to tell Ashley the truth about her feelings for David. Ebony wanted to tell Ashley the truth; she just didn't want it to be like this.

"Um, Ashley, I have a confession to make," Ebony whispered regretfully and barely audible to everybody in the room. Ashley looked up to indicate for her to continue and Ebony told Ashley about the night that she professed her love to David. She told her that she didn't do it with the intentions of him breaking up with her. Ebony then continued to tell Ashley about the realization she just came to -- how she was ignoring her feelings for David at the time because she didn't want to make the same mistake twice. Instead, she pushed David onto her. Clarity soon began to set in for Ashley. It was clear now that David and Ebony no longer talked as much and it had seemed to be so much tension between the two. Before Ebony could finish her confession and tell Ashley that she and David had agreed to be nothing more than friends, Ashley was in her face. *SLAP!* The sound of Ashley slapping Ebony in her face pierced through the room. Ashley had gotten across the room so fast, that it was nothing Keisha or Kelly could have done to stop her.

"How could you?" Ashley screamed vehemently at Ebony.

"Ashley STOP," Keisha screamed at Ashley as she frantically pulled her away from Ebony and sat her back down on Kelly's bed. "Ashley, in Ebony's defense, you knew that Ebony had feelings for David the whole time, even when she was denying them. You were so lonely and desperate at the time that you hooked up with David anyway. Now you want to sit here and play the victim role getting mad at Ebony when you played a major part in it too," Keisha yelled at Ashley. She was upset that Ashley had really just took it there physically with Ebony for something that she played just as much a hand.

"Keisha," Kelly gasped, "you are so out of line. You need to be yelling at Ebony and not Ashley." Kelly understood the point that Keisha was making, but Ebony was still wrong for her part in it, and Keisha was acting like Ebony didn't do anything wrong. In Kelly's eyes, Ebony started this whole predicament by pushing David onto Ashley. Kelly didn't care if Ebony just realized now that she had feelings for David; she should have just taken an L (loss) and kept her mouth shut, instead of telling David how she felt.

"What? I'm just telling her the truth, and she needs to accept the fact that she also had a part in this. Ebony already knows that she was wrong, so it's no need for me to yell at her," Keisha told Kelly defensively.

"Shut up, Keisha," Ashley screamed and then spitefully added. "You need to mind your own business, and focus all of that energy on your own personal life." There had been rumors floating around campus lately that Jaden was cheating on Keisha, but there was no proof so Keisha had been ignoring them, and chalked it up to people just hating. Still, she didn't appreciate the fact that Ashley tried to throw that into her face, and before Keisha had a chance to point out to Ashley that they were in her room, Kelly gave her a look that told her to let it go and not start up any more drama.

"Anyway, I guess this means that the two of you are together now, huh?" Ashley spat at Ebony, not forgetting about Ebony's confession in all of the other confusion. "No, Ashley. Like I was trying to tell you before you slapped me, David and I agreed that out of respect for you, we could never be more than just friends," Ebony whimpered as she tried to comfort her swelling lip.

"Hmm mm. Well tell me this, just how are you two going to be just 'friends' when both of ya'll are in love with each other? That doesn't work. I'm sorry Ebony, you're going to have to make a sacrifice: it's either our friendship or your friendship with David because you cannot have both," Ashley told Ebony spitefully. If Ashley was going to have to be lonely and miserable, then she wanted David and Ebony to feel the same way for causing her pain.

"Are you serious?" Keisha mumbled to herself. She couldn't believe that Ashley would give such an ultimatum. *They just said that they were never going to be nothing more than friends. Telling them that they can't see each other wasn't going to change anything,* Keisha thought to herself angrily. Kelly, on the other hand didn't see a problem with the ultimatum. Two people who were in love with each other could not be friends. It was as simple as that in Kelly's eyes.

"Ashley you know that's not right…" Keisha started off saying, but was cut off by Ebony.

"No Keisha, its okay; you don't have to defend me. I was wrong for hooking up Ashley with David in the first place. At the time, I was trying to force the feelings I had for him away and in the end I ended up hurting my cousin, who is also my best friend. If in order to make things right with Ashley that means that David and I can't be friends, then so be it. I'll cut David off as a friend," Ebony replied sorrowfully, wondering how she was going to break this news to David. Keisha just shook her head, as she looked over at Ashley who had a satisfied smirk on her face.

FEBRUARY

CHAPTER TWENTY-THREE

"What are ya'll getting into tonight?" Angel asked everybody as they chilled in her room, which seemed to be the only neutral spot lately. She was so glad that she had chosen to room by herself. Tonight was Valentine's Day, which fell on a Wednesday this year. Since the group seemed to be deteriorating before her eyes, Angel invited everybody over to chill in her room to see if she could patch things up on the day of love. Everything was going well until Angel asked that dreaded question. In an instant, the whole mood in the room shifted from upbeat chatter and the girls truly enjoying themselves to a dead silence with uncomfortable stares. It had slipped Angel's mind that David had just broken up with Ashley because he was in love with Ebony, which was one reason for the uncomfortable silence. Angel didn't know why Melissa got silent and fidgety. Angel figured it might have been because Melissa was alone and didn't have any guy to go out with tonight.

"Well, I'm going to be chilling in the room watching love movies, while you, Dana, and Kelly go out with ya'll men," Keisha joked, with an attempt to lighten up the mood. Jaden had an away game tomorrow and the team was leaving today, so Keisha and Jaden were going to celebrate Valentine's Day this weekend instead of tonight.

"Well I don't know, me and Aaron were supposed to have plans tonight, but he said he has to study later on. Melissa, are you going to be at this study session too? Since you and Aaron have become the best of buds lately," Kelly snidely asked Melissa. Melissa laughed to herself, and shook her head 'no,' deciding to take the high road this time. Melissa knew that Aaron had only told Kelly that because he had planned a special romantic dinner for her. If Aaron wasn't trying to surprise Kelly with it, Melissa would have thrown that back in her face.

"Well, I would probably be chilling with David right now, had he not broken up with me for Ebony," Ashley stated sarcastically still bitter over the break up. Keisha smacked her lips loudly and rolled her eyes at Ashley's sarcasm, while Ebony just ignored her. Ebony was starting to get used to it anyway. It had only been a couple of weeks since David had broken up with Ashley, so Ebony knew that it was going to take Ashley some time to get over him; so until then Ebony knew she was just going to have to put up with Ashley's rudeness.

"Keisha, I'm starting to get real tired of your little attitude," Ashley stated disgustedly, rolling her neck as she said it.

"Well, I'm starting to get *real* tired of you moping around here, trying to make everybody feel sorry for you. David dumped you, get over it. It is too many dudes on this campus to be sitting in here tripping off one. Dag! And the way you acting, you would think you and David were together for years; it was only like three months or so, chick. GET OVER IT!!!" Keisha told Ashley as her tone went from normal to screaming.

"Okay-y-y, umm…," Angel started saying, trying to think of a way to diffuse the situation before it escalated anymore.

"Look bitch, if I were you I wouldn't be sitting up here yelling at me. I would be out there"—Ashley pointed towards the door—"checking for my man. From what I heard the team doesn't leave until nine, which is another fours away. Since you're in here with us, then he's probably celebrating V-day with his other girl," Ashley replied with a malicious smirk. She had been delivering a lot of low blows lately out of her own bitterness.

"Whoa," Dana whispered to herself, as she put her head down and began to scratch the back of her head. Dana didn't want any parts of that argument. She and Keisha were just beginning to be on speaking terms again, so Dana pushed her chair back farther away from them and just sat back and watched the fireworks.

"*Bitch*, who are you calling a bitch?"—Keisha stood up— "You're just hating because you don't have a man anymore. Don't worry about my relationship with Jaden. Me and him are straight, and for your information, he's at the gym now with his coaches, not with another *chick*," Keisha spat as she squared up with Ashley, wanting her to jump out there so she could slap the mess out of her. Ashley just laughed in response, as if she knew something that Keisha didn't know, which pissed Keisha off even more. Before Keisha had a chance to act on that anger, Ebony went over to Keisha and made her sit back on Angel's bed where she was before, and attempted to calm her down. Angel couldn't believe that these were the same girls that last semester made a pact to never let anything get in between their friendship. She decided to now make a point to mention that.

"Man, eff that pact. As far as I'm concerned, Ashley and I

are no longer friends," Keisha stated as she made her way out of Angel's room and slammed the door behind her.

"That's cool, because I been stopped considering Keisha a friend,"—Ashley smirked—"Which is why I didn't tell her that I saw her man with another chick on my way over here." At that, Ashley laughed maliciously and made her way out of the room as well, but much calmer than Keisha's departure.

"Wow," was all Angel could muster as she looked around the room to see the others' reactions.

"Ugh, what do we do now?" Kelly asked the group. Dana and Ebony shrugged their shoulders, still in disbelief of everything that just went down.

"Well, in my opinion, I think we should just let them work it out. If we get involved, we're ultimately going to end up picking sides and it's just going to split our friendships up even more than they are now," Melissa stated plainly.

"Mmm hmm, just like you worked things out with me?" Kelly asked Melissa sarcastically, still mad that Melissa hadn't apologized to her for bidding on Mike.

"Well, whenever I tried to call you and apologize, you ignored my phone call and this is the first time that I've seen you since the beginning of the semester, so…" Melissa retorted, growing annoyed with Kelly's attitude.

"Whatever, Melissa, I don't even want to hear that, because you know where I live, and it's no reason why you couldn't have stopped by and apologized or at least attempted to work things out with our friendship," Kelly declared angrily.

"Whatever Kelly. It is what it is. For the record, when I bid on Mike I didn't know you were as in love with him as you are. I honestly thought it was just a fling, but I apologize if I hurt your feelings when I bid on him. As your friend, I wouldn't have done that had I known the truth then," Melissa told Kelly sincerely.

At first Melissa felt really bad about the whole bidding on Mike situation, and was beating herself up about possibly losing a friend. She had even attempted to contact Kelly and apologize to her, with no response. So, now, Melissa was starting to care less how things went between her and Kelly. The whole time that the two of them argued, the rest of the girls just sat back and watched the beginning of another friendship fall to pieces right before their eyes.

"Then why are you studying with my boyfriend behind my back? Were you confused about my relationship with Aaron as well?" Kelly yelled at Melissa heatedly.

"Hold up, you're making it seem like I tried to keep studying with Aaron a secret from you. If you had picked up your phone when I called, then you would have known. And then you acting like I'm trying to get at your man or something, which is so not the case," Melissa began to shout.

"Well, I don't know. You tried to get at Mike and you knew I used to mess with him, so why wouldn't you try and get at Aaron? You once said 'if I want something I go after it, regardless of if it's taken or not.' And those are *your* words, so you tell me!" Kelly stated angrily with her piercing eyes directed at Melissa.

"Kelly, I saw them at the library, and they were really just studying," Dana interrupted their argument, with an attempt to diffuse the situation a little bit. But then again, when Dana thought about it, it did seem like it was a lot of awkwardness between Aaron and Melissa when she sat down. *I hope Melissa isn't trying to get with Aaron*, Dana thought to herself wearily as she reflected on that night. Kelly ignored Dana, and continued her rampage.

"Oh, and let's not forget that you seem to open your legs up to any dude who looks at you for longer than thirty seconds. So for all I know you probably *did* sleep with Mike and now have your sights set on Aaron," Kelly spat out harshly.

"KELLY," Ebony gasped, not understanding how Kelly could say something so malicious.

"What? It's the truth, and all of ya'll know it," Kelly replied defensively.

"Word, Kelly? That's how you feel?" an upset Melissa stated as she nodded her head up and down trying to control her anger and prepared her things to leave. "It's cool. But for the record I didn't sleep with Mike, and I'm not trying to sleep with Aaron. But maybe I should since '*I can't seem to keep my legs closed.*'" Melissa then walked to the door to leave the room.

"Oh yeah, and if you didn't know, our friendship is done," Melissa declared with fiery eyes as she slammed the dorm room door on her way out.

"Whatever bitch, the friendship had been over in my eyes," Kelly mumbled to herself as she started gathering her things to leave as well.

"Kelly, I can't believe you said that to her. And honestly, it's not all her fault, you know. You never told us how much you cared about Mike, and from what we knew, that was just somebody who you had a little fling with. Then you started going with Aaron shortly afterwards, so how was she supposed to know that Mike was off limits, when you never even talked about him? You need to check yourself," Dana yelled heatedly at Kelly and then left out the room before Kelly could respond.

"Whatever, I don't need this. I'll see ya'll later," Kelly mumbled, starting to feel guilty about what she had said. Ebony was getting up trying to figure out what she was going to do with herself since everyone was storming out. *Well, so much for my attempt to patch everything up*, Angel thought to herself as she looked around her empty room after everybody left.

~~~~~~

This has to be the best Valentines Day date that I have ever been on, Dana thought to herself as she sat in the car with Jason, reflecting over the night's events. Earlier tonight had been way too much for Dana. Dana's night started off with Jason handing her a beautiful bouquet of roses, and taking her out to eat at the Cheesecake Factory. Afterwards, Jason took Dana to an exclusive park where they sat in his car and admired the stars through his sunroof. It was there that they exchanged their gifts. Dana had bought Jason a red, Rocawear t-shirt to go with his frat colors and to match the occasion. Jason bought Dana a beautiful sterling silver necklace with earrings to match. Dana was having so much fun that she wished the night would never end. Sadly, for Dana, it was getting close to that time, as she noticed the clock on his dashboard read midnight.

"I wish this night didn't have to end," Dana told Jason honestly.

"It doesn't have to," Jason stated with a mischievous grin.

"What do you mean?" Dana asked him naively, knowing darn well he wanted her to stay at his place tonight. Dana just wanted to hear him say it. She had been hoping all night that he would.

"I mean, I really like you and I would like to continue celebrating V-day at my place if it's all right with you," Jason answered genuinely.

"I would like that," Dana answered Jason truthfully, really beginning to fall for him.

"I was hoping you'd say that," Jason replied, and then gently kissed Dana on her lips.

When Jason and Dana arrived at Jason's apartment, Dana realized that he must have planned on her coming back to his place all along because there were rose pedals on his bed and candles strategically placed in his bedroom, which he began to light. Dana couldn't believe he went through that much trouble for her. If it were anybody else, Dana would have thought that they had ill intentions in mind, but Jason was different from the other guys that Dana had been with. Dana figured for Jason to go through all of this trouble that he must really like her. After Jason finished lighting the candles, he put on an R&B mix CD, and then put all of his attention on Dana.

"I've been looking forward to this for a long time," Jason whispered into Dana's ear as he began kissing on her neck. A soft moan escaped her lip, as he began to kiss downward. Before Dana could let Jason go any further, it was some things that they were going to have to discuss. Dana didn't plan on making the same mistake twice.

"Baby?" Dana whispered while pulling his head back up to eye level.

"Hunh?" Jason asked while still attempting to kiss on her.

"Before we do this, it's some things I have to say," Dana told him seriously, which caught his attention because he stopped kissing her altogether.

"What's up?"

"Well, if we have sex tonight, then I want something exclusive from you," Dana told Jason nervously, not sure how he would react to her declaration. Exclusive didn't necessarily mean a relationship; it just meant that Dana only planned on having sex with him and that she would like the same thing in exchange from him.

"I feel you, and I was going to ask the same of you," Jason replied sincerely.

Smiling and elated by his response, Dana threw her arms around him and started passionately kissing him.

"Close your eyes baby. I'm about to take you on the ride of your life," Jason whispered into Dana's ear.

~~~~~

Mmm, where am I? Angel wondered to herself as she rolled over and felt Shawn's arms around her. *Oh, that's right, I'm at the Marriott Hotel down the street from campus,* Angel thought to herself as the happenings of last night rushed back to her memory. After that crazy escapade between the girls happened in her room, she and Shawn shared a romantic dinner at a classy and expensive restaurant downtown. Afterwards, Shawn brought Angel to the Marriott, which was set up with beautiful bouquets of roses everywhere. To top that off, Shawn ordered a bottle of Moet and they toasted to a long lasting relationship. The night felt so special to Angel as no guy had ever gone out of his way that much just to make her happy. It was so sweet and touching that Angel decided then and there that he was the one whom she wanted to lose her virginity to. It was ironic, because the whole night Shawn was the perfect gentleman, and didn't once press Angel to have sex with him. Every time Angel and Shawn usually messed around, they would have a certain level that they would reach and then stop.

Last night when they had reached that level, Angel told him that she didn't want to stop and that she wanted him to go all the way and be her first. Instead of jumping right into it, like Angel had expected him to do, Shawn made sure that that was something that Angel was certain she wanted to do. Shawn made it a point to ask her four times just to make sure that Angel wouldn't wake up with any regrets in the morning. When he finally realized that Angel was a hundred percent sure, Shawn promised Angel that her first time was going to be special and a memorable time. Angel wished she could say that Shawn's promise had come true, but then she would be lying. Angel had expected her first time to be a magical night of bliss, but instead her first time hurt like hell, and it was only brief instances of pleasure behind the pain. Although Shawn said that it would get better the more she did it, she wasn't sure if she believed him. In addition, his words didn't take away the empty feeling that Angel felt in the bottom of her soul after the experience was over. After the act Shawn fell asleep blissfully, obviously satisfied, but Angel couldn't shake the sadness that soon overcame her as she lay there next to him in his arms. Nor could she explain the empty feeling that she still felt even as she woke up this morning and peeked over at Shawn who was still sleeping peacefully. All Angel knew was, if this was how sex was, then she didn't want to do it again.

CHAPTER TWENTY-FOUR

Ever since Valentine's night at the hotel a couple of weeks ago, things between Angel and Shawn had been kind of shaky. Shawn wasn't spending as much time with Angel as he used to, and he seemed to go out with his friends a lot more then he did before. Although they saw each other everyday it seemed like on most days it was only for Shawn to stop by and get some. When Angel complained about them not going out as much as they used to, Shawn claimed that because it was step season for his frat he was a lot busier and didn't have as much free time as he used to. Still, he promised her that as soon as the big step show was over in April that he would have a lot more time for her. His excuse appeased Angel, and she had left him alone about it. Plus, when he was with her, he was still his usual sweet attentive self, who spoiled and did whatever for her. The two of them had just finished up one of their lovemaking sessions at Shawn's apartment, and Angel was now waiting on Shawn to walk her back to her dorm. Although Angel had declared that that night at the hotel would be the last time that the two of them had sex, it definitely wasn't. At first Angel didn't want to have sex anymore, but did it only to please Shawn.

But soon after the first couple of times, Shawn was right, sex did get better for her; and soon they were doing it on a daily basis. However, she was still aware of the empty feeling afterward, but she was just starting to get used to it and considered it something that came along with sex. This reminded Angel that she was going to have to go to the health center and get some birth control pills. Shawn insisted sex was better without a condom, and since he was "clean" and he pulled out each time they had sex, he told her, she had nothing to worry about, but Angel didn't want any mishaps. When Angel had told the rest of the girls about losing her virginity, she received mixed reactions. Of course they were all shocked that she had lost her virginity, although some of them said they knew it was eventually going to happen. Dana and Melissa congratulated her and welcomed her to womanhood saying it was 'about time.' Kelly and Ashley were happy for her after she affirmed that Shawn didn't talk her into doing it, and that it was her choice. Keisha and Ebony on the other hand weren't as excited for her. Angel knew Ebony wasn't going to be happy for her because of her values, but she wasn't expecting that from Keisha. Over the past few months, Keisha had become one of Angel's closest friends out of the crew, so Keisha's opinion really mattered a lot to Angel. Angel still remembered everything Keisha told her:

> *I wish you would have waited to have sex,*
> *at least until you really got to know Shawn*
> *because losing your virginity is a serious*
> *thing and something that you can't undo.*
> *And honestly, sometimes I wish I were*
> *a virgin again because with sex comes*
> *emotions and desires that will never go*

away. Plus once you start having sex, it's something that quickly takes control of you and has you wanting to have sex all of the time. Trust me when I say that. I truly believe that this is why God intended for us to only have one partner and to only share that with our husbands. But don't get me wrong, I'm not judging you, I'm just giving you my opinion and as long as you're happy, that's all that matters to me."

After talking to Keisha and hearing her opinion, it really made Angel think about what she did because she was finding herself now yearning for sex on a daily basis. Angel also found herself growing more and more emotionally attached to Shawn lately. She didn't know why, but it seemed like the more and more they made love, the deeper she fell for him. She was now standing outside Shawn's apartment with him, growing impatient as she waited on him. He was chit chatting with Jason who also lived in Shawn's apartment building. Angel didn't understand why they didn't just wait until they got to step practice to talk since Jason was also on the step team with Shawn and he was headed there after he walked her to her dorm. Just as Angel was about to start complaining to Shawn and suggest that Jason just walk with them to her dorm, their conversation started getting interesting to Angel. She overheard Jason talking about Dana, and how much he liked her, but that was all she could hear. Angel was actually surprised that Jason was messing with Dana--especially since he used to have a huge crush on Keisha last semester and was always asking her what was up with Keisha. At that time, Keisha was messing with Jaden, so Angel never mentioned it to anybody. Angel never understood why it seemed like the same guys were always interested in both Keisha and Dana. As Angel inched closer to hear more of what they were talking about, Jason noticed and quickly cut the conversation short. That was the last thing Jason needed -- Angel running back and telling Dana everything that he said. Jason quickly changed the subject and this time included Angel in it.

"Hey Angel, you know me and your girl got a class together this semester," Jason told her with a smirk.

"Which one?" Angel asked with laugh because she had so many of them.

"Keisha," Jason answered as if it wasn't a big deal, which cut Angel's laughs short. Just then, it occurred to Angel that Keisha had told her about this cute dude named Jay in her class, and had asked Angel if she knew him. At the time Angel told her 'no' because she didn't refer to Jason as 'Jay,' so she didn't know who Keisha was talking about. But now it was all coming together, and Angel was going to have to let Keisha know ASAP that Jason is Dana's man and whatever flirting that they would exchange during class needed to stop. Since Keisha and Dana still weren't that tight, Dana never had a chance to introduce Jason to Keisha like she did with all the rest of the girls. Keisha didn't know what Jason looked like or who he was.

"Really? You know her and Dana are cool, right?" Angel asked Jason while giving him a disapproving look. Angel wanted to remind Jason that although Keisha might not know who he was in regards to Dana, that the two of them were still cool, and he better not try any slick stuff with Keisha behind Dana's back.

"Yeah, I know they're cool. I don't like Keisha like that

anymore; that's like my lil' homie," Jason lied to Angel with a big smile, and then gave her a playful shove. Angel didn't really believe him too much, but before she could grill him anymore, she saw a figure across the parking lot that caught her eye. It was a guy in a black fitted cap, and Northface jacket that looked awfully familiar. Jason quickly caught on to what Angel was staring at and noticed that the figure across the parking lot was Jaden with his ex, Monica.

It looks like Jaden, but why would Jaden be leaving out of the apartment with that upperclassmen chick? Angel thought to herself as she scrunched up her face. Angel had seen the chick around campus a few times, but didn't know who she was. After Angel had concluded that the guy definitely was Jaden, she decided to do a little more investigating of the situation, since there were rumors going around campus that Jaden was cheating on Keisha.

"Hey babe, who's that over there with Jaden?" Angel asked Shawn suspiciously. Shawn and Jason just exchanged furtive glances, and shook their heads.

~~~~~~

"Hey Melissa, what's up?" Aaron hesitantly greeted Melissa after their black experience class ended on Wednesday afternoon. After that night in the library, things between Melissa and Aaron had been a little awkward. They still talked from time to time in class, and Aaron had even shared with Melissa his Valentine's Day plans for Kelly, but that night at the library and what could have happened if Dana hadn't have come over, always stayed at the forefront of their minds.

"Hey Aaron," Melissa replied cautiously, as she gathered her things.

"This is silly. Nothing happened that night and nothing was going to happen that night. There's no reason we can't act normal around each other," Aaron told Melissa, as he grew tired of their awkward exchanges.

"I know, but that's not the reason I've been acting standoffish around you," Melissa told Aaron warily.

"What's up then? Did I do something to offend you?" Aaron asked Melissa perplexed and also embarrassed that he had inferred that she might be feeling awkward about that night. The truth was Aaron knew for a fact that if Dana wouldn't have come by then he probably was about to kiss Melissa, which he could never tell her. Aaron had felt so guilty about wanting to kiss Melissa that he had dropped the whole Mike situation with Kelly, and had even went all out for her for Valentines Day.

"Well, I don't know if you know this, but Kelly and I aren't friends anymore, so I figured she had prohibited you from being cool with me," Melissa told him, as she avoided eye contact with him. After Melissa's argument with Kelly that day, she did a lot of soul searching and thought about the hurtful things that Kelly had said to her. When Kelly had basically called her a slut, who couldn't keep her legs closed, it really hurt Melissa to the core. Unbeknownst to the girls, Melissa had stopped having sex period, since last semester after the J.O. rumors. Melissa recognized, then, that she was getting a little reckless with having sex and when she was telling Dana that she was worth more than how Ray treated her; she realized that she was also worth more then allowing just any ole' dude to have sex with her. Melissa figured that Kelly had told Aaron about how Melissa threatened to sleep with him, since Kelly had said that she couldn't keep her legs closed, which was the real reason that she had been acting weird around Aaron lately.

"Yeah, I heard,"—Aaron said with a hesitant laugh—"But Kelly doesn't control who I have as friends in my life. And I hope that doesn't affect us being friends," Aaron told Melissa sincerely. This led Melissa to believe that Kelly must not have told Aaron about the threat, which was like a weight being lifted off of Melissa's shoulders. That was the last thing she wanted Aaron to do: to look at her like some slut who would be trying to get with him.

"I would like that," Melissa responded with a sideways smile as she looked up at Aaron.

CHAPTER TWENTY-FIVE

Yes! I knew Jaden was going to slip up sooner or later. Just my luck it happened to be sooner, Jason thought to himself excitedly as Angel asked him and Shawn questions about who Jaden was with.

"Oh, that's Monica," Shawn answered Angel, nonchalantly, not trying to throw salt on Jaden's game. Monica wasn't just any ole girl though; she was Jaden's ex-girlfriend from freshmen year. Jason believed that Monica was the reason that Jaden couldn't seem to make a relationship last. She had been the only girl that Jaden didn't cheat on. They actually ended up breaking up because she cheated on him with a senior on the football team, who was supposed to go pro. The senior did end up going pro, but once he did, he dropped Monica and proposed to his main girl that Monica knew nothing about. That was karma for you!

"Ok, so why is Jaden over there with her," Angel asked Shawn, delving for more answers. Shawn wasn't going to tell her that answer though. It was the cardinal rule between boys to never snitch on your man cheating, even if you're cool with the girl that he was doing wrong; you don't snitch. That would just be plain ole' hating, which would ultimately get you blacklisted amongst your boys. For that reason, Shawn just shrugged his shoulders to signify that he didn't know. Jason mouthed 'good move' to Shawn behind Angel's back to give Shawn props for getting out of that one. Although, Jason liked Keisha and that was his homegirl, he would never mention Jaden's infidelities to her, for those same reasons. Ever since that day in class that Jason had introduced himself to Keisha as 'Jay,' they would sit next to each other during class and get something to eat at the dining hall afterwards. Jason saw Keisha as a really cool girl, and was starting to have trouble getting her off of his mind. At first it was just a strong physical attraction, mixed with some curiosity, but now Jason was starting to like her as a whole. This wasn't good considering that he had just got involved in an exclusive relationship with her friend, Dana. Jason had known, then, who Keisha was and that she hung out with Dana, which is why he introduced himself to her as Jay instead of Jason. Plus he had figured that he and Dana weren't going to get as serious as they were now, and he hadn't wanted to mess up his chances with Keisha, if he and Dana stopped talking. Jason was just telling Shawn about his dilemma before he noticed Angel snooping in from afar. Jason's predicament was that he was really feeling Dana, but he didn't want to settle down with her completely and miss out on an opportunity to be with Keisha. His logic was that when it hit the fan that Jaden was cheating on Keisha—which looked like it would be pretty soon, the way Jaden was parading around now with his ex—she would definitely leave him. Everybody knew Keisha had too much pride for that. Before Angel's tirade of questions about who Monica was, Shawn was just telling Jason that he should cut it off with Dana now, before Keisha realized that he was the same Jay that belonged to Dana. If that realization came about, he would lose his chances with Keisha completely. Before Jason saw Jaden and Monica, he was going to scratch Shawn's advice and just be with Dana, but now he wasn't so sure.

"What's good son?" Jaden greeted Shawn, jarring Jason out of his thoughts. Jaden then came over to Jason and gave him a brotherman handshake; the one that involved clasping each other's hands and giving one another a half hug. Jaden had seen Angel staring over at him and Monica with anger piercing her beautiful eyes, so he knew he had to walk over to where the three were standing and run damage control.

"Nothing much, about to walk Angel to her room and then go to step practice. What you up to, man?" Shawn replied while smirking knowingly at him, and then at Monica. Angel was too busy studying Monica's profile to notice. Monica was a highly attractive female, with high cheekbones and a short sophisticated haircut that she always had styled to a tee. The only problem that Monica had was that she knew it. She was a junior, and was known for only messing with the key players on campus. If a guy wasn't playing a sport or in a frat, then it was pointless to waste time trying to get her attention.

"What's up Jason," Monica said while walking over to Jason and giving him a flirtatious hug, which confused the heck out of Jason. Monica knew better than to flirt with any of Jaden's boys' period, let alone in front of him. Jaden didn't even flinch; he continued his round of greetings and gave Angel a hug. The real shocker to Jason was that Monica was even dealing with Jaden right now. She had once told Jason that she would never succumb to such a lowly status as being number two to any dude after the football player had dumped her. The even bigger shocker to Jason was that Jaden was with her. After Monica had her feelings hurt by the football player, she came squandering back to Jaden begging for another chance. To her dismay, Jaden played her out in front of all their friends and told her that he never wanted anything to do with her again. The two of them must have just recently become friends again because they hadn't been seen together since freshmen year. *Either Jaden's the exception to Monica's rule or Jaden plans on dumping Keisha for her*, Jason thought to himself as he admired Monica's beauty and entertained her flirting.

"Hey, girl," Jason greeted Monica back and gave her a hug.

"So, when are you going to take me out in that nice Lexus of yours?" Monica asked Jason, continuing to playfully flirt with him for Angel's benefit, more than Jason's. Jaden and Monica had planned out what they were going to do before they had even got anywhere near Angel, Shawn, and Jason. The last thing Jaden needed was for Angel to run back and tell Keisha that she saw him with some chick, and he saw her and didn't come over and speak to her. Especially with all of the rumors going around that Jaden was cheating on her already.

"Angel, this is my friend Monica," Jaden said introducing Monica to Angel, to show her that he had nothing to hide.

"Oh, nice to meet you," Angel said amicably, while observing how Jaden and Monica interacted on the sly.

"Where are ya'll headed off to?" Angel asked Jaden nonchalantly, trying to appear as if she wasn't getting into his business.

"Oh, I'm bout to take Monica up to the mall to pick up her check. If you talk to Keisha tell her I should be back in about an hour; I tried calling her cell phone, but she ain't picking up," Jaden told Angel deliberately. He knew that the second he left, Angel was going to pick up her phone to call Keisha and be like 'guess who I just saw?' If it was one thing that Jaden had, it was game—on and off the court.

"Well, I'ma get up with ya'll later," Jaden told the group as he and Monica made their way to his car.

"Ight son, be easy," Jason told them as he dapped Jaden up and shook his head. Shawn and Jason just shook their heads at Jaden's boldness, and before Angel could ask them any more questions, they started making their way over to her dorm, with her in tow.

CHAPTER TWENTY-FIVE

"I can't believe Jaden had the audacity to show off and introduce his other girl in front of you," Kelly told Angel as they walked through the mall on a mission. After Shawn and Jason had walked Angel back to her room, she called Kelly up and told her about everything that had just happened, which then lead to both of them to the conclusion to come to the mall and do some detective work. Kelly had found out from her brother that the girl, Monica, worked at Bebe, which was where the two were headed now.

"I know. He thinks he's slick, but I can tell by how she looked at him that they got something going on, but you know Keisha; unless you have full proof that Jaden's cheating she doesn't want to hear about it," Angel replied with slight irritation.

"Don't I know it," Kelly mumbled. The last time Kelly confronted Keisha about the various rumors going around campus about Jaden cheating and even told her about what Ashley saw, Keisha had brushed it off telling Kelly, *'If I got mad every time somebody told me that they saw Jaden with another girl, the relationship would have been over.'* Keisha then added confidently, *"I'm not one of these insecure chicks out here that need to know everything about their man."*

"Can you believe that heifer told me, *'Please, Don't tell me anything else about Jaden unless you see him having sex with another chick. Thanks!'"* Kelly told Angel while imitating Keisha in a stuck up shrill voice. Angel looked at Kelly for a second before they both burst into a fit of laughter.

"Shhhh, duck," Kelly hissed at Angel, and quickly pulled Angel down to the floor in front of the Bebe store window like a crazy person.

"What? Are you crazy?" Angel loudly whispered, bringing even more attention to them. Ignoring the uneasy stares that they were getting from the other people in the mall, Kelly quickly pointed towards the Bebe store window to Jaden and Monica who were inside holding hands.

"I can't believe this punta is out here blatantly cheating on our girl, knowing that anybody from campus can just walk by and see them," Angel stated angrily as she rose to go and confront them.

"Nah, chill let's follow them," Kelly whispered to her, as she held Angel back from going into the store and making a scene.

"You don't think we've seen enough?" Angel asked Kelly still outraged, but giving up her pursuit to confront Jaden.

"I do, but Keisha won't. So we need to get some hardcore proof," Kelly replied with a mischievous grin as she held up her digital camera that she thoughtfully brought for a situation like this.

"Why are we doing so much to prove to Keisha that Jaden's cheating? If she doesn't trust us as her friends to tell her the truth, then shouldn't that be her problem?" Angel asked indecisively as she contemplated if she should even go through so much trouble for somebody who might not believe her when it was all said and done.

Kelly looked off as if she was really considering what Angel had just asked and then replied, "If it was anybody else then I would agree, and say lets be out. But Keisha's different. You see, I remember her telling me this story about how she had a boyfriend who she really cared about, and one of her 'supposedly' good friends came to her and told her that he was cheating on her. When she heard that, she put all her trust into her friend and broke up with the dude, not even hearing him out. Then after a week or so, her friend ended up smashing the same dude behind her back, and had only told her those lies so that she could get with him. That's why I think Keisha has a hard time really trusting us. She even told us in the beginning that this is the first time that she's really had female friends. Plus, I know that she would do the same for us."

"Yeah, I guess you're right. One thing that college is teaching me is that everybody does not think like me. I think that you should trust your friends off the break, but that doesn't mean that everybody else is going to think the same way. They might have had situations in their lives that make them distrust people, and I have to take that into account," Angel replied sympathetically. The whole time the two had been talking, they had been following behind an unknowing Jaden and Monica, who was only a couple of stores ahead of them in the semi-crowded mall.

"You've done this before haven't you?" Kelly asked Angel giggling, as Angel pulled her into the Coach store that was to the right of them, so that the two of them couldn't see them.

"Maybe," Angel smiled innocently. "One time when I was in high school, my best friend said that she thought that my boyfriend was cheating on me with this girl that worked at the mall. So, one day after school we followed him to the mall, and followed him around the mall to see if he really was. It turns out that the girl he was with was his cousin, and he would just chill with her when she went on break. I found that piece of news out, after I embarrassed myself, by so called 'busting' him, which he then broke up with me for."

"Are you serious," Kelly shrieked in laughter.

"Yeah, it was cool though because I later found out that he was messing with somebody in the mall. It just so happened that that day it was his cousin whom he was with and not the other girl," Angel replied laughing.

"Girl, that is too funny," Kelly told her as she gasped between fits of laughter.

"Shh!" Angel said whispering to Kelly as they started getting closer to Jaden and Monica. They were now close enough to the two that they could hear what they were saying. Angel and Kelly had just followed the two into Nordstrom's, and when the two of them stopped to look at some shoes, the girls found a large mirror column to hide behind.

"When are you going to break up with your girlfriend?" the two of them heard Monica whine to Jaden.

"Look, I told you. I care about you, but I also care a lot about Keisha. So, if you want to be with me, then you have to deal with me being with her because I don't plan on breaking up with her anytime soon,"

"Is this dude serious," Angel smacked, forgetting that they were supposed to be incognito.

"Shh," Kelly hissed.

"Ight then. Peace," Monica told Jaden playfully as she pretended to walk away. She didn't get too far, as Jaden pulled her into his arms for a kiss. Kelly used this opportunity to take a picture of the two of them, or so she thought.

"I can't believe this," Kelly mumbled to herself.

"What's wrong, take the picture now why you have the chance," Angel whispered hurriedly.

"I can't my battery is dead," Kelly groaned, kicking herself that she didn't remember to put her digital camera on the charger after she used it earlier this week.

"Girl, you know you ain't goin' no where," Jaden told Monica with a hint of seriousness after their elongated kiss.

"I know, but if I'm going to be sharing you, then you're going to have to do some more for me then," Monica smiled seductively at Jaden as she pointed to some Coach shoes that she wanted. With nothing else said, Jaden pulled out a wad of money and gave Monica a couple hundred dollars, to Kelly and Angel's astonishment. With that, it was nothing more for the two of them to see.

"Did you see that?" Kelly asked Angel dumbfounded by what they had just witnessed. The two of them had just crept their way out of the Nordstrom's and were now making their way back down the mall corridor to the front mall entrance that they had came in.

"Yeah! I can't believe that girl, Monica, is okay with sharing somebody else's man. How stupid can she be?"

"I don't think she's stupid. I think she's actually pretty smart," Kelly replied nonchalantly.

"How so?" Angel asked her incredulously.

"Well, I'm pretty sure Monica knows that eventually Keisha is going to find out that Jaden is playing her, and that after Keisha finds out, Keisha is undoubtedly going to break up with Jaden. Then, Monica will be number one, and when Jaden enters the NBA draft at the end of the season, she'll be right by his side," Kelly stated knowingly.

"Dag, I didn't even think about it like that. I forgot that Keisha had mentioned that Jaden was going to forego his senior year, next year, and enter the draft since he's doing so well this season," Angel added as she sadly shook her head.

"Yeah, and if he keeps averaging thirty points a game like he's been doing, then he's sure to go in the first round. Shoot, that's probably why he's throwing money around like that," Kelly replied, referring to Jaden tossing Monica a couple hundred dollars.

"Nah, Jaden's people have money. I heard his father is like a CEO or something," Angel corrected her.

"Whatever, that doesn't really matter right now," Kelly huffed as they reached her car.

"I know. So what do we do now?" Angel asked her wearily.

"The only thing we can do"—Kelly told her as she dejectedly started her car—"We go back to campus and tell Keisha everything that we just saw, and hope to God that she believes us."

CHAPTER TWENTY-SIX

This is harder than I thought it was going to be, Kelly thought to herself, as she and Angel sat across from Keisha in their room thinking of the right way to tell her what they saw. It was a Saturday afternoon, and a few days had passed since Kelly and Angel had seen Jaden in the mall with Monica. The girls had anticipated telling Keisha the news that night, but Keisha had been nowhere to be found, and the two of them had agreed that it would be better if they told her together in person. They figured that if it came from the both of them at the same time, then it wouldn't seem like they were hating, but telling her out of love. The two of them had even planned out a game plan of how they were going to tell her and who was going to say what, but now that they were actually in front of her that game plan had gone out the door. Now Angel and Kelly sat there stammering and trying to come up with the best way to bring it up.

"So what's up? Ya'll said ya'll had something to tell me, but now ya'll are all quiet," Keisha told them with a light smile. Keisha had no idea what the girls wanted to talk to her about. She assumed that they probably were there to talk her into apologizing to Ashley for their blow-up, but Keisha had already decided that

that friendship had reached its end and it was nothing that they could say to convince her otherwise.

"Well, on Wednesday I saw Jaden in the parking lot of Shawn's apartment with some chick, Monica…" Angel started out saying before Keisha cut her off.

"Oh girl, I know about that already. Jaden had called me that day to let me know that he was taking Monica up to the mall to get her check. Is that what ya'll have to tell me? Sitting over there looking all nervous and stuff," Keisha replied while laughing, humored by the situation.

"So you're okay with Jaden hanging out alone with Monica?" Kelly asked Keisha confused, before they continued on with what they had to tell her.

"I mean, yeah. Jaden said that he and Monica are just close friends, so I can't really be mad at that. They were friends before I came along just like Mike and me were friends before he came along. So as long as he lets me know he's going out with her, I don't have any problems with it," Keisha stated naïvely.

Kelly and Angel exchanged hesitant glances to that response, to see if they should go on because they both knew that Jaden might have told her that he and Monica were just "friends," but they knew from firsthand that was far from the truth.

"Well, Keisha, there's more to the story than that," Angel told her cautiously and then hinted for Kelly to tell her the rest.

"I'm listening," Keisha told them as she sat at her computer and fished through Facebook—an online college network that allowed everybody to stay connected.

"Well,"—Kelly started, but then took a second to clear her throat—"later on that day we went to the mall and saw Jaden and

Monica looking like they were…more than friends."

"Is that so? So what were ya'll doing at the mall?" Keisha asked them suspiciously as she turned around to face them. Keisha wanted to trust them because they were her girls, but she had been with Jaden earlier that week after the incident and he had told her that he saw her friends snooping around at the mall and that they were probably going to tell her some hating stuff.

"Um, I know this is going to sound bad, but we had your best interest at heart," Angel began saying, but was cut off yet again by Keisha.

"So basically, ya'll went to snoop and spy on Jaden?" Keisha asked them raising her voice slightly as she pursed her lips waiting on their response.

"I wouldn't call it snooping or spying per se, but yeah. And for good reason though because we saw them kissing and he even gave the chick a couple hundred dollars for some shoes," Angel stated defensively.

"What shoes? These shoes?" Keisha asked them as she went to her closet and held out the Coach shoes that Monica had been looking at in the mall that day. *What? Now I'm confused,* Kelly thought to herself with her face scrunched up in total perplexity. Kelly wasn't the only one that was confused, as she looked over and saw that Angel wore the same bewildered expression on her face. "And as far as the kissing, Jaden said that the two of them had saw ya'll following behind them and that they decided to mess with ya'll and give ya'll what ya'll wanted to see," Keisha stated blandly.

"Nah, that was real Keisha, and you can't tell me that it wasn't. I don't care what he said," Angel expressed angrily, unable to believe the story that Jaden had told Keisha.

"Plus it was no way that they saw us following them. If they did see us, it was after their interaction and not beforehand. So, Jaden is obviously trying to get over on you, and I can't believe you're sitting up in here believing his lies," Kelly interjected as she began to get upset with Keisha's naïveté.

"See, I tried to give ya'll the benefit of the doubt, figuring that ya'll only did what ya'll did for my benefit. But what I'm not understanding now is why after I laid out the facts of what happened that day, ya'll are still sitting here trying to throw salt on my relationship?" Keisha asked them with slight irritation.

"Keisha, please listen to yourself. The facts? THE FACTS? Who has a girlfriend and passionately kisses somebody as a joke? Come on Keisha, let's think logically here," Kelly told Keisha condescendingly as she tapped her forehead with her forefinger.

"And Keisha, come on. You know we're your girls. What reason do the both of us have to hate on you and Jaden? None. I'm not getting anything out of this, and neither is Kelly. We spied on him for you and are telling you this because we don't want to see you get hurt," Angel told Keisha soothingly, trying to hide her irritation with Keisha's naïveté.

"Look, I want to believe you guys because I know you care...but then again it's like Jaden told me ya'll were going to say all of this. Ugh... and the last time I trusted a friend over a boyfriend I ended up getting my feelings hurt in the end." Keisha stated frustrated and not knowing who she should believe. "So I don't know who to believe or who I should trust, but what I do know is that I love Jaden and he loves me, and if he's cheating then it'll come to light. But until then please, *please,* just stay out of our relationship from now on and let me handle things," Keisha told the girls as a lone tear slid down her face. With that said, Keisha grabbed her purse and left the room, slowly closing the door behind her and leaving Kelly and Angel sitting in the room speechless.

~~~~~~~

Where is Keisha? Ebony thought to herself as she glanced down at her watch. Ebony was sitting at the XU basketball game, waiting for Keisha to arrive. It was the only way she got to see David, since Ashley had restricted her from seeing him. After that night of the break-up, Ebony had called David and let him know the devastating news that they wouldn't be able to even chill as friends. That was when they decided that if they couldn't see each other or talk, then Ebony could at least come to the basketball games with Keisha and see him there. That way she had a legitimate excuse to see him. So for the past couple of weeks that's what Ebony had been doing. Each player on the team received a certain amount of guest tickets to give out to family and friends that are right behind the bench. So Ebony and Keisha got to sit in the good seats instead of having to sit in the student section. At the moment, they were honoring the seniors on the team for senior night, since tonight's game was their last home game of the season. They had a really strong season; they only lost five games, and most of those losses were against teams ranked in the top ten. XU was ranked 15th in the country. Ebony was so proud of the team, which was funny because at first Ebony knew nothing about basketball and only came to the games as a way to see David. Now, as the realization set in that this would probably be the last game of the season that Ebony is able to attend, she couldn't even front, she was going to miss it. Ebony was especially going to miss her, Keisha, Jaden, and David going to eat after each home game. Whether they win or lose, they would always eat afterwards. It was a ritual they had started; a ritual that Ashley knew nothing about. And since Keisha and Ashley weren't cool, there was no way that Ashley would find out about it. Honestly, Ebony was starting to care less and grow weary of being concerned with Ashley. Although Ashley had told Ebony that if she cut David out of her life, then things would go back to normal, things hadn't. Half of the time Ashley pranced around like Ebony didn't even exist, and when she did pay attention to Ebony it was only to ask her for something. Ebony was truly beginning to lose her patience with Ashley. She didn't even do anything for real. Ebony could have gone cruddy and started a relationship with David right after the two of them broke up, but she didn't out of respect for Ashley. Although Ebony might have been wrong for professing her feelings to David that night and sharing a little kiss with him, it wasn't like she was the one who told David to break up with Ashley; he had come to that conclusion on his own.

"Oh say can yo-u-u se-e-e...." a petite white girl began to sing the national anthem. *Where is Keisha?* Ebony thought to herself and checked her watch again as she stood for the national anthem. Keisha never missed a game and was always there before the national anthem, so Ebony figured something must be wrong. Just as Ebony was about to take her cell phone out to call Keisha, she sat down next to Ebony with anger flaring in her eyes.

"What's wrong with you?" Ebony asked her cautiously.

"I don't feel like talking about it. I'll tell you later." Keisha huffed. *Okay! I won't say anything else to her for the rest of the game,* Ebony thought and then diverted all of her attention back to the court. Ignoring Keisha's attitude, Ebony sat back and enjoyed the game that was now underway.

MARCH

CHAPTER TWENTY-SEVEN

"Hey, how are you?" Melissa greeted Aaron as he walked into her dorm room. It was Saturday night and Aaron and Melissa had a quiz coming up in their Black Experience course. They were meeting to study for it now. Melissa's roommate had gone home for the weekend, so she figured that it would probably be fewer chances of any drama happening if they studied in her room. She didn't want to chance Kelly coming to the library to spy on her, especially after she heard about the Jaden escapade. Melissa had to laugh at that, every time she thought about it. She could just imagine the two of them all prissy, ducking and hiding whenever Jaden would turn in their direction.

"What are you over there chuckling about?" Aaron asked Melissa as he walked in and took a seat at Melissa's desk, which sat right next to her bed where she was sitting.

"I was just thinking about Kelly and Angel's detective escapade," Melissa told him with a smile.

"Yeah, I still can't believe they did all of that," Aaron said as he shook his head and laughed himself.

"Did you tell Ms. Double-O-Seven that you were studying in

here with me tonight?" Melissa teasingly asked Aaron, knowing that Kelly wouldn't approve.

"Um, sort of," Aaron answered with a mischievous smile.

"What's that mean?" Melissa asked him with a sideways glance and smile.

"It means that I told her I was meeting up with a study group, but I just left out that you were the only person in it," Aaron replied with a sheepish grin.

"Why didn't you tell her the truth?" Melissa asked him curiously as she intently gazed into his chestnut brown eyes.

"I just didn't want to give her anything to worry about," Aaron answered, turning his attention to her computer screen to break her intense stare. Aaron then pretended to search the Internet for the class syllabus, so that he could take away the lustful thoughts about Melissa that were starting to get the best of him. As hard as Aaron tried though, he couldn't help but to peak over at Melissa in her short cheerleading shorts that revealed her sexy, smooth legs. They were turning him on. Aaron was so caught up in his lustful thoughts that he didn't even realize that Melissa had asked him a question, and was still waiting for his response.

"Huh, what did you just say?" Aaron asked Melissa as he snapped his head up, and tried to focus on what she was now saying.

"Do you think it's something that she has to worry about?" Melissa repeated herself, but this time more seductively as she positioned herself directly across from him on her bed. Melissa would be lying if she said she didn't notice the hungry stare that Aaron had in his eyes as he glanced at her body, but Melissa didn't mind because she was just as attracted to him as he was to her. Melissa forgot all about Aaron belonging to Kelly as she admired the muscular arms that peaked out from his oversized white tee.

After he cleared his throat of an imaginary hairball, Aaron answered, "Maybe." This time Aaron dared not break the intense stare that they were having, and slowly stood up from his seat and leaned over to Melissa so that his face was millimeters away from hers. Unable to control herself for another second, Melissa pulled Aaron into her arms for a compulsive kiss that eventually led to the inevitable occurring.

I can't believe, I just cheated on Kelly, Aaron thought to himself guiltily as he searched for his shorts to put back on. The worst thing about it was that Aaron knew that something like this was going to happen at some point in time, especially after their last study session in the library. It was just something about the way Melissa carried herself, and how she attentively looked at him like everything that he said truly mattered to her. That aroused him so much. For that reason, Aaron knew he should have known better to agree to a study session in her dorm room. He didn't want to chance Kelly seeing them out somewhere studying or for somebody to run back and tell Kelly that they had seen them out somewhere studying -- especially when he had lied to Kelly about studying with Melissa, in the first place.

"What now?" Melissa whispered out loud, as she lay on her bed looking up at the ceiling. Aaron wasn't sure if she was directing that question to him or herself, but he was trying to figure out the same thing. Aaron loved Kelly too much to break up with her for Melissa, but he also knew that he was feeling Melissa too much to stop seeing her. This wasn't even counting that the sex was too good for him to hit it just once.

"Well, you know we can't tell anybody about this?" Aaron told

Melissa seriously.

"You don't have to tell me twice," Melissa stated grudgingly as she turned her body over to face him, still in disbelief that she had just had sex with Kelly's boyfriend. Aaron was now fully dressed and sitting in the chair next to her bed, staring off into the distance.

"I do know this. This can't happen again," Melissa stated seriously as she sat up and stared at him.

"I know," Aaron responded as he nodded his head up and down to emphasize his response as he stared back at her, knowing full well that it was very likely that it would probably happen again though.

~~~~~

The last couple of days had been so stressful for Keisha. She wasn't sure who she should believe: her friends or Jaden. Keisha knew that Angel and Kelly would have no reason to lie to her, but she also thought that her friend from back home, Nikki would never have a reason to lie to her either. That is, until Nikki did and Keisha listened to her. The following week Keisha saw Nikki bunned up with her ex-man. Keisha guessed she still had trust issues when it came to females. Ever since Kelly and Angel confronted her about Jaden cheating, Keisha had been staying in Mike's apartment while she figured out what she should do. Mike shared an apartment with one of his teammates, so the majority of the time Keisha had it to herself. The basketball team was playing in the NCAA tournament right now, so Mike and his roommate probably wouldn't be back for a while. That meant Keisha could stay as long as she wanted. When Keisha asked Mike what he thought about the situation, Mike said he was just as confused as her. Personally he hadn't seen Jaden cheat on Keisha or heard about him cheating, but Mike wouldn't put it past him or anybody else for that matter. Plus, Jaden knew better than to brag about getting with any other chicks around Mike because Mike didn't play that when it came to Keisha.

Right now, Keisha was in her boring ass accounting class passing notes with Jay. *He is so cool,* Keisha thought as she smiled over at him. If Keisha weren't with Jaden, she would definitely be trying to holler at Jay. Still the possibility was there if Jaden really was cheating on her. *Hmm, I wonder what Jay thinks about this situation.* Keisha and Jay had been chilling and conversing after class for about two months now, so Keisha deemed him trustworthy enough to ask for advice. So Keisha wrote him a note asking his opinion:

> *My friends told me that they've seen my*
> *boyfriend cheating on me, but he's telling me*
> *that they're lying. They said they saw him at*
> *the mall with this girl, but before they told*
> *me, he called me and claimed that they were*
> *following him so him and his friend put on a*
> *fake show for them to get back at them. I don't*
> *know who to believe. What do you think about*
> *the situation?*

As Keisha waited for his reply, she attempted to take notes since they did have an exam coming up soon.

"Keisha," Jay whispered to get Keisha's attention and passed the note back to her.

It read:

> *I don't want to tell you what to do, but I want*
> *you to honestly answer these questions: have*

*your friends ever given you a reason not to
trust them? Have they always been there for
you when you needed them? Have they ever
showed an interest in your man? And, why
would they lie to you? If you can answer these
questions in this order: no, yes, no, and they
wouldn't. Then maybe you need to re-evaluate
your relationship with your man.*

Well let's see, Keisha thought to herself as she went over Jay's questions in her mind. *No, Kelly and Angel have never given me a reason not to trust them. Yes, they have always been there for me when I needed them. No, they have never showed interest in my man. In fact they have been very supportive of me and Jaden.* The last question was the tricky one because Keisha couldn't understand why they would lie to her? *I don't know.* Keisha really wanted to trust them, but trusting them would mean admitting that Jaden was cheating on her. *And why would he cheat on me? But that's my pride talking. I guess Jay is right; I do need to re-evaluate my relationship with Jaden,* Keisha thought to herself humbly. Keisha had a lot of thinking to do when she got back to her room.

CHAPTER TWENTY-EIGHT

"I don't believe you. You had sex with him!" Dana shouted at Melissa incredulously. Melissa and Dana were sitting in Melissa's room early Tuesday afternoon, talking about Melissa's 'experience' with Aaron on Saturday night. Melissa knew that she and Aaron had agreed not to tell anybody, but she couldn't hold it in any longer. She called Dana over to discuss it. Melissa felt bad about having sex with Aaron, but it made her feel even worse when Dana said it like that.

"Yes," Melissa answered meekly.

"What were you thinking – especially after I just stood up for you, telling Kelly that you would never do anything like that to her?" Dana asked her unable to hide her disappointment. Dana had been chilling with Kelly and Angel over the weekend, and at first they had been discussing the Keisha situation. Then the conversation quickly turned to Melissa and how Aaron had been acting kind of funny after his last so-called study session. Dana persisted that Melissa would never do anything like that to her.

"I know girl, and I thank you for having my back like that. I don't even know what got into us. One minute we were talking and the next…" Melissa stated sadly as she dropped her head.

Melissa appeared genuine to Dana, but it didn't matter because the facts were still the same; she slept with Aaron, and friends just didn't do that. Dana wasn't even sure that she could look at Melissa the same. It was one thing to sleep around, but you don't sleep with your girl's boyfriend, even if you all did have a fight and claim that you're not friends anymore. That's still your girl! Dana couldn't say anything, but look over at Melissa disgustedly. Dana was sitting in the same chair that Aaron had been in, and Melissa was sitting on her bed now beginning to cry. Melissa had expected Dana to be upset but she didn't think that she would be this disappointed in her.

"One question: why would you suggest studying in your dorm?" Dana asked Melissa, with an attempt to make a little sense out of the situation.

"Um, we didn't want Kelly to see us studying together and cause more drama," Melissa answered sheepishly, knowing that in light of what just happened that reasoning sounded real shady.

"Melissa *are* you serious! So when Kelly asks why ya'll were in the room in the first place, you're going to say because ya'll were avoiding her so no more drama could occur?" Dana asked her with her face scrunched up, and then threw her hands up in frustration.

"No, because I'm not telling Kelly what happened. And neither are you," Melissa told Dana sternly, now sitting straight up to attention.

"Whatever Melissa, I'll give you until the end of this week to tell her. And if you don't tell her, then I am because that's just not right," Dana told Melissa with her eyes flaring from anger.

"Dana, please don't tell her. That was the first and last time that

that's going to happen. You don't want to ruin her happiness with Aaron because of one slip up. I don't even plan on studying with him again," Melissa pleaded, changing her approach. Before Dana could respond, her cell phone began to ring. As Dana flipped open her phone and saw the name pop onto the screen she couldn't help, but to allow a big smile to spread across her face.

"Hi, Jason," Dana said giddily into her cell phone, forgetting about the argument that she was just having with Melissa. Jason wanted to know if they could get together right now because he had to talk to her about something.

"Uh, okay. I'm over in Melissa's room now, but I was just about to leave," Dana told Jason as she gave Melissa an evil stare, and then hung up her phone.

"Melissa, all I have to say is if you don't tell Kelly about you and Aaron, then you can consider our friendship over with because I can't be friends with somebody who does that and then isn't woman enough to admit that she made a mistake," Dana told Melissa as she shook her head and walked out of the room, leaving a crying Melissa behind, even more confused than she was before.

~~~~~

The whole walk over to Jason's apartment, Dana was nervous for some reason. Now that she was sitting at the kitchen table looking into Jason's expressionless face, Dana could see that she had good reason to be.

"So what's up?" Dana asked Jason hesitantly to kill the dead silence that engulfed the room.

"I don't know how to say this…" Jason started wearily, still unable to believe that he was really about to do this. *Do I really want to end things with Dana just for a chance to get with Keisha?*

Jason asked himself. He still had time to change his mind because it wasn't a guarantee that Keisha would even like him when she and Jaden broke up. Hell, Keisha might even be one of those girls who stick with her man even after she finds out he's cheating on her; although, Jason highly doubted that. As Jason sat at the table across from Dana, looking into her uncertain, beautiful, brown eyes, he was beginning to rethink this gamble he was about to take. He was playing Russian roulette with hearts, even his. But on the other hand, Jason would risk anything for just a chance to have Keisha in his life in the future. He needed to end things with Dana now before it got back to Keisha that he and Dana were together because apparently Keisha still didn't know.

"What? What's wrong?" Dana asked Jason worriedly, making it even harder for Jason to say what he needed to say.

"I think that we need to take a break," Jason told a baffled Dana. Jason told Dana a break instead of full out breaking up with her because it still left an opening for him to come back if things didn't work out with Keisha down the road.

"What? I don't understand. I thought things were going good between us. Why do you want to take a break?" Dana asked Jason mystified. *This is going to be harder than I thought*, Jason thought as he watched her beautiful eyes began to tear up. Jason couldn't stand seeing a female cry, especially one that he cared about.

"I'm just feeling so stressed out by school, and it's that time of year when the frat starts entering into step shows, with practices every night. I just feel like I need to focus on myself right now and I don't want that to affect us down the road; especially since I know how much attention you need," Jason quickly lied, beginning to feel even worse.

"I don't need that much attention, baby! How about we just see if things work and if not we'll take a break then?" Dana asked hopefully. Jason really wanted to say 'okay,' but in order for his plan to work with Keisha, Jason knew he couldn't be seen around with Dana anymore—although they weren't really seen around campus together that much now. Now that Jason thought about it, Keisha wasn't the only one who didn't know about him and Dana. A lot of people didn't know, probably because they kept it on the low. It just made a relationship work better that way when everybody wasn't in your business. Although Angel had told Jason that Keisha and Dana were cool, he wasn't too concerned about that. From what he could tell they weren't that close anymore and they didn't even talk on a personal tip because Dana never even mentioned Keisha; nor Keisha, Dana. So as long as Jason continued to play the friendship role with Keisha, he knew he could slick talk his way in there with Keisha without Dana even being an issue.

"I'm sorry Boo, I really don't want to take a break, but I feel that it'll be what's best for both of us. Don't worry the break won't be that long, just until I get some things straightened out. Okay?" Jason told a bonafide lie. He couldn't stand seeing a female hurt, especially at his doing. After Jason spent twenty more minutes convincing Dana that a break would be the right thing for them right now, he escorted her out to the front of his apartment, and then came back up stairs to call his frat brother Shawn.

"It's on now," Jason smirked on the phone.

~~~~~

I thought Dana was my homegirl through thick and thin, but I see now that all I have is myself to lean on, Melissa cried to herself, as she laid in her bed, enclosed in complete darkness. The only sound in her room was her CD player softly playing Beyoncé's "Me, Myself, and I." Melissa hadn't expected Dana to be elated that she had slept with Aaron, but she at least expected Dana to stick by her side as her closest friend out of the crew. For Dana to give her that ultimatum was just plain messed up in Melissa's eyes. Melissa didn't want to lose Dana as a friend, but she couldn't betray Aaron either. Melissa didn't know what to do. *Beyoncé's right. All I got in the end is me, myself, and I. So, for now on I'm going to be my own best friend,* Melissa cried to herself, not really believing what she was saying, but it sounded good when Beyoncé said it. Melissa was beginning to feel sick to her stomach from trying to figure out what she should do. She strongly doubted that Dana was bluffing, and she knew that if she didn't tell Kelly herself, then Dana surely was. She had never felt this lonely in her life. She looked through her cell phone searching for somebody to call who would understand her side of the story and offer her comfort. As she passed by Angel and Ashley's name in her cell phone, she knew that she couldn't call any of them. If Dana, her closest friend out of the group, had reacted the way she did, then Melissa knew the others' reaction would be even less receptive. So, Melissa continued on her search through her phone. The next name that she came across was her mother's, but Melissa didn't have that close of a relationship with her mother or sister so she didn't expect for either of them to relate to her or give her the comfort that she needed. As Melissa came back across the A's in her cell phone contact list, she found herself dialing the number of the only person that she knew could understand the situation that she was in: Aaron.

"Hey Aaron," Melissa sniffled into the phone after he picked up.

"Hey, what's wrong?" Aaron asked Melissa concerned, after sensing the sadness in her voice.

"I just need somebody to talk to," Melissa admitted to him

"Go ahead."

"I would prefer to talk in person though. If you don't mind," Melissa quickly back- pedaled, not wanting to impose herself on him. She needed to get out of her room; it was starting to depress her.

"Oh, aight. Well Kelly just left and went over to her brother's crib, so why don't you come over here," Aaron suggested to Melissa, more concerned about her than the possibility of anybody else seeing her enter into his room.

"Okay, I'll be over there in a thirty," Melissa answered him, and hung up the phone.

CHAPTER TWENTY-NINE

"Keisha wake up! Telephone." Keisha heard Kelly scream into her ear. *What the hell is wrong with her? She sees I'm sleep. She should know better to than to wake me up for the stupid phone. Whoever it is could have called me back,* Keisha thought irately. It was ten in the morning and Keisha hadn't fallen asleep until late. She was still dead tired.

"Where's the phone?" Keisha grumbled as she sat up in her bed. Last night was Keisha's first night staying in her room since she got into the argument with Kelly and Angel. Although Keisha was back in her room, she still hadn't decided what side she should trust. For the most part she had been pretty much ignoring both parties of the situation until she figured out a solution to the problem. This meant that she also hadn't been out with Jaden since that night of the argument when she, Jaden, Ebony, and David had gone to eat that night after their game. It had been pretty easy avoiding Jaden though, since he was barely there. The team had made it past the first few rounds in the NCAA tournament and was now playing in the elite eight. Jaden only called Keisha to talk for five minutes, which was cool on her part.

"Here," Kelly snapped, giving Keisha the phone, and then got back into her bed, throwing Keisha the same amount of attitude that she just threw at her.

"Hello, is this Keisha Mitchell," a polite voice on the other end of the phone greeted Keisha. Sensing that this call might actually be serious, Keisha straightened up and cleared her throat.

"Yes, this is she," she answered, in her professional tone.

"Hi Keisha. This is nurse practitioner Suzan, and I'm calling from the health center in regard to your visit last week. The test we sent in has showed us that you have Chlamydia and we're going to need for you to come in as soon as possible."

"What? Are you sure? I can be there in ten minutes."

"Okay. I'll be here waiting for you," the nurse told Keisha and then hung up the phone. *I can't believe what she just told me,* Keisha thought to herself allowing herself to take it all in. All of a sudden Keisha felt a tear drop slither down her cheek, and then another one and another came, until Keisha was full out crying. *I can't believe I have Chlamydia. I've never had an STD in my life and now I get one while I have a boyfriend. That must mean that Kelly and Angel were telling the truth, and Jaden is cheating on me. I can't believe this. How could Jaden do this to me? And if he was going to cheat on me, he could have at least worn a damn condom,* the thoughts rumbled through Keisha's mind.

"What's wrong?" Keisha heard Kelly's soothing voice ask, as Kelly put her arms around Keisha in support. Kelly was by Keisha's side the second she saw the first teardrop slither down her face. Kelly had started to ignore the urgency she heard in Keisha's voice while Keisha was on the phone, but something made her turn back over in the bed and face Keisha.

"I guess Ebony was right that day she said you'll reap what you sow," Keisha said despondently, referring to when she helped spread the lie about Ray and P giving each other an STD.

"What are you talking about," Kelly asked Keisha, not understanding what Keisha meant.

"The health center said I have Chlamydia," Keisha answered and broke down some more.

"Are you serious?! But how?" Kelly asked confused and upset by what Keisha had just told her.

"Ya'll were right, Jaden must have been cheating on me and gave me a damn STD," Keisha murmured through her tears.

"Don't worry. It's going to be okay sweetie. Chlamydia isn't permanent, and it'll be gone in a week," Kelly said comforting Keisha.

Keisha didn't understand why Kelly was sitting here being so nice to her, after the way she had acted towards her.

"I'm so sorry, Kelly. I should have believed you." Keisha whimpered out, but was cut off.

"Shhh. It's okay. Don't worry about that right now. Let's just worry about getting you down to the health center and getting this taken care of."

"You're going to go with me?" Keisha asked her hopefully.

"Yes, and I'll stay right by your side the whole time," Kelly said caringly. At that moment Keisha finally knew what a true friend was, and she was so grateful to have Kelly in her life.

"Thank you," Keisha whimpered.

"You're welcome. Now get dressed."

~~~~~~

As Keisha and Kelly walked into the health center, Keisha's sadness was replaced with embarrassment. She couldn't help but to feel like everybody in the waiting room knew she was in there because she had an STD. Although Kelly reassured Keisha that nobody knew, and that there were plenty of reasons why people came to the health center, Keisha wasn't to sure. After signing her name in, Keisha just waited for her turn to go back. *Ugh! How could Jaden do this ish to me?* Keisha thought angrily. She trusted him and this was how he returned that trust, by cheating on her with some dirty bitch. Jaden was so lucky that he was on the road right now because if Keisha could see him right now, she didn't think she would be able to control her anger. *I might mess around and stab his ass,* Keisha thought, fuming. *Well, I may not do all of that, but he would feel my wrath.*

"Keisha Mitchell," Keisha heard the nurse call out. *Was it me or did she just announce my name a little bit too loud?* Keisha thought to herself as she cringed at hearing her name called that loud. It was bad enough that she had to be here, Keisha didn't need everybody in the damn waiting room to know her name.

"It'll be alright. I'll be right here after you get out," Kelly whispered to her before she got up.

"Hi, Keisha. How are you doing?" The nurse asked Keisha cheerfully. *Is she serious? How the hell does she expect for me to feel? She just called me and told me that I have an STD,* Keisha though to herself, while she tilted her head and gave the nurse the dumb look, in reply to her question. "Well, I know you would like for me to get straight to the point" the nurse said, and explained to Keisha how she could have contracted the disease and what Keisha needed to do to get rid of it. It was really no need for the nurse to explain to Keisha how she contracted it, because Keisha already knew: messing with Jaden's trifling ass. Keisha could remember that night like it was yesterday:

"Baby, put the condom on," Keisha moaned as he kissed on her neck and prepared to have sex with her raw.

"I don't have any more. Don't worry we have a mandatory STD test in the beginning of the season and I'm clean. And you know you're the only girl that I'm with." He whispered into her ear sincerely.

"Okay." Keisha replied naively. *How stupid could I have been, to believe that I was his only girl?*

"Well Keisha that's about it. I'm just going to walk you down to the pharmacy, and you can take the medicine right there. We're going to give you the liquid form of the medication, and you just have to drink the whole glass and after that, the bacteria should be gone in a week. So, I recommend that you don't have sex for a couple of weeks just to be on the safe side, and don't have sex with that partner unless you know for sure that he's received treatment as well," the nurse told Keisha and then walked her down to the pharmacy. *Well, she doesn't have to worry about me doing any one of those,* Keisha thought to herself. She didn't plan on having sex for a long while after this, let alone having sex with Jaden's trifling butt. It just wasn't worth it to her.

"Here you go," the pharmacist said to Keisha as she handed her the glass of powdered water, which was her medicine. *Eww, this stuff is nasty!* Keisha thought disgusted as she gulped down the last drop.

"Alright, that's it." As Keisha walked back out to the waiting room where Kelly was, Keisha wondered to herself why it seemed like everybody in this place was so cheery. Keisha couldn't wait to get this nightmare over with.

"You ready?" Keisha was making her way towards the door before she even heard her reply. She couldn't get out of that place quick enough.

"How was it?" Kelly asked Keisha consolingly after they had left out of the health center.

"It was what it was. I'm just glad it's over. Thank you for being here for me though," Keisha told Kelly sincerely, and then gave her a hug to reinforce what she was saying. "I'm sorry for how I acted. I've just had a lot of female friends in my past who I thought I could trust and when I did, they betrayed it when it came to guys. So, it's like I knew at heart that ya'll were telling the truth, but then I couldn't get past my old friends' sneakiness and trust ya'll. Can you forgive me?" Keisha asked Kelly as tears begin to fall from her eyes.

"Of course, sweetie. Come on let's get you back to the room."

"Okay." Keisha was going to accept all the love she could from her girls now.

~~~~~

"Girl, I can't believe Jason broke up with you claiming he needed a break," Ashley gushed to Dana. "These guys are just so trifling." Dana had just finished telling Ashley about what happened with Jason earlier today. They were sitting in the dining hall, discussing the situation. Usually, after something like this happened, Dana would run straight to Melissa, but after what Melissa had told her earlier today she didn't want anything to do with her right now. So she had called Ashley instead. Dana still couldn't believe that Melissa would sleep with Aaron. That was just dirty, even for Melissa. Dana had kept her word though, and didn't tell the others about what happened, yet. She planned on giving Melissa until Friday to tell Kelly, or else she would.

"I'm telling you it's probably another chick," Ashley told Dana, adamantly.

"Why do you think that?" Dana asked her quizzically.

"Because you said he had been acting funny for about a week, and then he came out of the blue and said he wanted a break. Plus, according to you, ya'll haven't had any problems with each other, and you were just telling me about how happy he makes you," Ashley answered knowingly, with no bitterness. At first Dana thought that Ashley was saying it out of bitterness because she still wasn't over David. Now that she thought about it, Ashley did make some sense.

"It sounds good, but I haven't seen Jason around any other chicks or heard about him being with any other chicks," Dana told her, rethinking Ashley's theory.

"Well, that's not exactly true," Ashley replied hesitantly, not knowing if she should tell Dana or not, what she had seen. This comment prompted Dana to give her the *'what the hell are you talking about'*, look.

"Well, I didn't want to say anything, but I did see Jason eating lunch with Keisha a few times in the dining hall. At the time, I didn't think anything about it, but now....," Ashley instigated.

"What are you talking about? Jason and Keisha don't even know each other. Plus everybody and their mother knows that Keisha is too infatuated with Jaden to be thinking about some other dude," Dana responded to Ashley, growing tiresome of her theories.

"Ight, you can believe that if you want. But everybody also knows that Jaden is cheating on Keisha, and it's just a matter of time before she breaks up with him. That may be the reason your boy decided to put you on break. Like you said Keisha doesn't know Jason as your boyfriend, but you can trust and believe that I've seen her and Jason eating together a few times in here," Ashley told Dana with a smirk as she rolled her neck with each sentence.

"Whatever," Dana told Ashley trying not to take what she said to heart. The only thing was that it was hard not to. Ashley was known for being blatantly honest, so if she said something then for the most part it was true. Dana didn't want to believe it because she and Keisha were just starting to get cool again after the Ray situation. Dana was wrong when it came to that situation but this time, if what Ashley said was true, she had a right to be angry at Keisha.

"Hmm, whatever huh? Where are you headed off to then?" Ashley asked Dana with a knowing grin as she watched Dana gather her belongings and get ready to leave.

"I'm just about to go over to Kelly's room. I have something I need to, uh, give her," Dana lied, knowing full well she was going over there to give Keisha a piece of her mind.

"Hmm mm, well tell *'Kelly'* I said 'hi,'" Ashley laughed, knowing the real reason Dana was going over there.

CHAPTER THIRTY

"I know you may not want to hear this right now, but everything happens for a reason," Ebony told Keisha soothingly. The girls were sprawled out in Keisha and Kelly's room, and Keisha had just finished telling Ebony and Angel about her health center visit, while Kelly sat next to her supportively. Keisha had called the two girls over after she had had time to reflect on the situation that she now found herself in. She purposefully left Ashley, Melissa and Dana out though, because she wasn't as close with them anymore and didn't want to share something so personal with them. At first, Keisha didn't plan on telling anybody else about what happened, but she learned that she needed friends in her life that she could lean on when she was going through something like this. At the moment, Keisha was glad that she did tell them, as they gave her words of encouragement and stuck by her side even after the way she had acted. Keisha knew now that these were her girls through thick and thin. Prior to her confession, Keisha apologized to the other girls for not believing them when they had told her that Jaden was cheating on her, and not trusting their friendship. In light of the situation, the girls had forgiven her whole-heartedly.

"I know and I already realized what that is," Keisha told Ebony solemnly. During Keisha's reflection time alone, Keisha found herself doing something that she hadn't done in a long, long, time. Keisha knelt down on the floor in front of her bed, clasped her hands together, bowed her head down and said a prayer to the Lord. Keisha prayed that the Lord would cleanse her of the sins that she committed against Him and her body. She prayed that He would forgive her for continuing to have sex freely, even though she knew it was wrong. Keisha even prayed for forgiveness for spreading that stupid rumor about Ray and P, feeling that she was now reaping what she sowed.

As she continued to pray, tears from her hazel eyes fell from her eyes onto her comforter. The more tears that seemed to fall, the lighter the weight on Keisha's shoulders began to feel to her. Keisha couldn't understand what was happening; it felt like the Lord was cleansing her with her tears. Keisha had never felt like that before, and at that moment she knew it was time for her to make a change in her life. She had a choice to make. She could either continue down the same path of destruction that she was on that brought her to contracting this disease and could lead to far worst, even death. Or she could give her life to Christ and look forward to eternal life. Keisha made the decision at that moment to choose eternal life with Jesus Christ. She knew it wasn't going to be easy changing her ways, but if Ebony could do it, then she had faith that she could too. At least she wasn't alone.

"Wow, that's deep," Angel told Keisha thoughtfully, after Keisha relayed what occurred during her reflection time to the girls.

"Yeah, I am so happy for you girl," Ebony told Keisha excitedly as she got up from her seat on the floor and ran over to the bed where Keisha was sitting and gave her a hug.

"Okay, okay, enough of the mushy stuff," Keisha joked, as she playfully pushed Ebony off of her, trying to downplay what she told them.

"No, for real Keisha that's a big step, and I'm happy that you came to that decision on your own," Ebony told Keisha seriously.

"I know girl, and I appreciate your support," Keisha told Ebony sincerely and then posed a question. "Ya'll know what's funny?"

"What's that?" Ebony asked curiously.

"Well, what God revealed to me during that time was that He had been calling me back to Him for a while, but I was too busy messing around with these dudes to hear Him. I even remember thinking to myself that the major thing that was holding me back from giving my life to Christ was my love for sex. I even remember myself saying that I would start living right after I get married because I love sex too much to give it up. It's crazy! But even then, I knew that was wrong, and had asked God to take away my strong desire for sex. That's one reason I know that this happened as an answer to my prayer; it was the only way that God was going to grab my attention enough for me to listen. I can't even be mad at Him for this happening because I brought it on myself. I should have listened to Him when He told me to stop having sex in the first place. I know one thing -- I am so thankful for God's grace because it could have been much worse," Keisha told the girls reflectively as she began to tear up a little bit.

"Amen to that girl because I already know...hmm girl, if it wasn't for his grace..." Ebony heaved a sigh as she shook her head and bit her lip. Just thinking about all the times God's grace saved her took her voice away.

~~~~~

It's so hard to believe we just lost to University of Maryland in the elite eight, Mike thought to himself as he sat silently on the bus ride back to school. They had been up by 10 points with 5 minutes left in the second half. Then everything seemed to just fall apart. It all started with Jaden's turnover; he attempted to give RaShawn a behind the back pass, but instead threw the ball out of bounds. After that, UMD went on a 12-0 run. Every shot that XU took after that turnover was not connecting. It wasn't until the last couple of minutes that somebody finally made a basket, but it was too late by then and UMD won, leaving Mike and his team standing there saddened by defeat. They were just pulling into the gym at school, where they all were getting dropped off. The whole bus ride from the airport was gravely silent. Nobody said a word to each other; the coaches weren't even talking amongst themselves. Everybody was just so disappointed by the loss because they knew that they shouldn't have lost. The first thing Mike planned on doing after he got off of the bus was going over to Keisha's room. In high school she was the only one who could always cheer Mike up after his team had lost a game. Plus, Keisha had left Mike an urgent message on his cell phone, instructing him to give her a call first thing when he got back to campus. *I wonder what's wrong with her*, Mike had thought to himself. When he asked Jaden about it, Jaden said he didn't know. *Oh well, I'll find out in a few.*

"Well guys, you played with your hearts out there and I am proud of ya'll. We may not have brought the title home, but when you get off this bus and go about your business, I want you to keep your heads held high," the head coach told the team after the bus finally stopped and they all began to gather their stuff. Mike assumed it was meant to pep them up, but he could really care less at this point. Mike's major concern at that point was just getting off of the bus, and getting away from the team for awhile.

"Thanks Coach," Mike told him mustering some appreciation, as he walked past him to get off of the bus. Before Mike headed to Keisha's dorm, he dapped up all of his teammates and said his goodbyes.

"Hey girl," Mike greeted Keisha on his cell phone. He had missed his best friend while he was away.

"Hey what's up? Where are you?"

"I'm on my way to your place. What was so urgent that you needed me to call you right away?" Mike asked her worried.

"Is anybody around you?"

"Nah. What's wrong?"

"Jaden cheated on me and gave me Chlamydia," Keisha told Mike soberly.

"What? Are you serious? I will beat his punk ass!" Mike yelled, ready to turn his truck around and go back to the gym to punish Jaden for giving his best friend a STD. Keisha was more than a friend to Mike, she was like a sister to him. So, for that Nigga to just cheat on her and give her a STD was definitely not cool; that kind of behavior called for repercussions in Mike's mind. Mike and Jaden weren't that tight that he would let him get away with that, so his ass was in for a rude awakening when Mike got his hands on him. Teammate or not, Mike didn't care. Family came first.

"No, Mike don't do that. Well not yet at least. I still haven't confronted him about it yet. I wanted to wait until he got back to bring it up," Keisha told him calmly. She was calmer than Mike expected her to be under these circumstances.

"Ight, but I'm surprised you weren't sitting out there waiting on the bus to arrive to jump down his throat," Mike told her with a slight chuckle, knowing how crazy Keisha could get when somebody crossed her.

Laughing Keisha responded, "Don't get me wrong, the thought did cross my mind. I've been doing some reflecting on myself and my life since I found out, and I know that wouldn't be the best way to handle things. Plus I don't need everybody up in my business and you know if I confronted him that way, everybody and their mama would know that I have an STD. I definitely don't need that." Keisha was exemplifying a lot of maturity, and Mike was impressed. He guessed college had matured them both in a lot of ways.

"Ight, that's cool. But let me know if you still want me to punish Jaden after you talk to him," Mike said playfully.

Giggling she replied, "I'll remember that."

"Well, I'm bout to find a parking spot now. I'll be up in your room in few minutes," Mike told her and hung up the phone.

~~~~~

"So, are you going to confront Jaden tonight?" Angel asked Keisha inquisitively. The two of them were now the only girls left in Keisha's room. Kelly had gone over to her brother's apartment, so that she could spend some time with him. Ebony had gone back to her room so that she could study. Angel was just going to stick around until Mike came up, since he had just called Keisha and said that he would be arriving in a few. Angel didn't want Keisha to be alone after what had happened.

"Nah, I'm going to wait until tomorrow to confront him. I want to have a clear head when I do it."

"I can understand that. I think that's probably the best thing to do," Angel told Keisha encouragingly. *Knock-Knock-Knock.* Keisha figured it was Mike at the door when she yelled come in. To her surprise, it was Dana. Keisha hadn't talked to Dana on a solo tip in a minute, so she was surprised to see her at the door.

"What's up Dana?" Keisha greeted Dana cautiously, not understanding what prompted her to show up unannounced. Although, Keisha and Dana weren't beefing anymore, they were far from being close to the point that Dana would just show up and chill.

"Hey Keisha, can I talk to you for a second?" Dana asked her, while eying Angel.

"Maybe I should leave," Angel announced, sensing that Dana might want to talk to Keisha on a solo tip.

"No, it's okay, you can stay," Dana told Angel as she motioned for her to sit back down.

"So, what's up?" Keisha asked Dana, while she stared at her serious expression. Keisha waited patiently for Dana to start, as she wondered what Dana could possibly have to talk to her about.

"Well, I wanted to know if it was true that you've been hanging out with Jason," Dana stammered out, rethinking her being there. Dana knew she shouldn't have let what Ashley said get to her, but she had found herself here anyway. She guessed it was too late now.

"Oh no," Angel mumbled to herself, knowing where this was headed. Shawn had told her earlier today that Jason had given Dana her walking papers, but wouldn't tell her the exact reasons why. Before Angel had a chance to call Dana and ask her about it, Keisha had called her over to her room to talk, so it totally slipped her mind just like it had slipped her mind to tell Keisha that 'Jay' was Dana's Jason. Angel was kicking herself for her forgetfulness.

"I don't even know Jason to hang out with him," Keisha answered Dana with a confused expression on her face.

"Ugh, yeah you do Keisha. Jason is Jay," Angel choked out, wishing she didn't have to break the news like this.

"What are you talking about Angel?" Keisha asked her even more confused and not really in the mood for anymore drama.

"Jay and Jason are the same people. Before when you asked me who 'Jay' was, I didn't realize that was who you were talking about because I never referred to him as Jay. I still didn't put two and two together until Jason told me that he had a class with you. I had meant to tell you, but I never got a chance to due to all of the other drama," Angel told Keisha apologetically, while giving both Keisha and Dana a remorseful smile.

"So that means you *have* been chilling with Jason,"—Dana pointed at Keisha, "and you knew about this Angel?" Dana asked and then turned her attention to Angel, as she shook her head with discontent. Keisha was too busy putting the pieces together in her head to hear anything that Dana had to say. Keisha had known that Jay—well, 'Jason'—seemed familiar somehow. The thing was Jason had never lied to Keisha, but he just evaded the truth. Keisha felt betrayed in a sense. As far as Keisha was now concerned, all guys were grimy, and she didn't want anything to do with them.

"It's not like that," Keisha heard Angel defending them in the background, which brought her out of her thoughts.

"ana, I don't know who your getting your info from, but the me and Jason ever did was hang out in the dining hall couple of times. Nothing more, nothing less. And honestly I have bigger worries in my life right now. Like breaking up with Jaden's trifling butt for giving me an STD, so I'm sorry that I can't entertain your trivial accusations, but I don't have the energy to argue with you tonight," Keisha stated, defeated. Keisha didn't mean for all of that to come out like it did, but she was too tired to fight anymore, and she wished things would just go back to the way they used to be; back when everybody was cool, and there were no silly arguments or drama penetrating through the group of friends.

"Oh my gosh, are you serious?!" Dana exclaimed, forgetting any feelings of discontent that she had had with Keisha a split second ago. Dana never personally transmitted an STD, but she knew that it was something that could happen to anybody and that Keisha had to be going through it right now. Dana agreed; the last thing that Keisha needed was Dana's drama. Dana then quickly walked over to Keisha's bed and gave her a hug, and told her that she would be here for her if she needed anything. At first Keisha didn't know how to respond to Dana's reaction, and sat there dumbfounded with her arms out in the air. Then after a couple of seconds passed by, Keisha decided to drop any animosity that she had been holding towards Dana, and hugged her back. That was a truce.

"Keisha, I have a confession," Dana announced sheepishly.

"What's up?" Keisha asked Dana calmly.

"Well, I just realized that the only reason that I've always acted the way I did towards you is because I've been jealous of you from that first day we met. I've always looked for reasons not to be your friend when you've always been a good friend to me. I know that sounds bad, but I guess that's just my insecurity and I'm trying to work on that. I say that to say I'm sorry and I hope that we can be *friends* again, like we were before," Dana humbl confessed to Keisha.

"I would like that," Keisha told Dana sincerely with a soft smile, and hugged her again. Keisha knew that Dana had a lot of pride, so it had to have taken a lot for her to confess that to her. Keisha appreciated it.

"Aww, you guys," Angel joked and faked like she was snapping a picture of the two of them.

"Shut up," they both playfully snapped at Angel, and each threw a pillow at her.

CHAPTER THIRTY-ONE

"Aaron, I don't know what to do," Mike heard Melissa sob into Aaron's shoulder. Mike was on his way up the stairs to Keisha's dorm room, and he was witnessing something that he wouldn't believe if he wasn't watching it with his own eyes. He usually didn't take the steps up to the fourth floor where Keisha lived. He usually took the elevators like everybody else, but tonight the elevators had been taking too long so he decided to make the trek up the steps. Mike figured that Aaron and Melissa had been betting on the fact that nobody took the stairs, as he stood in the stairwell watching the two from the level below them. Aaron placed a gentle kiss on Melissa's forehead that led to a soft kiss on her cheek and before Mike knew it, Aaron was now kissing Melissa passionately on her lips with no opposition from Melissa. For a second Mike thought he was seeing things; and he even rubbed his eyes to make sure that they weren't playing tricks on him. Mike couldn't believe that Aaron was cheating on Kelly right before his eyes and with Melissa at that. Right when Mike looked back up, he saw the two slither into the hallway to probably sneak into Aaron's room. Mike stood in shock for a couple of minutes before he made his way up the stairs and through the same door that the two of them had just gone through. He didn't know what shocked him more; the fact that Aaron was cheating on Kelly with Melissa, or the fact that he was bold enough to be doing it in the stairway of the dorm that Kelly also lived in. *Aaron goes hard; Kelly could come up to his room at any given moment and catch Melissa in there. This bamma must have some serious game,* Mike thought to himself shaking his head in disgust. The two of them had been so engulfed in each other that they hadn't even noticed Mike standing there gawking at them. *Aaron done slipped up around the wrong person; I've been waiting for something like this to happen,* Mike thought with mischievous smirk as he approached Keisha's door.

"What you out here grinning about?" Keisha asked Mike curiously, as she just opened her door to let Angel and Dana out. Mike couldn't help but to glance down the hall towards Aaron's door, and think about what great luck Aaron had. A few minutes later and Angel and Dana would have run into him and Melissa sneaking into his room.

"Nothing," Mike said, smiling back at Keisha and then embraced her lovingly, happy to see that she was in an upbeat mood.

"Ight, I'll see ya'll later," Keisha told the girls as her and Mike walked into her room.

"Was that *Dana*," Mike said as he playfully pointed towards the door and scrunched up his face in confusion.

"Yeah, me and her are cool again," Keisha replied, while laughing at his silliness.

"I'm not even going to ask," Mike responded, knowing there had to be a story to that. As Mike half listened to Keisha tell him about how she and Dana had reconciled, he contemplated to himself whether or not he should inform Keisha about what he just saw. Mike wanted to tell her the truth but, he knew Keisha, and he knew she would be down at Aaron's door right now causing a scene, which he didn't want to happen because Keisha had enough going on in her life. So Mike decided that he would handle the situation on his own.

"So, what happened regarding the other situation?" Mike asked Keisha sympathetically, still not able to believe that Jaden would do some mess like that. When you have a main girl, you always make sure that you wear a rubber with the girls on the side. *Hell you make sure you wear a rubber period! It's too many diseases going around out there, and AIDS is killing Niggas*, Mike thought to himself as Keisha went into her story of how the health center had called her and how she had to take the nasty medicine. Keisha then went into how she planned on confronting Jaden tomorrow about the whole situation. That's when Mike suggested to her that it would probably be best if she waited until tomorrow night after the basketball team's "celebration party." It wasn't much to celebrate in Mike's eyes, but some girls they knew were throwing a party to celebrate them making it that far and for having a great season.

"Why should I wait that long to confront him?" Keisha asked Mike, not understanding what he was getting at.

"Alright this is what I want you to do. I want you to tell Jaden that you are going home with Kelly tomorrow afternoon, and that you won't be back until late Thursday. Make up some lie about her going through some things and you having to be there for her. This way you'll catch him in the act of doing something, and he won't be able to flip it around on you."

"For what?" she asked, trying to figure out why she had to catch Jaden in the act and couldn't just outright tell him.

"You see most guys if you confront them about cheating—let alone them giving you a STD—even when they know they probably did, don't like to admit that they did. They try to flip the situation around on the girl. What they'll do is lie and say that the girl must have gotten it from somebody else because they're clean, blah blah blah. So, if you confront Jaden while he's in the act of cheating, it's no way that he can deny it," Mike told her convincingly.

"I don't know Mike. I don't feel like playing games," Keisha told him reluctantly, not sure about his plan.

"I know and it wouldn't be playing games. It would just be you delaying your talk until tomorrow night. Matter fact, you don't even have to tell him anything; I'll just let him know that you're not going to be around tomorrow. That way all you have to do is show up at his apartment to talk just like you were going to do anyway. But this way, you'll catch him in the act, and he won't be able to flip the script on you," Mike told Keisha, confident in his plan.

"Hmm, and how are you so sure that he's going to be doing something with somebody else tomorrow?" Keisha asked him skeptically.

"Because we just lost an important game, he'll be looking for comfort and you won't be there. Therefore, from what you told me, he seems to have at least one other female friend that he can choose from to comfort him tomorrow night. That's why all you have to do is wait until I call and give you the signal to go over to his apartment and walk in on him and whoever he's with," Mike asserted.

"I don't know…"

"Just trust me," Mike pleaded with his eyes.

"Alright, and only cause' you're my homie, who's never steered me wrong," Keisha told him with a loving smile.

"So, do you still want to talk about the basketball game?" Keisha asked Mike sympathetically, as she remembered the main reason he had called her earlier tonight.

"Nah, just sitting here talking to you has made me feel better," Mike told Keisha and gave her a hug. He had forgotten all about that stupid game as they sat there and discussed her situation with Jaden. The game pretty much paled in comparison to what Keisha was going through.

"Aww, okay. Well if you need me, I'm here for you," Keisha told Mike lovingly. *That's why I love Keisha so much because although she's going through this life-changing situation she is still taking time out to be there for me. Yeah, Jaden is about to go down,* Mike thought as he left her room and made his way back to his car.

~~~~~

How did I let this happen again? Aaron mumbled to himself as he sat up in his bed. The night had started off innocently enough until he received a phone call from a distraught Melissa. She sounded so defeated and down that, against his better judgment, he invited her over to his place because she said she needed to get out of her room. Aaron knew that being alone together in a room was the last place that they needed to be together. But there was no way that Aaron could say no to Melissa needing a friend to talk to, as he listened to her wounded voice. Aaron was a sucker for a crying female, especially when she meant something to him. Although Aaron had felt incredibly guilty about cheating on Kelly with one of her old friends, he couldn't ignore the twinge of sadness that he felt with knowing that he wasn't going to be able to see Melissa anymore. Over the last couple of months, Aaron had grown to care about Melissa as a friend, and was already missing her company. That was another reason when she called, a part of him was extremely excited to hear her voice and see her—even if it was just for one night. Thus, Aaron had instructed Melissa to take the stairs when she got into the dorm. Since Aaron knew nobody took the stairs in the towers, he predicted that she would go unseen. When Aaron had greeted Melissa in the stairwell, he didn't expect for the evening to end the way that it did. He thought that they would just be able to chill in the stairwell, and he could be a shoulder for her to cry on. At first Aaron had been furious about Melissa telling Dana what happened between them because he knew that Dana didn't make idle threats and his relationship with Kelly was as good as over. With Melissa standing there looking so helpless and beaten, all of Aaron's anger subsided and turned into sympathy. When Aaron kissed Melissa on her forehead the first time, it was to signify to her that he was there for her. However, after being that close to her again, the memories of the night that they had shared with each other popped back into his mind, which led him to continue to kiss downward to her cheek, and then finally to her lips. Aaron had become so lost in their kiss that he had forgotten where he was and as soon as he realized, he quickly escorted Melissa into his empty room so no one would stumble across them. Now, Aaron found himself lying in his bed, half-naked, with a completely naked Melissa fast asleep in his arms under his covers, wondering to himself: *What have I gotten myself into?*

CHAPTER THIRTY-TWO

What am I doing? Why did I let Mike talk me into confronting Jaden late tonight? Keisha thought to herself irritated as she nervously approached Jaden's apartment building. Mike had just called Keisha and told her that he was exiting the party with his so-called "friend" Monica. Mike had Jaden pegged to a T. He knew that if Keisha told Jaden that she was going to be at Kelly's house tonight, then Jaden would automatically run to the next chick in line. The plan that Keisha was implementing now was for her to wait in her dorm for Mike to give her the call that Jaden was leaving the party. Then Keisha was supposed to go over to his apartment, pretending to have just gotten back to campus. She would confront him then. Keisha was still hesitant about the plan because she wasn't a hundred percent sure that Jaden would go back to his apartment after he left the party, or that he would even come to the door when she knocked. As Keisha approached Jaden's apartment door, she soon found out that she had no reason to worry about either one. She knew Jaden was in there because Keisha could hear his favorite love song mix CD playing loudly through the door. It was the same CD that he would always put on when they used to "make love" in his room. Keisha didn't realize this was going to hurt so much, but hearing him play "their" CD for another female caused a rush of emotions to surface -- emotions that Keisha had been holding inside. After Keisha took some time to get her emotions together, she noticed that the two of them in their drunken haste hadn't shut the door all the way; it was cracked a little bit. Keisha took that as a sign to go with the element of surprise, instead of knocking. As Keisha crept into the dimly lit apartment, she could hear the faint sounds of moaning coming from the direction of Jaden's bedroom. As Keisha slowly slid open Jaden's bedroom door, she couldn't help the anger that was now boiling within her. Jaden and Monica were so encompassed in their love making session that they didn't even notice Keisha standing at the end of the bed watching them, with a crazed expression on her face. Keisha's facial expression resembled that of Lynn Whitfield's character in "A Thin Line between Love and Hate" with Martin Lawrence.

"Jaden I can't believe you would do me like this," Keisha whispered as she shook her head and turned off his CD player.

"What the…"Jaden mumbled as he looked up to see which one of his stupid friends was playing games. When Jaden realized it was Keisha, a look of pure shock crossed his face.

"Keisha? What are you doing here? I thought you were with Kelly tonight?" Jaden questioned Keisha after he got over the shock, as if she was the one who had some explaining to do and not him.

"Jaden you got some nerve. The question is who the hell is she, and why are you in here smashing this chick like I don't even exist?" Keisha fumed. She was contemplating if she should take the small lamp off of his dresser and launch it at his lying butt.

Keisha quickly decided against that, knowing that she didn't want that drama that would soon follow afterwards.

"Keisha, wait, I can explain," Jaden begged as he got out of the bed and searched his bedroom floor for some shorts to put on. Keisha noticed that Jaden wasn't wearing a condom either, which made her shake her head in disgust.

"Jaden why don't you just tell her the truth: you love me and don't want to be with her anymore. Dag," Monica yelled at Jaden, growing tired of being second fiddle to some freshmen chick.

"Dag Jaden, its one thing to cheat on me, but you had to go raw with the dirty trick too," Keisha yelled with a pained expression on her face. She ignored Monica's ravings.

"Who are you calling a 'dirty trick'?" Monica angrily yelled as she sat up in the bed, and searched for her clothes to put back on. At the moment, she was still under the covers naked like she hadn't a care in the world.

"Baby calm down, I can explain, let's just go out to the living room and talk," Jaden told Keisha as he grabbed her by the arms and tried to escort her out of his room into the living room.

"Don't touch me after you just had your hands all over that bitch," Keisha spat, as she roughly snatched her arms from him, but made her way out to the living room.

"Jaden you need to control your little young bitch, before I break my foot off in her…" Monica yelled, but was cut off by Jaden slamming the bedroom door.

This trifling Negro must really think I'm stupid, if he believes that he can explain his way out of this situation, Keisha thought to herself as she stared blankly at him.

"Baby, you see what happened was, after losing the game last night I just needed somebody to be here for me, and since you weren't here, Monica stepped in…" Jaden started, but was quickly cut off.

"Jaden, cut the bull. I don't know who you think I am, but you will not be flipping the script on me tonight. You cheated plain and simple. Just be a man and take responsibility for your actions," Keisha told him annoyed

"Ight, you're right, I cheated, but it was a mistake. Come on baby, you know I love you and I promise you this was the only time it happened," Jaden pleaded to an unwavering Keisha. Keisha held up her palm in response, gesturing for him to stop.

"Jaden, on some real, I really don't want to hear anymore because I am so tired of your lies. You and I both know that this wasn't the first and only time that you've cheated on me. But that's neither here nor there because I just came over here to let your trifling ass know that I am through with you and all of your games," Keisha let Jaden have it, as she waved her finger around to emphasize each point.

"Jaden, she's right just be honest and let her know that we've been sleeping around for months," Monica smirked maliciously. She had been secretively listening to their conversation the whole time from the other side of the bedroom door.

"Hmph, is that so? So you must be the dirty bitch that gave Jaden Chlamydia too, which explains how he passed it onto me," Keisha turned to Monica, and told her irately. That statement knocked the cocky smirk right off of Monica's face.

"Jaden what the hell is she talking about," Monica screamed at Jaden.

"I don't know what the hell she's talking about because I didn't give her anything. Trust me, I would know if I had that ish'," Jaden responded knowingly.

"Well, I'ma tell you like this. I got a call from the health center yesterday, telling me I have that mess, and you're the only person that I've been with. Therefore *you* gave it to me, and *you* need to get your trifling ass checked out tomorrow," Keisha yelled at him. With that said, Keisha yanked off the heart pendant necklace that he gave her, and threw it at him, leaving both him and Monica to argue over the news that she had just delivered.

~~~~~

With all of the drama going on with Keisha and Jaden, Mike had forgotten all about the secret that he was holding onto, involving Aaron and Melissa. Well, that was until Mike saw *her*. After Mike gave Keisha the call that Jaden was leaving the party with Monica, he left the party and began walking back to his dorm. That's when Mike saw *her* looking breathtakingly beautiful and innocent through the library window. Later that night, Mike had decided to just keep the secret to himself not really wanting to throw salt on another man's game, but as he watched *her* studying in the now empty library, he knew what he had to do.

"Hey Kelly," Mike greeted *her* nervously. This was the first time that Mike had approached Kelly since they got into it over her 'play sister.'

"Hi," Kelly responded happily, until she realized who had just spoken. That's when her face scrunched up with discomfort and uneasiness. "What can I do for you?" Kelly asked Mike passively as she redirected her focus back to her studies.

"What? I can't come over and say 'hi' to an old friend?" Mike asked her in mock seriousness, while wiping away a fake tear.

Mike was about to leave and forget about telling her what he had seen, when she surprised him and broke out a tiny smile.

"You're still silly I see. So how have you been Mike?" She smiled and gestured for him to sit down. Kelly had decided that she had held her grudge long enough, and now it was time to let bygones be bygones, especially after she remembered the conversation that she had had with Tiffany, her play-sister, last week. Tiffany had told Kelly that when she first saw Mike, she had had an instant attraction to him and didn't want to pass that up, which is why she slept with him that night. She quickly let Kelly know that that was all it was; just some great sex (as she put it). That night Kelly had got to see another side of Tiffany, one that she wished she never had to see. Tiffany wasn't the innocent big sister that Kelly had known her to be and she had reaffirmed that notion when she told Kelly that she should have gone ahead and got with Mike; that it would have been well worth it. So, after Kelly had that conversation with her, she had kind of been hoping to run into Mike, so that she could make amends with him. It was no need for her to still be mad at him over a situation that wasn't entirely his fault.

"I've been ight, I guess. And yourself?" Mike answered as he nervously sat down in a seat directly across from her. As Mike sat down, he began to feel all of the emotions for Kelly that he had tried to set aside rush back like a tidal wave. *What am I getting myself into?* Mike thought to himself, uncertain of his actions.

"Just ight?" Kelly asked Mike skeptically and ignored his question for her.

"Yeah," Mike answered, fawning confidence.

"You didn't look 'ight' when I saw XU lose to UMD in the Elite Eight on TV the other day," Kelly replied as she pulled

Mike's card. *Hmm, she got me*, Mike thought, smirking at how well Kelly seemed to know him. Since Keisha was going through so much drama of her own, Mike still hadn't got a chance to get the loss off of his chest.

"Well, now that you bring it up, I guess I'm not 'ight'. I'm still a little upset about the loss. But hey what can I do?" Mike told her hesitantly; he wasn't sure if he wanted to go into detail about how he was really feeling with her. Although talking to Kelly in the past had always been easy for Mike, and always made him feel better; he wasn't sure if that would be overstepping his boundaries now.

"You want to talk about it?" Kelly asked Mike sympathetically, in a voice as sweet as honey. As much as Mike wanted to talk about it, he couldn't help but to be curious and ask her where all of this was coming from. A few weeks ago, Mike couldn't have paid Kelly to speak to him and now she was sitting there willingly and offering to listen to his problems.

"Well, last week I talked to Tiffany about what happened between you and her. She told me that she was the one who was all up on you and that it was just a fling. She then emphasized that she wasn't really tripping off of it so I shouldn't be either,"—Kelly paused for a second and then continued—"I then told her about how I felt about you, and she was like I should have talked to her back then because she wouldn't have been mad. So I guess I owe you an apology," Kelly told Mike sheepishly.

"Whoa! So does that mean you'll give me a chance now?" Mike flirtatiously asked her; with a hopeful grin.

Laughing she replied, "You know I'm with Aaron."

For a second, Mike had forgotten all about that dude, and his whole purpose of coming into the library was to speak to her. *This is the perfect opening for me to tell her about what I saw,* Mike plotted to himself.

"Oh yeah. Well about Aaron…" Mike started tentatively, but he stopped when he saw the once happy expression on her face drastically change to one of distrust.

"What about Aaron?" Kelly asked Mike suspiciously, waiting to defend anything Mike was getting ready to say bad about Aaron.

"Uhh, nothing. He's a cool dude," Mike played it off, not wanting to say anything to harm their newly found friendship.

"Oh, okay-y," Kelly said confused by his response; but decided to just ignore it.

"So now that we're cool, when are you going to let me take you out? As friends of course," Mike playfully asked Kelly.

"Boy you are so crazy," Kelly laughed it off, not giving an answer either way. Mike decided to take that as a sign of hope and decided to just forget about his secret. The truth always seemed to come to light anyway. Now that Kelly was talking to him, Mike's new plan of action was to just wear her down. Mike knew that Kelly wouldn't be able to deny her feelings for him for long. He could tell by the way that she was staring at him, that she was still feeling him. She had a look in her eye that expressed complete desire for him. Mike knew that in due time Kelly would be his.

CHAPTER THIRTY-THREE

"I know that's not Kelly and Mike in front of me," Keisha mumbled to herself, as she squinted ahead to see if it was indeed the two of them. The two figures had their backs turned to Keisha, but she knew Kelly's dancer physique anywhere and it wasn't that many six-foot- something, black guys walking around campus, so Keisha knew it had to be the two of them. She was just confused to see them together and looking so buddy-buddy.

"Hey guys, what's up," Keisha greeted the two, with a surreptitious grin. She was surprisingly upbeat for somebody who just caught their boyfriend cheating on them.

"Hey girl, how did everything go?" Mike turned around and asked Keisha concerned, as he embraced her.

"Well, I caught him red-handed. Mike your plan worked to a T. Can you believe he still tried the flip the script on me, even after I caught him in the act?" Keisha asked them incredulously.

"Are you serious!?" Kelly replied disgusted.

"Yes girl, I caught this dude in mid-stroke and he going to claim that the only reason he was with her tonight was because I wasn't there for him after he lost last night -- talking about this was the only time," Keisha told them as she rolled her eyes.

"So what did you do after you walked in and caught them?" Mike asked her intrigued. Keisha then went on to tell the two every detail that happened from Jaden escorting her out of the room to her leaving him and Monica dumbfounded at the news she gave them.

"Dag, girl! You are better than me because I know if I would have walked in on Aaron cheating on me, all hell would have broke loose," Kelly promised.

Hmph, I guess all hell is about to break loose soon then, Mike mumbled to himself, as he looked off to the side.

"What you say, Mike," Keisha asked him, with a perturbed glance, not sure if she heard him clearly.

"Huh? Oh nothing, just that's crazy," Mike smiled innocently, attempting to cover up his slip of the tongue.

"So, what are ya'll about to get into?" Mike asked the two girls as he made an attempt to quickly change the subject.

"Dag, with all of the excitement going on, I forgot that I have dance practice tonight!" Kelly replied hurriedly, as she glanced down at her watch.

"What *kind of* dance practice you got going on this late at night?" Mike joked with a raised eyebrow. The only dancing he knew that went on at midnight was the kind at the strip club.

Laughing Kelly replied, "You are so stupid. Some of the girls in the dance department and I started our own dance group, and we're going to be performing at Spring Fest in a couple of weeks. The only time that we all had free in our schedule today was at midnight. Plus we don't have class tomorrow until one o'clock in the afternoon, so it's cool."

"Oh yeah, with everything going on, I forgot Spring Fest is

coming up soon," Keisha chimed in. Spring Fest was a big festival held on campus every year that consisted of vendors of every sort, carnival-like games, concerts, and just something that the whole student body could enjoy before finals started. It was actually on the weekend right before the first day of finals.

"Oh yeah, that's what's up. I heard they're going to have Kanye West performing at the concert this year," Mike told the girls excitedly.

"Yeah, it's going to be him and Sugar Ray," Kelly informed them. Kelly and her dance group were among the groups that were going to be opening for the major concert attractions.

"Who cares about Sugar Ray? I'm trying to see Kanyesie. I hope he brings Twista or maybe even Jay out with him," Mike said even more excited.

"Twista maybe, but you know this dude ain't bringing out Jay-Z," Keisha replied, as she looked at Mike incredulously; while Kelly laughed at their exchange.

"Well guys, I wish I could stay and chat some more, but I'm already 10 minutes late for my dance practice. Mike I'll see you later, and Keisha we can finish this conversation when I get back to the room if you're still up," Kelly told them and then ran towards the Student Center where her practice was being held at.

"So, when did you two get so chummy?" Keisha playfully asked Mike after Kelly was out of ear shot. She was not letting the fact that he and Kelly were carrying on a friendly conversation slip by her. The two of them were now walking slowly towards Keisha's dorm, enjoying the uncharacteristic warm March breeze as they chatted.

"She said that she talked to Tiffany and realized that she

shouldn't have brushed me off so quickly. She even apologized,"
Mike told Keisha as he smiled excitedly, although still puzzled at
the same time. "So after we got past that part in the conversation,
we've been talking like nothing even happened. I just wish she
would have talked to Tiffany before she started going with Aaron."

"Yeah well, just be happy that ya'll are on speaking terms.
You can't have your cake and eat it too," Keisha told him, warning
Mike not to push things.

"What does that mean? I've never understood that one. Why
can't I have my cake and eat it too. What am I supposed to do, just
look at it? And if that's the case, what's the point?" Mike asked
Keisha seriously. *Mike is too damn silly for his own good. He's
the only person I know who would overanalyze this old saying,*
Keisha thought to herself as she shook her head with a laugh at his
rambling.

"Shut up!" Keisha replied laughing. "Only you would take this
cliché and overanalyze it."

"Whatever, don't act like what I said don't make sense," Mike
responded playfully.

"Maybe a little bit," Keisha admitted, and then joined in on his
laughter.

~~~~~

Knock-Knock. The sound of Dana knocking on Melissa's
dorm room door reverberated through the hallway. With all of the
chaos that had been going on, it had taken Dana a week or so to
follow up on Melissa. It was a Sunday, and also the last day of
March. Dana had happened to be on her way back from church
with Ebony, Keisha, Angel, and Kelly. After the day's message on
judgment and forgiveness, Dana decided that she needed to stop

through and speak to Melissa. Church didn't usually move Dana, but the service that Ebony took them to at Zion Church had really spoken to her. From the sermon, Dana realized that if she expected God to forgive her many sins, then she had to forgive others. She also had no right to judge anybody else for their actions; only God could judge. The pastor had hit some other major points, but that was all Dana could remember; she was going to ask Ebony later for the notes. *I've never seen somebody taking notes so feverishly in church, like it was a class they were about to have an exam in until I met Ebony,* Dana thought to herself with a light chuckle.

"Hey," Melissa greeted Dana emotionless, assuming that Dana had only come by to make good on her threat.

"Hey, girl. Can we talk?" Dana asked Melissa softly. Melissa opened her door and extended her hand for Dana to come in.

"So talk," Melissa instructed Dana after Dana sat quietly for a couple of minutes.

"Well, I went to church with Ebony and them today…" Dana started saying only to be cut off by Melissa.

"Oh boy, don't tell me you're turning into one of them now," Melissa huffed and rolled her eyes.

"Anyway, like I was saying,"—Dana stated with some attitude—"today's sermon was on judgment and forgiveness, and from that I realized that I was wrong to judge you for what you did."

"Oh. So, what does that mean?" Melissa asked Dana suspiciously, knowing that she wasn't just going to up and let everything go.

"It means that I still think that you're wrong for what you did, and that you should tell Kelly, but I can't judge you for what you did. In the end, I will still be your girl no matter what happens," Dana told Melissa sincerely. Dana had missed her friendship with

Melissa. Melissa was the only one out of the 'crew' who really understood her, and she missed talking to her.

"What makes you think I want to be your friend anymore after how you walked out of here on me, like you did?" Melissa asked Dana, in mock seriousness.

"Oh. You don't want to be my friend?" Dana asked Melissa sadly as she looked down towards the floor not thinking that that would be an option, when she had walked over there. After a few moments, Melissa finally answered her.

"Nah, I'm just playing. Girl, I missed you so much," Melissa laughed as she got up from her seat on her bed and walked over to the desk where Dana was sitting. She gave Dana a huge hug, happy that they were friends again. Melissa had missed Dana as well.

"So what's new with you?" Melissa asked Dana, hoping to change the subject from her messing with Aaron behind Kelly's back. Truth was that what Melissa thought was going to be the last time over in Aaron's room, ended up being the start of a recurring thing. Now, Melissa found herself falling for Aaron, and it was no way that she was going to be able to relay that to Kelly without looking like the slut that Kelly had made her out to be. Besides, Aaron had been complaining about Kelly a lot lately, so Melissa figured that it would only be a matter of time until he broke up with her. Then she'd, have him to be all hers. Once that happened, it wouldn't matter anymore because Kelly wasn't her friend anyway. *Now, I just have to come up with a way for Dana to keep her big mouth shut and not tell Kelly or anybody else,* Melissa thought to herself mischievously, as she listened to Dana catch her up on all the things that she had missed.

APRIL

CHAPTER THIRTY-FOUR

The next couple of weeks flew by for Keisha, and now she was in her last day of classes. The last days of classes in college were nothing like they were in high school. In high school, you didn't even have to come to school on the last day, and if you did, it was just to socialize with your friends one last time before summer started. In college, they had final papers due, take-home exams due, and final group projects. It was crazy to Keisha! Each professor knew that his or her course was not the only course students were taking; yet they still piled on the workload and assigned everything to be due at the same time as the rest of the students' classes. Keisha had finally found out the key to being successful in college though. It was called time management; because the work wasn't that much harder than high school. It was just a matter of setting aside enough time to study for each class, and making sure to know when each assignment for each class was due. That's why Keisha was able to finish and turn in two of her final papers and a take-home exam early. This gave her plenty of time to prepare for her group presentation that she just presented in class and aced, which was pretty good for somebody whose last few weeks were filled to the capacity with drama. Unlike some other people in her class who waited until the last minute, Keisha had made it a point to finish her take-home exam and one of her papers when she had first heard about them. That helped her out a lot, so the only thing she had to do this past week was to prepare for her group presentation, which wasn't that hard because they would be presenting stuff on PowerPoint. Keisha only had one more exam left and that wasn't until the following Monday, during finals week. Her freshman year was almost over. The only thing left for her to do now was study for that last exam and start packing up her things. *That still feels funny to say because it feels like I just got here,* Keisha thought to herself as she walked into her bedroom and looked around nostalgically before beginning to pack.

~~~~~

My first year is almost over! Kelly thought as she made her way out of her dorm, and to her last freshman class of the day. Kelly was still kind of confused why they would make the last day of classes University wide a Tuesday of all days, but she guessed they wanted to give them a few days off before finals started on Monday. It still felt like the year flew by, even though some moments seemed like they would never end. Kelly was going to miss this place when she left to go home for the summer. *One thing that I'm not going to miss though is making this long ass walk across campus just to get to class*, Kelly thought to herself, as she continued her trek across campus in the heat. The walk wouldn't have been that bad if it wasn't almost ninety degrees right now. *I'm not the only person excited about today being the last day of classes,* Kelly considered as she looked around and noticed all of the excited faces around her. There were so many students out and about, smiling, and just plain ole lounging outside with friends. As many students as it was chilling outside, Kelly would have thought that classes had ended already. Then again, it was twelve thirty, so a lot of people were done with their classes for the day, which explained the abundance of students milling around. When Kelly finally reached her destination, there were only a couple people in the classroom. *I guess I'm early!* Kelly thought to herself and sat down in a seat a couple rows behind the front row. Today, the professor was going to do a review, so Kelly had to make sure that she could see and hear everything that he was going to put up on the board. As she sat and waited for class to begin, Kelly couldn't help but to think of Mike and how cool they had become lately. It felt so easy and flowed so nicely whenever she would have a conversation with him that she never wanted their talks to end. Kelly knew that she was with Aaron now and she loved Aaron to death, but she just couldn't help but to wonder how things would have been if she and Mike had ended up getting together. *What am I thinking? I'm in love with Aaron, and I'm with Aaron, so it doesn't matter what things would be like if Mike and me got together. I need to get a hold of myself, before I end up slipping up and doing something with Mike.* Kelly tried to shake the thoughts out of her head.

"Alright class, let's begin," Kelly's professor stated, beginning his lecture. For once Kelly was grateful for the interruption and the beginning of class. Kelly realized that she must have really zoned out those last five minutes because the class was now filled to capacity. It was funny because the whole semester this class had been empty to the core, but whenever a review was mentioned the class filled right up. *Alright, time to take notes.*

~~~~~

I am so excited right now; I just finished my last official class of the school year, Melissa cheered to herself. Now all she had left were three finals that started next Tuesday. Her last final was really late; it was on the last day of finals. That meant everybody else would be gone and she would still be there by herself. *Maybe I can get Aaron to stay those extra days with me. That's not a bad idea,* Melissa thought to herself as she walked up the stairs to his room. Melissa had called him before coming over to check if the coast was clear. Just as Melissa walked out from the stairwell and crept over to Aaron's door, prepared to knock, an angry Mike charged out of his room, almost knocking her down in the process. Instead of saying 'excuse me,' Mike just gave Melissa the evil eye and went about his business.

"What's his problem?" Melissa asked Aaron slightly annoyed as he rushed her into his room. Aaron then glanced surreptitiously out his door and looked both ways down the hallway to make sure nobody else was out there to see Melissa come in. After he closed the door, he broke down on his knees and told her what happened. Apparently, Mike saw Melissa and Aaron kissing one night in the stairs, and told Aaron that if he didn't tell Kelly about Melissa, then he would. On the outside Melissa appeared just as saddened by the new info as Aaron was, but on the inside she was elated. Now Melissa knew for sure that it was just a matter of time before either Kelly broke up with Aaron or vice versa, and then he would be all hers. Melissa was starting to grow tired of sharing him, although she knew Aaron didn't look at it that way. Aaron considered Melissa a good friend, and had told her that he didn't plan on leaving Kelly for her. He had even told Melissa that although he cared about her, he was in love with Kelly. Melissa had just ignored that tidbit of info, convincing herself that if Aaron was so 'in love' with Kelly then it was no way that he would be messing around with her behind Kelly's back.

"What should I do? I don't want to lose her," Aaron asked Melissa distressed. As he said those words out of his mouth, Melissa couldn't help but to snarl in his direction. Aaron couldn't see her though because he had his head pressed into her bosom.

"Baby, don't worry, everything will work itself out in the end," Melissa cooed in Aaron's ear, as she attempted to console him. Not wanting to discuss Kelly anymore, Melissa began to sensually kiss Aaron on his forehead. Then she started putting soft kisses all around his face until she reached his lips. Melissa could feel his body responding to her, as she moved from kissing on his lips to his neck.

"Just forget about everything that's going on, and let me make you feel better," Melissa seductively whispered into Aaron's ear as she began pulling his shirt off.

"Mm hmm," he moaned in ecstasy, forgetting all about Mike and his threats.

As Melissa watched Aaron sleep peacefully in her arms after yet another passionate 'love making' session, she began to plot a way for her and Mike to join forces. There was no reason that they couldn't be on the same team. After all, they both ultimately wanted the same thing; for Aaron and Kelly to break up so that they could have each person to themselves.

~~~~~

How did it get to this point? Ashley asked herself guiltily as she looked at her reflection in the mirror on the back of her dorm room door that Ebony had just slammed in her face. Stunned, Ashley found herself stuck in that stance as the nights happening ran over and over through her mind like it was a reoccurring dream. The guilt that she saw when looking at her reflection quickly turned into disgust. Disgust with the situation and more importantly disgusted with herself. Deep down, Ashley knew that she was wrong and responsible for allowing things to get to this point between her and Ebony, and she couldn't help but feel disgusted with herself for it. Ebony was her cousin for crying out loud! She was her cousin who had always been there for her and had her back through thick and thin, even when Ashley had done her dirty; as she was reminded of tonight. As Ashley begin to remember all of the times Ebony was there for her when they were growing up, even taking the fall for her with their parents a couple of times, the tears begin to trickle down her face even more. One by one, before the flood gates fully burst; breaking Ashley down to her knees with deep sobs. As she sobbed she couldn't help but to play the nights happenings through her mind one more time.

The night had started off pretty normal with Ebony lying on her bed searching the web on her laptop, while Ashley sat at a desk on her side of the room watching the movie Soul Food. From an onlooker, things would have seemed absolutely normal, but the two cousins knew better and knew that any wrong word could set things off that night. The tension in the room that night was thick enough to cut with a knife. Ebony had finally reached her fed up point with Ashley, and had vowed earlier that day that if Ashley came at her wrong at all, she was going to give her a piece of her mind, and stop holding back. Ebony was tired of apologizing over and over for a mistake that she had made; especially when Ashley had made plenty of mistakes in their past that Ebony warmly forgave her for each time. Ebony had had enough! Too bad Ashley wasn't aware of this before she made one of her infamous sarcastic remarks towards Ebony.

"What did you say?" Ebony snapped while eying Ashley, as she began to sit up in her bed to see if she had heard her clearly.

"I said this part of the movie reminds me of you. You know when the slut cousin slept with Terri's man, and got caught?" Ashley replied snidely, and dared Ebony with her eyes to comment. It was at that point that all hell broke loose. Ebony had tried her best to remain calm and patient with Ashley throughout this situation, like a "good Christian" should. But it was only so much that one person could take from a person, and Ebony had finally reached her breaking point.

"Ashley, I am tired of you sitting on your pedestal making me out to be the bad cousin, like you don't have any skeletons in your closet. And *you* of all people have the *audacity* to call me a slut?"— Ebony fumed as her necked rolled side to side, while she slowly walked closer to Ashley raising her voice with each step—"Let's talk about all the different guys you gave a 'piece' of yourself to this semester, only for them to toss you to the side when they were done and go wife up somebody else. If I recall correctly a couple of those guys might have had girlfriends." Ebony spat out nastily.

"Really Ebony, you wanna take it there?" Ashley asked Ebony with the same attitude that she was throwing at her as she stood up to face Ebony.

"Yeah! And while I'm there, let's talk about last summer, when *you* were sleeping around with Mandy's boyfriend behind *her* back, and had me covering for you all summer. I guess that slipped your mind, hunh? Or is it just because Mandy isn't family, that when you do it, it's okay?" Ebony yelled hysterically as she shoved Ashley down onto her bed.

"But that was different…" Ashley sputtered, making no attempts to get up from her bed; as she remembered the hurt that she had caused one of her good friends, Mandy, last summer. When Ashley had met Rasheed, she didn't know that he was Mandy's boyfriend. She thought they were just friends, and had begun to see him behind her back, never bothering to ask Mandy if she would mind. Then when she did finally find out that they were together, it was too late; she had already started falling for him. Instead of being honest with Mandy about it, she continued to see Rasheed behind her back until one of their mutual friends snitched on her. But through it all, Ebony had stood by her side, even when all her other friends stopped talking to her for awhile. This realization had Ashley second guessing all of the resentment she was holding towards Ebony.

"I bet. And I bet all the times you did me dirty in the past were different too. Yet I still forgave your selfish ass," Ebony screamed as all the months of built up anger poured out of her through her tears. It was just too much for Ebony to handle; and before she did something she knew she would regret she turned on her heal and stormed out of the room. Slamming the dorm room door behind her, leaving a teary eyed Ashley behind to seethe in what just happened.

CHAPTER THIRTY-FIVE

Wow! Look at all of the people out there, Kelly thought to herself as she peaked out at the crowd from behind the stage. Kelly knew a lot of people attended Spring Fest, but she hadn't expected to see that many people out there. *Aww, there's Keisha and Ebony coming out to show support.* Kelly tried to wave at them, but she didn't think that they saw her. As Kelly looked out into the crowd, she wondered where Aaron was. He had told her that he would be there extra early just so he could be in the front row supporting her, but Kelly didn't see him. *Oh well, he's probably somewhere out there; I know he wouldn't miss my big performance,* Kelly thought to herself as she nervously walked back over to where the rest of the dancers were. Kelly had choreographed her group's whole routine, so if they looked bad up there, it would reflect back on her, which was enough to have her sweating bullets -- that and the fact that they were about to perform it in front of ten thousand or more people. Kelly always got nervous though, right before she was about to go on, but it always disappeared magically when she got on stage.

"Hey girl!" Angel greeted Kelly excitedly and jarred her out of her nervous thoughts. Kelly looked up surprised to see Angel. She had forgotten that Angel was part of the show too. Angel was asked at the last minute to participate in a mini fashion show that was going to go on while some up-and-coming singer performed. They were going to walk down the stage and model while the singer performed in the background.

"Hey, what's up?"

"I'm just so excited right now. Do you see all of those people out there? This is going to be so much fun. I get such an adrenaline rush, every time I go out on stage and model," Angel told Kelly dreamily.

"You're not nervous?" Kelly asked her, hoping that she wasn't the only one.

"Not really. I'm used to this by now," Angel replied confidently. Angel had already done a few fashions shows in New York, so she was used to going out in front of a lot of people. Kelly had performed in front of huge crowds before, but just not in front of a bunch of her peers. Unlike today, Kelly was usually doing ballet or tap, and not a lot of her peers could appreciate that style of dance.

"All models approach the stage entrance," they heard the backstage coordinator call out.

"That's my cue, girl, I gotta go," Angel told Kelly and gave her a small wave good-bye.

"Good luck," Kelly called to her retreating back.

~~~~~

"Yeahhh, go girl!" Keisha screamed as Angel came out on stage and did her Naomi Campbell walk; she was looking so good up there. Keisha thought it was supposed to be an up- and-coming singer singing in the background, but whoever he was, was being out-did by all of the models who were walking down the long stage. *If I were him, I would come up to the front, so that everybody could see me instead of being back on the main stage part. But oh well, that's on him, Keisha thought nonchalantly.*

"Must you be so loud?" Ebony asked Keisha with a slight attitude, which in turn lead Keisha to scream louder just to spite her. Thinking Ebony was joking, a laughing Keisha responded, "You know I gotta cheer on my girl."

"Hmm, whatever," Ebony mumbled. Ebony knew she was being rude, but she just really didn't feel like being out there around all of those people after her big fight with Ashley last night.

"Girl what is wrong with you? You've been acting moody all afternoon," Keisha asked Ebony concerned, knowing that something had to be up for Ebony to act this out of character. Ebony hadn't told Keisha or any of the girls about her fight with Ashley, so Keisha didn't know what was going on. The only person Ebony had told about the fight was David. After she stormed out of her dorm room last night she had went down to Keisha's room but nobody was there. There was no way she was going back into her room that night. The next person that popped into her head that would fully understand what she was going through had been David. After she called him and met up with him over at his place, she divulged everything to him and had wound up talking to him all night. She ended up falling asleep over at his place.

"I know, girl, and I'm sorry. It's just that Ashley and I got into a horrible fight last night. I just really don't feel like being out here, but I also don't feel like going back to my room. I really don't want to see her right now." Ebony confessed to Keisha sheepishly. Although Ebony knew Keisha would more than likely be on her side, she couldn't help but feel guilty about the things that she had said to Ashley and for this time the fight being her fault.

"What happened?" Keisha asked Ebony soothingly, giving Ebony her undivided attention.

"If you don't mind I really don't feel like talking about it right now. Its just too much going on out here for me to have that deep of a conversation, you know?" Ebony told her as she uncomfortably looked around at the thousands of people having fun around her.

"I understand. We can talk about it later. In the meantime here's the key to my room. You can stay with us as long as you need to, until you feel comfortable going back to your room," Keisha told Ebony caringly as she took her dorm key off her key ring and handed it to Ebony.

"Thank you girl. I really appreciate this," Ebony replied drained, but breaking a slight smile at her friends understanding. "Oh look there's Kelly," Ebony pointed to the stage as Kelly and her group came out doing a nicely choreographed hip-hop routine.

"Wow! That was hot. I can't believe Kelly choreographed that whole dance. I didn't realize how talented Kelly was," Ebony stated amazed by Kelly's performance. Keisha on the other hand knew that Kelly was that talented and was just proud of her girl's success.

"I know, they tore it up," Keisha emphasized.

"Well girl I'm bout to head back to your room. I am so tired, me and David stayed up all night talking." Ebony slipped forgetting that she wanted to keep her night with David to herself. At least until she had a chance to go sit down and go over everything they had discussed in her mind.

"Hmm mmm, so what were you and David talking about all night to the wee hours of the morning?" Keisha teased Ebony, not missing her little slip up.

"I'll tell you all that when you come back to the room tonight," Ebony responded with a mischievous smile, and made her way back to the dorms before Keisha could ask any more questions.

"Hmph, let me find out!" Keisha mumbled to herself as she watched Ebony walk away. Happy that she was finally taken charge of her life again, and taking the reigns out of Ashley's hands. *It was a long time coming*, Keisha thought to herself as she looked up at the stage to enjoy the rest of the show. Keisha was now standing out in the crowd by herself, but she didn't mind. Angel and Kelly would be off of the stage in a few minutes, so she just continued to enjoy the great performances and the scenery. Keisha couldn't believe how many students of all ethnicities were out on the field where Spring Fest was being held. Spring fest was held outside of the XU recreation center on the large vacant field behind it. On a normal day, the field was usually used for intramural soccer games and such, but today it was occupied by over ten thousand people: students, vendors, and visitors. Keisha couldn't help but to marvel at all of the different activities that were going on around her. Keisha laughed at the twenty-something students who were jumping in the moon bounce like they were five years old, and smiled as a cute Asian couple took a picture with the school mascot right next to her.

"Hey what's up? Who are you here with?" Jason greeted Keisha and looked around to see if she was with anybody else. Keisha slightly jumped at the sound of his voice. She had been so enveloped in the scenery that she hadn't seen him creep up on her.

"You okay," Jason asked Keisha with the cutest smile. A smile that had Keisha forgetting that Jay was Dana's old boo, for a second. Just for a second though! Keisha still hadn't gotten the chance to confront 'Jay' or should she say 'Jason' about why he didn't tell Keisha that he was with Dana, since he missed the last few classes they had together.

"Yeah, I'm fine. I was just deep in thought and you scared me," Keisha told Jason, trying to laugh off her embarrassment. "But to answer your question, I was here with Ebony but she went back to the dorm to lie down. Now I'm just waiting for Kelly and Angel to come from backstage, and for Dana to get here," Keisha threw that out there to catch his reaction. He was obviously playing it off since he acted like he didn't even know Dana.

"Oh okay, I came up here with my boys," Jason stated hesitantly as he pointed over to Shawn and a couple of other guys in their frat paraphernalia. Keisha throwing Dana's name out there had surprised Jason and messed up his whole game plan. Jason had planned on walking over to her, asking her about Jaden. By now, he knew they had broken up. After he played the sympathetic friend role he was going to ask her if she would like to hang out sometime since their class was about to be over. Now that Keisha had mentioned that Dana was on her way out there, Jason had to quickly come up with a new game plan.

"So how come you never told me that you were messing with Dana?" Keisha asked Jason, cutting straight to the point. She stared him down waiting for an honest answer. Jason's face dropped for a second, but then he quickly recovered it with a shy smile. *Damn, what did I get myself into*, Jason thought to himself as he tried to think of quick answer to tell Keisha that wouldn't mess up his chances with her. Who was he kidding, the second Keisha said that Dana was meeting her out there; Jason's chances were gone. So Jason just decided to lay it all out there, and see where it would take him.

"I have a secret. I know this may sound kind of corny considering the circumstances, but I've been feeling you since the first time I saw you, and that's why I never told you about Dana. When I heard that you and Dana weren't cool like that at the time, and she never mentioned you, I didn't feel like it was something that I had to reveal to you. I understand if you're upset and don't want to be my friend anymore," Jason told Keisha sincerely, hoping that she would respect his honesty. Keisha didn't know how to respond to him. Part of her was flattered by his sincerity, but the other part knew that she couldn't mess with anybody that used to be with her girl. It was too many guys out there for her to go like that.

"Aww that's sweet Jason," Keisha responded with a sideways smile, giving Jason some hope. "But Dana's my girl and there is no way that I could talk to you after you used to mess with her. I guess I'll see you around," Keisha stated with a smirk, as she turned on her heels and went to meet Kelly and Angel, whom she could now spot in the crowd. Glancing back only to give Jason a small wave goodbye, she left him standing there with a wounded look on his face and his feelings hurt.

"Dag, so much for that plan," Jason mumbled to himself as he approached his boys.

"So what happened, son?" Shawn pulled Jason to the side and asked him after he walked back over to them. It was still a secret that Jason was trying to holler at Keisha, since majority of the guys in his crew were tight with Jaden. Jason hardly heard Shawn, though, as he pulled out his cell to call Dana, and see if he could get another chance.

"Hello," Dana answered in a smooth, sexy voice that Jason had come to love so much. *I don't know what I was thinking, ditching Dana for a chance with Keisha*, Jason thought as he began apologizing to Dana for telling her that he needed a break. Jason went on to tell her that his schedule wasn't too busy for her, and that he missed her in his life.

"Aww, Jason. That would be so sweet if you hadn't had just tried to get with Keisha," Dana spat the end out like she had a bad taste in her mouth. *Click!* The sound of Dana hanging up on him was all Jason heard next. *Damn, all of this just cause I decided to put another female in front of the one I had*, Jason mumbled to himself, kicking himself for messing up what he had with Dana. *You win some, you lose some and this time, I definitely lost.*

CHAPTER THIRTY-SIX

"Hey girl," Kelly greeted Keisha with a hug. She and Angel had just gotten off stage from performing. It had been such an adrenaline rush for Kelly that she felt like she could just dance forever.

"Where's Ebony?" Angel asked Keisha as she looked around the premises to see if she could spot her.

"Oh. Ebony left right after ya'll got off stage. She was really tired, but wanted me to tell ya'll she enjoyed ya'll performance," Keisha informed the other girls, leaving out the fight with Ashley part, not knowing if Ebony wanted everybody else to know yet.

"Hey guys," Dana greeted the girls happily and exchanged a knowing glance with Keisha, before they both burst out laughing.

"What's so funny?" Angel quizzed the two, wanting to be let in on the joke.

"Tell me why Jason just tried to holler at Keisha, and then when she turned him down, he gonna call me up talking about he misses me and he wants to be with me now," Dana smacked as she rolled her eyes.

"What did you tell him?" Keisha asked nosily.

"I told him that would be cool...if he hadn't have just tried to holler at my girl. And then I hung up on that loser," Dana responded laughing as she high-fived Keisha. Usually Dana would have been upset by a dude she had really been feeling trying to holler at Keisha, but this time it was cool because ever since Dana had started going to church with Ebony and Keisha on a regular basis, she felt more at peace with herself. Dana realized that she had been using guys to make herself feel beautiful and purposeful, but that feeling could only come from a relationship with God, and feeling beautiful could only come from within. Once she grasped a hold of that, everything in her life began to take on a whole new light. God really did change things.

"I know that's right, girl," Kelly said as she snapped her fingers in agreement.

"Man these dudes are so stupid these days. He should have already known it was going to get back to you," Angel huffed as she shook her head at Jason, whom they could see standing a couple of feet away.

"Speaking of stupid dudes, have ya'll seen Aaron?" Kelly asked the group as she searched the premises looking for him.

"Nah. Call him. I'm sure he's here somewhere. You know that boy wouldn't miss his boo's performance," Keisha assured Kelly.

"And why is he stupid?" Dana asked Kelly, hoping that Kelly was getting tired of Aaron, so she wouldn't have to tell her about Melissa sleeping with him. Dana had promised to give Melissa until the last week of school, that way it wouldn't affect Kelly's finals, but she wasn't sure how long she could keep this information from Kelly and the rest of the girls.

"Oh I was just joking," Kelly answered Dana with a smile. Just as Kelly was about to call Aaron, she saw him strolling over to them with a huge grin on his face.

"See I told you he was around," Keisha told Kelly confidently.

"Hey ya'll!" Aaron greeted Keisha, Dana and Angel.

"Hey baby," he whispered in Kelly's ear as he gave her a hug and a kiss on the forehead.

"Hey boo, I was just thinking about you. Did you like my performance?" Kelly asked him anxiously. Kelly knew that they had done great up there, but Aaron's opinion really meant a lot to her.

"I missed it," Aaron replied barely audible.

"Excuse me?" Kelly asked him, slightly annoyed. "I don't think I heard you correctly. Did you just say you missed my performance?" Aaron couldn't even look Kelly in the eye, as he nodded his head 'yes' in reply. If Kelly knew the real reason why Aaron had missed the performance, she would be doing a lot more than yelling at him. Aaron had got 'tied' up in Melissa's room, after he had stopped through there to drop off her book for Black Experience. Aaron had only planned on being over there long enough to say 'hi' and drop the book off. But Melissa had other plans in mind, as she opened the door with a sexy lingerie ensemble on. Aaron tried to deny her, but his libido won out, and after he left her room he had to run back to his room, shower, and change. He had more sense than to come out to Spring Fest smelling like sex, which was why he had arrived so late.

"Why did you miss it?" Kelly asked Aaron with an attitude, unable to hide her disappointment. Kelly couldn't believe this! The main person that she had wanted to see her performance had missed it. Although Aaron had seen Kelly perform before on numerous occasions, today was important to her because this was the first time that she got to choreograph a routine and perform it in front of a wide spread audience.

"Uh, we'll be over here," Keisha signaled to the right, as she, Dana and Angel awkwardly made their way towards one of the food vendors.

"Hmm, he's in trouble," Kelly heard Angel whisper as the girls walked away. *Angel's right, this Negro is in trouble. He better have a damn good excuse for missing my performance because he can't say that he forgot what time I was supposed to go on because Spring Fest and performing is all that I've talked about for the past few weeks. He knew how much this meant to me,* Kelly fumed waiting for Aaron's response.

~~~~~

While all of the other girls were out enjoying Spring Fest, Ashley was in her room packing up her stuff to go home. She didn't like the person that college had turned her into, and was ready to go back home to Atlanta to do some deep soul searching. Ashley could not wait until her freshmen year was over. She only had one final to take on Monday and that would be a reality for her. At first Ashley was going to call her girls and let them know that she was leaving earlier than planned, but she couldn't bring herself to face them. She just was not feeling the person that she had turned into. Besides, Ashley wasn't even sure if she was going to come back next school year.

"Ight, mom. Thanks. I'll see you tomorrow," Ashley told her mother as she hung up the phone. Mrs. Johnson would be staying at the Hyatt Regency Hotel next to campus tomorrow night. After Ashley's final on Monday morning they would be driving back to Atlanta together. Mrs. Johnson had witnessed enough quarrels between these two to know that they would be able to work it out on their own, so she opted to stay out of the fight and obliged her daughter's wishes. She assumed the two would be friends again, once the summer break began. Ashley wasn't too sure about that, but only time would tell.

~~~~~~

"Did you not hear me? I said, why did you miss my performance?" Kelly asked Aaron getting loud and irritated that he still hadn't answered her.

"Baby I'm sorry. I was working on a final group project that is due on Monday, and we lost track of time. I got out here as soon as I could though," Aaron lied quickly. Kelly couldn't put her finger on it, but her intuition was telling her that he wasn't being completely honest with her.

"Come on baby, let's not fight on the last week of school. You know we only have a few more days left to enjoy each other's company without our parents around. Let's not ruin it over something that can't be changed," Aaron whispered sweetly into Kelly's ear and then gave her a passionate kiss, which tempted Kelly to just let it go. Kelly figured that it was no point in her tripping off of it anymore since it wasn't like she was going to break up with him over it. *Why do I have this weird feeling like somebody's staring at me?* Kelly thought to herself as she looked around the field to see who was staring at her.

"Why is she staring at us like that?" Kelly asked out loud, completely irked, as she saw Melissa staring at the two of them. Kelly curled her lip up in a grimace towards Melissa and rolled her eyes towards her, hoping that she would go mind her business. When Aaron turned around and saw who Kelly was talking about, a frown automatically came across his face. He couldn't believe this chick had followed him out there. Aaron knew then that he was going to have to put an end to his affair with Melissa. He would just wait until Kelly left for the summer break, that way Melissa couldn't tell Kelly anything.

"I don't know. What am I a psychic now?" Aaron snapped at Kelly, displacing his annoyance.

"What's your problem? It was a rhetorical question. I didn't expect you to answer," Kelly huffed and rolled her eyes at him. She was growing tired of his snappy comments. *Stuff is changing between us; two fights in five minutes,* Kelly thought to herself as she shook her head. Before she could comment on her thoughts, Aaron pointed towards the stage to signal that Kanye was about to come on. Kelly still felt like she should say something, but decided against it. Not wanting to start a third argument, she focused all of her attention on to the stage and enjoyed the concert.

MAY

CHAPTER THIRTY-SEVEN

Wow! I can now officially say that I am done with my freshman year here at XU, Keisha thought proudly. She just had her last final earlier and aced it. It felt so good for her to be done with everything finally. Keisha still couldn't believe she was going home tomorrow, but she was glad that the day was finally here. This had been a fun school year and all, but it had also been a stressful one filled with plenty of drama. Keisha missed being in Maryland and was homesick for her family and friends. Not to mention, after these finals and final projects, Keisha just needed a break from school. She couldn't wait to go home tomorrow. Keisha had even been packed up since this weekend. Everybody else out of the crew was leaving on Wednesday or Thursday. Keisha could have chosen to chill a few days longer, but she knew she would chill with her "friends" sometime this summer. Otherwise, she would holler at them next school year. It was as simple as that. Anyway, she was riding home with Mike and he really wanted to leave Tuesday morning after his last exam. He only had a couple of weeks to chill at home before coming back to school for summer classes and basketball stuff.

"Girl I can't believe you're about to leave me tomorrow," Kelly whined to Keisha; getting misty-eyed.

"Aww, girl you know I'ma get up with you over the summer," Keisha assured Kelly, as she got up and gave her a hug. They were sitting in their dorm room, reminiscing over the school year while Kelly continued to pack up her belongings.

"I know, but I'm going to miss being able to just sit up all night and have girl talk with you."

"Aww I know," Keisha replied starting to get teary-eyed herself. "You know what we should do?"

"What?"

"We should have a last girl's night in our room tonight. Just tell everybody to come over and chill."

"Yeah that *sounds* good. What about Ebony and Ashley though? And Melissa?" Kelly asked Keisha with a concerned facial expression.

"I mean, if me and Dana killed the beef, then you can surely kill the beef with Melissa, and as far as Ashley and Ebony are concerned, they're family, and ain't no beef going to change that," Keisha stated plainly.

"Yeah ight," Kelly replied nonchalantly. "Melissa can come, but just for the record, we don't have a beef, we're just not friends. It's a difference."

"Whatever chick. Just be nice to the girl when she comes over tonight," Keisha laughed at Kelly, and ignored her nonchalant tone as she began to call all of the girls and invite them over for one last sleepover.

~~~~~

"I can't believe this is really our last night together, guys,"

Angel told the group as tears began to slide down her cheek. Angel had always been one of the more sensitive girls out of the crew.

"Oh boy, let's not start the water works just yet. The night just started," Keisha told Angel playfully. All the girls, excluding Ashley and Melissa, were in Keisha and Kelly's room for one last sleepover before everybody went home for summer break. Keisha and Kelly were lying in their respective beds, while Dana, Angel and Ebony were on the floor lying on a jumbo- sized air mattress.

"I know, but I was just thinking about all the fun times we had together and all the things we been through this year," Angel told the group reminiscently.

"Yeah, we have been through a lot," Dana agreed, as she looked over and smiled at Keisha.

"Hey where are Ashley and Melissa?" Angel asked the girls as she checked her watch. The sleepover was supposed to start at eight, and it was now nine o'clock.

"Ashley's not coming," Ebony stated hesitantly.

"Why not?" Kelly asked her confused. She knew that Ashley had her beef with Ebony and wasn't really getting along with Keisha, but she figured that she would at least show face for their last group gathering.

"She went home earlier today," Ebony informed the group. "The only reason I even know that was because my Aunt was waiting in the room for me after my final."

"Dag, it's like that? She couldn't even say bye to nobody," Dana said while shaking her head, with her feelings slightly hurt. Ebony just shrugged her shoulders in response. She didn't know why Ashley left so abruptly. Yeah they had a fight, but they had had plenty of fights this year and Ashley never just left like that.

Ebony had no words for it.

"So, I guess Melissa's not showing up either," Keisha assumed as she looked at the clock on her nightstand.

"Yeah, she had told me she wasn't coming. I didn't want to say anything because I thought she might change her mind," Dana admitted. She thought about her conversation she had with Melissa earlier that day. Melissa had told Dana angrily that she didn't know why they were inviting her to a sleepover when she hadn't even heard from any of them in a month and to let them know that she would not be in attendance. Dana tried to convince her that it would be a good time to clear the air with everybody, but Melissa wasn't trying to hear it.

"So much for our pact," Kelly chuckled, referring to the pact that they had made at the end of first semester claiming, *"From now until forever that, we will always be friends and never let anything come between us."*

"Well, honestly when I think about that pact, it was doomed from the beginning because it was before we all really knew each other," Dana declared to the girls.

"That's true," Kelly co-signed with a sigh.

"How about this time instead of making a silly pact 'to be friends to the end', we just learn from our past mistakes. Let's promise to be upfront with each other, to not keep any secrets, and to just always be there for each other no matter what," Angel suggested to the group and received the agreement of the others through head nods.

"That's good Angel because I guess if I would have just been upfront with myself and Ashley, then we would still be tight right now," Ebony admitted sadly; as she thought about her ruined relationship between her and her cousin.

"Yeah, and if I would have been upfront with Melissa about my feelings for Mike, she and I would probably still be cool," Kelly confessed to the group. After Kelly's confession, Dana's secret that she was holding for Melissa began to really eat her up inside, but she pushed the feeling away not wanting to betray Melissa.

"Yeah. I'm just happy that Dana and I"—Keisha said pointing at Dana—"could work out our issues," Keisha told the group with a smile.

"I know girl, me too," Dana replied and went over to Keisha's bed to give her a hug.

"I can't wait until next school year," Ebony declared as she looked around at her girls. She was begrudging going home to Atlanta, not knowing how things were going to be with her and Ashley beefing.

"Girl, chill because I can't wait until summer break. Three months of fun in the sun with no worrying about studying or exams," Dana retorted playfully.

"I'm with Dana. I'm looking forward to this summer break. I do know one thing regarding next year, ya'll are going to see a different me. I'm going to be looking like Ebony next year," Keisha joked.

"What are you talking about, looking like me?" Ebony laughed, not knowing what Keisha was talking about; which took her away from her thoughts of home.

"I'm about to be more focused and into the church, and I'm giving up sex until marriage. And ya'll can quote me on that," Keisha announced while Kelly and Angel exchanged knowing glances.

"You know what, I'm with you Keisha. I've decided earlier

today that I'm swearing off sex," Dana proclaimed to the group.

"Yeah right, as much as ya'll love sex, I really don't see that happening," Kelly stated doubtfully.

"Whatever. You can say what you want, but I'm telling you now I'm done with it until marriage. If it's one thing that I've learned this year, it's that nothing good comes from sex. I mean, let's be real. Look at all of the guys ya'll have had sex with, where are they now? I know that none of the guys that I've been with are in my life now," Dana told the girls seriously, as her eyes flashed around the room looking at each one.

"That's true girl because when it comes down to it, Jesus is the only one who will always be there for you no matter what; which is why my trust is with Him," Keisha stated in agreement with Dana. Although Dana and Keisha sounded serious right now, Kelly doubted that either one would be able to hold off all summer on sex; and chalked it up to them just getting out of bad relationships. Kelly kept her thoughts to herself though, not really in the mood to start a big debate about it.

"I know that's right," Ebony shouted in agreement. Ebony was so happy that Keisha and Dana both had decided to change their lifestyles, especially since she knew she had a big part to play in that. For the past month or so, Keisha and Dana both had been going to church with Ebony on a regular basis, and had even went up to the altar to commit their lives to Christ the previous Sunday.

"Guys, I think Aaron is losing interest in me," Kelly stated plainly out of the blue, after the previous conversation died down.

"What makes you think that?" Keisha asked Kelly confused not knowing where that was coming from. Dana, on the other hand, began to feel real guilty about the secret that she was holding from her girls, because she knew where it was coming from.

"It's like the last month or so, he's just been acting really weird and distant. It's like one moment he's the sweet caring Aaron that I know and love, and the next second he's defensive and standoffish. I just don't know what to do," Kelly confessed to the group.

"Have you tried talking to him?" Angel asked her.

"Yeah, but every time I bring it up, he's like 'let's just enjoy the last few days up here together and worry about that later.'"

"Girl, he's probably cheating." Keisha stated matter-of-factly. Keisha's opinion was kind of jaded to Kelly. After Keisha had caught Jaden cheating on her, she thought everybody was cheating.

"Nah I don't really think Aaron is cheating on me. He's with me all of the time. And even if he were, I would have heard *something*. You know?" Kelly confidently told the girls.

Dana couldn't take it anymore. She was going to explode if she didn't get this secret out of her.

"Kelly, Keisha might actually be right on this one," Dana told Kelly cautiously as she tried to think of the best way to tell her that Melissa had been sleeping with Aaron. Melissa had only told Dana about that one time that she slept with him, but Dana knew Melissa well enough to know that she was still messing around with Aaron. Dana could tell by the way Melissa had been jealously staring at Aaron at Spring Fest, which led Dana to believe that Aaron was late because his 'group project' with Melissa had run over.

"Dana what are you talking about?" Kelly asked Dana amused, still doubting that Aaron was cheating on her.

"Well, I don't know how to say this…," Dana started out hesitantly, still trying to find the right words to say to Kelly.

"Girl just spit it out," Kelly smirked feeling like Dana was probably just overreacting over something she had probably seen.

"Well…Melissa had confessed to me…that she had slept with Aaron, after one of their study sessions," Dana told Kelly sullenly. To Dana's surprise, Kelly wasn't at all affected by the news and even had a smile on her face.

"You don't really believe her do you?" Kelly asked Dana with a smirk. "Melissa probably only told you that to make me feel bad. I strongly doubt that Aaron had sex with Melissa."

"Kelly how can you be so sure?" Keisha asked Kelly wearily, believing that it was a possibility that Aaron and Melissa had slept together.

"Because at that last gathering we had, she had threatened to sleep with Aaron, in order to piss me off. And I know Aaron, and he wouldn't cheat on me with one of my friends, or old friends," Kelly stated confidently, as the rest of the girls looked at her with doubt in their eyes.

"Ight, if you don't believe me then ask Aaron about it, and I'll bet you he'll begin stuttering about it," Dana predicted.

"Nah, I got an even better idea," Keisha smiled mischievously. "What you need to do is tell Aaron that you're going to go home tomorrow for break instead of Wednesday like you had planned. Then, call him and pretend like you just made it home, when in reality you're still going to be on campus. Then wait about an hour, and stop by his room later on that night claiming that you missed him or something and wanted to surprise him. That way if nobody's in there, you have an excuse for showing up at his room when you said you were going to be home. However, if he is cheating with Melissa, then he's most likely going to try and get some time in with her before they leave for break."

"Keisha, I think you've been spending a little too much time with Mike. That sounds like the crazy scheme he told you to do with Jaden." Kelly replied cynically.

"Hey, the crazy scheme worked too," Keisha replied with smirk.

"That is true," Angel replied with a laugh.

"Yeah, it sounds like a pretty good plan," Dana co-signed nodding her head at Keisha to give her, her props.

"Am I the only one who remembers the pact that we just made? Or did ya'll all forget that we just agreed to be upfront with one another and not keep any secrets?" Ebony asked the group disapprovingly.

"Exactly! We made a pact that we would be upfront with everybody in here"—Keisha pointed to everybody in the room— "and not keep secrets. Melissa and Aaron are not in this room," Keisha responded playfully while laughing which caused the rest of the girls to break out in laughter.

"Anyway, are you going to go through with the plan or not?" Keisha asked Kelly persistently.

"Ight, but what if he's not in the room at all," Kelly asked Keisha, deciding to hear her plan out.

"That's why you'll call him on his room phone, to let him know that you supposedly made it home safely, and if he answers then you'll know that he's in, but if he doesn't then you just call his cell phone and find out what he's doing for the rest of the night. There aren't any parties going on this week and a lot of people are leaving tomorrow. It's no reason he shouldn't be in his room," Keisha answered Kelly confidently.

"I don't know," Kelly replied hesitantly. "It all sounds good, but if I do all of that and he's not cheating on me, then I'm going to feel guilty that I distrusted him." At that point, Dana washed her hands of it. She did her friendship duty and put the truth out there. Now it was up to Kelly to believe the truth or not.

"Well, you don't have to go through with it, sweetie. But it's a sure fire way to find out what's really going on with him," Keisha told Kelly frankly.

"Ight, I'll worry about that tomorrow. Let's just enjoy the rest of our night together," Kelly pleaded to the group, not wanting to discuss the possibility of Aaron cheating on her with Melissa of all people. To back up what she just said, Kelly got up and turned the radio on, which prompted the rest of the girls to get up and start dancing.

"What are you doing?" Kelly asked Keisha, laughing as she watched Keisha attempt to do her own version of the chicken head dance, since she couldn't do the real dance.

"Don't hate," Keisha replied laughing, as the other girls started imitating her. It was a good ending to a fun night.

CHAPTER THIRTY-EIGHT

"I can't believe you're leaving me," Kelly cried softly as she gave Keisha a final hug goodbye. They had just finished putting all of Keisha's stuff into Mike's truck, which was packed to the brim.

"Aww, you got me crying now," Keisha whined playfully as she pulled away from their heartfelt hug.

"I'm going to miss your stuck up butt," Kelly playfully retorted.

"I'm going to miss you too, loser. You're like the sister I never had," Keisha told Kelly sincerely and gave her one last hug before she went to say her goodbyes to Ebony, Angel and Dana, who had also come out this morning to bid Keisha goodbye.

"I guess this is goodbye," a smooth masculine voice said next to Kelly. As Kelly looked over to see who was talking to her, Mike quickly swept her up in his arms and gave her a kiss, before she could get a reply out of her mouth. Kelly didn't know whether or not she should kiss him back or slap him. Her mind was telling her to pull away, but her heart wouldn't let her. After being lost in the moment, Kelly came to her senses and remembered that she did have a boyfriend and they were in front of her dorm, which her boyfriend also lived in. She quickly pulled away.

"Shh, before you get mad I just want to tell you something," Mike whispered into Kelly's ear to stop her from going off on him. "I never met a female like you before and I probably won't ever again. You are the only female that I can see myself being with. Just promise me one thing."

"What's that?" Kelly asked, hypnotized by his voice.

"Promise me that when Aaron messes up, I'm the first one you call."

"You say it like you know he's going to mess up?" Kelly asked him perturbed. Mike didn't respond to her comment he just gave her a knowing smile and got into his truck. Keisha had informed Mike of the plan that they had concocted to catch Aaron cheating, so Mike had made it a point to mention it to Melissa. Now it was only a matter of time before Kelly became his.

"Bye everybody," Keisha yelled as she got into the passenger side of the truck.

"Bye," they all yelled back in unison. Kelly couldn't help but to think back to how wonderful Mike's lips felt on hers, as she watched his truck drive off into the horizon. It was like his lips were made for the sole purpose of kissing her. The kiss had almost made Kelly forget all about Aaron. Almost!

"Hmmm, chica. Tsk, tsk, tsk," Angel scolded Kelly teasingly as Ebony laughed in the background.

"I don't know why you don't just break up with Aaron, and get with Mike. You know that's who you've wanted to be with from jump," Angel informed Kelly with a hint of her Puerto Rican accent slipping out.

"Because I love Aaron; and what we have is real. If Mike and I got together, it would have been based on passion and that's it. That's all fine physically, but you can't base a relationship solely on passion."

"If you say so," Angel replied, rolling her eyes, disregarding what Kelly had just said.

"Well, its early girls. I'm 'bout to go back to sleep. I'll get up with ya'll later," Dana informed the group as she made her way over to her dorm.

"Yeah me, too," Angel co-signed.

"Ight girls," Kelly said yawning herself, and waved goodbye to them.

"And then there were two," Ebony joked as they got off the elevator and headed to their rooms. As Kelly walked into her room, she couldn't shake what Mike had said to her from her mind. *'Promise me that when Aaron messes up, I'm the first one you call.'* It wasn't even what he said to her that was bothering Kelly. It's more of how he said it, like he was certain that Aaron was going to mess up. Kelly decided to take that as sign to go ahead with Keisha's elaborate plan. Before she could change her mind, Kelly called Aaron and told him that she was going to be leaving for break tonight instead of tomorrow morning. It wasn't a total lie though. Kelly was going to be taking half of her stuff home today. *Oh well, it's too late now.*

~~~~~

I can't believe my girl left this morning, Angel thought sadly. It was going to be weird for Angel not to be able to just go over to Keisha's dorm room when she needed somebody to talk to. Angel was going to miss all of her girls over the summer because back home she didn't really have that many female friends to hang out with. They were all too petty and jealous, so Angel kind of stuck to herself. Angel had never met a group of girls like them that she just automatically clicked with. After last night, Angel realized the girls had become like sisters to her. She definitely planned on getting with all of them over the summer -- especially since Kelly and Dana lived only 30 minutes away from her. She knew Keisha would be up to visit a lot. Ebony and Ashley were kind of far, but Angel planned to make a trip to ATL at least once during the summer. Right now, Angel was just leaving Kelly and Ebony's dorm. She had to go over there and say goodbye to them this afternoon. Angel was supposed to be leaving tomorrow morning, but her mother wasn't going to be able to pick her up tomorrow so she was coming this evening. Angel couldn't wait to see her mom. It felt like forever since she'd been home. Angel especially couldn't wait for that home-cooked meal that her mom had been promising her, because this dining hall food was no competition when it came to that. Before Angel made her way back to her room to get the rest of her stuff together, she had an appointment at the health center. Angel assumed that she caught a stomach virus or something because she had been throwing up every morning for the last few days now and she heard something was going around campus. She had wanted to come in sooner, but today was the earliest they could take her. Everybody was probably trying to get in to the health center before they went home for break, since it was free.

"Angel Gonzalez," Angel heard the nurse call her name. *About time! I feel like I've been waiting here forever,* Angel mumbled to herself. She couldn't understand doctor's offices; they tell you to be there at a certain time, but then they never call you back to the room on time. What's the purpose of giving you an appointment time?

"So what brings you in here today?" the nurse practitioner asked Angel pleasantly.

"Well, I've been throwing up the last few mornings, and I know I heard it's a stomach virus going around and just wanted to get it checked out."

"Okay." The nurse performed a regular check-up, and asked Angel to pee in a cup. After Angel did, the nurse told her to get dressed and left Angel in the room for about ten minutes. *I don't know why it's taking her so long. All she's going to do is prescribe me some medicine to take, probably an antibiotic or something,* Angel grumbled as she checked her watch for the umpteenth time. Her mother expected everything to be packed and ready to go when she arrived, so Angel didn't have time to be fooling around in the health center when she still had a bunch of stuff to pack.

"Angel, when was your last period?" the nurse asked Angel when she finally walked back into the room, startling Angel to death. She didn't even hear her come back in. *What? Why does she need to know that?*

"Uhh, I'm not really sure. My period is so erratic. Sometimes it'll come on after a month, and then other times it may be two months," Angel replied baffled and slightly annoyed by the question.

"Well, I just gave you a pregnancy test, and it came out positive," the nurse told Angel cautiously. She always hated breaking that news to young, college women. *NOOOOOO!!!!* Angel inwardly screamed. *This cannot be happening to me.*

"No, that can't be true," Angel told the nurse and started

crying. *What am I going to do? I can't afford to take care of a baby! What about my goals and my dreams?*

"There are options nowadays for young ladies." The nurse started talking about "the options," but Angel was too distraught to listen. Besides the only option she had was having the baby. Neither Angel, nor her family believed in abortions, and it was no way they were going to give it up for adoption. Now Angel had to figure out how she was going to break the news to Shawn.

~~~~~

After Angel had finally pulled herself together, she called Shawn and told him that they needed to talk. She was supposed to see him after she left the health center anyway, so now she was waiting outside of his apartment for him on the front steps.

"Hey baby, what's wrong?" Shawn greeted Angel, with a hug.

"Baby let's sit down," Angel told him and then guided him towards a bench that was on the other side of the parking lot.

"Angel, what's wrong?" Shawn asked her concerned, but growing slightly annoyed. He didn't have time for her to be playing games.

"I-I-I'm pr-e-egnant," Angel stammered out, after they had finally sat down; tears beginning to stream down her face. Shawn's face dropped in pure shock, causing him to become unusually silent.

"Shawn. Say something!" Angel demanded. Out of all the possible reactions, she wasn't expecting that one.

"Are you sure you're pregnant. It could just be stress," Shawn told her trying to convince himself more so than her.

"No. I'm PREGNANT. The health center just confirmed that," Angel snapped; her sadness quickly changing to anger. She had told him to use a condom, but no-o-o, 'it felt so much better without one.'

"Can you say it any louder? I don't think those people over there heard you," Shawn hissed as he pointed in the direction of some upperclassmen lounging around on the benches about ten feet across from them.

"Look right now, I really don't give a damn about those people over there or what they think," Angel proclaimed fiercely.

"Okay baby. Calm down, it's going to be okay," Shawn told her soothingly. *There's the sweet Shawn I know. I was wondering what happened to him,* Angel thought as she finally started to feel better about the situation.

"It's alright baby. I'll take care of everything. Just let me know how much it cost."

"What the hell are you talking about? What makes you think I'm not going to keep it?" Angel screeched. Angel couldn't believe him, she felt like she didn't even know him anymore. Her daddy was right; a man does show his true colors when a serious problem occurs.

"Well, all I'm saying is that I'm not ready for a baby, and I definitely don't have the funds to take care of one. I mean, I just have too much going on for myself right now, to allow a baby to ruin it. So it's a no-brainer," Shawn stated bluntly; like it was something that he had been through before.

"Well you should have thought about that ish' before you had sex with me raw," Angel screamed, and then left him sitting there stunned as she walked away devastated.

~~~~~

I can't believe I'm going through with this, Kelly thought nervously to herself as she crept down the hallway to Aaron's room. Earlier that night Kelly had said a fake 'goodbye' to Aaron, claiming that she was leaving for summer break, although she wasn't really leaving until tomorrow. She had taken some of her stuff home earlier since she only lived thirty minutes away, so it wasn't a complete lie. It was now midnight, and Kelly was just arriving back to campus. She had called Aaron an hour ago to let him know that she had 'made it home safe' and was going to sleep. Little did he know she was really on campus about to come pay him a visit. Aaron had claimed that he was in his room about to do the same. Ever since Kelly had gotten off the phone with Aaron, all of the different possible outcomes had been playing through her mind. There was the one when he'll open the door and she would see Melissa sitting half-naked on his bed. Then there was the one when he opens the door and is elated to see her, and says he was so lonely without her. Kelly was hoping for the latter. When Kelly approached his door, her instincts told her not to knock immediately. So instead of knocking, she tilted her ear towards the door to hear if she heard anything suspicious. Just as Kelly was about to give up on that, she heard talking and then a girl giggling. *I can't believe he has a girl in his room*, Kelly murmured to herself. It had to be Aaron in there with her because he didn't have a roommate.

"Okay, let's not jump to conclusions," Kelly mumbled to herself as she paced back and forth down the hallway. It could always just be one of his female friends that live on this floor that Kelly knew; he did hang out with them occasionally. *Knock- knock.* Kelly had to have waited like two minutes with no reply. *Maybe he didn't hear me. KNOCK- KNOCK.* Kelly knocked louder this time.

This time she heard shuffling and whispering, but still nobody came to open the door. *Is this dude serious? He's just going to have some female up in his room, and then not answer the door when I knock. Oh hell nah,* Kelly fumed and then began banging on the door with no reply still. *That's okay. I'll just sit my ass right here in front of the door. They have to come out at some point in time.*

~~~~~

"Stop Aaron, that tickles," Melissa shrilled and giggled playfully as Aaron continued to tickle her. They had just finished one of their passionate 'love making' sessions, and were now just relaxing on his bed. Aaron had planned on telling Melissa that the affair that they were having was going to end tonight, but Melissa had other plans. Aaron had started out the night yelling at Melissa for showing up at Spring Fest and staring at him while he was with Kelly. The whole time he had been yelling at Melissa, she had been smiling seductively at him, while slowly and seductively slipping off her clothes. By the time Aaron had finished yelling at Melissa and telling her that it was best that they didn't talk anymore, Melissa was down to her bra and panties. Aaron had tried to resist her seductress ways but for some reason, no matter how hard Aaron tried to resist her, he always gave in; and this night was no different. After their 'love making' session Aaron had agreed to letting Melissa spend the night in his room, since Kelly and most of her friends had already gone home for the break. *Knock-knock.*

Aaron wondered who that was as he stuck his index finger over his mouth, to signal for Melissa to not say anything. Aaron planned on just ignoring whoever it was; he was much too comfortable lying there with Melissa in his arms. Besides he didn't need anybody to accidentally peep his or her head inside of his room and see Melissa lying in his bed. This game Aaron was playing was beginning to get tough to keep up with. It was too hard to juggle between two girls that he really cared about. Just the other day, he hurt Kelly's feelings because he missed her performance at Spring Fest. If he hadn't been messing around with Melissa that afternoon, he would have been there, for sure. Over summer break, Aaron was going to have to do some serious soul searching and decide which girl he wanted to keep.

KNOCK-KNOCK. The person knocked louder. *This person doesn't seem to be going away,* Aaron thought as he got out of his bed and put some sweat pants on. He was about to go check through his peephole and see who it was at the door.

"Who is that?" Melissa whispered.

"Shh, I'm 'bout to check it out," Aaron whispered back and tip toed over to the peephole. *Oh Shit! It's Kelly!! What the hell do I do now?* Aaron mentally screamed to himself, as he began to panic. *BANG-BANG-BANG.* The sound of Kelly banging on the door vibrated throughout the whole room. The look of sheer fear on Aaron's face must have concerned Melissa because she was now standing by his side, in a tank and boy shorts.

"Who is it?" Melissa whispered with a confused expression on her face after she looked out the peephole and didn't see anybody. *What does she mean who is it? I know she sees Kelly standing on the other side of the door,* Aaron thought to himself annoyed. Irked by her demeanor, Aaron hastily moved her out of his way and looked through the peephole again. But this time he didn't see anybody. *Where'd she go?* Aaron thought to himself frantically.

"Kelly was at the door," Aaron hissed at Melissa to explain why he was so frantic.

"Well she's not there anymore," Melissa replied nonchalantly and made her way back to the bed.

"But she might come back. So you got to leave now before she does," Aaron told Melissa and hurriedly gathered her things together.

"Are you seriously kicking me out?" Melissa asked Aaron, hurt and angered by his actions. Aaron knew it was messed up, but Melissa knew from the beginning what she was getting herself into. It was too late to cry about it now. After Melissa quickly dressed, and had all of her things together Aaron opened the door for her to leave.

"Oh shit!!" Aaron mumbled to himself as he saw Kelly sitting patiently against the wall in front of his door. There was nothing he could say or do as she sat there staring at him angrily. As Aaron started to weep inwardly over hurting the person who had loved him unselfishly, Aaron couldn't help but notice a smirk of contentment spread across Melissa's face.

EPILOGUE

KEISHA

Freshman year! What a year! It seems like just yesterday I was making this three hour trek up to New Jersey for my first year of college, not knowing what to expect. Now I'm making it once again for my sophomore year, but this time I'm going up more mature and less naïve then last year. As I get closer and closer to campus, I can't help but to reminisce on the times that I had up there last year. I would say drama filled definitely summed up that school year. Ha-ha! But, one positive thing that did stem from all of that drama was me reaching my goal that I set for myself that first day I arrived on campus. Not only did I achieve that goal of making one lasting friendship, but I made five of them. I love those girls to death, and I can say that we will be friends for life. I guess you can call us a true click now, or the 'Freshmen Honeys' as the fellas on campus used to call us. Then again, we're not freshmen anymore! Looking back over that crazy school year, we had some fun times together. We had some rough times too. All in all, it was a great experience and I wouldn't trade it in for the world -- although I do wish I would've handled some things differently. Well, that's life, and when I think about it, I'm happy that I went through what I went through. It's made me a much stronger and wiser woman in the end. All that's in the past now, and it's up to me to make this year a much better one then last year. That's why I decided at the end of last year to change my lifestyle. Kelly doubted me at that last sleepover when I announced that I was going to change my life and live right for God but I've upheld what I've said and haven't had sex this whole summer. I can't front though, it was the hardest thing I've had to do, and I know it's only going to get harder once I get to XU with all of the temptation walking around. If its one thing I've learned from Ebony, it's that with God all things are possible. Ebony thought that she and Ashley would never be cool again, after that whole David situation. Yet, when she got back home to Atlanta for the summer, Ashley was at her house waiting for her, apology in tow. They made up right there on the spot, and promised to never fight like that again. Ashley even called me to apologize for the way that she was acting. I told her it wasn't all her fault. I may be stubborn at times, but I do know when I'm wrong, and I admitted that I should have minded my own business and kept my mouth shut. After she agreed we made up and became friends again. Yup, just like that! It's really no point in holding grudges, especially when it comes to true friends, whom you know will have your back when times get tough. Just thinking about that conversation brings a smile to my face. Now that they're cool again, I wonder what's going to happen between Ebony and David. With Ashley giving her the green light, things might finally pop off for them. Hmm, I guess only time will tell. Speaking of things popping off, I still can't believe Melissa was sleeping with Aaron.

When Kelly called me crying telling me that what Dana told us was true -- that Aaron had been sleeping with Melissa, it took everything in me not to grab Mike and have him drive me back up there to whip Melissa's ass. It's one thing to go at Mike, but to get with Aaron! That's just dirty. I think after that, Dana's probably the only one out of the crew still cool with that chick. I'm sure Melissa could care less, which is why she had a satisfied smirk on her face when Kelly caught them. Kelly couldn't believe that one of her 'used-to-be' good friends could do something like that to her. Shoot, I couldn't believe it either! Kelly started to punish Melissa right then and there, but she realized that it just wasn't worth it and decided to kill her with words instead.

"Well Melissa, How does it feel? How does it feel to have proved yourself to be the slut that you are -- reaching the all time low of sleeping with one of your friends' boyfriends? Although you may say that we're not 'friends', I'm pretty sure that we were still on speaking terms when this ish' started between you two. I want you to know that I'm not tripping off of it because Niggas come a dime a dozen, but true friends only come once in a blue moon. And I have five lovely friends who are going to have my back when I get home. As for you, I can't say the same. Once they find out what you did, they will never trust you to be their friend again. I hope it was worth it." With that said Kelly turned on her heal and wiped that smirk right off of Melissa's face, leaving her standing there speechless and hurt. I'm not sure what happened with Melissa and Aaron, because I sure haven't spoken to either one. From what Kelly told me, Aaron has been calling her damn near everyday to ask her for forgiveness. I don't know if that means he left Melissa alone or not. I guess I'll find out soon enough when I get back to campus. I'm sure it'll be

a hot topic -- especially since one of the nosiest girls on our floor peeped the whole scene as it played out that night, probably ecstatic that she had chosen not to leave until the last day. Speaking of another hot topic, I can't believe Angel's pregnant and the messed up thing is that I didn't even find out about it from her. Shawn told some of his boys, and through the grapevine it got back to me. I couldn't believe it at first, until I called her and she confirmed it. Poor Angel! All it took was one reckless night of passion for her to end up pregnant and for her to see the true side of Shawn. After receiving a multitude of advice from her family and friends, Angel made one of the hardest decisions of her life - whether or not she should keep the baby. Against Shawn's wishes, Angel decided to have the baby. Her parents are devout Catholics and would have disowned her if she had decided to have an abortion. I wish I could say I knew how she was doing now, or if she was coming back to school this semester or not but I can't. I haven't spoken to Angel since that day she confirmed she was pregnant. It's like she cut off all her school ties. I still call her every once in awhile to leave a message letting her know that if she needs anything she can always call me. What's really messed up though is that now that everybody found out Angel's pregnant, Shawn's going around telling all his boys that the kid isn't his. He's saying he's not going to give her any type of help until the baby is born and he gets a paternity test. Some men can be so trifling! He knows that he was her only one. That's why you have to be careful of the company you keep. And while we're on that subject, it looks like Dana's back to keeping bad company but she'll learn. This year should prove to be a very interesting one. All I got to say is if you thought freshmen year was filled with drama, then you can only imagine what sophomore year has in store!!!!

~~~~~

Find out what happens to Keisha and the rest of the gang in 'Sophomore Blues', the sequel to 'Freshmen Honeys'.